THE DON CAMILLO
OMNIBUS

THIS omnibus edition, issued in 1955, is for
members of The Companion Book Club,
8 Long Acre, London, W.C.2, from which
address particulars of membership may be
obtained. The book is published by arrange-
ment with the original publishers, Victor
Gollancz Ltd.

"A blessed companion is a book"—JERROLD

THE
DON CAMILLO
OMNIBUS

★

GIOVANNI GUARESCHI

The Little World of Don Camillo
Don Camillo and the Prodigal Son
Don Camillo's Dilemma

THE COMPANION BOOK CLUB
LONDON

Contents

★

INTRODUCTION

My LIFE began on the 1st of May, 1908, and between one thing and another, it still goes on.

My parents had decided that I should become a naval engineer and so I ended up studying law and thus, in a short time, I became famous as a signboard artist and caricaturist. Since no one at school had ever made me study drawing, drawing naturally had a particular fascination for me and, after doing caricatures and public advertisements, I studied wood-carving and scenic design.

At the same time I kept busy as a doorman in a sugar refinery, a superintendent of a parking lot for bicycles, and since I knew nothing at all about music I began to give mandolin lessons to some friends. I had an excellent record as a census-taker. I was a teacher in a boarding school and then I got a job correcting proofs on a local newspaper. To supplement my modest salary I began to write stories about local events and since I had a free day on Sunday I took over the editorship of the weekly magazine which came out on Monday. In order to get it together as quickly as possible I wrote three-quarters of it.

One fine day I took a train and went to Milan, where I wormed my way into a humorous magazine called *Bertoldo*. Here I was forced to stop writing, but I was allowed to draw. I took advantage of this by drawing in white on black paper, something which created vast depressed areas in the magazine.

I was born in Parma near the Po River; people born in this area have heads hard as pig iron and I succeeded in becoming editor-in-chief of *Bertoldo*. This is the magazine in which Saul Steinberg, who at that time was studying architecture in Milan, published his first drawings and for which he worked until he left to go to America.

For reasons entirely beyond my control, the war broke out and one day in 1942 I went on a terrific drunk because my brother was lost in Russia and I couldn't find out anything about him. That night I went up and down the streets of Milan shouting things which filled several sheets of legal-size paper—as I found out the next day when I was arrested by the political police. Then a lot of people worried about me and they finally got me released. However, the political police wanted me out of circulation and so had me called into the army, and on the 9th of September, 1943, with the fall of Fascism I was taken prisoner again, this time at Alessandria in Northern Italy by the Germans. Since I did not want to work for the Germans, I was sent to a Polish concentration camp. I was in various German concentration camps until April, 1945, when my camp was taken over by the English and after five months I was sent back to Italy.

The period I spent in prison was the most intensely active of my life. In fact I had to do everything to stay alive and succeeded almost completely by dedicating myself to a precise programme which is summarized in my slogan, "I will not die even if they kill me."

When I returned to Italy I found that many things were changed, especially the Italians, and I spent a good deal of time trying to figure out whether they had changed for the better or for the worse. In the end I discovered that they had not changed at all, and then I became so depressed that I shut myself in my house.

Shortly thereafter a new magazine called *Candido* was established in Milan and, working for it, I found myself up to my eyes in politics, although I was then, and still am, an independent. Nevertheless, the magazine values my contributions very highly—perhaps because I am editor-in-chief.

I remember distinctly the 23rd of December, 1946. Because of Christmas, the work had to be in "ahead of time," as the penpushers put it. At that time, beside editing the magazine *Candido*, I wrote stories for *Oggi*, another weekly put out by the same publisher. On December 23, then, I was up to my ears in trouble. When evening came I had done my piece for *Oggi* and it had been set up by the printer, but the last page of *Candido* was still unfinished.

"Closing up *Candido*!" shouted the copy boy.

What was I to do? I lifted the piece out of *Oggi*, had it reset in larger type and put it into my own paper.

"God's will be done!" I exclaimed.

And then, since there was another half-hour before the deadline of *Oggi*, I wrote a hasty story to fill the gap.

"God's will be done!" I said again.

And God must have willed exactly what proceeded to

6

happen. For God is no punctilious penpusher. Because, if I had heeded all the good advice poured into my ear, Don Camillo, Peppone and all the other characters in this book would have perished on the day they were born, that December 23, 1946. For the very first story of the series was written for *Oggi*, and if it had appeared there, it would have gone the way of its predecessors, and no one would have heard of it again.

The background of these stories is my home, Parma, the Emilian Plain along the Po where political passion often reaches a disturbing intensity, and yet these people are attractive and hospitable and generous and have a highly developed sense of humour. It must be the sun, a terrible sun which beats on their brains during the summer, or perhaps it is the fog, a heavy fog which oppresses them during the winter.

There, my friends, is the story of how the priest and the mayor of a village in the Po River valley were born. It is not that I claim to be their "creator"; all I did was put words into their mouths. The river country of *The Little World* created them; I crossed their path, linked their arms with mine and made them run through the alphabet, from one end to another. In the last weeks of 1951, when the mighty river over-ran its banks and flooded the fields of the happy valley, readers from other countries sent me blankets and parcels of clothing marked "For the people of Don Camillo and Peppone." Then, briefly, I imagined that instead of being an unimportant fool I was an important one.

When I was a little boy I used to sit on the bank of the mighty river and say to myself: "Who knows? Perhaps when I'm grown up I'll manage to get to the other side." My greatest dream was to own a bicycle. Now I am forty-seven years old and the bicycle is mine. Often I go to sit on the river bank where I sat as a boy. And as I chew a blade of grass I can't help thinking: "After all, this side is the better." I listen to the stories borne down the mighty river, and people say:

"He grows more absurd every year!"

Which isn't true, because I was absurd from the very beginning. Thanks be to God.

G. G.

THE LITTLE
WORLD OF DON CAMILLO

translated by
UNA VINCENZO TROUBRIDGE

THE LITTLE WORLD

THE LITTLE world of Don Camillo is to be found in almost any village on that stretch of plain in Northern Italy. There, between the Po and the Apennines, the climate is always the same. The landscape never changes and, in country like this, you can stop along any road for a moment and look at a farmhouse sitting in the midst of maize and hemp—and immediately a story is born.

Why do I tell you this instead of getting on with my story? Because I want you to understand that, in the Little World between the river and the mountains, many things can happen that cannot happen anywhere else. Here, the deep, eternal breathing of the river freshens the air, for both the living and the dead, and even the dogs, have souls. If you keep this in mind, you will easily come to know the village priest, Don Camillo, and his adversary, Peppone, the Communist Mayor. You will not be surprised that Christ watches the goings-on from a big cross in the village church and not infrequently talks, and that one man beats the other over the head, but fairly—that is, without hatred—and that in the end the two enemies find they agree about essentials.

And one final word of explanation before I begin my story. If there is a priest anywhere who feels offended by my treatment of Don Camillo, he is welcome to break the biggest candle available over my head. And if there is a Communist who feels offended by Peppone, he is welcome to break a hammer and sickle on my back. But if there is anyone who is offended by the conversations of Christ, I can't help it; for the one who speaks in this story is not Christ, but my Christ —that is, the voice of my conscience.

11

A CONFESSION

DON CAMILLO had been born with a constitutional preference
for calling a spade a spade. Upon a certain occasion when
there had been a local scandal involving landowners of ripe
age and young girls of his parish, he had, in the course of his
Mass, embarked upon a seemly and suitably generalised
address, when he had suddenly become aware of the fact that
one of the chief offenders was present among the foremost
ranks of his congregation. Flinging all restraint to the four
winds and also flinging a hastily snatched cloth over the head
of the Crucified Lord above the high altar in order that the
divine ears might not be offended, he had set his arms firmly
akimbo and had resumed his sermon. And so stentorian had
been the voice that issued from the lips of the big man and
so uncompromising had been his language that the very roof
of the little church had seemed to tremble.

When the time of the elections drew near Don Camillo
had naturally been explicit in his allusions to the local
leftists. Thus there came a fine evening when, as he was going
home at dusk, an individual muffled in a cloak sprang out of
a hedge as he passed by and, taking advantage of the fact
that Don Camillo was handicapped by his bicycle and by a
large parcel containing seventy eggs attached to its handlebars, belaboured him with a heavy stick and promptly
vanished as though the earth had swallowed him.

Don Camillo had kept his own counsel. Having arrived
at the presbytery and deposited the eggs in safety, he had

gone into the church to discuss the matter with the Lord, as was his invariable habit in moments of perplexity.

"What should I do?" Don Camillo had inquired.

"Anoint your back with a little oil beaten up in water and hold your tongue," the Lord had replied from above the altar. "We must forgive those who offend us. That is the rule."

"Very true, Lord," agreed Don Camillo, "but on this occasion we are discussing blows, not offences."

"And what do you mean by that? Surely you are not trying to tell me that injuries done to the body are more painful than those aimed at the spirit?"

"I see your point, Lord. But You should also bear in mind that in the beating of me, who am Your minister, an injury has been done to Yourself also. I am really more concerned on Your behalf than on my own."

"And was I not a greater minister of God than you are? And did I not forgive those who nailed me to the Cross?"

"There is never any use in arguing with You!" Don Camillo had exclaimed. "You are always in the right. Your will be done. We must forgive. All the same, don't forget that if these ruffians, encouraged by my silence, should crack my skull, the responsibility will lie with You. I could cite several passages from the Old Testament. . . ."

"Don Camillo, are you proposing to instruct me in the Old Testament? As for this business, I assume full responsibility. Moreover, strictly between Ourselves, the beating has done you no harm. It may teach you to let politics alone in my house."

Don Camillo had duly forgiven. But nevertheless one thing had stuck in his gullet like a fish bone; curiosity as to the identity of his assailant.

Time passed. Late one evening, while he sat in the confessional, Don Camillo discerned through the grille the countenance of the local leader of the extreme leftists, Peppone.

That Peppone should come to confession at all was a sensational event, and Don Camillo was proportionately gratified.

"God be with you, brother; with you who, more than any other man, have need of His holy blessing. It is a long time since you last went to confession?"

13

"Not since 1918," replied Peppone.

"You must have committed a great number of sins in the course of those twenty-eight years, with your head so crammed with crazy notions. . . ."

"A good few, undoubtedly," sighed Peppone.

"For example?"

"For example, two months ago I gave you a hiding."

"That was serious indeed," replied Don Camillo, "since in assaulting a minister of God, you have attacked God Himself."

"But I have repented," exclaimed Peppone. "And, moreover, it was not as God's minister that I beat you, but as my political adversary. In any case, I did it in a moment of weakness."

"Apart from this and from your membership of your accursed Party, have you any other grave sins on your conscience?"

Peppone spilled all the beans.

Taken as a whole, his offences were not very serious, and Don Camillo let him off with a score of Paters and Aves. Then, while Peppone was kneeling at the altar rails performing his penance, Don Camillo went and knelt before the crucifix.

"Lord," he said. "You must forgive me, but I am going to beat him up for You."

"You are going to do nothing of the kind," replied the Lord. "I have forgiven him and you must forgive him also. All things considered, he is not a bad soul."

"Lord, you can never trust a Red! They live by lies. Only look at him; Barabbas incarnate!"

"It's as good a face as most, Don Camillo; it is your heart that is venomous!"

"Lord, if I have ever served you well, grant me just one small grace: let me at least break this candle on his shoulders. Dear Lord, what, after all, is a candle?"

"No," replied the Lord. "Your hands were made for blessing, not for striking."

Don Camillo sighed heavily.

He genuflected and left the sanctuary. As he turned to make a final sign of the cross he found himself exactly behind Peppone who, on his knees, was apparently absorbed in prayer.

"Lord," groaned Don Camillo, clasping his hands and

14

gazing at the crucifix. "My hands were made for blessing, but not my feet!"

"There is something in that," replied the Lord from above the altar, "but all the same, Don Camillo, bear it in mind: only one!"

The kick landed like a thunderbolt and Peppone received it without so much as blinking an eye. Then he got to his feet and sighed with relief.

"I've been waiting for that for the last ten minutes," he remarked. "I feel better now."

"So do I!" exclaimed Don Camillo, whose heart was now as light and serene as a May morning.

The Lord said nothing at all, but it was easy enough to see that He too was pleased.

A BAPTISM

ONE DAY the church was unexpectedly invaded by a man and two women, one of whom was Peppone's wife.

Don Camillo, who from the top of a pair of steps was cleaning St. Joseph's halo with Brasso, turned round and inquired what they wanted.

"There is something here that needs to be baptised," replied the man, and one of the women held up a bundle containing a baby.

"Whose is it?" inquired Don Camillo, coming down from his steps.

"Mine," replied Peppone's wife.

"And your husband's?" persisted Don Camillo.

"Well, naturally! Who else do you suppose gave it to me?" retorted Peppone's wife indignantly.

"No need to be offended," observed Don Camillo on his way to the sacristy. "Haven't I been told often enough that your Party approves of free love?"

As he passed before the high altar Don Camillo knelt down and permitted himself a discreet wink in the direction of the Lord. "Did you hear that one?" he murmured with a joyful grin. "One in the eye for the Godless ones!"

"Don't talk rubbish, Don Camillo," replied the Lord irritably. "If they had no God, why should they come here to get their child baptised? If Peppone's wife had boxed your ears it would only have served you right."

"If Peppone's wife had boxed my ears I should have taken

16

the three of them by the scruff of their necks and . . ."

"And what?" inquired the Lord severely.

"Oh, nothing; just a figure of speech," Don Camillo hastened to assure Him, rising to his feet.

"Don Camillo, watch your step," said the Lord sternly.

Duly vested, Don Camillo approached the font. "What do you wish to name this child?" he asked Peppone's wife.

"Lenin Libero Antonio," she replied.

"Then go and get him baptised in Russia," said Don Camillo calmly, replacing the cover on the font.

The priest's hands were as large as shovels and the three left the church without protest. But as Don Camillo was attempting to slip into the sacristy he was arrested by the voice of the Lord.

"Don Camillo, you have done a very wicked thing. Go at once and bring those people back and baptise their child."

"But Lord," protested Don Camillo, "you really must bear in mind that baptism is not a jest. Baptism is a very sacred matter. Baptism is . . ."

"Don Camillo," the Lord interrupted him. "Are you attempting to teach me the nature of baptism? Did I not invent it? I tell you that you have been guilty of gross presumption, because, suppose that child were to die at this moment, it would be your fault if it failed to attain Paradise!"

"Lord, do not let us be melodramatic," retorted Don Camillo. "Why in the name of Heaven should it die? It's as pink and white as a rose!"

"Which means exactly nothing!" the Lord admonished him. "What if a tile should fall on its head or it should suddenly have convulsions? It was your duty to baptise it."

Don Camillo raised protesting arms: "But Lord, just think it over. If it were certain that the child would go to Hell, we might stretch a point; but seeing that despite being the son of that nasty piece of work he might very easily manage to slip into Paradise, how can You ask me to risk anyone going there with such a name as Lenin? I'm thinking of the reputation of Paradise."

"The reputation of Paradise is my business," shouted the Lord angrily. "What matters to me is that a man should be a decent fellow and I care less than nothing whether his name be Lenin or Button. At the very most, you should have pointed out to those people that saddling children with fantastic names may involve them in annoyances when they grow up."

"Very well," replied Don Camillo. "I am always in the wrong. I must see what I can do about it."

Just at that moment someone came into the church. It was Peppone, alone, with the baby in his arms. He closed the church door and bolted it.

"I do not leave this church," he said, "until my son has been baptised with the name that I have chosen."

"Look at that," whispered Don Camillo, smiling as he turned towards the Lord. "Now do You see what these people are? One is filled with the holiest intentions and this is how they treat you."

"Put yourself in his place," replied the Lord. "One may not approve his attitude, but one can understand it."

Don Camillo shook his head.

"I have already said that I do not leave this place unless you baptise my son as I demand!" repeated Peppone. Whereupon, laying the bundle containing the baby upon a bench, he took off his coat, rolled up his sleeves and advanced threateningly.

"Lord," implored Don Camillo. "I ask You! If You think it just that one of your priests should give way to the threats of a layman, then I must obey. But in that event, if to-morrow they should bring me a calf and compel me to baptise it You must not complain. You know very well how dangerous it is to create precedents."

"All right," replied the Lord, "but in this case you must try to make him understand...."

"And if he hits me?"

"Then you must accept it. You must endure and suffer as I did."

Don Camillo turned to his visitor. "Very well, Peppone," he said. "The baby will leave the church baptised, but not by that accursed name."

"Don Camillo," stuttered Peppone, "don't forget that my stomach has never recovered from that bullet that I stopped in the mountains. If you hit low, I shall go for you with a bench."

"Don't worry, Peppone. I can deal with you entirely in the upper storeys," Don Camillo assured him, landing him a neat one above the ear.

18

They were both burly men with muscles of steel, and their blows fairly whistled through the air. After twenty minutes of silent and furious combat, Don Camillo distinctly heard a voice behind him. "Now, Don Camillo! The point of the jaw!" It came from the Lord above the altar. Don Camillo struck hard and Peppone crashed to the ground.

He remained where he lay for some ten minutes; then he sat up, got to his feet, rubbed his jaw, shook himself, put on his jacket and reknotted his red handkerchief. Then he picked up the baby. Fully vested, Don Camillo was waiting for him, steady as a rock, beside the font. Peppone approached him slowly.

"What am I to name him?" asked Don Camillo.

"Camillo Libero Antonio," muttered Peppone.

Don Camillo shook his head. "No; we will name him Libero Camillo Lenin," he said. "Yes, Lenin. When you have a Camillo around, such folk as he are quite helpless."

"Amen," muttered Peppone, gently prodding his jaw.

When all was done and Don Camillo passed before the altar the Lord smiled and remarked: "Don Camillo, I am bound to admit that in politics you are My master."

"And also in fisticuffs," replied Don Camillo with perfect gravity, carelessly fingering a large lump on his forehead.

ON THE TRAIL

DON CAMILLO had let himself go a bit in the course of a little sermon with a local background, allowing himself some rather pointed allusions to *"certain people"* and it was thus that on the following evening, when he seized the ropes of the church bells—the bell-ringer having been called away on some pretext—all hell broke out. Some damned soul had tied crackers to the clappers of the bells. No harm done, of course, but there was a shattering din of explosions, enough to give the ringer heart failure.

Don Camillo had not said a word. He had celebrated the evening service in perfect composure, before a crowded congregation from which not one was absent, with Peppone in the front row and every countenance a picture of fervour. It was enough to infuriate a saint, but Don Camillo was no novice in self-control and his audience had gone home disappointed.

As soon as the big doors were closed, Don Camillo snatched up an overcoat and on his way out went to make a hasty genuflection before the altar.

"Don Camillo," said the Lord, "put it down."

"I don't understand," protested Don Camillo.

"Put it down!"

Don Camillo drew a heavy stick from beneath his coat and laid it in front of the altar.

"Not a pleasant sight, Don Camillo."

"But, Lord! It isn't even oak; it's only poplar, light and supple . . ." Don Camillo pleaded.

"Go to bed, Don Camillo, and forget about Peppone."

Don Camillo had raised his arms and had gone to bed with a temperature. And so when on the following evening Peppone's wife made her appearance at the presbytery, he leaped to his feet as though a cracker had gone off under his chair.

"Don Camillo," began the woman, who was visibly greatly agitated. But Don Camillo interrupted her "Get out of my sight, sacrilegious creature!"

"Don Camillo, never mind about that foolishness. At Castellino there is that poor wretch who tried to do in Peppone! They have turned him out!"

Don Camillo lighted a cigar. "Well, what about it, comrade? I didn't make the amnesty. And in any case, why should you bother about it?"

The woman started to shout. "I'm bothering because they came to tell Peppone, and Peppone has gone rushing off to Castellino like a lunatic. And he has taken his tommy-gun with him!"

"I see; then you have got concealed arms, have you?"

"Don Camillo, never mind about politics! Can't you understand that Peppone is out to kill? Unless you help me, my man is done for!"

Don Camillo laughed unpleasantly. "Which will teach him to tie crackers to the clappers of my bells. I shall be pleased to watch him die in gaol! You get out of my house!"

Ten minutes later, Don Camillo, with his skirts tucked up almost to his neck, was pedalling like a lunatic along the road to Castellino astride a racing bicycle belonging to the son of his sacristan.

There was a splendid moon and when he was about four miles from Castellino Don Camillo saw by its light a man sitting on the low parapet of the little bridge that spans the Fossone. He slowed down, since it is always best to be prudent when one travels by night, and halted some ten yards from the bridge, holding in his hand a small object that he happened to have discovered in his pocket.

"My lad," he inquired, "have you seen a big man go by on a bicycle in the direction of Castellino?"

"No, Don Camillo," replied the other quietly.

Don Camillo drew nearer, "Have you already been to Castellino?" he asked.

"No. I thought it over. It wasn't worth while. Was it my fool of a wife who put you to this trouble?"

"Trouble? Nothing of the kind . . . a little constitutional!"

"Have you any idea what a priest looks like on a racing bicycle?" sniggered Peppone.

Don Camillo came and sat beside him on his wall. "My son, you must be prepared to see all kinds of things in this world."

Less than an hour later, Don Camillo was back at the presbytery and went to make his report to the Lord.

"All went well according to Your instructions."

"Well done, Don Camillo, but would you mind telling me who it was that instructed you to take him by the feet and tumble him into the ditch?"

Don Camillo raised his arms. "To tell you the truth, I really can't remember exactly. As a matter of fact, he appeared to dislike the sight of a priest on a racing bicycle, so it seemed only kind to prevent him from seeing it any longer."

"I understand. Has he got back yet?"

"He'll be here soon. Seeing him fall into the ditch, it struck me that as he would be coming home in a rather damp condition he might find the bicycle in his way, so I thought it best to bring it along with me."

"Very kind of you, I'm sure, Don Camillo," said the Lord with perfect gravity.

Peppone appeared just before dawn at the door of the presbytery. He was soaked to the skin, and Don Camillo asked if it was raining.

"Fog," replied Peppone with chattering teeth. "May I have my bicycle?"

"Why, of course. There it is."

"Are you sure there wasn't a tommy-gun tied to it?"

Don Camillo raised his arms with a smile. "A tommy-gun? And what may that be?"

"I," said Peppone as he turned from the door, "have made one mistake in my life. I tied crackers to the clappers of your bells. It should have been half a ton of dynamite."

Errare humanum est," remarked Don Camillo.

EVENING SCHOOL

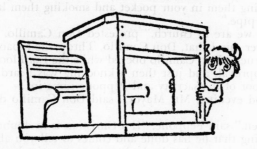

IN THE empty church, by the faint light of the two altar candles, Don Camillo was chatting with the Lord about the outcome of the local elections.

"I wouldn't presume to criticize Your actions," he wound up, "but I should never have allowed Peppone to become mayor with a council in which only two people really know how to read and write properly."

"Culture is entirely without importance, Don Camillo," replied the Lord with a smile. "What counts is ideas Eloquent speeches get nowhere unless there are practical ideas at the back of them. Before judging, suppose we put them to the test."

"Fair enough," conceded Don Camillo. "I really said what I did because, in the event of the lawyer's party coming out top, I had already been given assurances that the bell tower of the church would be repaired. In any case, should it fall down, the people will have compensation in watching the construction of a magnificent People's Palace with dancing, sale of alcoholic liquors, gambling and a theatre for variety entertainments."

"And a lock-up for such venomous reptiles as Don Camillo," added the Lord.

Don Camillo lowered his head. "Lord, You misjudge me," he said. "You know what a cigar means to me? Well look: this is the only cigar I possess, and look what I am doing with it."

He pulled a cigar out of his pocket and crumbled it in his enormous hand.

"Well done," said the Lord, "Well done. Don Camillo. I accept your penance. Nevertheless, I should like to see you throw away the crumbs, because you would be quite capable of putting them in your pocket and smoking them later on in your pipe."

"But we are in church," protested Don Camillo.

"Never mind that, Don Camillo. Throw the tobacco into that corner." Don Camillo obeyed while the Lord looked on with approval, and just then a knocking was heard at the little door of the sacristy and Peppone came in.

"Good evening, Mr. Mayor," said Don Camillo deferentially.

"Listen," said Peppone. "If a Christian is in doubt about something that he has done and comes to tell you about it, and if you found that he had made some mistakes, would you point them out to him or would you simply leave him in ignorance?"

Don Camillo protested indignantly: "How can you dare to doubt the honesty of a priest? His primary duty is to point out clearly all the penitent's mistakes."

"Very well, then," exclaimed Peppone. "Are you quite ready to hear my confession?"

"I am ready."

Peppone pulled a large sheet of paper from his pocket and began to read: "Citizens, at the moment when we are hailing the victorious affirmation of our Party . . ."

Don Camillo interrupted him with a gesture and went to kneel before the altar. "Lord," he murmured, "I am no longer responsible for my actions."

"But I am," said the Lord promptly. "Peppone has outwitted you, and you must play fair and do your duty."

"But, Lord," persisted Don Camillo. "You realize, don't You, that You are making me work on behalf of the Agit-Prop?"

"You are working on behalf of grammar, syntax and spelling, none of which is either diabolical or sectarian."

Don Camillo put on his spectacles, grasped a pencil and set to work on the tottering periods of the speech that Peppone was to make on the following day. Peppone read it through intently.

"Good," he approved. "There is only one thing that I do

24

not understand. Where I had said: '*It is our intention to extend the schools and to rebuild the bridge over the Fossalto,*' you have substituted: '*It is our intention to extend the schools, repair the church tower and rebuild the bridge over the Fossalto.*' Why is that?"

"A mere matter of syntax," explained Don Camillo gravely.

"Blessed are those who have studied Latin and who are able to understand niceties of language," sighed Peppone. "And so," he added, "we are to lose even the hope that the tower may collapse on to your head!"

Don Camillo raised his arms. "We must all bow before the will of God!"

When he returned from accompanying Peppone to the door, Don Camillo came to say good night to the Lord.

"Well done, Don Camillo," said the Lord with a smile. "I was unjust to you and I am sorry you destroyed your last cigar. It was a penance that you did not deserve. Nevertheless, we may as well be frank about it: Peppone was a skunk not to offer you even a cigar, after all the trouble you took!"

"Oh, all right," sighed Don Camillo, fishing a cigar from his pocket and preparing to crush it in his big hand.

"No, Don Camillo," smiled the Lord. "Go and smoke it in peace. You have earned it."

"But..."

"No, Don Camillo; you didn't steal it. Peppone had two cigars in his pocket. Peppone is a Communist. He believes in sharing things. In skilfully relieving him of one cigar, you only took your fair share."

"You always know best," exclaimed Don Camillo with deep respect.

OUT OF BOUNDS

Don Camillo was in the habit of going to measure the famous crack in the church tower, and every morning his inspection met with the same result: the crack had not increased in width, but neither had it diminished. Finally, he lost his temper and one day he dispatched the sacristan to the headquarters of the Commune.

"Go and tell the mayor to come at once and look at this damage. Explain that the matter is serious."

The sacristan went and returned.

"Peppone says that he will take your word for it that it is a serious matter. In any case, he also said that if you really want to show him the crack, you had better take the tower to him in his office. He will be available there until five o'clock."

Don Camillo did not bat an eyelid: all he said was: "If Peppone or any member of his gang has the courage to turn up at Mass to-morrow we shall see something sensational. But they know it, and not one of them will put in an appearance."

The next morning there was no sign of a Red in church, but five minutes before Mass was due to begin the sound of marching was heard upon the flags before the church door. In perfect formation all the Reds, not only those of the village but also those of neighbouring cells, every man jack of them including the cobbler, Bilò, who had a wooden leg, and Roldo dei Prati, who was shivering with fever, came marching proudly towards the church, led by Peppone. With perfect composure they took their seats in church, sitting in a solid phalanx with faces as ferocious as the cruiser *Potemkin*.

When Don Camillo had finished his sermon, a very cultured exposition of the parable of the good Samaritan, he followed it by a brief exhortation to the faithful.

"As you all know, a most dangerous crack is threatening the security of the church tower. I therefore appeal to you, my dear brethren in the faith, to come to the assistance of the house of God. In using the term 'brethren in the faith' I am addressing those decent folk who come here with a desire to draw near to God, and not certain individuals who come only in order to parade their militarism. To such as these it can matter nothing should the tower fall to the ground."

The Mass over, Don Camillo settled himself at a table near the presbytery door and the congregation filed past him, but not a soul left the place. One and all, having made the expected donation, remained on the little *piazzetta* in front of the church to watch developments. And last of all came Peppone, followed by his battalion in perfect formation. They drew up to a defiant halt before the table.

Peppone stepped forward proudly.

"From this tower, in the past, the bells have hailed the dawn of freedom, and from it, to-morrow, they shall welcome the glorious dawn of the proletarian revolution," said Peppone to Don Camillo as he laid on the table before him three large red handkerchiefs full of money.

Then he turned on his heel and marched away, followed by his gang. And Roldo dei Pratti was shaking with fever and could scarcely remain on his feet, but he held his head erect, and the crippled Bilò, as he passed Don Camillo, stamped his wooden leg defiantly in perfect step with his comrades.

When Don Camillo went to the Lord to show Him the basket containing the money and told Him that there was more than enough for the repair of the tower, the Lord smiled in astonishment.

"You were quite right, Don Camillo."

"Naturally," replied Don Camillo. "Because you understand humanity, but I know Italians."

Up to that moment Don Camillo had behaved well. But he made a mistake when he sent a message to Peppone to the effect that he had much admired the military smartness of his men, but that he advised him to give them more intensive drilling in right-about-turn and the double, of which they would have urgent need on the day of the proletarian revolution.

This was deplorable, and Peppone prepared to retaliate.

Don Camillo was an honest man, but in addition to an overwhelming passion for shooting he possessed a splendid double-barrelled gun and a good supply of cartridges. Moreover, Baron Stocco's private shoot lay only three miles from the village and constituted a permanent temptation, because not only game but even the neighbouring poultry had learned that they were in safety behind his fence of wire netting and once within it could thumb their noses at anyone who wished to wring their necks.

It was therefore not at all astonishing that on a certain evening Don Camillo, his skirts bundled into an enormous pair of breeches and his face partly concealed beneath the brim of an ancient felt hat, should find himself actually on the business side of the baron's fence. The flesh is weak and the flesh of the sportsman particularly so.

Nothing to be surprised at, therefore, if Don Camillo fired a shot that brought down a hare almost under his nose. He thrust it into his game-bag and was beating a retreat when he suddenly found himself face to face with another invader. Ramming his hat down over his eyes, he butted the stranger in the stomach with the intention of knocking him out, since it was undesirable that the countryside should learn that their parish priest had been caught poaching.

Unfortunately, his adversary conceived the same idea at precisely the same moment and the two heads met with a crash so tremendous that both parties found themselves sitting on the ground seeing stars.

"A pate as hard as that can only belong to our beloved mayor," muttered Don Camillo as his vision began to clear.

"A pate as hard as that can only belong to our beloved parish priest," replied Peppone, scratching his head. For Peppone also was poaching on forbidden ground and also had a hare in his game-bag, and his eye gleamed as he surveyed Don Camillo.

"Never would I have believed," said Peppone, "that the very man who preaches respect for other people's property would be found breaking through the fences of a preserve in order to go poaching.

"Nor would I have believed that our chief citizen, our comrade mayor . . ."

"Citizen, yes, but also comrade," Peppone interrupted, "and therefore perverted by those diabolic theories that aim at the fair distribution of all property, and therefore acting more logically in accordance with his known views than the reverend Don Camillo, who, for his part . . ."

Someone was approaching them and had drawn so near that it was quite impossible to take to their heels without the risk of stopping a charge of shot, since on this occasion the intruder happened to be a gamekeeper.

"We've got to do something!" whispered Don Camillo. "Think of the scandal if we are recognized!"

"Personally, I don't care," replied Peppone with composure. "I am always ready to answer for my actions."

The steps drew nearer and Don Camillo melted against a large tree trunk. Peppone made no attempt to move, and when the gamekeeper appeared with his gun over his arm Peppone greeted him:

"Good evening."

"What are you doing here?" inquired the gamekeeper.

"Looking for mushrooms."

"With a gun?"

"As good a means as another."

The means whereby a gamekeeper can be rendered relatively innocuous are also fairly simple. If one happens to be standing behind him, it suffices to muffle his head unexpectedly in an overcoat and give him a good rap on the head. Advantage can then be taken of his moment of unconsciousness in order to reach the hedge and scramble over it. Once over, all is well.

Don Camillo and Peppone found themselves sitting behind a bush a good mile away from the Baron's estate:

"Don Camillo!" sighed Peppone. "We have committed a serious offence. We have raised our hands against one in authority! That is a felony."

Don Camillo, who had in point of fact been the one to raise them, broke out into a cold sweat.

"My conscience troubles me," pursued the tormentor. "I shall have no peace remembering so horrible a thing. How shall I dare present myself before a minister of God to ask forgiveness for such a misdeed? Accursed be the day when I lent an ear to the infamous lures of the Muscovite doctrine, forgetting the holy precepts of Christian charity!"

Don Camillo was so deeply humiliated that he wanted to cry. On the other hand, he also wanted desperately to land one good crack on the pate of his perverted adversary, and as Peppone was well aware of the fact, he left off.

"Accursed temptation!" he shouted suddenly, pulling the hare out of his bag and hurling it from him.

"Accursed indeed!" shouted Don Camillo, and, hauling out his own hare, he flung it far into the snow and walked away with bent head. Peppone followed him as far as the cross-road and then turned to the right.

"By the way," he asked, pausing for a moment, "could you tell me of a reputable parish priest in this neighbourhood to whom I could go and confess this sin?"

Don Camillo clenched his fists and walked straight ahead.

When he had gathered sufficient courage to present himself before the Lord above the altar, Don Camillo spread his arms wide.

"I didn't do it to save myself, Lord," he said. "I did it simply because, had it become known that I go poaching, the Church would have been the chief sufferer from the scandal." But the Lord remained silent, and in such cases Don Camillo acquired a quartan ague and put himself on a diet of bread and water for days and days, until the Lord felt sorry for him and said: "Enough."

This time, the Lord said nothing until the bread-and-water diet had continued for seven days. Don Camillo had reached the stage where he could only remain standing by leaning against a wall and his stomach was fairly bawling with hunger.

Then Peppone came for confession.

"I have sinned against the law and Christian charity," said Peppone.

"I know it," replied Don Camillo.

"Moreover, as soon as you were out of sight, I went back and collected both the hares and I have roasted one and jugged the other."

"Just what I supposed you would do," murmured Don Camillo. And when he passed the altar a little later, the Lord smiled at him, not so much on account of his prolonged fast as in consideration of the fact that Don Camillo, when he had murmured, "Just what I supposed you would do," had felt no desire to hit Peppone but had experienced profound shame at the remembrance that on that same evening he himself had had a momentary temptation to do exactly the same thing.

"Poor Don Camillo," whispered the Lord tenderly. And Don Camillo spread out his arms as though he wished to say that he did his best and that if he sometimes made mistakes it was not deliberately.

"I know, I know, Don Camillo," replied the Lord. "And now get along and eat your hare—for Peppone has left it for you, nicely cooked, in the presbytery kitchen."

THE TREASURE

ONE DAY Smilzo made his appearance at the presbytery. He was a young ex-partisan who had been Peppone's orderly during the fighting in the mountains and the latter had now taken him on as messenger to the Commune. He was the bearer of a handsome letter printed in Gothic lettering on hand-made paper and with the Party heading.

"Your honour is invited to grace with his presence a ceremony of a social nature which will take place tomorrow at ten o'clock a.m. in Piazza della Libertà. The Secretary of the Section, Comrade Bottazzi, Mayor, Giuseppe."

Don Camillo looked severely at Smilzo. "Tell Comrade Peppone Mayor Giuseppe that I have no wish to go and listen to the usual imbecilities against reaction and the capitalists. I already know them by heart."

"No," explained Smilzo. "This is no affair of political speeches. This is a question of patriotism and social activities. If you refuse it means that you know nothing of democracy."

Don Camillo nodded his head slowly. "If that is so," he said, "then I have nothing more to say."

"Very good. And the leader says you are to come in uniform and to bring all your paraphernalia."

"Paraphernalia?"

"Yes: the pail and the brush; there is something to be blessed."

Smilzo permitted himself to speak in such a manner to Don Camillo precisely because he was Smilzo—that is to say, the lean one, and so built that by virtue of his amazing swiftness of movement he had been able in the mountains to slip between bullet and bullet without coming to harm. By the time, therefore, that the heavy book flung at him by Don Camillo reached the spot where his head had been, Smilzo had already left the presbytery and was pedalling away for dear life.

Don Camillo got up, rescued the book and went to let off steam to the Lord at the altar.

"Lord," he said, "is it conceivable that I should be unable to find out what those people are planning to do to-morrow? I never knew anything so mysterious. What is the meaning of all these preparations? All those branches that they are sticking into the ground round the meadow between the pharmacy and the Baghetti's house? What kind of devilry can they be up to?"

"My son, if it were devilry, first of all they wouldn't be doing it in the open and secondly they wouldn't be sending for you to bless it. Be patient until to-morrow."

That evening Don Camillo went to have a look round but he saw nothing but branches and decorations surrounding the meadow and nobody appeared to know anything.

When he set out next morning, followed by two acolytes, his knees were trembling. He felt that something was not as it should be, that there was treachery in the air.

He returned an hour later, shattered and with a temperature.

"What has happened?" inquired the Lord from the altar.

"Enough to make one's hair stand on end," stammered Don Camillo. "A terrible thing. A band, Garibaldi's hymn, a speech from Peppone and the laying of the foundation stone of 'The People's Palace'! And I had to bless the stone while Peppone chuckled with joy. And the ruffian asked me to say a few words, and I had to make a suitable little address because, although it is a Party activity, the rascal dressed it up as a social undertaking."

Don Camillo paced to and fro in the empty church. Then he came to a standstill in front of the Lord. "A mere trifle," he exclaimed. "An assembly hall, reading-room, library, gymnasium, dispensary and theatre. A skyscraper of two

33

floors with adjacent ground for sports and *bocce*. And the whole lot for the miserable sum of ten million lire."

"By no means dear, given the present prices," observed the Lord.

Don Camillo sank down upon a bench. "Lord," he sighed dolefully, "why have You done this to me?"

"Don Camillo, you are unreasonable."

"No: I am not unreasonable. For ten years I have been praying to You on my knees to find me a little money so that I could establish a library, an assembly hall for the young people, a playground for the children with a merry-go-round and swings and possibly a little swimming pool like they have at Castellino. For ten years I have lowered myself making up to swine of bloated landowners when I should have liked to box their ears every time I saw them. I must have got up quite two hundred lotteries and knocked at quite two thousand doors, and I have nothing at all to show for it. Then along comes this excommunicate mounte-bank, and behold ten million lire drop into his pockets from heaven."

The Lord shook His head. "They didn't fall from heaven," he replied. "He found them underground. I had nothing to do with it, Don Camillo. It is entirely due to his own personal initiative."

Don Camillo spread out his arms. "Then it is simple enough and the obvious deduction is that I am a poor fool."

Don Camillo went off to stamp up and down his study in the presbytery, roaring with fury. He must exclude the possibility that Peppone had got himself that ten million by holding people up on the roads or by robbing a bank. "That fellow, in the days of the liberation, when he came down from the mountains and it seemed as if the proletarian revolution might break out at any moment, must have played upon the funk of those cowards of gentry and squeezed their money out of them."

Then he reflected that at that time there had been no gentry in the neighbourhood, but that, on the other hand, there had been a detachment of the British Army which had arrived simultaneously with Peppone and his men. The British had taken possession of the gentry's houses, taking the place of the Germans, who, having spent some time in the countryside, had thoroughly cleared those houses of everything of any value. It was therefore out of the question that Peppone should have obtained his ten million by looting.

Possibly the money had come from Russia? He burst out laughing: was it likely that the Russians should give a thought to Peppone?

At last he returned to the church. "Lord," he begged from the foot of the altar, "won't You tell me where Peppone found the money?"

"Don Camillo," replied the Lord with a smile, "do you take Me for a private detective? Why ask God to tell you the truth when you have only to seek it within yourself? Look for it, Don Camillo, and meanwhile, in order to distract your mind, why not make a trip to the town?"

On the following evening, having returned from his excursion to the town, Don Camillo presented himself before the Lord in a condition of extreme agitation.

"What has upset you, Don Camillo?"

"Something quite crazy," exclaimed Don Camillo breathlessly. "I have met a dead man! Face to face in the street!"

"Don Camillo, calm yourself and reflect: usually the dead whom one meets face to face in the streets are alive."

"This one cannot be!" shouted Don Camillo. "This one is dead as mutton, and I know it because I myself carried him to the cemetery."

"If that is the case," replied the Lord, "then I have nothing more to say. You must have seen a ghost."

Don Camillo shrugged his shoulders. "Of course not! Ghosts have no existence except in the foolish pates of hysterical women!"

"And therefore?"

"Well . . ." muttered Don Camillo.

Don Camillo collected his thoughts. The deceased had been a thin young man, not a native of the village, who had come down from the mountains with Peppone and his men. He had been wounded in the head and was in a bad state, and they had fixed him up in the former German headquarters, which had become the headquarters of the British Command. Peppone had established his own office in the room next to that of the invalid. Don Camillo remembered it all clearly: the villa was surrounded by sentries three deep and not a fly could leave it unperceived, because the

British were still fighting nearby and were particularly careful of their own skins.

All this had happened one morning, and on the same evening the young man had died. Peppone had sent for Don Camillo towards midnight, but by the time he had got there the young man had been already in his coffin. The British didn't want the body in the house, and so, at about noon, the coffin, covered with the Italian flag, was carried out of the villa by Peppone and his most trusted men. A detachment of British soldiers had kindly volunteered to supply the military honours.

Don Camillo recalled that the ceremony had been moving: all the village had walked behind the coffin, which had been placed on a gun carriage. He himself had made the address before the body was lowered into the grave, and people had actually wept. Peppone, in the front row, had sobbed.

"When I put my mind to it, I certainly know how to express myself!" said Don Camillo to himself complacently, recalling the episode. Then he returned to his original train of thought. "And in spite of all that, I am prepared to take my oath that the young man whom I met to-day in the town was the same as the one I followed to the grave." He sighed. "Such is life!"

The following day Don Camillo sought out Peppone at his workshop, where he found him lying on his back underneath a car.

"Good morning, Comrade Mayor. I have come to tell you that for the past two days I have been thinking over your description of your People's Palace!"

"And what do you think of it?" jeered Peppone.

"Magnificent! It has made me decide to start work on that scheme of a little place with a bathing-pool, garden, sports ground, theatre, etcetera, which, as you know, I have had in mind for twenty years past. I shall be laying the foundation stone next Sunday. It would give me great pleasure if you, as mayor, would attend the ceremony."

"Willingly: courtesy for courtesy."

"In the meanwhile, you might try to cut down the plans for your own place a bit. It looks like being too big for my personal taste."

Peppone stared at him in amazement. "Don Camillo, are you demented?"

"Not more than I was when I conducted a funeral and

36

made a patriotic address over a coffin that can't have been securely closed, because only yesterday I met the corpse walking about the town."

Peppone ground his teeth. "What are you trying to insinuate?"

"Nothing: only that that coffin to which the British presented arms was full of what you found in the cellars of the Villa Dotti, where the German Command had hidden it. And that the dead man was alive and concealed in the attic."

"A-a-h!" howled Peppone. "The same old story! An attempt to malign the partisan movement!"

"Leave the partisans out of it. I take no interest in them!"

And he walked away while Peppone stood muttering vague threats.

That same evening, Don Camillo was awaiting him at the presbytery when he arrived accompanied by Brusco and two other prominent supporters—the same men who had acted as coffin-bearers.

"You," said Peppone, "can drop your insinuations. It was all of it stuff looted by the Germans—silver, cameras, instruments, gold, etcetera. If we hadn't taken it, the British would have had it. Ours was the only possible means of getting it out of the place. I have here witnesses and receipts: nobody has touched so much as a lira. Ten million was taken and ten million will be spent for the people."

Brusco, who was hot-tempered, began to shout that it was God's truth and that he, if necessary, knew well enough how to deal with certain people.

"So do I," Don Camillo replied calmly. He dropped the newspaper which he had been holding extended in front of himself and thus allowed it to be seen that under his right arm-pit he held the famous tommy-gun that had once belonged to Peppone.

Brusco turned pale and retreated hastily, but Peppone extended his arms. "Don Camillo, it doesn't seem to me that there is any need to quarrel."

"I agree," replied Don Camillo. "The more easily as I am entirely of your opinion. Ten million was acquired and ten million should be spent on the people. Seven on your People's Palace and three on my recreation centre for the people's children. Suffer the little children to come unto me. I ask only what is my due."

The four consulted together for a moment in undertones. Then Peppone spoke: "If you hadn't got that damnable thing in your hands, I should tell you that your suggestion is the filthiest blackmail in the universe.

On the following Sunday Peppone, together with all the village council, assisted at the laying of the foundation stone of Don Camillo's recreation centre. He also made a short speech. However, he found a means of whispering in Don Camillo's ear:

"It might be better to tie this stone round your neck and throw you into the Po."

That evening Don Camillo went to make his report to the Lord above the altar.

"Well; what do You think about it?" he said in conclusion.

"Exactly what Peppone said to you. That if you hadn't got that damnable thing in your hands, I should say that it was the filthiest blackmail in the universe."

"But I have nothing at all in my hands except the cheque that Peppone has just given me."

"Precisely," whispered the Lord. "And with that three million you are going to do so many beautiful things, Don Camillo, that I haven't the heart to scold you."

Don Camillo genuflected and went off to bed to dream of a garden full of children—a garden with a merry-go-round and a swing, and seated on the swing Peppone's youngest son chirping joyfully like a fledgling.

RIVALRY

A BIG noise from the town was expected on a visit, and people were coming from all the surrounding cells. Therefore Peppone decreed that the ceremony should be held in the big square, and he not only had a large platform, decorated with red, set up, but he got hold of one of those trucks with four great loudspeakers and all the electric mechanism inside them for amplifying the voice. And so, on the afternoon of that Sunday, the big square was crammed to overflowing with people, and so also was the church square, which happened to be adjacent.

Don Camillo had shut all the doors and withdrawn into the sacristy, so as to avoid seeing or hearing anything which would work him up into a temper. He was actually dozing when a voice like the wrath of God roused him with a jerk as it bellowed: *"Comrades! . . ."*

It was as though the walls had melted away.

Don Camillo went to work off his indignation at the high altar. "They must have aimed one of their accursed loud-speakers directly at the church," he exclaimed. "This is nothing short of violation of domicile."

"What can you do about it, Don Camillo? It is progress," replied the Lord.

After a preface of generalizations, the voice had got down to business and, since the speaker was an extremist, he made no bones about it.

We must remain within the law and we shall do so!
Even at the cost of taking up our weapons and of using

39

the firing squad for all the enemies of the people! . . ."

Don Camillo was pawing the ground like a restive horse. "Lord, only listen to him!"

"I hear him, Don Camillo. I hear him only too well."

"Lord, why don't You drop a thunderbolt among all that rabble?"

"Don Camillo, let us remain within the law. If, in order to drive the truth into the head of one who is in error, your remedy is to shoot him down, where was the use of My allowing Myself to be crucified?"

Don Camillo threw up his hands. "You are right, of course. We can do nothing but wait for them to crucify us also."

The Lord smiled. "If, instead of speaking first and then thinking over what you have said, you thought first and did the speaking afterwards, you might avoid having to regret the foolish things you have said."

Don Camillo bowed his head.

". . . as for those who, hiding in the shadow of the Crucifix, attempt with the poison of their ambiguous words to spread dissension among the masses of the workers . . ." The voice of the loudspeaker, borne on the wind, filled the church and shook the blue, red and yellow glass in the Gothic windows. Don Camillo grasped a heavy bronze candlestick and, brandishing it like a club, strode with clenched teeth in the direction of the church door.

"Don Camillo, stop!" cried the Lord. "You will not leave the church until everyone has gone away."

"Oh, very well," replied Don Camillo, putting back the candlestick in its place. "I obey." He strode up and down the church and finally halted in front of the Lord. "But in here I can do as I please?"

"Naturally, Don Camillo; here you are in your own house and free to do exactly as you wish. Short of climbing up to a window and firing at the people below."

Three minutes later, Don Camillo, leaping and bounding cheerfully in the bell-chamber of the church tower, was performing the most infernal carillon that had ever been heard in the village.

The orator was compelled to interrupt his speech and turned to the local authorities who were standing with him on the platform. "He must be stopped" he cried indignantly.

Peppone agreed gravely, nodding his head. "He must

indeed," he replied, "and there are just two ways of stopping him. One is to explode a mine under the church tower and the other is to bombard it with heavy artillery."

The orator ordered him to stop talking nonsense. Surely it was easy enough to break in the door of the tower and climb the stairs.

"Well," said Peppone calmly. "One goes up by ladders from landing to landing. Look, comrade, do you see those projections just by the big window of the belfry? They are the steps that the bell-ringer has removed as he went up. By closing the trap-door of the top landing, he is cut off from the world."

"We might try firing at the windows of the tower!" suggested Smilzo.

"Certainly," agreed Peppone: "but we should have to be certain of knocking him out with the first shot, otherwise he also would begin firing, and then there might be trouble."

The bells ceased ringing and the orator resumed his speech and all went well only so long as he was careful to say nothing of which Don Camillo disapproved. If he did so, Don Camillo immediately began the counter-argument with his bells, leaving off only to resume as soon as the orator left the straight and narrow path again. And so on until the peroration was merely pathetic and patriotic and was therefore respected by the admonitory bells.

That evening Peppone met Don Camillo. "Take care, Don Camillo, that this baiting does not bring you to a bad end."

"There is no baiting involved," replied Don Camillo calmly. "You blow your trumpets and we ring our bells. That, comrade, is democracy. If, on the other hand, only one person is allowed to perform, that is a dictatorship."

Peppone held his peace, but one morning Don Camillo got up to find a merry-go-round, a swing, three shooting-galleries, an electric track, the "wall of death" and an indefinite number of other booths established within exactly half a yard of the line that divided the church square from the public square.

The owners of the "amusement park" showed him their permits, duly signed by the mayor, and Don Camillo retired without comment to his presbytery. That evening pandemonium broke out: barrel organs, loudspeakers, gunfire, shouting and singing, bells, whistling, roaring, braying and bellowing.

Don Camillo went to protest before the Lord. "This is a lack of respect towards the house of God."

"Is there anything about it that is immoral or scandalous?" asked the Lord.

"No—merry-go-rounds, swings, little motor cars, chiefly children's amusements."

"Well, then, it is simply democracy."

"But this infernal din?" protested Don Camillo.

"The din also is democracy, provided it remains within the law. Outside church territory, the mayor is in command, my son."

The presbytery stood some thirty yards farther forward than the church, having one of its sides adjoining the square, and exactly underneath one of its windows a strange apparatus had been erected that immediately aroused Don Camillo's curiosity. It was a kind of small column about three feet high, topped by a sort of stuffed mushroom covered with leather. Behind it was another column, taller and more slender, upon which was a large dial bearing figures from 1 to 1,000. It was an instrument for the trial of strength: a blow was struck at the mushroom and the dial recorded its force. Don Camillo, squinting through the cracks of the shutters, began to enjoy himself. By eleven o'clock in the evening the highest number recorded was 750, and that stood to the credit of Badile, the Gretti's cowman, who had fists like sacks of potatoes. Then quite suddenly Comrade Peppone made his appearance surrounded by his satellites.

All the people came running to see, crying, "Go on, Peppone. Go to it!" And Peppone removed his jacket, rolled up his sleeves and took his stand opposite the machine, measuring the distance with his clenched fist. There was total silence and even Don Camillo felt his heart hammering.

Peppone's fist cleft the air and struck the mushroom.

"Nine hundred and fifty," yelled the owner of the machine. "Only once before have I seen any man get that score, and he was a longshoreman in Genoa." The crowd howled with enthusiasm.

Peppone put on his coat again, raised his head and looked at the window behind which Don Camillo was concealed. "To anyone whom it may concern," he remarked loudly, "I might say that a blow that registers nine hundred and fifty is no joke!"

Everyone looked up at Don Camillo's window and

sniggered. Don Camillo went to bed with his legs shaking under him. On the next evening he was there again, watching from behind his window and waiting feverishly for the clock to strike eleven. Once again Peppone arrived with his staff, took off his coat, rolled up his sleeve and aimed a mighty blow at the mushroom.

"Nine hundred and fifty-one!" howled the crowd. And once again they looked up at Don Camillo's window and sniggered. Peppone also looked up.

"To anyone whom it may concern," he remarked loudly, "I might say that a blow that registers nine hundred and fifty-one is no joke!"

Don Camillo went to bed that night with a temperature.

Next day he went and knelt before the Lord. "Lord," he sighed. "I am being dragged over the precipice!"

"Be strong and resist, Don Camillo!"

That evening Don Camillo went to his peephole in the window as though he were on his way to the scaffold. Rumour had spread like wildfire and the whole countryside had come to see the performance. When Peppone appeared there was an audible whisper of "Here he is!" Peppone looked up, jeering, took off his coat, raised his fist and there was silence.

"Nine hundred and fifty-two!"

Don Camillo saw a million eyes fixed upon his window, lost the light of reason and hurled himself out of the room.

"To anyone whom . . ." Peppone did not have time to finish his remarks about a blow that registered nine hundred and fifty-two: Don Camillo already stood before him. The crowd bellowed, and then was suddenly silent.

Don Camillo threw out his chest, took a firm stance, threw away his hat and crossed himself. Then he raised his formidable fist and struck hard.

"One thousand!" yelled the crowd.

"To anyone whom it may concern, I might say that a blow that registers one thousand is no joke," remarked Don Camillo.

Peppone had grown rather pale, and his satellites were glancing at him doubtfully, hesitating between resentment and disappointment. Other bystanders were chuckling delightedly. Peppone looked Don Camillo straight in the eyes and took off his coat again. He stepped in front and raised his fist.

"Lord!" whispered Don Camillo hastily.

Peppone's fist cleft the air.

"A thousand," bawled the crowd and Peppone's body-guard rejoiced.

"At one thousand all blows are formidable," observed Smilzo. "I think we will leave it at that."

Peppone moved off triumphantly in one direction while Don Camillo moved off triumphantly in the other.

"Lord," said Don Camillo when he knelt before the crucifix. "I thank You. I was scared to death."

"That you wouldn't make a thousand?"

"No; that that pig-headed fool wouldn't make it too. I should have had it on my conscience."

"I knew it; and it was lucky that I came to your help," replied the Lord, smiling. "Moreover, Peppone also, as soon as he saw you, nearly died of fear lest you shouldn't succeed in reaching nine hundred and fifty-two."

"Possibly!" muttered Don Camillo, who now and then liked to appear sceptical.

CRIME AND PUNISHMENT

ON EASTER morning, Don Camillo, leaving his home at an early hour, was confronted at the door of the presbytery by a colossal chocolate egg tied up with a handsome riband of red silk. Or, rather, by a formidable egg that resembled a chocolate one, but was merely a two-hundred-pound bomb shorn of its fins and painted a rich brown.

The war had not omitted to pass over Don Camillo's parish, and planes had visited it on more than one occasion, dropping bombs. A number of these had remained unexploded, half buried in the ground or actually lying on the surface, since the planes had flown low. When all was over, a couple of engineers had arrived from somewhere or other, exploded the bombs lying far from any building and dismantled those too close to occupied places. These they had collected to be disposed of later. One bomb had fallen upon the old mill, destroying the roof and remaining wedged between a wall and a main beam and it had been left there because the house was derelict and the dismantled bomb no longer dangerous. It was this bomb that had been transformed into an Easter egg by unknown hands.

"Unknown," let us say, as a figure of speech, since there was the inscription: "Happy Eester" (with two e's), and there was also the red riband. The business had been carefully organized, because when Don Camillo turned his eyes away from the strange egg, he found the church square thronged with people. These scoundrels had all conspired to be present in order to enjoy Don Camillo's discomfiture.

Don Camillo felt annoyed and allowed himself to kick the object, which, naturally, remained immovable.

"It's pretty heavy!" someone shouted.

"Needs the bomb-removal squad!" suggested another voice.

There was a sound of sniggering.

"Try blessing it and see if it doesn't walk off of its own accord!" cried a third voice.

Don Camillo went pale and his knees began to tremble. Slowly he bent down and with his immense hands grasped the bomb at its two extremities. There was a deathly silence. The crowd gazed at Don Camillo, holding their breaths, their eyes staring in something akin to fear.

"Lord!" whispered Don Camillo desperately.

"Heave ho, Don Camillo!" replied a quiet voice that came from the high altar.

The bones of that great frame literally cracked. Slowly and implacably Don Camillo straightened his back with the enormous mass of iron welded to his hands. He stood for a moment contemplating the crowd and then he set out. Every step fell like a ton weight. He left the church square and step by step, slow and inexorable as Fate, Don Camillo crossed the big square. The crowd followed in silence, amazed. On reaching the far end of the square, opposite the Party headquarters, he stopped. And the crowd also stopped.

"Lord," whispered Don Camillo desperately.

"Heave ho, Don Camillo!" came a rather anxious voice from the now-distant high altar of the church.

Don Camillo collected himself, then in one sudden movement he brought the great weight up to the level of his chest. Another effort and the bomb began slowly to rise higher, watched by the now-frightened crowd.

Now Don Camillo's arms were fully extended and the bomb poised above his head. For one moment he held it there, then he hurled it from him and it landed on the ground exactly in front of the door of the Party headquarters.

Don Camillo looked at the crowd: "Returned to sender," he observed in a ringing voice. "Easter is spelt with an A. Correct and re-deliver."

The crowd made way for him and Don Camillo returned triumphantly to the presbytery.

Peppone did not re-deliver the bomb. With two helpers he loaded it on to a cart and it was removed and thrown down a disused quarry at a distance from the village. The bomb rolled down a slope but did not reach the bottom, because it was arrested by a tree stump and remained wedged in an upright position.

Three days later it happened that a goat approached the quarry and discovered an alluring patch of fresh grass at the roots of the tree stump. In cropping the grass, it pushed the bomb which resumed its descent and, having travelled some two yards, struck a stone and exploded with terrific violence. In the village, at a considerable distance, the windows of thirty houses were shattered.

Peppone arrived at the presbytery a few moments later, gasping, and found Don Camillo going upstairs.

"And to think," groaned Peppone, "that I spent an entire evening hammering at those fins!"

"And to think that I . . ." moaned Don Camillo, and could get no further because he was visualizing the scene in the square.

"I'm going to bed . . ." gasped Peppone.

"I was on my way there . . ." gasped Don Camillo.

He had the crucifix from the high altar brought to him in his bedroom.

"Forgive me if I put You to this inconvenience," murmured Don Camillo, whose temperature was raging, "but I had to thank You on behalf of the whole village."

"No need of that, Don Camillo," replied the Lord with a smile. "No need of that."

One morning shortly after this, on leaving the house, Don Camillo discovered that during the night someone had defaced the white wall of the presbytery by writing upon it in red letters two feet high the words: *Don Camàlo*, which means stevedore, and undoubtedly referred to his recent feat of strength.

With a bucket of whitewash and a large brush Don Camillo set to work to efface the inscription, but in view of the fact that it was written in aniline red, the application of whitewash was completely useless and the letters only glared more balefully through any number of coats. Don Camillo had to resort to scraping, and the job took him quite half the day.

47

He made his appearance before the Lord above the altar as white as a miller all over but in a distinctly black frame of mind. "If I can only find out who did it," he said, "I shall thrash him until my stick is worn away."

"Don't be melodramatic, Don Camillo," the Lord advised him. "This is some urchin's doing. After all, no one has really insulted you."

"Do you think it seemly to call a priest a stevedore?" protested Don Camillo. "And then, it's the kind of nickname that, if people get hold of it, may stick to me all my life."

"You've got broad shoulders, Don Camillo," the Lord consoled him with a smile. "I never had shoulders like yours and yet I bore the Cross without beating anybody."

Don Camillo agreed that the Lord was in the right. But he was not satisfied, and that evening, instead of going to his bed, he took up his station in a strategic position and waited patiently. Towards two o'clock in the morning an individual made his appearance in the church square and, having placed a small pail on the ground beside him, set to work carefully upon the wall of the presbytery. But without giving him time even to complete the letter D, Don Camillo overturned the pail on his head and sent him flying with a terrific kick in the pants.

Aniline dye is an accursed thing, and Gigotto (one of Peppone's most valued henchmen), on receiving the baptism of red paint, remained for three days concealed in his house scrubbing his face with every conceivable concoction, after which he was compelled to go out and work. The facts had already become generally known and he found himself greeted with the nickname of "Redskin." Don Camillo fanned the flames until a day came when, returning from a visit to the doctor, he discovered too late that the handle of his front door had received a coating of red. Without uttering so much as one word, Don Camillo went and sought out Gigotto at the tavern and with a blow that was enough to blind an elephant liberally daubed his face with the paint collected from the door handle. Naturally, the occurrence immediately took on a political aspect and, in view of the fact that Gigotto was supported by half a dozen of his own party, Don Camillo was compelled to use a bench in self-defence.

The six routed by the bench were seething with fury. The tavern was in an uproar and the same evening some unknown person serenaded Don Camillo by throwing a fire-work in front of the presbytery door.

People were getting anxious and it needed but a spark to set fire to the tinder. And so, one fine morning, Don Camillo received an urgent summons to the town because the bishop wished to speak to him.

The bishop was old and bent, and in order to look Don Camillo in the face he had to raise his head considerably. "Don Camillo," said the bishop, "you are not well. You need to spend a few months in a beautiful mountain village. Yes, yes; the parish priest at Puntarossa has died recently, and so we shall kill two birds with one stone: you will be able to reorganize the parish for me and at the same time you will re-establish your health. Then you will come back as fresh as a rose. You will be supplied by Don Pietro, a young man who will make no trouble for you. Are you pleased, Don Camillo?"

"No, Monsignore; but I shall leave as soon as Monsignore wishes."

"Good," replied the bishop. "Your discipline is the more meritorious inasmuch as you accept without discussion my instructions to do something that is against your personal inclinations."

"Monsignore, you will not be displeased if the people of my parish say that I have run away because I was afraid?"

"No," replied the old man, smiling. "Nobody on this earth could ever think that Don Camillo was afraid. Go with God, Don Camillo, and leave benches alone; they can never constitute a Christian argument."

The news spread quickly in the village. Peppone had announced it in person at a special meeting. "Don Camillo is going," he proclaimed. "Transferred to some God-forsaken mountain village. He is leaving to-morrow afternoon at three o'clock."

"Hurrah!" shouted the entire meeting. "And may he croak when he gets there. . . ."

"All things considered, it's the best way out," said Peppone. "He was beginning to think he was the King and the Pope rolled into one, and if he had stayed here we should have had to give him a super dressing-down. This saves us the trouble."

"And he should be left to slink away like a whipped cur,"

49

howled Brusco. "Make the village understand that there will be trouble for anyone who is seen about the church square from three to half-past."

The hour struck and Don Camillo went to say goodbye to the Lord above the altar. "I wish I could have taken You with me," sighed Don Camillo.

"I shall go with you just the same," replied the Lord. "Don't you worry."

"Have I really done anything bad enough to deserve being sent away?" asked Don Camillo.

"Yes."

"Then they really are all against me," sighed Don Camillo.

"All of them," replied the Lord. "Even Don Camillo himself disapproves of what you have done."

"That is true enough," Don Camillo acknowledged. "I could hit myself."

"Keep your hands quiet, Don Camillo, and a pleasant journey to you."

In a town fear can affect 50 per cent of the people, but in a village the percentage is doubled. The roads were deserted. Don Camillo climbed into the train, and when he watched his church tower disappear behind a clump of trees he felt very bitter indeed. "Not even a dog has remembered me," he sighed. "It is obvious that I have failed in my duties and it is also obvious that I am a bad lot."

The train was a slow one that stopped at every station, and it therefore stopped at Boschetto, a mere cluster of four houses three or four miles from Don Camillo's own village. And so, quite suddenly, Don Camillo found his compartment invaded; he was hustled to the window and found himself face to face with a sea of people who were clapping their hands and throwing flowers.

"Peppone's men had said that if anyone in the village showed up at your departure it meant a hiding," the steward from Stradalunga was explaining, "and so, in order to avoid trouble, we all came on here to say goodbye to you."

Don Camillo was completely dazed and felt a humming in his ears, and when the train moved off the entire compartment was filled with flowers, bottles, bundles and parcels of all sizes, while poultry with their legs tied together clucked and protested from the baggage nets overhead.

But there was still a thorn in his heart. "And those others?

50

They must really hate me to have done such a thing! It wasn't even enough for them to get me sent away!"

A quarter of an hour later the train stopped at Bosco-planche, the last station of the Commune. There Don Camillo heard himself called by name, and going to the window beheld Mayor Peppone and his entire *giunta*. Mayor Peppone made the following speech:

"Before you leave the territory of the Commune, it seems to us proper to bring you the greetings of the population and good wishes for a rapid recovery, the which will enable a speedy return to your spiritual mission."

Then, as the train began to move, Peppone took off his hat with a sweeping gesture and Don Camillo also removed his hat and remained standing at the window with it posed in the air like a statue of the Risorgimento.

The church at Puntarossa sat on the top of the mountain and looked like a picture postcard. When Don Camillo reached it he inhaled the pine-scented air deeply and exclaimed with satisfaction:

"A bit of rest up here will certainly do me good, the which will enable a speedy return to my spiritual mission."

And he said it quite gravely, because to him that "the which" was of more value than the sum of all Cicero's orations.

RETURN TO THE FOLD

THE PRIEST who had been sent to supply the parish during Don Camillo's political convalescence was young and delicate. He knew his business and he spoke courteously, using lovely, polished phrases that appeared to be newly minted. Naturally, even though he knew that he was only in temporary occupation, this young priest established some small changes in the church such as any man feels to be necessary if he is to be tolerably at his ease in strange surroundings.

We are not making actual comparisons, but it is much the same when a traveller goes to an hotel. Even if he is aware that he will remain there only for one night, he will be inclined to move a table from left to right and a chair from right to left, because each one of us has a strictly personal concept of aesthetic balance and colour and experiences discomfort on every occasion when, being at liberty to do so, he does not exert himself to create such harmony as he desires.

It therefore happened that on the first Sunday following the new priest's arrival the congregation noticed two important innovations: the great candlestick that supported the big paschal candle with its floral decorations and which had always stood on the second step at the Gospel side of the altar had been shifted to the Epistle side and placed in front of a small picture representing a saint—a picture which had previously not been there.

Out of curiosity, together with respect to the new parish priest, the entire village was present, with Peppone and his henchmen in the foremost ranks.

"Have you noticed," muttered Brusco to Peppone with a stifled snigger, pointing out the candlestick, "changes!"

"M-m-m," mumbled Peppone irritably. And he remained irritable until the priest came down to the altar rails to make the customary address.

Then Peppone could bear no more, and just as the priest was about to begin, he detached himself from his companions, marched steadily towards the candlestick, grasped it firmly, carried it past the altar and placed it in its old position upon the second step to the left. Then he returned to his seat in the front row and with knees wide apart and arms folded stared arrogantly straight into the eyes of the young priest.

"Well done!" murmured the entire congregation, not excepting Peppone's political opponents.

The young priest, who had stood open-mouthed watching Peppone's behaviour, changed colour, stammered somehow through his brief address and returned to the altar to complete his Mass.

When he left the church he found Peppone waiting for him with his entire staff. The church square was crowded with silent and surly people.

"Listen here, Don—Don whatever you call yourself," said Peppone in an aggressive voice, "Who is this new person whose picture you have hung on the pillar to the right of the altar?"

"Santa Rita da Cascia," stammered the little priest.

"Then let me tell you that this village has no use for Santa Rita da Cascia or anything of the kind. Here everything is better left as it was before."

The young priest spread out his arms. "I think I am entitled . . ." he began, but Peppone cut him short.

"Ah, so that's how you take it? Well, then let us speak clearly: this village has no use for a priest such as you."

The young priest gasped. "I cannot see that I have done anything . . ."

"Then I'll tell you what you have done. You have committed an illegal action. You have attempted to change an order that the permanent priest of the parish had established in accordance with the will of the people."

"Hurrah!" shouted the crowd, including the reactionaries.

The little priest attempted a smile. "If that is all the

53

trouble, everything shall be put back exactly as it was before. Isn't that the solution?"

"No," thundered Peppone, flinging his hat behind him and placing his enormous fists on his hips.

"And may I be allowed to ask why?"

Peppone had reached the end of his supplies of diplomacy. "Well," he said, "if you really want to know, it is not a solution because if I give you one on the jaw I shall send you flying at least fifteen yards, while if it were the regular incumbent he wouldn't move so much as an inch!"

Peppone stopped short of explaining that in the event of his hitting Don Camillo once, the latter would have hit him half a dozen times in return. He left it at that, but his meaning was clear to all his hearers with the exception of the little priest, who stared at him in amazement.

"But, excuse me," he murmured. "Why should you have any wish to hit me?"

Peppone lost patience. "Who in the world wants to hit you? There you are again, running down the left-wing parties! I used a figure of speech merely in order to explain our views. Is it likely that I should waste my time hitting a scrap of a priest like you!"

On hearing himself termed a "scrap of a priest," the young man drew himself up to his full five feet four inches and his face grew purple till the very veins in his neck swelled.

" 'Scrap of a priest' you may call me," he cried in a shrill voice, "but I was sent here by ecclesiastical authority and here I shall remain until ecclesiastical authority sees fit to remove me. In this church you have no authority at all! Santa Rita will stay where she is and, as for the candlestick, watch what I am going to do!"

He went into the church, grasped the candlestick firmly and after a considerable struggle succeeded in removing it again to the Epistle side of the altar in front of the new picture.

"There!" he said triumphantly.

"Very well!" replied Peppone, who had observed his actions from the threshold of the church door. Then he turned to the crowd which stood in serried ranks in the church square, silent and surly, and shouted: "The people will have something to say to this! To the town hall, all of you, and we will make a demonstration of protest."

"Hurrah!" howled the crowd.

Peppone elbowed his way through them so that he could lead them, and they formed up behind him yelling and brandishing sticks. When they reached the town hall, the yells increased in volume, and Peppone yelled also, raising his fist and shaking it at the balcony of the council chamber.

"Peppone," shouted Brusco in his ear, "are you crazy? Stop yelling! Have you forgotten that you yourself are the mayor?"

"Hell! . . ." exclaimed Peppone. "When these accursed swine make me lose my head I remember nothing!" He ran upstairs and out on to the balcony, where he was cheered by the crowd including the reactionaries.

"Comrades, citizens," shouted Peppone. "We will not suffer this oppression that offends against our dignity as free men! We shall remain within the bounds of the law so long as may be possible, but we are going to get justice even if we must resort to gunfire! In the meantime I propose that a committee of my selection shall accompany me to the ecclesiastical authorities and impose in a democratic manner the desires of the people!"

"Hurrah!" yelled the crowd, completely indifferent to logic or syntax. "Long live our Mayor Peppone!"

When Peppone and his committee stood before the bishop he had some difficulty in finding his voice, but at last he got going.

"Excellence," he said, "that priest that you have sent us is not worthy of the traditions of the leading parish of the district."

The bishop raised his head in order to see the top of Peppone. "Tell me now: what has he been doing?"

Peppone waved his arms. "For the love of God! Doing? He hasn't done anything serious. . . . In fact, he hasn't done anything at all.... The trouble is that ... Oh, well, Eminence, he's only a half man ... you know what I mean, a priestling; when the fellow is all dressed up—your Eminence must excuse me, but he looks like a coat-hanger loaded with three overcoats and a cloak!"

The old bishop nodded his head gravely. "But do you," he inquired very graciously, "establish the merits of priests with a tape measure and a weighing machine?"

"No, Excellence," replied Peppone. "We aren't savages! But all the same, how shall I put it—even the eye needs some satisfaction, and in matters of religion it's the same as with a doctor, there's a lot to be said for personal sympathies and moral impressions!"

The old bishop sighed. "Yes, yes. I understand perfectly. But all the same, my dear children, you had a parish priest who looked like a tower and you yourselves came and asked me to remove him!"

Peppone wrinkled his forehead. "Monsignore," he explained solemnly, "it was a question of a *casus belli*, an affair *sui generis*, as they say. Because that man was a multiple offence in the way he exasperated us by his provocative and dictatorial poses."

"I know, I know," said the bishop. "You told me all about it when you were here before, my son, and, as you see, I removed him. And that was precisely because I fully understood that I had to deal with an unworthy man. . . ."

"One moment, if you will excuse me," Brusco interrupted. "We never said that he was an unworthy man! . . ."

"Well, well; if not 'an unworthy man,'" continued the bishop, "at any rate an unworthy priest inasmuch as . . ."

"I beg your pardon," said Peppone, interrupting him. "We never suggested that as a priest he had failed in his duty. We only spoke of his serious defects, of his very serious misdeeds as a man."

"Exactly," agreed the old bishop. "And as, unfortunately, the man and the priest are inseparable, and a man such as Don Camillo represents a danger to his neighbours, we are at this very moment considering the question of making his present appointment a permanent one. We will leave him where he is, among the goats at Puntarossa. Yes, we will leave him there, since it has not yet been decided whether he is to be allowed to continue in his functions or whether we shall suspend him *a divinis*. We will wait and see."

Peppone turned to his committee and there was a moment's consultation, then he turned again to the bishop.

"Monsignore," he said in a low voice, and he was sweating and had gone pale, as though he found difficulty in speaking audibly, "if the ecclesiastical authority has its own reasons for doing such a thing, of course that is its own affair. Nevertheless, it is my duty to warn your Excellency that until our regular parish priest returns to us, not a soul will enter the church."

The bishop raised his arms. "But, my sons," he exclaimed,

56

"do you realize the gravity of what you are saying? This is coercion!"

"No, Monsignore," Peppone explained, "we are coercing nobody, because we shall all remain quietly at home, and no law compels us to go to church. Our decision is simply a question of availing ourselves of democratic liberty. Because we are the only persons qualified to judge whether a priest suits us or not, since we have had to bear with him for nearly twenty years."

"*Vox populi vox Dei*," sighed the old bishop. "God's will be done. You can have your reprobate back if you want him. But don't come whining to me later on about his arrogance."

Peppone laughed. "Eminence! The rodomontades of a type such as Don Camillo don't really break any bones. We came here before merely as a matter of simple political and social precaution, so as to make sure that Redskin here didn't lose his head and throw a bomb at him."

"Redskin yourself!" retorted the indignant Gigotto, whose face Don Camillo had dyed with aniline red and whose head had come in contact with Don Camillo's bench. "I never meant to throw any bombs. I simply threw a firework in front of his house to make him realize that I wasn't standing for being knocked on the head even by the reverend parish priest in person."

"Ah! Then it was you, my son, who threw the firework?" inquired the old bishop indifferently.

"Well, Excellence," mumbled Gigotto, "you know how it is. When one has been hit on the head with a bench one may easily go a bit too far in retaliation."

"I understand perfectly," replied the bishop, who was old and knew how to take people in the right way.

Don Camillo returned ten days later.

"How are you?" inquired Peppone, meeting him just as he was leaving the station. "Did you have a pleasant holiday?"

"Well, it was a bit dreary up there. Luckily I took my pack of cards with me and worked off my restlessness playing patience," replied Don Camillo. He pulled a pack of cards from his pocket. "Look," he said. "But now I shan't need them any more." And delicately, with a smile, he tore the pack in two as though it were a slice of bread.

"We are getting old, Mr. Mayor," sighed Don Camillo.

"To hell with you and with those who sent you back here!" muttered Peppone, turning away, the picture of gloom.

Don Camillo had a lot to tell the Lord above the altar. Then at the end of their gossip he inquired, with an assumption of indifference:

"What kind of a fellow was my supply?"

"A nice lad, cultured and with a nice nature. When anyone did him a good turn, he didn't bait them by tearing up a pack of cards under their noses."

"Lord!" exclaimed Don Camillo, raising his arms. "I don't suppose anyone here ever did him a good turn, anyway. And then there are people who have to be thanked like that. I'll bet You that now Peppone is saying to his gang: 'And he tore the whole pack across, zip, the misbegotten son of an ape!' And he is thoroughly enjoying saying it! Shall we have a wager?"

"No," replied the Lord with a sigh; "because that is exactly what Peppone is saying at this moment."

THE DEFEAT

THE WAR to the knife that had now been in progress for nearly a year was won by Don Camillo, who managed to complete his recreation centre while Peppone's People's Palace still lacked all its locks.

The recreation centre proved to be a very up-to-date affair: a hall for social gatherings, dramatic performances, lectures and suchlike activities, a library with a reading and writing room and a covered area for physical training and winter games. There was in addition a magnificent fenced sports ground with a gymnasium, running track, bathing pool and a children's playground with giant-stride, swings, etcetera. Most of the paraphernalia was as yet in an embryonic stage, but the important thing was to have made a start.

For the inauguration ceremony Don Camillo had prepared a most lively programme: choral singing, athletic competitions and a game of football. For the latter Don Camillo had succeeded in mustering a really formidable team, a task to which he had brought so impassioned an enthusiasm that in the course of the team's eight months of training the kicks administered by him alone to the eleven players were far more numerous than those that all those players put together had succeeded in giving to the ball.

Peppone knew all this and was deeply embittered. He could not endure the thought that the party that genuinely represented the people must play second fiddle in the celebration organized by Don Camillo on the people's behalf.

And when Don Camillo sent to inform him that in order to demonstrate his "sympathetic understanding of the more ignorant social strata of the village" he was willing to allow a match between their Dynamos football team and his own Galliards, Peppone turned pale, summoned the eleven lads of the local sports squadron and made them stand to attention against the wall while he made them the following address: "You are to play against the priest's team. You have got to win or I shall smash in every one of your faces. The Party orders it for the honour of a down-trodden people!"

"We shall win!" replied the eleven, sweating with terror.

As soon as this scene was reported to him Don Camillo mustered the Galliards and addressed them as follows.

"We are not here among uncouth savages such as your opponents," he said, smiling pleasantly. "We are capable of reasoning like sensible and educated gentlemen. With the help of God, we shall beat them six goals to none. I make no threats; I merely remind you that the honour of the parish is in your hands. Also in your feet.

"Therefore let each of you do his duty as a good citizen. Should there be some Barabbas among you who is not ready to give his all even to the last drop of his blood, I shall not indulge in Peppone's histrionics with regard to the smashing of faces. I shall merely kick his backside to a jelly!"

The entire countryside attended the inauguration, led by Peppone and his satellites with blazing red handkerchiefs round their necks. In his capacity as *mayor*, he expressed his satisfaction at the event and as *personal representative of the people* he emphasized his confident belief that the occasion they were celebrating would not be made to serve "unworthy ends of political propaganda such as were already being whispered of by ill-intentioned persons."

During the performance of the choral singers, Peppone was able to point out to Brusco that, as a matter of fact, singing was also a sport, inasmuch as it developed the expansion of the lungs, and Brusco, with seeming amiability, replied that in his opinion the exercise would prove even more efficacious as a means of physical development for Catholic youth if they were taught to accompany it with gestures adapted to the improvement not only of their lung power, but also of the muscles of their arms.

During the game of basket-ball, Peppone expressed a

sincere conviction that the game of ping-pong had also not only an undeniable athletic value, but was so graceful that he was astonished not to find it included in the programme.

In view of the fact that these comments were made in voices that were easily audible half a mile away, the veins of Don Camillo's neck were very soon swelled to the size of cables. He therefore awaited with indescribable impatience the hour of the football match, which would be that of his reply.

At last it was time for the match. White jerseys with a large "G" on the breast for the eleven Galliards. Red jerseys bearing the hammer, sickle and star combined with an elegant "D" adorned the eleven Dynamos.

The crowd cared less than nothing for symbols, anyway, and hailed the teams after their own fashion: "Hurrah for Peppone!" or "Hurrah for Don Camillo!" Peppone and Don Camillo looked at one another and exchanged slight and dignified bows.

The referee was a neutral: the clockmaker Binella, a man without political opinions. After ten minutes' play the sergeant of carabinieri, pale to the gills, approached Peppone, followed by his two equally pallid subordinates.

"Mr. Mayor," he stammered, "don't you think it would be wise for me to telephone to the town for reinforcements?"

"You can telephone for a division for all I care, but if those butchers don't let up, nobody will be able to avoid there being a heap of corpses as high as the first-floor windows! Not His Majesty the King himself could do a thing about it, do you understand," howled Peppone, forgetting the very existence of the republic in his blind fury.

The sergeant turned to Don Camillo, who was standing a few feet away. "Don't you think . . . . ?" he stuttered, but Don Camillo cut him short.

"I," he shouted, "simply think that nothing short of the personal intervention of the United States of America will prevent us all from swimming in blood if those accursed bolsheviks don't stop disabling my men by kicking them in the shins!"

"I see," said the sergeant, and went off to barricade himself into his quarters, although perfectly aware that the common sequel of such behaviour is a general attempt to close the festivities by setting fire to the barracks of the carabinieri.

The first goal was scored by the Galliards and raised a howl that shook the church tower. Peppone, his face distorted with rage, turned on Don Camillo with clenched fists as though about to attack him. Don Camillo's fists were already in position. The two of them were within a hair's-breadth of conflict, but Don Camillo observed out of the tail of his eye that all other eyes present were fixed upon them.

"If we begin fighting, there'll be a free-for-all," he muttered through clenched teeth to Peppone.

"All right, for the sake of the people."

"For the sake of the faith," said Don Camillo.

Nothing happened. Nevertheless, Peppone, when the first half ended a few moments later, mustered the Dynamos. "Fascists!" he said to them in a voice thick with contempt. Then, seizing hold of Smilzo, the centre-forward: "As for you, you dirty traitor, suppose you remember that when we were in the mountains I saved your worthless skin no less than three times. If in the next five minutes you haven't scored a goal, I'll attend to that same skin of yours!"

Smilzo, when play was resumed, got the ball and set to work. And work he did, with his head, with his legs and with his knees. He even bit the ball, he spat his lungs out and split his spleen, but at the fourth minute he sent the ball between the posts.

Then he flung himself on to the ground and lay motionless. Don Camillo moved over to the other side of the ground lest his self-control should fail him. The Galliards' goalkeeper was in a high fever from sheer funk.

The Dynamos closed up into a defensive phalanx that seemed impregnable. Thirty seconds before the next break, the referee whistled and a penalty was given against the Galliards. The ball flew into the air. A child of six could not have muffed it at such an angle. Goal!

The match was now over. The only task remaining for Peppone's men was that of picking up their injured players and carrying them back to their pavilion. The referee had no political views and left them to it.

Don Camillo was bewildered. He ran off to the church and knelt in front of the altar. "Lord," he said, "why did You fail to help me? I have lost the match."

"And why should I have helped you rather than the others? Your men had twenty-two legs and so had they, Don Camillo, and all legs are equal. Moreover, they are not My business. I am interested in souls. *Da mihi animam, caetera tolle*. I leave the bodies on earth. Don Camillo, where are your brains?"

"I can find them with an effort," said Don Camillo. "I was not suggesting that You should have taken charge of my men's legs, which in any case were the best of the lot. But I do say that You did not prevent the dishonesty of one man from giving a foul unjustly against my team."

"The priest can make a mistake in saying Mass, Don Camillo. Why must you deny that others may be mistaken while being in good faith?"

"One can admit of errors in most circumstances, but not when it is a matter of arbitration in sport! When the ball is actually there . . . Binella is a scoundrel . . ." He was unable to continue because at that moment the sound of an imploring voice became progressively audible and a man came running into the church, exhausted and gasping, his face convulsed with terror.

"They want to kill me," he sobbed. "Save me!"

The crowd had reached the church door and was about to irrupt into the church itself. Don Camillo seized a candlestick weighing half a quintal and brandished it menacingly.

"Back, in God's name, or I strike!" he shouted. "Remember that anyone who enters here is sacred and immune!"

The crowd hesitated.

"Shame on you, you pack of wolves! Get back to your lairs and pray God to forgive you your savagery."

The crowd stood in silence, heads were bowed, and there was a general movement of retreat.

"Make the sign of the cross," Don Camillo ordered them severely, and as he stood there brandishing the candlestick in his huge hand he seemed a very Samson.

Everyone made the sign of the cross.

"Between you and the object of your brutality is now that sign of the cross that each one of you has traced with his own hand. Anybody who dares to violate that sacred barrier is a blasphemer. *Vade retro!*" He himself stood back and closed the church door, drawing the bolt, but there was no need. The fugitive had sunk on to a bench and was still panting. "Thank you, Don Camillo," he murmured.

Don Camillo made no immediate reply. He paced to and fro for a few moments and then pulled up opposite the man. "Binella!" said Don Camillo in accents of fury. "Binella,

63

here in my presence and that of God you dare not lie! There was no foul! How much did that reprobate Peppone give you to make you call a foul in a drawn game?"

"Two thousand five hundred lire."

"M-m-m-m!" roared Don Camillo, thrusting his fist under his victim's nose.

"But then . . ." moaned Binella.

"Get out," bawled Don Camillo, pointing to the door.

Once more alone, Don Camillo turned towards the Lord. "Didn't I tell you that the swine had sold himself? Haven't I a right to be enraged?"

"None at all, Don Camillo," replied the Lord. "You started it when you offered Binella two thousand lire to do the same thing. When Peppone bid five hundred lire more, Binella accepted the higher bribe."

Don Camillo spread out his arms. "Lord," he said, "but if we are to look at it that way, then I emerge as the guilty man!"

"Exactly, Don Camillo. When you, a priest, were the first to make the suggestion, he assumed that there was no harm in the matter, and then, quite naturally, he took the more profitable bid."

Don Camillo bowed his head. "And do you mean to tell me that if that unhappy wretch should get beaten up by my men, it would be my doing?"

"In a certain sense, yes, because you were the first to lead him into temptation. Nevertheless, your sin would have been greater if Binella, accepting your offer, had agreed to cheat on behalf of your team. Because then the Dynamos would have done the beating up and you would have been powerless to stop them."

Don Camillo reflected awhile. "In fact," he said, "it was better that the others should win."

"Exactly, Don Camillo."

"Then, Lord," said Don Camillo, "I thank you for having allowed me to lose. And if I tell you that I accept the defeat as a punishment for my dishonesty, You must believe that I am really penitent. Because, to see a team such as mine who might very well—and I am not bragging—play in Division B, a team that, believe me or not, could swallow up and digest a couple of thousand Dynamos in their stride, to see them beaten . . . is enough to break one's heart and cries for vengeance to God!"

"Don Camillo!" the Lord admonished him, smiling.

"You can't possibly understand me," sighed Don Camillo. "Sport is a thing apart. Either one cares or one doesn't. Do I make myself clear?"

"Only too clear, my poor Don Camillo. I understand you so well that . . . Come now, when are you going to have your revenge?"

Don Camillo leaped to his feet, his heart swelling with delight. "Six to nothing!" he shouted. "Six to nought that they never even see the ball! Do You see that confessional?"

He flung his hat into the air, caught it with a neat kick as it came down and drove it like a thunderbolt into the little window of the confessional.

"Goal!" said the Lord, smiling.

THE AVENGER

SMILZO RODE up on his racing bicycle and braked it in the American manner, which consists of letting the backside slip off the seat backwards and sit astride the wheel.

Don Camillo was reading the newspaper, seated upon the bench in front of the presbytery. He raised his head. "Does Stalin hand you down his trousers?" he inquired placidly.

Smilzo handed him a letter, touched his cap with a fore finger, leaped on to his bicycle and was just about to disappear round the corner of the presbytery when he slowed down for an instant. "No, the Pope does that," he bawled, then stood on his pedals and was gone in a flash.

Don Camillo had been expecting the letter. It contained an invitation to the inauguration ceremony of the People's Palace with a programme of the festivities enclosed. Speeches, reports, a band and refreshments. Then, in the afternoon: *"Great Boxing Match between the Heavyweight Champion of the Local Section, Comrade Bagotti Mingo, and the Heavyweight Champion of the Provincial Federation, Comrade Gorlini Anteo."*

Don Camillo went off to discuss the event with the Lord above the altar. "Lord!" he exclaimed when he had read the programme aloud. "If this isn't vile! If Peppone hadn't been an utter boor, he would have staged the return match between the Galliards and the Dynamos instead of this pummelling bout! And so I shall ..."

"And so you will not even dream of going to tell him one

66

word of what you would like to say; and in any case you're entirely wrong," the Lord interrupted him. "It was perfectly logical of Peppone to try to do something different. Secondly, it was also logical that Peppone should not expose himself to inaugurating his venture with a defeat. Even if we suppose that his champion may lose, he would be none the worse: one comrade fights another; it all remains in the family. But a defeat of his team by yours would be detrimental to the prestige of his party. Don Camillo, you must admit that Peppone couldn't possibly have staged a return match against your team."

"And yet," exclaimed Don Camillo, "I did stage a match against his team, and what's more, I lost it!"

"But Don Camillo," put in the Lord gently, "you don't represent a party. Your lads were not defending the colours of the Church. They were merely defending the prestige of a sporting team, of a pleasant combination that had been organized under the patronage of the parish church. Or do you perhaps think that that Sunday afternoon defeat was a defeat for the Catholic faith?"

Don Camillo began laughing. "Lord," he protested, "You wrong me if you accuse me of any such idea. I was only saying, as a sportsman, that Peppone is a boor. And so you will forgive me if I can't help laughing when his famous champion gets such a drubbing that by the third round he won't know his own name."

"Yes, I shall forgive you, Don Camillo. But I shall find it less easy to forgive your taking pleasure in the spectacle of two men belabouring each other with their fists."

Don Camillo raised his arms. "I have never done anything of the kind and would never lend my presence to countenance such manifestations of brutality as serve only to foster that cult of violence which is already too deeply rooted in the minds of the masses. I am in full agreement with You in condemning any sport in which skill is subordinated to brute force."

"Bravo, Don Camillo," said the Lord. "If a man feels the need to limber his muscles, it is not necessary to fight with his neighbour. It suffices if, having put on a pair of well-padded gloves, he takes it out on a sack of sawdust or a ball suspended somewhere."

"Exactly," agreed Don Camillo, crossing himself hastily and hurrying away.

"Will you satisfy my curiosity, Don Camillo?" exclaimed the Lord. "What is the name of that leather ball which you have had fixed with elastic to the ceiling and the floor of your attic?"

"I believe it is called a 'punching ball,'" muttered Don Camillo, halting for a moment.

"And what does that mean?"

"I don't know any English," replied Don Camillo, making good his escape.

Don Camillo attended the inaugural ceremony of the People's Palace and Peppone accompanied him personally upon a tour of the entire concern; it was all obviously thoroughly up-to-date.

"What do you think of it?" asked Peppone, who was burbling with joy.

"Charming!" replied Don Camillo, smiling cordially. "To tell you the truth, I should never have thought that it could have been designed by a simple builder such as Brusco."

"True enough!" muttered Peppone, who had spent God only knew how much in order to have his project realized by the best architect in the town.

"Quite a good idea to make the windows horizontal instead of perpendicular," observed Don Camillo. "The rooms can be less lofty without its being too obvious. Excellent. And this I suppose is the warehouse."

"It is the assembly room," Peppone explained.

"Ah! And have you put the armoury and the cells for dangerous adversaries in the basement?"

"No," replied Peppone. "We haven't any dangerous adversaries; they are all harmless little folk that can remain in circulation. As for an armoury, we thought that in case of need we could make use of yours."

"An admirable idea," agreed Don Camillo politely. "You have been able to see for yourself how well I look after the tommy-gun which you entrusted to my care, Mr. Mayor."

They had pulled up in front of a huge picture representing a man with a heavy walrus moustache, small eyes and a pipe. "Is that one of your dead leaders?" inquired Don Camillo respectfully.

"That is someone who is among the living and who when he comes will drive you to sit on the lightning conductor of your own church," explained Peppone, who had reached the end of his tether.

"Too high a position for a humble parish priest. The highest position in a small community always pertains to the mayor, and from now onwards I put it at your complete disposal."

"Are we to have the honour of your presence among us at the boxing match to-day, reverend sir?" asked Peppone, thinking it best to change the subject.

"Thank you, but you had better give my seat to someone who is better qualified than I am to appreciate the innate beauty and deeply educational significance of the performance. But I shall at any rate be available at the presbytery in the event of your champion requiring the Holy Oils. You have only to send Smilzo, and I can be with you within a couple of minutes."

During the afternoon Don Camillo chatted for an hour with the Lord and then asked to be excused: "I am sleepy and I shall take a nap. And I thank You for making it rain cats and dogs. The crops need it."

"And, moreover, according to your hopes, it will prevent many people coming from any distance to see Peppone's celebrations," added the Lord. "Am I right?"

Don Camillo shook his head.

The rain, heavy though it was, had done no harm at all to Peppone's festivities: people had flocked from every section of the countryside and from all the nearer communes, and the gymnasium of the People's Palace was as full as an egg. "Champion of the Federation" was a fine title, and Bagotti was undeniably popular in the region. And then it was also in some sense a match between town and country and that aroused interest.

Peppone, in the front row close under the ring, surveyed the crowd triumphantly. Moreover, he was convinced that, at the worst, Bagotti could only lose on points, which, in such circumstances, would be almost as good as a victory.

On the stroke of four o'clock, after an outburst of applause and yelling sufficient to bring down the roof, the gong was sounded and the audience began to get restless and excitable.

It became immediately apparent that the provincial champion surpassed Bagotti in style, but on the other hand Bagotti was quicker, and the first round left the audience breathless. Peppone was pouring with sweat and appeared to have swallowed dynamite.

69

The second round began well for Bagotti, who took the offensive, but quite suddenly he went down in a heap and the referee began the count.

"No," bawled Peppone leaping to his feet. "It was below the belt!"

The federal champion smiled sarcastically at Peppone. He shook his head and touched his chin with his glove.

"No!" bellowed Peppone in exasperation, drowning the uproar of the audience. "You all saw it! First he hit him low and when the pain made him double up he gave him the left on the jaw! It was a foul!"

The federal champion shrugged his shoulders and sniggered, and meanwhile the referee, having counted up to ten, was raising the victor's hand to show that he had won when the tragedy occurred.

Peppone flung away his hat and in one bound was in the ring and advancing with clenched fists upon the federal champion: "I'll show you," he howled.

"Give it to him, Peppone," yelled the infuriated audience.

The boxer put up his fists and Peppone fell upon him like a Panzer and struck hard. But Peppone was too furious to retain his judgment, and his adversary dodged him easily and landed him one directly on the point of the jaw. Nor did he hesitate to put all his weight into it, as Peppone stood there motionless and completely uncovered: it was like hitting a sack of sawdust.

Peppone slumped to the ground and a wave of dismay struck the audience and smote them to a frozen silence. But just as the champion was smiling compassionately at the giant lying prone on the mat, there was a terrific yell from the crowd as a man entered the ring. Without even troubling to remove a drenched waterproof or his cap, he seized a pair of gloves lying on a stool in the corner, pulled them on without bothering to secure them and, standing on guard squarely before the champion, aimed a terrific blow at him. The champion dodged it, naturally, but failed to get in a return, as his opponent was ready for him. The champion danced round the man, who did no more than revolve slowly, and at a given moment the champion launched a formidable blow. The other seemed barely to move, but with his left he parried while his right shot forward like a thunderbolt. The champion was already unconscious as he fell and lay as if asleep in the middle of the ring.

70

The audience went crazy.

It was the bell-ringer who brought the news to the presbytery and Don Camillo had to leave his bed in order to open the door because the sacristan appeared to be insane and, had he not been allowed to pour out the whole story from A to Z, there seemed every reason for fearing that he might blow up. Don Camillo went downstairs to report to the Lord.

"Well?" the Lord inquired. "And how did it go off?"

"A very disgraceful brawl; such a spectacle of disorder and immorality as can hardly be imagined!"

"Anything like that business when they wanted to lynch your referee?" asked the Lord indifferently.

Don Camillo laughed. "Referee, my foot! At the second round Peppone's champion slumped like a sack of potatoes. Then Peppone himself jumped into the ring and went for the victor. Naturally, since, although he is strong as an ox, he is such a dunderhead that he pitches in without judgment, like a Zulu or a Russian, the champion gave him one on the jaw that laid him out like a ninepin."

"And so this is the second defeat his section has suffered."

"Two for the section and one for the federation," chuckled Don Camillo. "Because that was not the end! No sooner had Peppone gone down than another man jumped into the ring and fell upon the victor. Must have been somebody from one of the neighbouring communes, I imagine, a fellow with a beard and a moustache who put up his fists and struck out at the federal champion."

"And I suppose the champion dodged and struck back and the bearded man went down also and added his quotum to the brutal exhibition," the Lord remarked.

"No! The man was as impregnable as an iron safe. So the champion began dodging round trying to catch him off-guard, and finally, zac! he put in a straight one with his right. Then I feinted with the left and caught him square with the right and left the ring!"

"And what had you to do with it?"

"I don't understand."

"You said: 'I feinted with the left and caught him square with the right.' "

"I can't imagine how I came to say such a thing."

The Lord shook His head. "Could it possibly be because you yourself were the man who struck down the champion?"

71

"It would not seem so," said Don Camillo gravely. "I have neither beard nor moustache."

"But those, of course, could be assumed so that the crowd should not suspect that the parish priest is interested in the spectacle of two men fighting in public with their fists!"

Don Camillo shrugged. "All things are possible, Lord, and we must also bear in mind that even parish priests are made of flesh and blood."

The Lord sighed.

"We are not forgetting it, but we should also remember that if parish priests are made of flesh and blood they themselves should never forget that they are also made of brains. Because if the flesh-and-blood parish priest wishes to disguise himself in order to attend a boxing match, the priest that is made of brains prevents him from giving an exhibition of violence."

Don Camillo shook his head. "Very true. But You should also bear in mind that parish priests, in addition to flesh and blood and brains, are also made of yet another thing. And so, when that other thing sees a mayor sent flat on the mat before all his own people by a swine from the town who has won by striking below the belt (which is a sin that cries to heaven for vengeance), that other thing takes the priest of flesh and blood and the priest of brains by the throat and sends the lot of them into the ring."

The Lord nodded. "You mean to say that I should bear in mind that parish priests are also made of heart?"

"For the love of heaven," exclaimed Don Camillo. "I should never presume to advise You. But I would venture to point out that none of those present is aware of the identity of the man with the beard."

"Nor am I aware of it," replied the Lord with a sigh; "but I should like to know whether you have any idea of the meaning of those words 'punching ball'?"

"My knowledge of the English language has not improved, Lord," replied Don Camillo.

"Well, then we must be content without knowing even that," said the Lord, smiling. "After all, culture in the long run often seems to do more harm than good. Sleep well, federal champion."

NOCTURNE WITH BELLS

FOR SOME time Don Camillo had felt that he was being watched. On turning round suddenly when he was walking along the street or in the fields he saw no one, but felt convinced that if he had looked behind a hedge or among the bushes he would have found a pair of eyes and all that goes with them.

When leaving the presbytery on a couple of evenings he not only heard a sound from behind the door, but he caught a glimpse of a shadow.

"Let it be," the Lord had replied from above the altar when Don Camillo had asked Him for advice. "Eyes never did anyone any harm."

"But it would be useful to know whether those two eyes are going about alone or accompanied by a third, for instance one of 9-calibre," sighed Don Camillo. "That is a detail not without its own importance."

"Nothing can defeat a good conscience, Don Camillo."

"I know, Lord," sighed Don Camillo once more, "but the trouble is that people don't usually fire at a conscience, but between the shoulders."

However, Don Camillo did nothing about the matter and a little time elapsed, and then late one evening when he was sitting alone in the presbytery reading, he unexpectedly "felt" the eyes upon him.

There were three of them, and raising his head slowly he saw first of all the black eye of a revolver and then those of Biondo.

"Do I lift my hands?" inquired Don Camillo quietly.

"I don't want to do you any harm," replied Biondo, thrusting the revolver into his jacket pocket. "I was afraid you might be scared when I appeared unexpectedly and might start shouting."

"I understand," replied Don Camillo. "And did it never strike you that by simply knocking at the door you could have avoided all this trouble?"

Biondo made no reply; he went and leaned over the windowsill. Then he turned round suddenly and sat down beside Don Camillo's little table. His hair was ruffled, his eyes deeply circled and his forehead was damp with sweat.

"Don Camillo," he muttered from behind clenched teeth, "that fellow at the house near the dyke; it was I that did him in."

Don Camillo lighted a cigar. "The house near the dyke?" he said quietly. "Well, that's an old story; it was a political affair and came within the terms of the amnesty. What are you worrying about? You're all right under the law."

Biondo shrugged his shoulders. "To hell with the amnesty," he said furiously. "Every night when I put my light out I can feel him near my bed, and I can't understand what it means."

Don Camillo puffed a cloud of blue smoke into the air. "Nothing at all, Biondo," he replied with a smile. "Listen to me: go to sleep with the light on."

Biondo sprang to his feet. "You can go and jeer at that fool Peppone," he shouted, "but you can't do it to me!"

Don Camillo shook his head. "Firstly, Peppone is not a fool; and, secondly, where you are concerned there is nothing that I can do for you."

"If I must buy candles or make an offering to the church, I'll pay," shouted Biondo, "but you've got to absolve me. And in any case I'm all right legally!"

"I agree, my son," said Don Camillo mildly. "But the trouble is that no one has ever yet made an amnesty for consciences. Therefore, so far as we are concerned, we muddle along in the same old way, and in order to obtain absolution it is necessary to be penitent and then to act in a manner that is deserving of forgiveness. It's a lengthy affair."

Biondo sniggered. "Penitent? Penitent of having done in that fellow? I'm only sorry I didn't bag the lot!"

"That is a province in which I am completely incom-

74

petent. On the other hand, if your conscience tells you that you acted rightly, then you should be content," said Don Camillo, opening a book and laying it in front of Biondo. "Look, we have very clear rules that do not exclude the political field. Fifth: thou shalt not kill. Seventh: thou shalt not steal."

"What has that got to do with it?" inquired Biondo in a mystified voice.

"Nothing," Don Camillo reassured him, "but I had an idea that you told me that you had killed him, under the cloak of politics, in order to steal his money."

"I never said so!" shouted Biondo, pulling out his pistol and thrusting it into Don Camillo's face. "I never said so, but it's true! And if it's true and you dare to tell a living soul I shall blow you to pieces!"

"We don't tell such things even to the Eternal Father," Don Camillo reassured him; "and in any case He knows them better than we do."

Biondo appeared to quiet down. He opened his hand and looked at his weapon. "Now look at that!" he exclaimed, laughing. "I hadn't even noticed that the safety catch was down."

He raised the catch with a careful finger.

"Don Camillo," said Biondo in a strange voice, "I am sick of seeing that fellow standing near my bed. There are only two ways for it: either you absolve me or I shoot you." The pistol shook slightly in his hand and Don Camillo turned rather pale and looked him straight in the eyes.

"Lord," said Don Camillo mentally, "this is a mad dog and he will fire. An absolution given in such conditions is valueless. What do I do?"

"If you are afraid, give him absolution," replied the voice of the Lord.

Don Camillo folded his arms on his breast.

"No, Biondo," said Don Camillo.

Biondo set his teeth. "Don Camillo, give me absolution or I fire."

"No."

Biondo pulled the trigger and the trigger yielded, but there was no explosion.

And then Don Camillo struck, and his blow did not miss the mark, because Don Camillo's punches never misfired.

Then he flung himself up the steps of the tower and rang

the bells furiously for twenty minutes. And all the country-side declared that Don Camillo had gone mad, with the exception of the Lord above the altar, who shook His head, smiling, and Biondo, who, tearing across the fields like a lunatic, had reached the bank of the river and was about to throw himself into its dark waters. Then he heard the bells.

So Biondo turned back because he had heard a Voice that he had never known. And that was the real miracle, because a pistol that misfires is a material event, but a priest who begins to ring joybells at eleven o'clock at night is quite another matter.

MEN AND BEASTS

LA GRANDE was an enormous farm with a hundred cows, steam dairy, orchards and all the rest of it. And everything belonged to old Pasotti, who lived alone at the Badia with an army of retainers. One day these retainers set up an agitation and, led by Peppone, went *en masse* to the Badia and were interviewed by old Pasotti from a window.

"May God smite you," he shouted, thrusting out his head. "Can't a decent man have peace in this filthy country?"

"A decent man, yes," replied Peppone, "but not profiteers who deny their workmen what is their just due."

"I only admit of dues as fixed by the law," retorted Pasotti, "and I am perfectly within the law."

Then Peppone told him that so long as he refused to grant the concessions demanded, the workers of La Grande would do no work of any kind or description. "So you can feed your hundred cows yourself!" Peppone concluded.

"Very well," replied Pasotti. He closed the window and resumed his interrupted slumbers.

This was the beginning of the strike at La Grande, and it was a strike organized by Peppone in person, with a squad of overseers, regular watches, pickets and barricades. The doors and windows of the cowsheds were nailed up and seals placed upon them.

On the first day the cows lowed because they had not been milked. On the second day they lowed because they had not been milked and because they were hungry and on the third day thirst was added to all the rest and the lowing could be heard for miles around. Then Pasotti's old servant came out

77

by the back door of the Badia and explained to the men on picket duty that she was going into the village to the pharmacy to buy disinfectants. "I have told the master that he can't possibly want to get cholera from the stench when all the cows have died of starvation."

This remark caused quite a lot of head-shaking among the older labourers, who had been working for more than fifty years for Pasotti and who knew that he was incredibly pig-headed. And then Peppone himself stepped in to say, with the support of his staff, that if anyone dared to go near the cowshed he would be treated as a traitor to his country.

Towards the evening of the fourth day, Giacomo, the old cowman from La Grande, made his appearance at the presbytery.

"There is a cow due to calve and she is crying out fit to break your heart, and she will certainly die unless someone goes to help her; but if anyone attempts to go near the cow-shed they will break every bone in his body."

Don Camillo went and clung to the altar rails. "Lord," he said to the crucified Lord, "You must hold on to me or I shall make the march on Rome!".

"Steady, Don Camillo," replied the Lord gently. "Nothing is ever gained by violence. You must try to calm these people so that they will hear reason, and avoid exasperating them to acts of violence."

"Very true," sighed Don Camillo. "One must make them listen to reason. All the same, it seems a pity that while one is preaching reason the cows should die."

The Lord smiled. "If, by the use of violence, we succeed in saving a hundred beasts and kill one man and if, on the other hand, by using persuasion we lose the beasts, but avoid the loss of that man, which seems to you preferable: violence or persuasion?"

Don Camillo who, being filled with indignation, was loath to renounce his idea of a march on Rome, shook his head. "Lord, You are confusing the issue: this is not only a question of the loss of a hundred beasts, but also of the public patrimony; and the death of those beasts is not simply a personal disaster for Pasotti: it is also a loss for every one of us, good and bad. And it may also easily have repercussions such as may further exacerbate existing differences and create a conflict in which not only one man may die, but twenty."

The Lord was not of his opinion. "But if, by reasoning, you avoid one man being killed to-day, couldn't you also, by reasoning, avoid others being killed to-morrow? Don Camillo, have you lost your faith?"

Don Camillo went out for a walk across the fields because he was restless, and so it happened that quite by chance his ears began to be assailed more and more painfully by the lowing of the hundred cows at La Grande. Then he heard the voices of the men on picket duty at the barricades and at the end of ten minutes he found himself crawling inside and along the great cement irrigation pipe that passed underneath the wire netting at the boundaries of La Grande, and which was fortunately not in use at the moment.

"And now," thought Don Camillo, "it only remains for me to find someone waiting at the end of this pipe to knock me on the head." But there was nobody there and Don Camillo was left in peace to make his way cautiously along the entire length of the pipe in the direction of the farm.

"Halt!" said a voice presently, and Don Camillo made one leap out of the end of his pipe to shelter behind a tree trunk.

"Halt or I fire!" repeated the voice which came from behind another tree trunk on the farther side of the pipe.

It was an evening of coincidences, and Don Camillo, quite by chance, found himself grasping an appliance made of steel. He manipulated a certain movable gadget and replied:

"Be careful, Peppone, because I also shall fire."

"Ah!" muttered the other. "I might have known that I should find you mixed up in this business."

"Truce of God," said Don Camillo; "and if either of us breaks it he is damned. I am now going to count and when I say 'three' we both jump into that ditch."

"You wouldn't be a priest if you weren't so mistrustful," replied Peppone, and at the count of three he jumped and they found themselves sitting together at the bottom of the ditch.

From the cowshed came the desperate lowing of the cows, and it was enough to make one sweat with anguish. "I suppose you enjoy such music," muttered Don Camillo. "A pity that it will stop when all the cows have died. You're a fine fellow to hold on, aren't you? Why not persuade the labourers to burn the crops and also the barns that contain them. Just think now of poor Pasotti's fury if he were driven to take refuge in some Swiss hotel and to spend those few millions that he has deposited over there."

"He would have to reach Switzerland first!" growled Peppone threateningly.

"Exactly!" exclaimed Don Camillo. "It's about time we did away with that old Fifth Commandment which forbids us to kill! And when one comes eventually face to face with Almighty God one will only have to speak out bluntly: 'That's quite enough from you, my dear Eternal Father, or Peppone will proclaim a general strike and make everyone fold their arms!' By the way, Peppone, how are you going to get the cherubim to fold their arms? Have you thought of that?"

Peppone's roar vied with that of the expecting cow, whose complaints were heartrending. "You are no priest!" he vociferated. "You are the chief of the *Ghepeù*!"

"The *Gestapò*," Don Camillo corrected him. "The *Ghepeù* is your affair."

"You go about by night, in other people's houses, clutching a tommy-gun like a bandit!"

"And what about you?" inquired Don Camillo mildly.

"I am in the service of the people!"

"And I am in God's service!"

Peppone kicked a stone. "No use trying to argue with a priest! Before you have uttered two words they have dragged in politics!"

"Peppone," began Don Camillo gently, but the other cut him short:

"Now don't you begin jawing about the national patrimony and rubbish of that kind or as there is a God above I shall shoot you!" he exclaimed.

Don Camillo shook his head. "No use trying to argue with a Red. Before you have uttered two words they drag in politics!"

The cow that was about to calve complained loudly.

"Who goes there?" came a sudden voice from someone very close to the ditch. Then Brusco, Il Magro and Il Bigio made their appearance.

"Go and take a walk along the road to the mill," Peppone ordered them.

"All right," replied Brusco; "but who are you talking to?"

"To your damned soul," roared Peppone furiously.

"That cow that is going to calve is fairly bellowing," muttered Brusco.

"Go and tell the priest about it!" bawled Peppone. "And let her rot! I am working for the interests of the people, not of cows!"

"Keep your hair on, chief," stammered Brusco, making off hastily with his companions.

"Very well, Peppone," whispered Don Camillo; "and now we are going to work for the interests of the people."

"What do you intend to do?"

Don Camillo set out quietly along the ditch towards the farm and Peppone told him to halt or he would get what he was asking for between the shoulders.

"Peppone is as stubborn as a mule," said Don Camillo calmly, "but he doesn't shoot at the backs of poor priests who are doing what God has commanded them to do."

Then Peppone swore blasphemously and Don Camillo turned on him in a flash. "If you don't stop behaving like a balky horse, I shall give you one on the jaw exactly as I did to your celebrated federal champion. . . ."

"You needn't tell me: I knew all along that it could only be you. But that was quite another matter."

Don Camillo walked along quietly, followed by the other muttering and threatening to shoot. As they approached the cowshed another voice called to them to halt.

"Go to hell!" replied Peppone. "I am here myself now, so you can get along to the dairy."

Don Camillo did not even vouchsafe a glance at the cowshed door with its seals. He went straight up the stairs to the hay-loft above it and called in a low voice: "Giacomo."

The old cowman who had come to see him earlier and had related the story of the cow rose out of the hay. Don Camillo produced an electric torch and, shifting a bale of hay, revealed a trapdoor.

"Go down," said Don Camillo to the old man, who climbed down and disappeared for a considerable time.

"She's had her calf all right," he whispered when he returned. "I've seen a thousand of them through it and I know more than any vet."

"Now go along home," Don Camillo told the old man, and the old man went.

Then Don Camillo opened the trap-door again and sent a bale of hay through the opening. "What do you think you are doing?" asked Peppone, who had so far remained hidden.

"Help me to throw down these bales and then I'll tell you."

Grumbling as he did so, Peppone set to work chucking down the bales, and when Don Camillo had let himself down after them into the cowshed, Peppone followed him.

Don Camillo carried a bale to a right-hand manger and broke its lashings. "You'd better attend to the left-hand mangers," he said to Peppone.

"Not if you murder me!" shouted Peppone, seizing a bale and carrying it to the manger.

They worked like an army of oxen. Then there was the business of making the beasts drink and, since they were dealing with a modern cowshed with its drinking troughs placed along its outer walls, it was a matter of making one hundred cows right-about-turn and then belabouring their horns to stop them from drinking themselves to death.

When all was finished it was still pitch dark in the cowshed, but that was merely because all the shutters of the windows had been sealed from the outside.

"It's three o'clock in the afternoon," said Don Camillo, looking at his watch. "We shall have to wait until evening before we can get out!"

Peppone was biting his own fists with fury, but there was nothing for it but patience. When evening fell, Peppone and Don Camillo were still playing cards by the light of an oil lamp.

"I'm so hungry I could swallow a bishop whole!" exclaimed Peppone savagely.

"Hard on the digestion, Mr. Mayor," replied Don Camillo quietly, though he himself was faint with hunger and could have devoured a cardinal. "Before saying you are hungry, you should wait until you have fasted for as many days as these beasts."

Before leaving they again filled all the mangers with hay. Peppone tried to resist, saying that it was betraying the people, but Don Camillo was inflexible.

And so it happened that during the night there was a deathly silence in the cowshed, and old Pasotti, hearing no more lowing from the cows, became afraid that they must be so far gone that they had not even the strength to complain. In the morning he made a move to treat with Peppone, and with a little give and take on both sides the strike was settled and things resumed their normal course.

THE PROCESSION

EVERY YEAR, at the time of the blessing of the village, the crucified Lord from above the altar was carried in procession as far as the river bank, where the river also was blessed in order that it should refrain from excesses and behave decently.

Once again it seemed as though everything would take place with the customary regularity and Don Camillo was thinking over the final touches to be given to the programme of the celebrations when Brusco made his appearance at the presbytery.

"The secretary of our local section," said Brusco, "sends me to inform you that the entire section will take part in the procession complete with all its banners."

"Convey my thanks to Secretary Peppone," replied Don Camillo. "I shall be only too happy for all the men of the section to be present. But they must be good enough to leave their banners at home. Political banners have no place in religious processions and must not appear in them. Those are the orders that I have received."

Brusco retired, and very soon Peppone arrived, red in the face and with his eyes popping out of his head.

"We are just as much Christians as all the rest of them!" he shouted, bursting into the presbytery without even knocking on the door. "In what way are we different from other folk?"

"In not taking off your hats when you come into other people's houses," said Don Camillo quietly.

Peppone snatched his hat from his head.

"Now you are just like any other **Christian**," said Don Camillo.

"Then why can't we join the procession with our flag?" shouted Peppone. "Is it the flag of thieves and murderers?"

"No, Comrade Peppone," Don Camillo explained, lighting his cigar. "But the flag of a party cannot be admitted. This procession is concerned with religion and not with politics."

"Then the flags of Catholic Action should also be excluded!"

"And why? Catholic Action is not a political party, as may be judged from the fact that I am its local secretary. Indeed, I strongly advise you and your comrades to join it."

Peppone sniggered. "If you want to save your black soul, you had better join our party!"

Don Camillo raised his arms. "Supposing we leave it at that," he replied, smiling. "We all stay as we are and remain friends."

"You and I have never been friends," Peppone asserted.

"Not even when we were in the mountains together?"

"No! That was merely a strategic alliance. For the triumph of our arms, it is allowable to make an alliance even with priests."

"Very well," said Don Camillo calmly. "Nevertheless, if you want to join in the procession, you must leave your flag at home."

Peppone ground his teeth. "If you think you can play at being Duce, reverendo, you're making a big mistake!" he exclaimed. "Either our flag marches or there won't be any procession!"

Don Camillo was not impressed. "He'll get over it," he said to himself. And in fact, during the three days preceding the Sunday of the blessing, nothing more was said about the argument. But on the Sunday, an hour before Mass, scared people began to arrive at the presbytery. Early that morning Peppone's satellites had called at every house in the village to warn the inmates that anyone who ventured to take part in the procession would do so at the risk of life and limb.

"No one has said anything of the kind to me," replied Don Camillo, "I am therefore not interested."

The procession was to take place immediately after Mass,

and while Don Camillo was vesting for it in the sacristy he was interrupted by a group of parishioners.

"What are we going to do?" they asked him.

"We are going in procession," replied Don Camillo quietly.

"But those ruffians are quite capable of throwing bombs at it," they objected. "You cannot expose your parishioners to such a risk. In our opinion, you ought to postpone the procession, give notice to the public authorities of the town, and have the procession as soon as there are sufficient police on the spot to protect the people."

"I see," remarked Don Camillo. "And in the meantime we might explain to the martyrs of our faith that they made a big mistake in behaving as they did and that, instead of going off to spread Christianity when it was forbidden, they should have waited quietly until they had police to protect them."

Then Don Camillo showed his visitors the way to the door, and they went off, muttering and grumbling.

Shortly afterwards a number of aged men and women entered the church. "We are coming along, Don Camillo," they said.

"You are going straight back to your houses!" replied Don Camillo. "God will take note of your pious intentions, but this is decidedly one of those occasions when old men, old women and children should remain at home."

A number of people had lingered in front of the church, but when the sound of firing was heard in the distance (occasioned by Brusco letting off a tommy-gun into the air as a demonstration), even the group of survivors melted away, and Don Camillo, appearing upon the threshold of the sacristy, found the square as bare as a billiard table.

"Are we going now, Don Camillo?" inquired the Lord from above the altar. "The river must be looking beautiful in this sunshine and I shall really enjoy seeing it."

"We are going all right," replied Don Camillo. "But I am afraid that this time I shall be the entire procession. If You can put up with that . . ."

"Where there is Don Camillo, he is sufficient in himself," said the Lord, smiling.

Don Camillo hastily put on the leather harness with the support for the foot of the Cross, lifted the enormous crucifix from the altar and adjusted it in the socket. Then he sighed:

87

"All the same, they need not have made this cross quite so heavy."

"You're telling Me!" replied the Lord, smiling. "Didn't I carry it to the top of the hill, and I never had shoulders such as yours."

A few moments later Don Camillo, bearing his enormous crucifix, emerged solemnly from the door of the church.

The village was completely deserted; people were cowering in their houses and watching through the cracks of the shutters.

"I must look like one of those friars who used to carry a big black cross through villages smitten by the plague," said Don Camillo to himself. Then he began a psalm in his ringing baritone, which seemed to acquire volume in the silence.

Having crossed the square, he began to walk down the main street, and here again there was emptiness and silence. A small dog came out of a side street and began quietly to follow Don Camillo.

"Get out!" muttered Don Camillo.

"Let it alone," whispered the Lord from His Cross, "and then Peppone won't be able to say that not even a dog walked in the procession."

The street curved at its end and then came the lane that led to the river bank. Don Camillo had no sooner turned the bend when he found the way unexpectedly obstructed. Two hundred men had collected and stood silently across it with straddled legs and folded arms. In front of them stood Peppone, his hands on his hips.

Don Camillo wished he were a tank. But since he could only be Don Camillo, he advanced until he was within a yard of Peppone and then halted. Then he lifted the enormous crucifix from its socket and raised it in his hands, brandishing it as though it were a club.

"Lord," said Don Camillo. "Hold on tight; I am going to strike!"

But there was no need, because, having in a flash grasped the situation, the men withdrew to the sides of the road, and as though by enchantment the way lay open before him.

Only Peppone, his arms akimbo and his legs wide apart, remained standing in the middle of the road. Don Camillo replaced the crucifix in its socket and marched straight at him, and Peppone moved to one side.

88

"I'm not shifting myself for your sake, but for His," said Peppone, pointing to the crucifix.

"Then take that hat off your head!" replied Don Camillo without so much as looking at him.

Peppone pulled off his hat and Don Camillo marched solemnly through two rows of Peppone's men.

When he reached the river bank he stopped. "Lord," said Don Camillo in a loud voice, "if the few decent people in this filthy village could build themselves a Noah's Ark and float safely upon the waters, I would ask You to send such a flood as would break down this bank and submerge the whole countryside. But as these few decent folk live in brick houses exactly similar to those of their rotten neighbours, and as it would not be just that the good should suffer for the sins of scoundrels such as the Mayor Peppone and his gang of Godless brigands, I ask You to save this countryside from the waters and to give it every prosperity."

"Amen," came Peppone's voice from just behind him.

"Amen," came the response from behind Peppone of all the men who had followed the crucifix.

Don Camillo set out on the return journey and when he reached the threshold of the church and turned round so that the Lord might bestow a final blessing upon the distant river, he found standing before him: the small dog, Peppone, Peppone's men and every inhabitant of the village, not excluding the chemist, who was an atheist, but who felt that never in his life had he dreamed of a priest such as Don Camillo who could make even the Eternal Father quite tolerable.

THE MEETING

As soon as Peppone read a notice pasted up at the street corners to the effect that a stranger from the town had been invited by the local section of the Liberal Party to hold a meeting in the square, he leaped into the air.

"Here, in the Red stronghold! Are we to tolerate such a provocation?" he bawled. "We shall very soon see who commands here!"

Then he summoned his general staff and the stupendous occurrence was studied and analysed. The proposal to set fire immediately to the headquarters of the Liberal Party was rejected. That of forbidding the meeting met with the same fate.

"There you have democracy!" said Peppone sententiously. "When an unknown scoundrel can permit himself the luxury of speaking in a public square!"

They decided to remain within the bounds of law and order: general mobilization of all their members, organization of squads to supervise things generally and avoid any ambush. Occupation of strategic points and protection of their own headquarters. Pickets were to stand by to summon reinforcements from neighbouring sectors.

"The fact that they are holding a public meeting here shows that they are confident of overpowering us," said Peppone. "But in any case they will not find us unprepared."

Scouts placed along the roads leading to the village were to report any suspicious movement, and were already on duty from early Saturday morning, but they failed to sight so much as a cat throughout the entire day. During the night Smilzo discovered a questionable cyclist, but he proved to be only a normal drunk. The meeting was to take place in the course of Sunday afternoon, and up to three o'clock not a soul had put in an appearance.

"They will be coming by the three-fifty-five train," said Peppone. And he placed a large contingent of his men in and around the railway station. The train steamed in and the only person who got out was a thin little man carrying a small fibre suitcase.

"It's obvious that they got wind of something and didn't feel strong enough to meet the emergency," said Peppone.

At that moment the little man came up to him and, taking off his hat, politely inquired whether Peppone would be so kind as to direct him to the headquarters of the Liberal Party.

Peppone stared at him in amazement. "The headquarters of the Liberal Party?"

"Yes," explained the little man. "I am due to make a short speech in twenty minutes' time, and I should not like to be late."

Everyone was looking at Peppone and Peppone scratched his head. "It is really rather difficult to explain, because the centre of the village is over a mile away."

The little man made a gesture of anxiety. "Will it be possible for me to find some means of transport?"

"I have a lorry outside," muttered Peppone, "if you care to come along."

The little man thanked him. Then, when they got outside and he saw the lorry full of surly faces, red handkerchiefs and Communist badges, he looked at Peppone.

"I am their leader," said Peppone. "Get up in front with me."

Halfway to the village Peppone stopped the engine and examined his passenger, who was a middle-aged gentleman, very thin and with clear-cut features.

"So you are a Liberal?"

"I am," replied the gentleman.

"And you are not alarmed at finding yourself alone here among fifty Communists?"

"No," replied the man quietly. A threatening murmur came from the men in the lorry.

"What have you got in that suitcase?"

91

The man began to laugh and opened the case.

"Pyjamas, pair of slippers and a tooth-brush," he exclaimed.

Peppone pushed his hat on to the back of his head and slapped his thigh.

"You must be crazy!" he bellowed. "And may one be allowed to inquire why you aren't afraid?"

"Simply because I am alone and there are fifty of you," the little man explained quietly.

"What the hell has that got to do with it?" howled Peppone. "Doesn't it strike you that I could pick you up with one hand and throw you into that ditch?"

"No; it doesn't strike me," replied the little man as quietly as before.

"Then you really must either be crazy or irresponsible, or deliberately out to gull us."

The little man laughed again. "It is much simpler than that," he said. "I am just an ordinary, decent man."

"Ah, no, my good sir!" exclaimed Peppone leaping to his feet. "If you were an ordinary, decent man, you wouldn't be an enemy of the people! A slave of reaction! An instrument of capitalism!"

"I am nobody's enemy and nobody's slave. I am merely a man who thinks differently from you."

Peppone started the engine and the lorry dashed forward. "I suppose you made your will before coming here?" he jeered as he jammed his foot on the accelerator.

"No," replied the little man unperturbed. "All I have is my work, and if I should die I couldn't leave it to anyone else."

Before entering the village Peppone pulled up for a moment to speak to Smilzo, who was acting as orderly with his motor-bike. Then, by way of several side streets, they reached the headquarters of the Liberal Party. Doors and windows were closed.

"Nobody here," said Peppone gloomily.

"They must all be in the square, of course. It is already late," retorted the little man.

"I suppose that's it," replied Peppone, winking at Brusco.

When they reached the square Peppone and his men got out of the lorry and surrounded the little man and thrust a way through the crowd to the platform. The little man climbed on to it and found himself face to face with two thousand men, all wearing the red handkerchief.

The little man turned to Peppone, who had followed him on to the platform. "Excuse me," he inquired, "but have I by any chance come to the wrong meeting?"

"No," Peppone reassured him. "The fact is that there are only twenty-three Liberals in the whole district, and they don't show up much in a crowd. To tell you the truth, if I had been in your place, it would never have entered my head to hold a meeting here."

"It seems obvious that the Liberals have more confidence in the democratic discipline of the Communists than you have," replied the little man.

Peppone looked disconcerted for a moment then he went up to the microphone. "Comrades," he shouted, "I wish to introduce to you this gentleman who will make you a speech that will send you all off to join the Liberal Party."

A roar of laughter greeted this sally, and as soon as it died down the little man began speaking.

"I want to thank your leader for his courtesy," he said, "but it is my duty to explain to you that his statement does not tally with my wishes. Because if, at the end of my speech, you all went to join the Liberal Party, I should feel it incumbent upon me to go and join the Communist Party, and that would be against all my principles."

He was unable to continue, because just at that moment a tomato whistled through the air and struck him in the face.

The crowd began jeering and Peppone went white. "Anyone who laughs is a swine!" he shouted into the microphone, and there was immediate silence.

The little man had not moved, and was trying to clean his face with his hand. Peppone was a child of instinct, and quite unconsciously was capable of magnificent impulses; he pulled his handkerchief from his pocket, then he put it back again and unknotted the vast red handkerchief from his neck and offered to the little man.

"I wore it in the mountains," he said. "Wipe your face."

"Bravo, Peppone!" thundered a voice from the first-floor window of a neighbouring house.

"I don't need the approval of the clergy," replied Peppone arrogantly, while Don Camillo bit his tongue with fury at having let his feelings get the better of him.

The little man shook his head, bowed and approached the microphone.

"There is too much history attached to that handkerchief for me to soil it with the traces of a vulgar episode that belongs to the less heroic chronicles of our times," he said. "A handkerchief such as we use for a common cold suffices for such a purpose."

Peppone flushed scarlet and also bowed, and then a wave of emotion swept the crowd and there was vigorous applause while the hooligan lad who had thrown the tomato was kicked off the square.

The little man resumed his speech calmly. He was quiet, without any trace of bitterness; smoothing off corners, avoiding contentious arguments, being fully aware that should he let himself go, he could do so with impunity and would therefore be guilty of taking a cowardly advantage of the situation. At the end, he was applauded, and when he stepped down from the platform a way was cleared before him.

When he reached the far end of the square and found himself beneath the portico of the town hall, he stood helplessly with his suitcase in his hand, not knowing where to go or what to do. At that moment Don Camillo hurried up and turned to Peppone, who was standing just behind the little man. "You've lost no time, have you, you Godless rascal, in making up to this Liberal priest-eater."

"What?" gasped Peppone, also turning towards the little man. "Then you are a priest-eater?"

"But . . ." stammered the little man.

"Hold your tongue," Don Camillo interrupted him. "You ought to be ashamed, you who demand a free church in a free state!"

The little man attempted to protest, but Peppone cut him short before he could utter a word. "Bravo!" he bawled. "Give me your hand! When a man is a priest-eater he is my friend, even if he is a Liberal reactionary!"

"Hurrah!" shouted Peppone's satellites.

"You are my guest!" said Peppone to the little man.

"Nothing of the kind," retorted Don Camillo. "This gentleman is my guest. I am not a boor who fires tomatoes at his adversaries!"

Peppone pushed himself menacingly in front of Don Camillo.

"I have said that he is my guest," he repeated fiercely.

"And as I have said the same thing," replied Don Camillo, "it means that if you want to come to blows with me about it, you can have those that are due to your ruffianly Dynamos!"

Peppone clutched his fists.

"Come away," said Brusco. "In another minute you'll be at fisticuffs with the priest in the public square!"

In the end, the matter was settled in favour of a meeting on neutral territory. All three of them went out into the country to luncheon with Gigiotto, a host completely indifferent to politics, and thus even the democratic encounter led to no results of any kind.

ON THE RIVER BANK

BETWEEN ONE and three o'clock of the afternoon in the month of August, the heat in these districts that lie under hemp and buckwheat is something that can be both seen and felt. It is almost as though a great curtain of boiling glass hung at a few inches from one's nose. If you are crossing a bridge and you look down into the canal, its bed is dry and cracked with here and there a dead fish, and when from the road along the river bank you look at a cemetery you almost seem to hear the bones rattling beneath the boiling sun.

Along the main road you will meet an occasional wagon piled high with sand, with the driver sound asleep lying face downwards on top of his load, his stomach cool and his spine incandescent, or sitting on the shaft fishing out pieces from half a water melon that he holds on his knees like a bowl. Then when you come to the big bank, there lies the great river, deserted, motionless and silent, and it seems not so much a river as a cemetery of dead waters.

Don Camillo was walking in the direction of the big river, with a large white handkerchief inserted between his head and his hat. It was half-past one of an August afternoon and, seeing him thus, alone upon the white road under the burning rays of the sun, it was not possible to imagine anything blacker or more blatantly priest-like.

"If there is at this moment anyone within a radius of twenty miles who is not asleep, I'll eat my hat," said Don Camillo to himself. Then he climbed over the bank and sat down in the shade of a thicket of acacias and watched the water shining through the interstices of the foliage. Presently he took off his clothes, folding each garment carefully, and, rolling them all into a bundle that he hid among the bushes and wearing only his drawers, went and flung himself into the water.

Everything was perfectly quiet; no one could possibly have seen him, because, in addition to selecting the hour of siesta, he had also chosen the most secluded spot In any case, he was prudent and at the end of half an hour he climbed out of the water among the acacias and reached the bush where he had hidden his clothes, only to discover that the clothes were no longer there.

Don Camillo felt his breath fail him.

There could be no question of theft: nobody could possibly covet an old and faded cassock. It must mean that some devilry was afoot. And in fact at that very moment he heard voices approaching from the top of the bank. As soon as Don Camillo was able to see something he made out a crowd of young men and girls, and then he recognized Smilzo as their leader and was seized with an almost uncontrollable desire to break a branch from the acacias and use it on their backs. But he fully realized that he would only be gratifying his adversaries: what they were playing for was to enjoy the spectacle of Don Camillo in his drawers.

So he dived back into the water and, swimming beneath the surface, reached a little island in the middle of the river. Creeping ashore, he disappeared among the reeds.

But although his enemies had been unable to see him land they had become aware of his retreat and had now flung themselves down along the bank and lay waiting for him, laughing and singing.

Don Camillo was in a state of siege.

How weak is a strong man when he feels himself to be ridiculous! Don Camillo lay among the reeds and waited. Lying there unseen and yet able to see, he beheld the arrival of Peppone followed by Brusco, Bigio and his entire staff. Smilzo explained the situation with many gestures and there was much laughter. Then came more people and Don Camillo realized that the Reds were out to make him pay dearly for all past and present accounts and that they had hit upon the best of all systems because, when anyone has made himself ridiculous, nobody is ever afraid of him again, not even if his fists weigh a ton and he represents the Eternal Father. And in any case it was all grossly unfair because Don Camillo had never wished to frighten anyone except the devil. But somehow politics had contrived so to distort facts that the Reds had come to consider the parish priest as their enemy and to say that if things were not as they wished it was all the fault of the priests. When things go wrong it always seems less important to seek a remedy than to find a scapegoat.

"Lord!" said Don Camillo. "I am ashamed to address You in my drawers, but the matter is becoming serious and if it is not a mortal sin for a poor parish priest who is dying of the heat to go bathing, please help me, because I am quite unable to help myself."

The watchers had brought flasks of wine, parcels of food and an accordion. The river bank had been transformed into a beach and it was obvious that they had not the faintest intention of raising the siege. Indeed, they had extended it to beyond the celebrated locality of the ford, two hundred yards of shore consisting of shrubs and undergrowth. Not a soul had set foot in this area since 1945, because the retreating Germans had destroyed all the bridges and mined both banks at the ford. After a couple of disastrous attempts, the mine-removal squads had merely isolated the area with posts and barbed wire.

There were none of Peppone's men in that region: they were unnecessary, as no one but a lunatic would think of going near the mine-field. There was thus nothing to be done, because should he attempt to land beyond the watchers downstream, Don Camillo would find himself in the middle of the village and any attempt to get ashore upstream would lead him into the mine-field. A priest wearing only his drawers could not permit himself such luxuries.

Don Camillo did not move: he remained lying on the damp earth, chewing a reed and following his own train of thought.

"Well," he concluded, "a respectable man remains a respectable man even in his drawers. The important thing is that he should perform some reputable action and then his clothing ceases to have any importance."

The daylight was now beginning to fail and the watchers on the bank were lighting torches and lanterns. As soon as the green of the grass became black, Don Camillo let himself

98

down into the water and made his way cautiously upstream until his feet touched bottom at the ford. Then he struck out for the bank. No one could see him, as he was walking rather than swimming, only lifting his mouth out of the water at intervals to get his breath.

Here was the shore. The difficulty was to leave the water without being seen; once among the bushes, he could easily reach the bank and by running along it duck under the rows of vines and through the buckwheat and so gain his own garden.

He grasped a bush and raised himself slowly, but just as he had almost achieved his end, the bush came up by the roots and Don Camillo fell back into the water. The splash was heard and people came running. But in a flash Don Camillo had leaped ashore and had vanished among the bushes.

There were loud cries and the entire crowd surged towards the spot just as the moon rose to give its light to the spectacle.

"Don Camillo!" bawled Peppone, thrusting his way to the front of the crowd. "Don Camillo!" There was no reply and a deathly silence fell upon all those present.

"Don Camillo!" yelled Peppone again. "For God's sake don't move! You are in the mine-field!"

"I know I am," replied the voice of Don Camillo quietly from behind a shrub in the midst of the sinister shrubbery.

Smilzo came forward carrying a bundle. "Don Camillo," he shouted. "It was a rotten joke. Keep still and here are your clothes."

"My clothes? Oh, thank you, Smilzo. If you will be so kind as to bring them to me."

A branch was seen to move at the top of a bush some distance away. Smilzo's mouth fell open and he looked round at those behind him. The silence was broken only by an ironical laugh from Don Camillo.

Peppone seized the bundle from Smilzo's hand. "I'll bring them, Don Camillo," said Peppone, advancing slowly towards the posts and the barbed wire. He had already thrown a leg over the barrier when Smilzo sprang forward and dragged him back.

"No, chief," said Smilzo, taking the bundle from him and entering the enclosure. "He who breaks, pays."

The people shrank back, their faces were damp with sweat,

and they held their hands over their mouths. Amid a leaden silence Smilzo made his way slowly towards the middle of the enclosure, placing his feet carefully.

"Here you are," said Smilzo, in the ghost of a voice as he reached Don Camillo's bush.

"Good!" muttered Don Camillo. "And now you can come round here. You have earned the right to see Don Camillo in his drawers." Smilzo obeyed him.

"Well? And what do you think of a parish priest in drawers?"

"I don't know," stammered Smilzo. "I've stolen trifles and I've hit a fellow now and again, but I've never really done any harm to anyone."

"*Ego te absolvo,*" replied Don Camillo, making the sign of the cross on his forehead. They walked slowly towards the bank and the crowd held its breath and waited for the explosion.

They climbed over the barbed wire and walked along the road, Don Camillo leading and Smilzo, at his heels, still walking on tiptoe as though he had not left the mine-field, because he no longer knew what he was doing. Suddenly he collapsed on to the ground. Peppone, who at twenty paces distance was leading the rest of the people, picked up Smilzo by the collar as he went by and dragged him along like a bundle of rags, without once taking his eyes from Don Camillo's back. At the church door Don Camillo turned round for a moment, bowed politely to his parishioners and went into the church.

The others dispersed in silence and Peppone remained standing alone before the church staring at the closed door and still clutching the collar of the unconscious Smilzo. Then he shook his head, and he also turned and went his way, still dragging his burden.

"Lord," whispered Don Camillo to the crucified Lord, "one must serve the Church, even by protecting the dignity of a parish priest in his drawers."

There was no reply.

"Lord," whispered Don Camillo anxiously. "Did I really commit a mortal sin in going to bathe?"

"No," replied the Lord; "but you did commit a mortal sin when you dared Smilzo to bring you your clothes."

"I never thought he would do it: I was thoughtless, but not deliberately wicked."

From the direction of the river came the sound of a distant explosion. "Every now and then a hare runs through the mine-field, and then . . ." Don Camillo explained in an almost inaudible voice. "So we must conclude that You . . ."

"You must conclude nothing at all, Don Camillo," the Lord interrupted him with a smile. "With the temperature you are running at this moment your conclusions would scarcely be of any value."

Meanwhile, Peppone had reached the door of Smilzo's home. He knocked, and the door was opened by an old man who made no comment as Peppone handed over his burden. And it was at that moment that Peppone also heard the explosion, shook his head and remembered many things. Then he took Smilzo back from the old man for a moment and boxed his ears until his hair stood on end.

"Forward!" murmured Smilzo in a faraway voice as the old man once more took charge of him.

101

RAW MATERIAL

ONE AFTERNOON Don Camillo, who for a week past had been in a chronic state of agitation and had done nothing but rush to and fro, was returning from a visit to a neighbouring village. As soon as he reached his own parish he was compelled to alight from his bicycle because some men had appeared since his departure and were digging a ditch right across the road.

"We are putting in a new drain," a workman explained, "by the mayor's orders."

Then Don Camillo went straight to the village hall, and when he found Peppone he lost his temper.

"Are we all going off our heads?" he exclaimed. "Here you are, digging this filthy ditch and don't you know that this is Friday?"

"Well!" replied Peppone with every appearance of astonishment. "And is it forbidden to dig a ditch on a Friday?"

Don Camillo roared: "But have you realized that we are within less than two days of Sunday?"

Peppone looked worried. He rang a bell, and it was answered by Bigio. "Listen, Bigio," said Peppone. "The reverendo says that since today is Friday, it lacks less than two days to Sunday. What do you think about it?"

Bigio appeared to reflect very gravely. Then he pulled out a pencil and made calculations on a piece of paper. "Why," he said presently, "taking into consideration that it is now four o'clock in the afternoon and therefore within eight hours of midnight, it will actually be Sunday within thirty-two hours from the present time."

Don Camillo had watched all these manoeuvres and was by now almost foaming at the mouth. "I understand!" he shouted. "This is all a put-up job in order to boycott the bishop's visit."

"Reverendo," replied Peppone, "where is the connection between our local sewage and the bishop's visit? And also, may I ask what bishop you are speaking of and why he should be coming here?"

"To the devil with your black soul!" bawled Don Camillo. "That ditch must be filled in at once, or else the bishop will be unable to pass on Sunday!"

Peppone's face looked completely blank. "Unable to pass? But then how did you pass? There are a couple of planks across the ditch, if I am not mistaken."

"But the bishop is coming by car," exclaimed Don Camillo. "We can't ask the bishop to get out of his car and walk!"

"You must forgive me. I didn't know that bishops were unable to walk," retorted Peppone. "If that is so, then it is quite another matter. Brusco, call up the town and tell them to send us a crane immediately. We'll put it near the ditch, and as soon as the bishop's car arrives the crane can grapple on to it and lift it over the ditch without the bishop having to leave it. Have you understood?"

"Perfectly, chief. And what colour crane shall I ask for?"

"Tell them chromium or nickel-plated; it will look better."

In such circumstances even a man who lacked Don Camillo's armour-plated fists might have been tempted to come to blows. But it was precisely in such cases as these that Don Camillo, on the contrary, became entirely composed. His argument was as follows: "If this fellow sets out so blatantly and deliberately to provoke me it is because he hopes that I shall lose my temper. Therefore, if I give him one on the jaw I am simply playing his game. As a fact, I should not be striking Peppone, but a mayor in the exercise of his functions, and that would make an infernal scandal and create an atmosphere not only hostile to me personally, but also to the bishop."

"Never mind," he said quietly. "Even bishops can walk."

Speaking in church that evening, he literally implored all

his congregation to remain calm and to concentrate upon asking God to shed light upon the mind of their mayor in order that he might not attempt to ruin the impending ceremony, breaking up the procession and compelling the faithful to pass one at a time over a couple of insecure boards. And they must also pray God to prevent this improvised bridge from breaking under the undue strain and thus turning a day of rejoicing into one of mourning.

This diabolical address had its calculated effect upon all the women of the congregation who, on leaving the church, collected in front of Peppone's house and carried on to such effect that at last Peppone came to a window and shouted that they could all go to hell and that the ditch would be filled in.

And so all was well, but on Sunday morning the village streets were adorned with large printed posters:

> *"Comrades!*
>
> *"Alleging as a pretext of offence the initiation of work of public utility, the reactionaries have staged an unseemly agitation that has offended our democratic instincts. On Sunday our borough is to receive a visit from the representative of a foreign power, the same in fact who has been, indirectly, the cause of the aforementioned agitation. Bearing in mind your just resentment and indignation, we are anxious to avoid, on Sunday, any demonstration which might complicate our relations with strangers. We therefore categorically exhort you to keep your reception of this representative of a foreign power within the limits of a dignified indifference.*
>
> *"Hurrah for the Democratic Republic! Hurrah for the Proletariat! Hurrah for Russia!"*

This exhibition was further enlivened by a throng of Reds, who, it was easy to understand, had been specially mobilized with orders to parade the streets with *"dignified indifference,"* wearing red handkerchiefs or red ties.

Don Camillo, very white about the gills, went for a moment into the church, and was about to hurry away when he heard the Lord calling him. "Don Camillo, why are you in such a hurry?"

"I have to go and receive the bishop along the road," Don Camillo explained. "It is some distance, and then there are so many people about wearing red handkerchiefs that if the bishop does not see me immediately he will think that he has come to Stalingrad."

"And are these wearers of red handkerchiefs foreigners or of another religion?" asked the Lord.

"No; they are the usual rascals that You see before You from time to time, here in the church."

"Then if that is the case, Don Camillo, it would be better for you to take off that affair that you have strapped on under your cassock and to put it back in the cupboard." Don Camillo removed the tommy-gun and went to put it away in the sacristy.

"You can leave it there until I tell you to take it out again," commanded the Lord, and Don Camillo shrugged his shoulders.

"If I am to wait until You tell me to use a tommy-gun, we shall be in the soup!" he exclaimed. "You aren't likely ever to give the word, and I must confess that in many instances the Old Testament..."

"Reactionary!" smiled the Lord. "And while you are wasting your time in chattering, your poor old defenceless bishop is the prey of savage Russian Reds!"

This was a fact: the poor old defenceless bishop was indeed in the hands of the Red agitators. From as early as seven o'clock in the morning, the faithful had flocked to both sides of the main road, forming two long and impressive walls of enthusiasm, but a few minutes before the bishop's car was sighted Peppone, warned by a rocket fired by his outpost to signal the passing by of the enemy, gave the order to advance and by a lightning manoeuvre the Red forces rushed forward half a mile, so that, upon his arrival, the bishop found the entire road a mass of men wearing red handkerchiefs. People wandered to and fro and clustered into gossiping groups, displaying a sublime indifference towards the difficulties of the bishop's driver, who was compelled to proceed at a foot's pace, clearing a passage by continuous use of his horn.

This was in fact the *"dignified indifference"* ordained by the headquarters staff. Peppone and his satellites, mingling with the crowd, were chuckling with delight.

The bishop (that celebrated and very aged man, white-haired and bent, whose voice, when he spoke, appeared to come not from his lips, but from another century) immediately understood the *"dignified indifference"* and, telling his driver to stop the car (which was an open tourist model), made an abortive movement to open the door, allowing it to seem as if he lacked the necessary strength. Brusco, who was standing nearby, fell into the trap and when he realized his mistake, because of the kick Peppone had landed on his shin, it was too late and he had already opened the door.

"Thank you, my son," said the bishop. "I think it would be better if I walked to the village."

"But it is some distance," muttered Bigio, also receiving a kick on the shin.

"Never mind," replied the bishop, laughing, "I shouldn't like to disturb your political meeting."

"It is not a political meeting," explained Peppone gloomily. "They are only workers quietly discussing their own affairs. You'd better stay in your car."

But by now the bishop was standing in the road and Brusco had earned another kick because, realizing that he was unsteady on his feet, he had offered the support of his arm.

"Thank you, thank you so much, my son," said the bishop, and he set out, having made a sign to his secretary not to accompany him, as he wished to go alone.

And it was in this manner, at the head of the entire Red horde, that he reached the zone occupied by Don Camillo's forces and beside the bishop were Peppone, his headquarters staff, and all his most devoted henchmen, because, as Peppone had very wisely pointed out, the slightest gesture of discourtesy shown by any hot-headed fool to the representative of a foreign power would have given the reactionaries the opportunity of their lives.

"The order remains and will remain unchanged," concluded Peppone. *"Dignified indifference."*

The instant he sighted the bishop Don Camillo rushed towards him. "Monsignore," he exclaimed with great agitation, "forgive me, but it was not my fault! I was awaiting you with all the faithful, but at the last moment . . ."

"Don't worry," smiled the bishop. "The fault has been entirely my own, because I took it into my head to leave the car and take a walk. All bishops, as they get old, become a little crazy!"

The faithful applauded, the bands struck up and the bishop looked about him with obvious enjoyment. "What a lovely village!" he said as he walked on. "Really lovely, and so beautifully neat and clean. You must have an excellent local administration."

"We do what we can for the good of the people," replied Brusco, receiving his third kick from Peppone.

The bishop, on reaching the square, immediately noticed the fountain and halted.

"A fountain in a village of the Bassa!" he exclaimed. "That must mean that you have water!"

"Only a matter of bringing it here, Eminence," replied Bigio, to whom belonged the chief credit of the enterprise. "We laid three hundred yards of pipes and there, with God's help, was the water."

Bigio got his kick in due time and then, as the fountain was situated opposite the People's Palace, the bishop noticed the large new edifice and was interested. "And what is that handsome building?"

"The People's Palace," replied Peppone proudly.

"But it is really magnificent!" exclaimed the bishop.

"Would you care to go over it?" said Peppone on an impulse, while a terrible kick on the shins made him wince. That particular kick had come from Don Camillo.

The bishop's secretary, a lean young man with spectacles perched upon a big nose, had hurried forward to warn him that this was an unsuitable departure from routine, but the bishop had already entered the building. And they showed him everything: the gymnasium, the reading-room, the writing-room, and when they reached the library he went up to the book-shelves and studied the titles of the books. Before the bookcase labelled "Political," which was filled with propagandist books and pamphlets, he said nothing but only sighed, and Peppone, who was close to him, noticed that sigh.

"Nobody ever reads them, Monsignore," whispered Peppone.

He spared his visitor the inspection of the offices, but could not resist the temptation to show off the tea-room, which was the object of his special pride, and thus the bishop, on his way out, was confronted by the enormous portrait of the man with the big moustache and the small eyes.

"You know how it is in politics," said Peppone in a confidential voice. "And then, you may believe me, he isn't really such a bad fellow."

"May God in His mercy shed light upon his mind also," replied the bishop quietly.

Throughout all this business Don Camillo's psychological position was peculiar. Because, while he was foaming at the mouth with indignation at the presumption upon the bishop's kindness that dared to inflict upon him an inspection of the People's Palace, which was a foundation that surely cried to God for vengeance, on the other hand he was proud that the bishop should know how progressive and up-to-date a village he had come to visit. Moreover, he was not displeased that the bishop should realize the strength of the local leftist organization, since it could only enhance the merits of his own recreation centre in the bishop's eyes.

When the inspection was at an end Don Camillo approached the bishop. "It seems a pity, Monsignore," he said, so loudly that Peppone could not fail to hear him, "it seems a pity that our mayor has not shown you the arsenal. It is believed to be the most fully supplied of the entire province."

Peppone was about to retort, but the bishop forestalled him. "Surely not so well supplied as your own," he replied, laughing.

"Well said," exclaimed Bigio.

"He even has an S.S. mortar buried somewhere," added Brusco.

The bishop turned towards Peppone's staff. "You would insist on having him back again," he said; "and now you can keep him. Didn't I warn you that he was dangerous?"

"He doesn't manage to scare us," said Peppone with a grin.

"Keep an eye on him, all the same," the bishop advised him.

Don Camillo shook his head. "You will always have your joke, Monsignore!" he exclaimed. "But you can have no idea what these people are like!"

On his way out, the bishop passed the newsboard, saw the poster and paused to read it.

"Ah," he remarked, "you are expecting a visit from the representative of a foreign power! And who may that be, Don Camillo?"

"I know very little of politics," replied Don Camillo. "We must ask the gentleman who is responsible for the poster. Mr. Mayor, Monsignore wishes to know who is the representative of a foreign power who is mentioned in your manifesto?"

"Oh," said Peppone, after a moment's hesitation. "The usual American."

"I understand," replied the bishop. "One of those Americans who are looking for oil in these parts. Am I right?"

"Yes," said Peppone. "It's a downright scandal: any oil there may be belongs to us."

"I quite agree," said the bishop with the utmost gravity. "But I think you were wise to tell your people to limit their reactions to a dignified indifference. In my view, we should be foolish to quarrel with America. Don't you agree?"

Peppone spread out his arms. "Monsignore," he said, "you know how it is: one puts up with as much as can be borne and then comes the final straw!"

When the bishop arrived in front of the church he found all the local children from Don Camillo's recreation centre mustered in a neat formation, singing a song of welcome. Then an immense bouquet of flowers was seen to detach itself from the formation, and when it came to a halt in front of the bishop the flowers moved upwards and revealed a tiny child, so lovely and with such beautiful curls and clothes that all the women present went nearly out of their minds. There was complete silence while the infant, without pause or punctuation and in a voice as clear and pure as a little spring of water, recited a poem in the bishop's honour. After which everyone present applauded the child vociferously, exclaiming that he was adorable.

Peppone went up to Don Camillo. "Dastard!" he hissed in his ear. "You have taken advantage of a child's innocence in order to make me ridiculous before everybody! I shall break every bone in your body. And as for that brat, I shall show him where he gets off. You have contaminated him, and I shall chuck him into the river!"

"Good hunting!" replied Don Camillo. "He's your own son, and you can do as you like with him."

And it really was a shocking episode, because Peppone, carrying off the poor child to the river like a bundle, compelled him after fearful threats to recite three times over the poem in honour of the bishop . . . of that poor old weak and ingenious bishop who, being the *representative of a foreign power*" (the Vatican), had been received, according to plan, with "*dignified indifference.*"

THE BELL

DON CAMILLO, after a week during which he had attacked
Bigio at least three times daily wherever he met him, shouting that he and all his breed of house-painters were highway
robbers and lived only by extortion, had at last succeeded in
agreeing with him on a price for whitewashing the outside
walls of the presbytery. And now, from time to time, he went
to sit for a while upon the bench in the church square so
that he might enjoy the spectacle of those gleaming white
walls that, together with the newly painted shutters and the
climbing jasmine over the doorway, made a really beautiful
effect.

But after each gratifying contemplation, Don Camillo
turned to look at the church tower and sighed heavily, thinking of Geltrude. Geltrude had been carried off by the
Germans, and Don Camillo had therefore now been fretting
for her for nearly three years. For Geltrude had been the
largest of the church bells, and only God could provide the
necessary cash for the purchase of another bell of her lordly
proportions.

"Stop brooding, Don Camillo," said the Lord above the
altar one day. "A parish can get along very nicely even if
the church tower lacks one of its bells. In such a matter, noise
is not everything. God has very sharp ears and can hear
perfectly well even if He is called by a bell the size of a hazel
nut."

"Of course He can," replied Don Camillo with a sigh. "But

110

men are hard of hearing, and it is chiefly to call them that bells are needed: the masses do listen to those who make the loudest noise."

"Well, Don Camillo, peg away and you'll succeed."

"But, Lord, I have tried everything. Those who would like to give haven't the money, and the rich won't shell out even if you put a knife to their throats. I've been very near success a couple of times with the football pools. . . . A pity! If only someone had given me the shadow of a tip—just one name and I could have bought a dozen bells. . . ."

The Lord smiled. "You must forgive My carelessness, Don Camillo. You want Me in the coming year to keep My mind on the football championship? Are you also interested in the lottery?"

Don Camillo blushed. "You have misunderstood me," he protested. "When I said 'someone' I hadn't the faintest intention of alluding to You! I was speaking in a general sense."

"I am glad of that, Don Camillo," said the Lord with grave approval. "It is very wise, when discussing such matters, always to speak in a general sense."

A few days later Don Camillo received a summons to the villa of the Signora Carolina, the lady of Boscaccio, and when he came home he was fairly bursting with joy: "Lord!" exclaimed Don Camillo, halting breathlessly before the altar. "To-morrow You will see before You a lighted candle of twenty pounds' weight. I am going now to the town to buy it, and if they haven't got one, I shall have it specially made."

"But, Don Camillo, where will you get the money?"

"Don't You worry, Lord. You shall have Your candle if I have to sell the mattress off my bed to pay for it! Look what You have done for me!"

Then Don Camillo calmed down a little. "The Signora Carolina is giving an offering to the church of all the money needful for casting a new Geltrude!"

"And how did she come to think of it?"

"She said she had made a vow," explained Don Camillo, "to the effect that if the Lord helped her to bring off a certain business deal she would give a bell to the church. Thanks to Your intervention, the deal was successful, and within a month's time Geltrude will once more lift up her voice to Heaven! I am going now to order the candle!"

The Lord checked Don Camillo just as he was making off under full steam.

"No candles, Don Camillo," said the Lord severely. "No candles."

"But why?" demanded Don Camillo in amazement.

"Because I do not deserve them," replied the Lord. "I have given the Signora Carolina no help of any kind in her affairs. I take no interest in competition or in commerce. If I were to intervene in such matters, the winner would have reason to bless Me, while the loser would have cause to curse Me. If you happen to find a purse of money, I have not made you find it, because I did not cause your neighbour to lose it. You had better light your candle in front of the middleman who helped the Signora Carolina to make a profit of nine million. I am not myself a middleman."

The Lord's voice was unusually severe and Don Camillo was filled with shame.

"Forgive me," he stammered. "I am a poor, obtuse, ignorant country priest and my brain is filled with fog and foolishness."

The Lord smiled. "Don't be unjust to Don Camillo," He exclaimed. "Don Camillo always understands Me, and that is clear proof that his brain is not filled with fog. Very often it is precisely the intellect that fogs the brain. It is not you who have sinned; indeed, your gratitude touches Me because in any small matter that gives you pleasure you are always ready to perceive the kindness of God. And your joy is always honest and simple, as it is now in the thought of once more having your bell. And as it is also in your desire to thank Me for having enabled you to have it. But the Signora Carolina is neither simple nor honest when she sets out to acquire money by enlisting God's help in her shady financial transactions."

Don Camillo had listened silently and with his head bowed. Then he looked up. "I thank You, Lord. And now I shall go and tell that usurer that she can keep her money! My bells must all be honest bells. Otherwise it would be better to die without ever again hearing Geltrude's voice!"

He wheeled round, proud and determined, and the Lord smiled as He watched him walk away. But as Don Camillo reached the door, the Lord called him back.

"Don Camillo," said the Lord. "I am perfectly aware of all that your bell means to you, because I can always read your mind at any moment, and your renunciation is so fine and noble that in itself alone it would suffice to purify the bronze of a statue of Antichrist. *Vade retro, Satana!* Get out of here quickly or you will compel Me to grant you not only your bell, but who knows what other development."

Don Camillo stood quite still. "Does that mean I can have it?"

"It does. You have earned it."

In such contingencies Don Camillo invariably lost his head. As he was standing before the altar he bowed, spun on his heel, set off at a run, pulled himself up halfway down the nave and finally skidded as far as the church door. The Lord looked on with satisfaction, because even such antics may at given moments be a manner of praising God.

And then a few days later there occurred an unpleasant incident. Don Camillo surprised an urchin busily engaged in adorning the newly whitened walls of the presbytery with a piece of charcoal and saw red. The urchin made off like a lizard, but Don Camillo was beyond himself and gave chase.

"I shall collar you if I burst my lungs!" he yelled.

He set off on an infuriated pursuit across the fields and at every step his ire increased. Then suddenly the boy, finding his escape blocked by a thick hedge, stopped, threw up his arms to shield his head and stood still, too breathless to utter a word.

Don Camillo bore down on him like a tank and, grasping the child's arm with his left hand, raised the other, intending dire punishment. But his fingers closed on an arm so slender and emaciated that he let go and both his own arms fell to his sides.

Then he looked more attentively at the boy and found himself confronted by the white face and terrified eyes of Straziami's son.

Straziami was the most unfortunate of all Peppone's faithful satellites, and this not because he was an idler: he was in fact always in search of a job. The trouble lay in the fact that, having secured one, he would stick to it quietly for one day and on the second he would have a row with his employer, so that he seldom worked more than five days a month.

"Don Camillo," the child implored him, "I'll never do it again!"

113

"Get along with you," said Don Camillo abruptly.

Then he sent for Straziami, and Straziami strode defiantly into the presbytery with his hands in his pockets and his hat on the back of his head.

"And what does the people's priest want with me?" he demanded arrogantly.

"First of all that you take off your hat or else I'll knock it off for you; and, secondly, that you stop hectoring, because I won't put up with it."

Straziami himself was as thin and as colourless as his son and a blow from Don Camillo would have felled him to the ground. He threw his hat on to a chair with an elaborate assumption of boredom.

"I suppose you want to tell me that my son has been defacing the Archbishop's Palace? I know it already; some-one else told me. Your grey Eminence need not worry: this evening the boy shall have his hiding."

"If you dare so much as to lay a finger on him, I'll break every bone in your body," shouted Don Camillo. "Suppose you give him something to eat! Haven't you realized that the wretched child is nothing but a skeleton?"

"We aren't all of us the pets of the Eternal Father," began Straziami sarcastically.

But Don Camillo interrupted him: "When you do get a job, try to keep it instead of getting thrown out on the second day for spouting revolution!"

"You look after your own bloody business!" retorted Straziami furiously. He turned on his heel to go, and it was then that Don Camillo caught him by the arm. But that arm, as his fingers grasped it, was as wasted as that of the boy and Don Camillo let go of it hastily.

Then he went off to the Lord above the altar. "Lord," he exclaimed, "must I always find myself taking hold of a bag of bones?"

"All things are possible in a country ravaged by so many wars and so much hatred," replied the Lord with a heavy sigh. "Suppose you tried keeping your hands to your-self?"

Don Camillo went next to Peppone's workshop and found him busy at his vice.

"As mayor it is your duty to do something for that un-happy child, Straziami's," said Don Camillo.

"With the funds available to the commune, I might possibly be able to fan him with the calendar on that wall," replied Peppone.

"Then do something as chief of your beastly Party. If I am not mistaken, Straziami is one of your star scoundrels."

"I can fan him with the blotter from my desk."

"Heavens above! And what about all the money they send you from Russia?"

Peppone worked away with his file. "The Red Tzar's mails have been delayed," he remarked. "Why can't you lend me some of the cash you get from America?"

Don Camillo shrugged his shoulders. "If you can't see the point as mayor or as Party leader, I should have thought you might understand as the father of a son (whoever may be his mother!) the need for helping that miserable child who comes and scribbles on the presbytery wall. And by the way, you can tell Bigio that unless he cleans my wall free of charge I shall attack your Party from the Demo-Christian newsboard."

Peppone carried on with his filing for a bit; then he said: "Straziami's boy isn't the only one in the commune who needs to go to the sea or to the mountains. If I could have found the money, I should have established a colony long ago."

"Then go and look for it!" exclaimed Don Camillo. "So long as you stay in this office and file bolts, mayor or no mayor, you won't get hold of money. The peasants are stuffed with it."

"And they won't part with a cent, reverendo. They'd shell out fast enough if we suggested founding a colony to fatten their calves! Why don't you go yourself to the Pope or to Truman?"

They quarrelled for two hours and very nearly came to blows at least thirty times. Don Camillo was very late in returning to the presbytery.

"What has happened?" asked the Lord. "You seem upset."

"Naturally," replied Don Camillo. "When an unhappy priest has had to argue for two hours with a Communist mayor in order to make him understand the necessity for founding a seaside colony, and for another two hours with a miserly woman capitalist to get her to fork out the money required for that same colony, he may justly feel a bit gloomy."

"I understand you," replied the Lord.

115

Don Camillo hesitated. "Lord," he said at last, "You must forgive me if I have dragged even You into this business of the money."

"Me?"

"Yes, Lord. In order to compel that usurer to part with her cash, I had to tell her that I saw You in a dream last night and that You told me You would rather her money went for a work of charity than for the buying of the new bell."

"Don Camillo! And after that you have the courage to look Me in the eyes?"

"Yes," replied Don Camillo calmly. "The end justifies the means."

"Machiavelli doesn't strike me as being one of those sacred scriptures upon which you should base your actions," exclaimed the Lord.

"Lord," replied Don Camillo, "it may be blasphemy to say so, but even he can sometimes have his uses."

"And that is true enough," agreed the Lord.

Ten days later when a procession of singing children passed by the church on their way to the colony Don Camillo hurried out to say goodbye and to bestow stacks of little holy pictures. And when he came to Straziami's boy at the end of the procession, he frowned at him fiercely. "Wait until you are fat and strong and then we shall have our reckoning!" he threatened.

Then, seeing Straziami, who was following the children at a little distance, he made a gesture of disgust. "Family of scoundrels," he muttered as he turned his back and went into the church.

That night he dreamed that the Lord appeared to him and said that He would sooner the Signora Carolina's money were used for charity than for the purchase of a bell.

"It is already done," murmured Don Camillo in his sleep.

FEAR

PEPPONE FINISHED reading the newspaper that had come by the afternoon post and then spoke to Smilzo, who was awaiting orders perched on a high stool in a corner of the workshop.

"Go and get the car and bring it here with the squadron in an hour's time."

"Anything serious?"

"Hurry up!" shouted Peppone.

Smilzo started up the lorry and was off, and within three-quarters of an hour he was back again with the twenty-five men of the squadron. Peppone climbed in and they were very soon at the People's Palace.

"You stay here and guard the car," Peppone ordered Smilzo, "and if you see anything odd, shout."

When they reached the assembly room Peppone made his report. "Look here," he said, thumping with his big fist upon the news-sheet, which bore enormous headlines, "matters have reached a climax: we are for it. The reactionaries have broken loose, our comrades are being shot at and bombs are being thrown against all the Party headquarters." He read aloud a few passages from the paper, which was in point of fact the *Milano Sera,* a Milanese evening publication.

"And note that we are told these things not by one of our Party papers! This is an independent newspaper and it is telling the truth, because you can read it all clearly printed under the headlines!"

"Just think of it!" growled Brusco. "If one of those independent papers that always favour the right so damnably and oppose us whenever they can, is compelled to publish such things, only think how much worse the reality must be! I can't wait to read to-morrow's *Unità*!"

Bigio shrugged his shoulders. "It'll probably be tamer than this," he said. "*Unità* is run by comrades who are active, but all of them educated persons of culture who are learned in philosophy, and they always tend to minimize such matters, so as to avoid exciting the people."

"Yes; educated folk who are careful to observe rules and do nothing illegal," added Pellerossa.

"More like poets than anything else!" concluded Peppone. "But all the same they are people who, once they do pick up a pen, strike so hard that they would knock out the Eternal Father!"

They continued to discuss the situation, reading over again the principal statements in the Milanese paper and commenting upon what they had read. "It is obvious that the Fascist revolution has already begun," said Peppone. "At any moment, here where we stand, we may expect the flying squads to burn the Co-operatives and the people's houses and beat folk up and purge them. This paper mentions 'Fascist cells' and 'storm-troopers'; there is nothing equivocal about it. If it were a case of simple *qualunquismo*,[1] capitalism or monarchism they would speak of reactionaries, of 'nostalgists,' etcetera. But here they put it perfectly clearly and bluntly as 'fascism' and 'flying squads.' And bear in mind that it's an independent paper. We must be ready to face up to any eventuality."

Lungo gave it as his opinion that they ought to move first before the others got going: they knew perfectly well every individual reactionary in the commune. "We should go to every house in turn and pull them out and beat them up, and we should do it without any further talk."

"No," Brusco objected. "It seems to me that we should be putting ourselves in the wrong from the start. Even this paper says that we should reply to provocation, but not invite it. Because if we give provocation, we give them the right to retaliate."

Peppone agreed. "If we are to beat up anybody we should do it with justice and democratically."

[1] Italian party entitled "L'Uomo Qualunque": equivalent to "The Man in the Street."

They went on talking more quietly for another hour and were suddenly roused by an explosion that shook the windows. They all rushed out of the building and found Smilzo lying full length behind the lorry, as though he were dead, with his face covered with blood. They handed over the unconscious man to his wife's care and leaped into the lorry.

"Forward!" bawled Peppone as Lungo bent to the wheel. Off went the lorry at full tilt and it was not until they had covered a couple of miles that Lungo turned to Peppone.

"Where are we going?"

"That's just it," muttered Peppone. "Where are we going?"

They stopped the car and collected themselves. Then they turned round and went back to the village and drew up in front of the Demo-Christian headquarters. There they found a table, two chairs and a picture of the Pope, and all these they threw out of the window. Then they climbed into the lorry again and set out firmly for Ortaglia.

"Nobody but that skunk Pizzi would have thrown the bomb that killed Smilzo," said Pellerossa. "He swore vengeance on us that time when we quarrelled over the labourers' strike. 'We shall see!' he said."

They surrounded the house, which was isolated, and Peppone went in. Pizzi was in the kitchen stirring the *polenta*. His wife was laying the table and his little boy was putting wood on the fire.

Pizzi looked up, saw Peppone and immediately realized that something was wrong. He looked at the child, who was now playing on the floor at his feet. Then he looked up again.

"What do you want?" he asked.

"They have thrown a bomb in front of our headquarters and killed Smilzo!" shouted Peppone.

"Nothing to do with me," replied Pizzi. The woman caught hold of the child and drew back.

"You said that you would make us pay dearly when we came up against you over the labourers' strike. You are a reactionary swine, anyway." Peppone bore down on him menacingly, but Pizzi stepped back a pace and, catching up a revolver that lay on the mantelpiece, he pointed it at Peppone.

"Hands up, Peppone, or I shoot you!"

At that moment somebody who was hiding outside threw open the window, fired a shot and Pizzi fell to the ground. As he fell his revolver went off and the bullet lost itself among the ashes on the hearth. The woman looked down at her husband's body and put her hand in front of her mouth. The child flung himself on his father and began screaming.

Peppone and his men climbed hastily into the lorry and went off in silence. Before reaching the village, they stopped, got out and proceeded separately on foot.

There was a crowd in front of the People's Palace, and Peppone met Don Camillo coming out of it. "Is he dead?" Peppone asked.

"It would take a lot more than that to kill a fellow of his stamp," replied Don Camillo chuckling. "Nice fool you've made of yourself destroying the table at the Demo-Christian headquarters. They won't half laugh at you!"

Peppone looked at him gloomily. "There isn't much to laugh at, when people begin throwing bombs."

Don Camillo looked at him with interest. "Peppone," he said. "One of two things: either you are a scoundrel or a fool."

In point of fact, Peppone was neither. He quite simply did not know that the explosion had not been caused by a bomb, but by one of the retreaded tyres of the lorry from which a piece of rubber had struck the unfortunate Smilzo in the face.

He went to look underneath the lorry and saw the disembowelled tyre and then thought of Pizzi lying stretched out on the kitchen floor, of the woman who had put her hand to her mouth to stifle her screams and of the screaming child.

And meanwhile people were laughing. But within an hour the laughter died down because a rumour had spread through the village that Pizzi had been wounded.

He died next morning, and when the police went to question his wife the woman stared at them with eyes that were blank with terror.

"Didn't you see anyone?"

"I was in the other room; I heard a shot and ran in and found my husband lying on the ground. I saw nothing else."

"Where was the boy?"

"He was already in bed."

120

"And where is he now?"

"I've sent him to his grandmother."

Nothing more could be learned. The revolver was found to have one empty chamber, the bullet that had killed Pizzi had hit him in the temple and its calibre was identical with that of those remaining in the revolver. The authorities promptly decided that it was a case of suicide.

Don Camillo read the report and the statements made by various persons to the effect that Pizzi had been worried for some time past by the failure of an important deal in seeds, and had been heard to say on several occasions that he would like to make an end of it all. Then Don Camillo went to discuss the matter with the Lord.

"Lord," he said unhappily, "this is the first time in my parish that someone has died to whom I cannot give Christian burial. And that is right enough, I know, because he who kills himself kills one of God's children and loses his soul, and, if we are to be severe, should not even lie in consecrated ground."

"That is so, Don Camillo."

"And if we decide to allow him a place in the cemetery, then he must go there alone, like a dog, because he who renounces his humanity lowers himself to the rank of a beast."

"Very sad, Don Camillo, but so it is."

The following morning (it happened to be a Sunday) Don Camillo, in the course of his Mass, preached a terrible sermon on suicide. It was pitiless, terrifying and implacable.

"I would not approach the body of a suicide," he said in his peroration, "not even if I knew that my doing so would restore him to life!"

Pizzi's funeral took place on that same afternoon. The coffin was pushed into a plain third-class hearse which set out jerkily followed by the dead man's wife and child and his two brothers in a couple of two-wheeled carts. When the convoy entered the village people closed their shutters and peeped through the cracks.

Then suddenly something happened that struck everybody speechless. Don Camillo unexpectedly made his appearance, with two acolytes and the cross, took up his station in front of the hearse and preceded it on foot, intoning the customary psalms.

On reaching the church square, Don Camillo beckoned

to Pizzi's two brothers, and they lifted the coffin from the hearse and carried it into the church, and there Don Camillo said the office for the dead and blessed the body. Then he returned to his position in front of the hearse and went right through the village, singing. Not a soul was to be seen.

At the cemetery, as soon as the coffin had been lowered into the grave, Don Camillo drew a deep breath and cried in a stentorian voice: "May God reward the soul of his faithful servant, Antonio Pizzi."

Then he threw a handful of earth into the grave, blessed it and left the cemetery, walking slowly through the village depopulated by fear.

"Lord," said Don Camillo when he reached the church, "have You any fault to find with me?"

"Yes, Don Camillo, I have: when one goes to accompany a poor dead man to the cemetery one should not carry a pistol in one's pocket."

"I understand, Lord," replied Don Camillo. "You mean that I should have kept it in my sleeve so as to be more accessible."

"No, Don Camillo, such things should be left at home, even if one is escorting the body of a . . . suicide."

"Lord," said Don Camillo after a long pause, "will you have a bet with me that a commission composed of my most assiduous bigots will write an indignant letter to the bishop, to the effect that I have committed a sacrilege in accompanying the body of a suicide to the cemetery?"

"No," replied the Lord. "I won't bet, because they are already writing it."

"And by what I have done I have drawn upon myself the hatred of everyone: of those who killed Pizzi, of those who, while well aware, like everybody else, that Pizzi had been murdered, found it inconvenient that doubts should be raised regarding his suicide. Even of Pizzi's own relations who would have been glad to have it believed that there was no suspicion that he had not killed himself. One of his brothers asked me: 'But isn't it forbidden to bring a suicide into the church?' Even Pizzi's own wife must hate me, because she is afraid, not for herself, but for her son, and is lying in order to defend his life."

The little side door of the church creaked and Don Camillo looked round as Pizzi's small son entered. The boy came forward and halted in front of Don Camillo.

"I thank you on behalf of my father," he said in the grave, hard voice of a fully grown man. Then he went away as silent as a shadow.

"There," said the Lord, "goes someone who does not hate you, Don Camillo."

"But his heart is filled with hatred of those who killed his father, and that is another link in an accursed chain that no one succeeds in breaking. Not even You, who allowed Yourself to be crucified for these mad dogs."

"The end of the world is not yet," replied the Lord serenely. "It has only just begun, and up There time is measured by millions of centuries. You must not lose your faith, Don Camillo. There is still any amount of time."

THE FEAR CONTINUES

AFTER THE publication of his parish magazine, Don Camillo found himself quite alone.

"I feel as though I were in the middle of a desert," he confided to the Lord. "And it makes no difference even when there are a hundred people around me, because although they are all there, within half a yard of me, there seems to be a thick wall of glass that divides us. I hear their voices, but as though they came from another world."

"It is fear," replied the Lord. "They are afraid of you."

"Of me!"

"Of you, **Don Camillo.** And they hate you. They were living warmly and comfortably in their cocoon of cowardice. They were perfectly aware of the truth, but nobody could compel them to recognize it, because nobody had proclaimed it publicly. You have acted and spoken in such a manner that they are now forced to face up to it, and it is for that reason that they hate and fear you. You see your brothers who, like sheep, are obeying the orders of a tyrant, and you cry: 'Wake up out of your lethargy and look at those who are free; compare your lives with those of people who enjoy liberty!' And they will not be grateful to you but will hate you, and if they can they will kill you, because you compel them to face up to what they already knew but for love of a quiet life pretended not to know. They have eyes, but they will not see. They have ears, but they will not hear.

You have given publicity to an injustice and have placed these people in a serious dilemma: if you hold your tongue you condone their imposition; if you don't condone it you must speak out. It was so much easier to ignore it. Does all this surprise you?"

Don Camillo spread out his arms. "No," he said. "But it would have surprised me had I not known that You were crucified for telling people the truth. As it is, it merely distresses me."

Presently there came a messenger from the bishop. "Don Camillo," he explained, "Monsignore has read your parish magazine and is aware of the reactions it has aroused in the parish. The first number has pleased him, but he is exceedingly anxious that the second number shouldn't contain your obituary. You must see to it."

"That matter is independent of the will of the publishers," replied Don Camillo, "and therefore any request of the kind should be addressed not to me, but to God."

"That is exactly what Monsignore is doing," explained the messenger, "and he wished you to know it."

The sergeant of police was a man of the world: he met Don Camillo by chance in the street. "I have read your magazine and the point you make about the tyre tracks in the Pizzi's yard is very interesting."

"Did you make a note of them?"

"No," replied the sergeant. "I didn't make a note of them because directly I saw them I had casts taken of them then and there and happened to discover, quite by chance, when I was comparing the casts with the wheels of various local cars, that those tracks had been made by the mayor's lorry. Moreover, I observed that Pizzi had shot himself in the left temple when he was holding the revolver in his right hand. And when I hunted among the ashes in the fireplace I found the bullet that left Pizzi's revolver when Pizzi fell, after the other bullet had been fired at him through the window."

Don Camillo looked at him sternly. "And why have you not reported all this?"

"I have reported it in the proper quarter, reverendo. And I was told that if, at such a moment, the mayor was arrested, the matter would immediately assume a political significance. When such things get mixed up with politics there are complications. It is necessary to wait for an opportunity, and you, Don Camillo, have supplied it. I have no wish to shift my responsibility on to other shoulders; I merely want to avoid the danger that the whole business should get bogged because there are people who wish to make a political issue of it."

Don Camillo replied that the sergeant had acted most correctly.

"But I can't detail two constables to guard your back, Don Camillo."

"It would be a blackguardly attack!"

"I know it; but all the same I would surround you with a battalion if it were in my power," muttered the sergeant.

"It isn't necessary, sergeant. Almighty God will see to it."

"Let's hope He'll be more careful than He was of Pizzi," the sergeant retorted.

The following day the inquiries were resumed and a number of landowners and leaseholders were interrogated. As Verola, who was among those questioned, protested indignantly, the sergeant replied very calmly.

"My good sir: given the fact that Pizzi had no political views and that nobody robbed him of anything, and given also the fact that certain new evidence tends to suggest a murder rather than a suicide, we must exclude the supposition that we are dealing with either a political crime or a robbery. We must therefore direct our inquiries towards those with whom Pizzi had business or friendly relations and who may have borne him a grudge."

The matter proceeded in this manner for several days and the persons questioned were furiously angry.

Brusco also was infuriated, but he held his tongue.

"Peppone," he said at last. "That devil is playing with us as though we were kids. You'll see. When he has questioned everybody he can think of, including the midwife, in a couple of weeks' time he'll be coming to you with a smile to ask whether you have any objection to his questioning one of our people. And you won't be able to refuse, and he will begin his questioning and out will come the whole business."

"Don't be ridiculous," shouted Peppone. "Not even if they tore out my nails."

"It won't be you that they'll question, or me, or the others we are thinking of. They'll go straight for the one who will spill everything. They'll tackle the man who fired the shot."

Peppone sniggered. "Don't talk rubbish! When we ourselves don't know who did it!"

And thus it was. Nobody had seen which of the twenty-five men of the squadron had done the deed. As soon as Pizzi had fallen, they had all of them climbed into the lorry and later on had separated without exchanging a single word. Since then nobody had even mentioned the matter.

Peppone looked Brusco straight in the eyes. "Who was it?" he asked.

"Who knows. It may have been you yourself."

"I," cried Peppone. "And how could I do it when I wasn't even armed?"

"You went alone into Pizzi's house and none of us could see what you did there."

"But the shot was fired from outside, through the window. Someone must know who was stationed at that window."

"At night all cats are grey. Even if someone did see, by now he has seen nothing at all. But one person did see the face of the man who fired, and that was the boy. Otherwise his people wouldn't have said that he was in bed. And if the boy knows it then Don Camillo also knows it. If he hadn't known he wouldn't have said or done what he has said and done."

"May those who brought him here roast in Hell!" bawled Peppone.

Meanwhile, the net was being drawn closer and closer and every evening, as a matter of discipline, the sergeant went off to inform the mayor of the progress of the inquiries.

"I can't tell you more at the moment, Mr. Mayor," he said one evening, "but we know where we are at last; it seems that there was a woman in the case."

Peppone merely replied, "Indeed!" but he would gladly have throttled him.

It was already late in the evening and Don Camillo was finding jobs for himself in the empty church. He had set up a pair of steps on the top step of the altar, for he had discovered a crack in the grain of the wood of one of the crucifix and having filled it up was now applying a little brown paint to the white plaster of the stopping.

At a certain moment he sighed and the Lord spoke to him in an undertone. "Don Camillo, what is the matter? You haven't been yourself for several days past. Are you feeling unwell? Is it perhaps a touch of influenza?"

"No, Lord," Don Camillo confessed without raising his head. "It is fear."

"You are afraid? But of what, in heaven's name?"

"I don't know. If I knew what I was afraid of I shouldn't be frightened," replied Don Camillo. "There is something wrong, something in the air, something against which I can't defend myself. If twenty men came at me with guns I shouldn't be afraid. I should only be angry because they were twenty and I was alone and had no gun. If I found myself in the sea and didn't know how to swim I'd think: 'There now, in a few moments I shall drown like a kitten!' and that would annoy me very much but I should not be afraid. When one understands a danger one isn't frightened. But fear comes with dangers that are felt but not understood. It is like walking with one's eyes bandaged on an unknown road. And it's a beastly feeling."

"Have you lost your faith in your God, Don Camillo?"

"*Da mihi animam, caetera tolle.* The soul is of God, but the body is of the earth. Faith is a great thing, but this is a purely physical fear. I may have immense faith, but if I remain for ten days without drinking I shall be thirsty. Faith consists in enduring that thirst in serenity as a trial sent by God. Lord, I am willing to suffer a thousand fears such as this one for love of You. But nevertheless I am afraid."

The Lord smiled.

"Do You despise me?"

"No, Don Camillo; if you were not afraid, what value would there be in your courage?"

Don Camillo continued to apply his paint-brush carefully to the wood of the crucifix and his eyes were fixed upon the Lord's hand, pierced by the nail. Suddenly it appeared to him that this hand came to life, and at exactly that moment a shot resounded through the church.

Somebody had fired through the window of the little side chapel.

A dog barked, and then another; from far away came the brief burst of a tommy-gun firing. Then there was silence once more. Don Camillo gazed with scared eyes into the Lord's face.

"Lord," he said, "I felt Your hand upon my forehead."

"You are dreaming, Don Camillo."

Don Camillo lowered his eyes and fixed them upon the

hand pierced by the nail. Then he gasped and the brush and the little pot of paint fell from his fingers.

The bullet had passed through the Lord's wrist.

"Lord," he said breathlessly, "You pushed back my head and Your arm received the bullet that was meant for me!"

"Don Camillo!"

"The bullet is not in the wood of the crucifix!" cried Don Camillo. "Look where it went!"

High up to the right and opposite the side chapel hung a small frame containing a silver heart. The bullet had broken the glass and had lodged itself exactly in the centre of the heart.

Don Camillo ran to the sacristy and fetched a long ladder. He stretched a piece of string from the hole made by the bullet in the window to the hole made in the silver heart. The line of the string passed at a distance of about twelve inches from the nail in the Lord's hand.

"My head was just there," said Don Camillo, "and Your arm was struck because You pushed my head backwards. Here is the proof!"

"Don Camillo, don't get so excited!"

But Don Camillo was beyond recovering his composure, and had he not promptly developed a fierce temperature the Lord only knew what he might have done. And the Lord obviously did know it, because He sent him a fever that laid him low in his bed as weak as a half-drowned kitten.

The window through which the shot had been fired gave on to the little enclosed plot of land that belonged to the church, and the police sergeant and Don Camillo stood there examining the church wall.

"Here is the proof," said the sergeant, pointing to four holes that were clearly visible upon the light distemper just below the window-sill. He took a penknife from his pocket, dug into one of the holes and presently pulled out some object.

"In my opinion, the whole business is quite simple," he explained. "The man was standing at some distance away and fired a round with his tommy-gun at the lighted window. Four bullets struck the wall and the fifth hit the glass and went through it."

Don Camillo shook his head. "I told you that it was a

pistol shot and fired at close range. I am not yet so senile as to be unable to distinguish a pistol shot from a round of machine-gun fire! The pistol shot came first and was fired from where we are standing. Then came the burst from the tommy-gun from farther away."

"Then we ought to find the cartridge case nearby," retorted the sergeant; "and it isn't anywhere to be seen!"

Don Camillo shrugged his shoulders. "You would need a musical critic from La Scala to distinguish by the key tone whether a shot comes from an automatic or from a revolver! And if the fellow fired from a pistol he took the cartridge case with him."

The sergeant began to nose round and presently he found what he was looking for on the trunk of one of the cherry trees that had been planted in a row some five or six paces from the church.

"One of the bullets has cut the bark," he said. And it was obvious that he was right. He scratched his head thoughtfully.

"Well," he said, "we may as well play the scientific detective!"

He fetched a pole and stuck it into the ground close to the church wall, in front of one of the bullet holes. Then he began to walk to and fro with his eyes fixed on the damaged cherry tree, moving to right or left until the trunk was in a direct line covering the pole by the wall. Thus he ultimately found himself standing in front of the hedge and beyond the hedge were a ditch and a lane.

Don Camillo joined him and, one on either side of the hedge, they carefully examined the ground. They went on searching for a while, and after about five minutes Don Camillo said: "Here it is," and held up a tommy-gun cartridge case. Then they found the other three.

"That proves I was right," exclaimed the sergeant. "The fellow fired from here through the window."

Don Camillo shook his head. "I've never used a tommy-gun," he said, "but I know that with other guns, bullets never describe a curve. See for yourself."

Just then a constable came up to inform the sergeant that everyone in the village was quite calm.

"Many thanks!" remarked Don Camillo. "Nobody fired at any of them! It was me that they shot at!"

The sergeant borrowed the constable's rifle and lying

flat on the ground aimed in the direction of the upper pane of the chapel window where, so far as his memory served him, he thought the bullet had struck it.

"If you fired now, where would the bullet go?" asked Don Camillo.

It was an easy reckoning, mere child's play: a bullet fired from where they were and passing through the chapel window would have hit the door of the first confessional on the right-hand side, at about three yards' distance from the church door.

"Unless it was a trained bullet, it couldn't have gone past the altar, not if it split itself!" said the sergeant. "Which only goes to show," he went on, "that any matter in which you are mixed up is always enough to make one tear out one's hair! You couldn't be contented with one assailant! No, sir: you must have two of them. One that fires from behind the window and another that fires from behind a hedge a hundred and fifty paces away."

"Oh well, that's how I'm made," replied Don Camillo. "I never spare expense!"

That same evening Peppone summoned his staff and all the local Party officials to headquarters.

Peppone was gloomy. "Comrades," he said, " a new event has occurred to complicate the present situation. Last night some unknown person shot at the so-called parish priest and the reaction is taking advantage of this episode in order to raise its head and throw mud at the Party. The reaction, cowardly as always, has not the courage to speak out openly, but, as we would expect, is whispering in corners and trying to saddle us with the responsibility for this attack."

Lungo held up his hand and Peppone signed to him that he could speak.

"First of all," said Lungo, "we might tell the reactionaries that they had better offer proof that there really has been an attempt on the priest's life. Since there seem to have been no witnesses, it might easily be that the reverend gentleman himself fired off a revolver in order to be able to attack us in his filthy periodical! Let us first of all obtain proof!"

"Excellent!" exclaimed his audience. "Lungo is perfectly right!"

Peppone intervened. "One moment! What Lungo says is fair enough, but we should not exclude the possibility that what we have heard is the truth. Familiar as we all are with

Don Camillo's character, it can hardly be said, honestly, that he is in the habit of using underhand methods . . ."

Peppone was in his turn interrupted by Spocchia, the leader of the cell at Milanetto. "Comrade Peppone, do not forget that once a priest always a priest! You are letting yourself be carried away by sentimentality. Had you listened to me, his filthy magazine would never have seen the light and to-day the Party would not have had to endure all the odious insinuations with regard to Pizzi's suicide! There should be no mercy for the enemies of the people! Anyone who has mercy on the people's enemies betrays the people!"

Peppone crashed his fist down on the table. "I don't require any preaching from you!" he bawled.

Spocchia seemed unimpressed. "And, moreover, if instead of opposing us you had let us act while there was still time," he shouted, "we shouldn't now be held up by a crowd of accursed reactionaries! I . . ."

Spocchia was a thin young man of twenty-five and sported an immense head of hair. He wore it brushed back, waved on top of his head and smooth at the sides, forming a kind of upstanding crest such as is affected by louts in the north and by the boors of Trastevere. He had small eyes and thin lips.

Peppone strode up to him aggressively. "You are a half-wit!" he said, glaring at him. The other changed colour, but made no reply.

Returning to the table, Peppone went on speaking. "Taking advantage of an episode that is based only upon the statement of a priest," he said, "the reaction is putting forward fresh speculations to the discredit of the people. The comrades need to be more than ever determined. To such ignoble suggestions they . . ."

Quite suddenly something happened to Peppone that had never happened to him before: Peppone began *listening to himself*. It seemed to him as though Peppone were among his audience listening to what Peppone was saying:

". . . *and their bodies sold, the reaction paid by the enemies of the proletariat, the labourers starved . . .*" Peppone listened and gradually he seemed to be listening to another man. ". . . *the Savoy gang . . . the lying clergy . . . the black government . . . America . . . plutocracy . . .*"

"What in the world does plutocracy mean? Why is that fellow spouting about it when he doesn't even know what it means?" Peppone was thinking. He looked round him and saw faces that he barely recognized. Shifty eyes, and the most treacherous of all were those of young Spocchia. He thought of the faithful Brusco and looked for him, but Brusco stood at the far end of the room, with folded arms and bent head.

"But let our enemies learn that in us the Resistance has not weakened. . . . The weapons that we took up for the defence of our liberty . . ." And now Peppone heard himself yelling like a lunatic, and then the applause brought him back to himself.

"Splendid!" whispered Spocchia in his ear as they went downstairs. "You know, Peppone, it only needs a whistle to set them going. My lads could be ready in an hour's time."

"Good! Excellent!" replied Peppone, slapping him on the shoulder. But he would gladly have knocked him down. Nor did he know why.

He remained alone with Brusco and at first they were silent. "Well!" exclaimed Peppone at last. "Have you lost your wits? You haven't even told me whether I spoke well or not?"

"You spoke splendidly," replied Brusco, "wonderfully. Better than ever before." Then the curtain of silence fell back heavily between them.

Peppone was doing accounts in a ledger. Suddenly he picked up a glass paperweight and threw it violently on to the ground, bellowing a long, intricate and infuriated blasphemy. Brusco stared at him.

"I made a blot," explained Peppone, closing the ledger.

"Another of that old thief Barchini's pens," remarked Brusco, being careful not to point out to Peppone that, as he was writing in pencil, the explanation of the blot did not hold water.

When they left the building and went out into the night they walked together as far as the crossroads and there Peppone pulled up as though he had something that he wished to tell Brusco. But he merely said: "Well; see you to-morrow."

"To-morrow then, Chief. Good night."

"Good night, Brusco."

MEN OF GOODWILL

CHRISTMAS WAS aproaching, and it was high time to get the figures of the Crib out of their drawer so that they might be cleaned, touched up here and there and any stains carefully removed. It was already late, but Don Camillo was still at work in the presbytery. He heard a knocking on the window and on seeing that it was Peppone went to open the door.

Peppone sat down while Don Camillo resumed his work and neither of them spoke for quite a long time.

"Hell and damnation!" exclaimed Peppone suddenly and furiously.

"Couldn't you find a better place to blaspheme in than my presbytery?" inquired Don Camillo quietly. "Couldn't you have got it off your chest at your own headquarters?"

"One can't even swear there any longer," muttered Peppone. "Because if one does, someone asks for an explanation."

Don Camillo applied a little white lead to St. Joseph's beard. "No decent man can live in this filthy world!" exclaimed Peppone after a pause.

"How does that concern you?" inquired Don Camillo. "Have you by any chance become a decent man?"

"I've never been anything else."

"There now! And I should never have thought it." Don Camillo continued his retouching of St. Joseph's beard. Then he began to tidy up the saint's clothing.

"How long will you be over that job?" asked Peppone angrily.

"If you were to give me a hand, it would soon be done."

Peppone was a mechanic and he possessed hands as big as shovels and enormous fingers that gave an impression of clumsiness. Nevertheless, when anybody wanted a watch repaired, they never failed to take it to Peppone. Because it is a fact that it is precisely such bulky men that are best adapted to the handling of minute things. Peppone could streamline the body of a car or the spokes of a wheel like a master painter.

"Are you crazy! Can you see me touching up saints!" he muttered. "You haven't by any chance mistaken me for a sacristan?"

Don Camillo fished in the bottom of the open drawer and brought forth a pink-and-white object about the size of a sparrow: it was in fact the Holy Infant Himself.

Peppone hardly knew how he came to find it in his hands, but he took up a little brush and began working carefully. He and Don Camillo sat on either side of the table, unable to see each other's faces because of the light of the lamp between them.

"It's a beastly world," said Peppone. "If you have something to say you daren't trust anyone. I don't even trust myself."

Don Camillo appeared to be absorbed in his task: the Madonna's whole face required repainting.

"Do you trust me?" he asked casually.

"I don't know."

"Try telling me something and then you will know."

Peppone completed the repainting of the Baby's eyes, which were the most difficult part. Then he touched up the red of the tiny lips. "I should like to give it all up," said Peppone, "but it can't be done."

"What prevents you?"

"Prevents me? With an iron bar in my hand, I could stand up to a regiment!"

"Are you afraid?"

"I've never been afraid in my life!"

"I have, Peppone. Sometimes I am frightened."

Peppone dipped his brush in the paint. "Well, so am I, sometimes," he said, and his voice was almost inaudible.

Don Camillo sighed. "The bullet was within four inches

of my forehead" said Don Camillo. "If I hadn't drawn my head back at that exact moment I should have been done for. It was a miracle."

Peppone had completed the Baby's face and was now working with pink paint on His body.

"I'm sorry I missed," he mumbled, "but I was too far off and the cherry trees were in the way." Don Camillo's brush ceased to move.

"Brusco had been keeping watch for three nights round the Pizzi house to protect the boy. The boy must have seen who it was that fired at his father through the window, and whoever did it knows that. Meanwhile I was watching your house. Because I was certain that the murderer must know that you also knew who killed Pizzi."

"The murderer: who is he?"

"I don't know," replied Peppone. "I saw him from a distance creeping up to the chapel window. But I wasn't in time to fire before he did. As soon as he had fired I shot at him and I missed."

"Thank God," said Don Camillo. "I know how you shoot, and we may say that there were two miracles."

"Who can it be? Only you and the boy can tell."

Don Camillo spoke slowly. "Yes, Peppone, I do know; but nothing in this world could make me break the secrecy of the confessional."

Peppone sighed and continued his painting.

"There is something wrong," he said suddenly. "They all look at me with different eyes now. All of them, even Brusco."

"And Brusco is thinking the same thing as you are, and so are the rest of them," replied Don Camillo. "Each of them is afraid of the others and every time any one of them speaks he feels as if he must defend himself."

"But why?"

"Shall we leave politics out of it, Peppone?"

Peppone sighed again. "I feel as if I were in gaol," he said gloomily.

"There is always a way out of every gaol in this world," replied Don Camillo. "Gaols can only confine the body, and the body matters so little."

The Baby was now finished and it seemed as if His clear, bright colouring shone in Peppone's huge dark hands. Peppone looked at Him and he seemed to feel in his palms the living warmth of that little body. He forgot all about being in gaol.

He laid the Baby delicately upon the table and Don Camillo placed the Madonna near Him.

"My son is learning a poem for Christmas," Peppone announced proudly. "Every evening I hear his mother teaching it to him before he goes to sleep. He's a wonder!"

"I know," agreed Don Camillo. "Look how beautifully he recited the poem for the bishop!"

Peppone stiffened. "That was one of the most rascally things you ever did!" he exclaimed. "I shall get even with you yet."

"There is plenty of time for getting even, or for dying," Don Camillo replied.

Then he took the figure of the ass and set it down close to the Madonna as she bent over Her Child. "That is Peppone's son, and that is Peppone's wife, and this one is Peppone," said Don Camillo, laying his finger on the figure of the ass.

"And this one is Don Camillo!" exclaimed Peppone, seizing the figure of the ox and adding it to the group.

"Oh, well! Animals always understand one another," said Don Camillo.

And though Peppone said nothing he was now perfectly happy, because he still felt in the palm of his hand the living warmth of the pink Baby; and for a time the two men sat in the dim light looking at the little group of figures on the table and listening to the silence that had settled over the Little World of Don Camillo, and that silence no longer seemed ominous but instead full of peace.

DON CAMILLO
AND THE PRODIGAL SON

translated by
FRANCES FRENAYE

THE THIRTEENTH-CENTURY ANGEL

WHEN OLD Bassini died they found written in his will: "I bequeath everything I have to the parish priest, Don Camillo, to be spent for gilding the angel on the church tower so that I can see it shining all the way from Heaven and recognize the place where I was born."

The angel was at the top of the bell tower and, from below, it did not appear to be very large. But when they had erected scaffolding and climbed up to see, they found it was almost the size of a man and would require quite an amount of gold leaf to cover it. An expert came from the city to examine the statue at close hand, and he came down a few minutes later in a state of great agitation.

"It's the Archangel Gabriel in beaten copper," he explained to Don Camillo. "A beautiful thing, straight from the thirteenth century."

Don Camillo looked at him and shook his head.

"Neither the church nor the tower is more than three hundred years old," he objected.

But the expert insisted that this didn't matter.

"I've been in business forty years, and I've gilded I can't tell you how many statues. If it isn't thirteenth-century, I'll do the job for you free."

Don Camillo was a man who preferred to keep his feet firmly on the ground, but curiosity drove him to climb with the expert to the top of the tower and look the angel in the face. There he gaped in astonishment, for the angel was very beautiful indeed. He, too, was agitated when he came down, because he couldn't imagine how such a work of art had come to be on the bell tower of a humble country church. He dug into the parish archives, but found no account of it whatsoever. The next day the expert came back from the city with two gentlemen who went with him to the top of the tower, and they backed up his opinion that the statue was beyond a shadow of doubt thirteenth-century. They were two professors in the line of art, two important names, and Don Camillo could not find words with which to thank them.

"It's quite wonderful!" he exclaimed. "A thirteenth-century angel on the tower of this poor little church! It's an honour for the whole village."

That afternoon a photographer came to take pictures of the statue from every possible angle. And the next morning a city newspaper carried an article, with three illustrations, which said it was a crime to leave such a treasure exposed to the four winds, when it was part of the nation's cultural heritage and should be kept under shelter. Don Camillo's ears turned crimson as he read.

"If those city rascals think they're going to take our angel away, then they can think again," he said to the masons who were strengthening the scaffolding.

"That's right," said the masons. "It's ours, and nobody has a right to touch it."

Then some more important people arrived upon the scene, including representatives of the bishop, and as soon as they came down from looking at the angel they all told Don Camillo that it was a shame to leave it there, exposed to the weather.

"I'll buy him a raincoat," Don Camillo said in exasperation, and when they protested that this was an illogical thing to say he retorted with considerable logic: "In public squares all over the world statues have stood for centuries amid the raging elements and no one has dreamed of putting them under shelter. Why should we have to tuck our angel away? Just go and tell the people of Milan that the Madonnina on that cathedral of theirs is falling to pieces and they ought to take it down and put it under cover. Don't you know that they'd give you a good, swift kick if you suggested anything of the kind?"

"The Madonnina of Milan is a very different matter," said one of the important visitors.

"But the kicks they give in Milan are very much like those

we give here!" Don Camillo answered, and because the villagers crowding around him on the church square punctuated his last remark with a "That's right!" no one pursued the subject further.

Some time later the city newspaper returned to the attack. To leave a beautiful thirteenth-century angel on the church tower of a valley village was a crime. Not because anyone wanted to take the angel away, but because the village could make good money from tourists if only it were in a more accessible place. No art-lover was going to travel so far, simply in order to stand in the square and gape up at a statue on top of a tower. They ought to bring the angel down into the church, have a cast made, and then an exact copy which they could gild and put in its place.

After people in the village had read that newspaper article, they began to mumble that there was something to it, and the local Communists, under the leadership of Mayor Peppone, couldn't very well miss the opportunity to comment on "a certain reactionary who should have been born in the Middle Ages." As long as the angel stayed up on the tower, no one could appreciate its beauty. Down in the church it would be in plain sight, and there would be no loss to the tower if another angel were to replace it. Don Camillo's most prosperous parishioners talked it over with him, and eventually he admitted that he might have been in the wrong. When the angel was taken down the whole village gathered in the square, and it had to be left there for several days because people wanted to see and touch it. They came from miles around, for word had spread that the angel had miraculous powers. When the time came to make the cast, Don Camillo said stubbornly: "The angel's not to budge. Bring your tools and do the job here."

After the settlement of old Bassini's estate, it was found that he had left enough money to gild a dozen angels, and so there was plenty to spend on the bronze copy. The copy itself finally arrived from the city, all covered with gold, and everyone proclaimed it a masterpiece. People compared the measurements, inch by inch, and found that they tallied exactly.

"If the original were gilded too," they said, "no one could tell them apart."

However, Don Camillo felt some scruples about his failure to carry out the terms of old Bassini's will.

"I'll have the original gilded, then," he said. "There's plenty of money."

But the people from the city intervened and said the original mustn't be tampered with. They presented a number of arguments, but Don Camillo had ideas of his own.

"It isn't a question of art," he insisted. "Bassini left me the money for the express purpose of gilding the angel on the tower. This is the angel he meant, and if I don't have it gilded, then I'm betraying his trust."

The new angel was hoisted to the top of the tower, and the experts proceeded to gild the old one. It was placed in a niche near the door, and everyone gaped at it in its shiny new dress.

The night before the unveiling of both statues, Don Camillo could not sleep. Finally he got up and went over to the church to look at the original angel.

"Thirteenth-century," he said to himself, "and this little church no more than three hundred years old! You existed four hundred years before the tower was built. How did you ever get up there?"

Don Camillo stared at the great wings of the Archangel Gabriel and ran his big hand over his perspiring face. How could a heavy copper angel like this one have flown up to the top of a tower? Now he stood in a niche, behind a glass door that could be opened and shut for protection. Impulsively Don Camillo took a key out of his pocket and opened the door. How could an angel that had lived on top of a tower stay shut up in a box? Surely he must be suffocating for want of air. And Don Camillo remembered the text of old Bassini's will: "I bequeath everything I have to the parish priest, Don Camillo, to be spent for gilding the angel on the church tower so that I can see it shining all the way from Heaven and recognize the place where I was born."

"And now he doesn't see his angel at all," Don Camillo reflected. "He sees a false angel in its place. That isn't what he wanted."

Don Camillo was very troubled, and when that happened he went to kneel at the feet of Christ on the big cross over the altar.

"Lord," he said, "why did I cheat old Bassini? What made me give in to those rascals from the city?"

The Lord did not answer, and so Don Camillo went back to the angel.

144

"For three hundred years you've watched over this valley and its people. Or perhaps for seven hundred years. Who knows? For this church may have been built on the ruins of one much older. You have saved us from famine and plague and war. Who can say how many gales and bolts of lightning you have turned away? For three, or perhaps seven hundred years, you have given the village's last farewell to the souls of the dead as they rose up into Heaven. Your wings have vibrated to the sound of the bells, whether they called men to rejoice or to mourn. Yes, centuries of joy and sorrow are in your wings. And now you are shut up in a gilded cage, where you will never see the sky or the sun again. Your place has been usurped by a false city angel, whose only memories are the swear words of unionized foundry workers. You took shape from an unknown thirteenth-century craftsman with faith to inspire his hammer, while the usurper was turned out by some monstrously unholy machine. How can a pitiless, mechanical creature like that protect us? What does he care for our land and its people?"

It was eleven o'clock at night and the village lay wrapped in silence and fog from the river when Don Camillo went out of the church and into the darkness.

Peppone was not in a good humour when he answered the knock at his door.

"I need you," said Don Camillo. "Put on your coat and follow me."

When they were inside the church the priest pointed to the captive angel.

"He protected your father and mother and their fathers and mothers before them. And he must watch over your son. That means going back to where he was before."

"Are you mad?" asked Peppone.

"Yes," said Don Camillo. "But I can't do it alone. I need the help of a madman like you."

The scaffolding was still up all around the tower. Don Camillo tucked his cassock into his trousers and began to climb, while Peppone followed him with a rope and pulley. Their madness lent them the strength of a dozen men. They lassooed the angel, detached it from its pedestal and lowered it to the ground. Then they carried it into the church, took the original angel out of the niche and put the false one in its place.

145

Five men had worked at hoisting the false angel up to the top of the tower, but now the two of them managed to do it alone. They were soaked with fog and perspiration and their hands were bleeding from the rope.

It was five o'clock in the morning. They lit a fire in the rectory and downed two or three bottles of wine in order to collect their thoughts. At this point they began to be afraid. Day was breaking, and they went to peer out of the window. There was the angel, high above them, on top of the tower.

"It's impossible," said Peppone.

Suddenly he grew angry and turned upon Don Camillo.

"Why did you rope me into it?" he asked him. "What damned business is it of mine?"

"It isn't damned business at all," Don Camillo answered. "There are too many false angels loose in the world working against us already. We need true angels to protect us."

Peppone sneered.

"Silly religious propaganda!" he said, and went away without saying goodbye.

In front of his own door, something made him turn around and look up into the sky. There was the angel, shining in the first light of dawn.

"Hello there, Comrade!" Peppone mumbled serenely, taking off his cap to salute him.

Meanwhile Don Camillo knelt before the crucifix at the altar and said:

"Lord, I don't know how we did it!"

The Lord did not answer, but he smiled, because He knew very well how.

THE DANCE OF THE HOURS

LA ROCCA, the tower which was the centre of the township and the seat of the Town Hall, was in a sad state of disrepair. When one day a squad of masons appeared upon the scene and began to throw up scaffolding round the tower, everybody said: "It's about time!"

It wasn't a question of looks, because in the Po River valley aesthetics matter very little, and a thing is beautiful when it is well made and serves its purpose. But everybody had occasion at one time or another to go to the Town Hall, and they didn't like the prospect of having a brick or a fragment of cornice fall upon their heads.

When the scaffolding was up, the masons swathed the façade with cloth so that no plaster wou'd fall on the passers-by and then began the repairs. These went on for about a month, until one night everything was taken down, and the next morning the people of the village, along with a number of strangers who had come to the weekly market-day, found the tower completely restored. The masons knew their trade and had done a good job. Of course, they couldn't leave politics out of it and so they had hung up a big sign, near the top, which said: *"This public work was NOT financed by the Marshall Plan."*

Don Camillo was among the crowd that had gathered in the square and when Peppone saw him he edged up behind his back and sprang on him the question: "Well, what have you got to say?"

Don Camillo did not even turn round. "A good job," he

said. "Too bad that the looks of it should be ruined by that sign."

Peppone turned to a group of his gang, who just happened to be standing by.

"Did you hear? He says that the looks of the thing are ruined by the sign. Do you know, I very nearly agree!"

"Where artistic matters are concerned, the priest's word carries a lot of weight," Smilzo put in. "I think he's right."

They discussed it further, and finally Peppone said:

"Someone go and tell them to take down that sign. That'll prove we're not like certain people who claim to be infallible."

A couple of minutes later, someone loosened a rope, and the sign came down. And then appeared the real surprise: a magnificent new clock. For years and years the clock on the bell tower of the church had been the only public timepiece in the village, but now there was another on the Town Hall.

"You can't appreciate it fully in the daytime," Peppone explained. "But the dial is transparent and lighted from inside, so that by night you can read the time from a mile away."

Just then there was a vague noise from the top of La Rocca and Peppone shouted:

"Silence!"

The square was full of people, but they all fell silent to hear the new clock strike ten. Hardly had the echoes died away, when the clock on the church tower began to ring out the same hour.

"Wonderful," said Don Camillo to Peppone. "Only your clock is nearly two minutes fast."

Peppone shrugged his shoulders.

"One might just as well say that your clock is nearly two minutes slow."

Don Camillo did not lose his aplomb.

"One might just as well say so, but it's inadvisable. My clock is exact to the second, just as it has been for the last thirty or forty years, and there was no use in squandering public funds for a new one on the Town Hall."

Peppone wanted to say any number of things, but there were so many he choked, and the veins of his neck stood out like ropes. Smilzo rushed into the breach, raising one finger.

"You're angry because you wanted to have a monopoly

on time! But time doesn't belong exclusively to the clergy!
It belongs to the people!'"

The new clock struck a quarter past the hour, and once
more the square was silent. First one and then two minutes
went by.

"It's more inaccurate than before!" exclaimed Don
Camillo. "Now it's a full two minutes fast."

People took big silver watches out of their vest pockets
and began to argue. It was all very strange, because before
this none of them had ever cared about minutes at all.
Minutes and seconds are strictly city preoccupations. In the
city people hurry, hurry so as not to waste a single minute,
and fail to realize that they are throwing a lifetime away.

When the Town Hall clock struck half-past ten, and the
bell tower followed, two minutes later, there were two
schools of opinion. The conflict was not a violent one, because it remained within the circumference of the opposing
parties' vest pockets. But Smilzo had warmed up to all the
implications, and shouted:

"On the day when La Rocca clock strikes the hour of the
people's revolution, some people are going to find out that
they're not two minutes but two centuries behind!"

Smilzo always talked like that, but this time he made
the mistake of shaking a threatening finger under Don
Camillo's nose. And Don Camillo made an unequivocal
answer. He stretched out his hand, pulled Smilzo's cap down
over his eyes and then did the classical turn of the screw,
leaving the visor at the back of his neck. Peppone stepped
forward.

"What would you say if anyone played that trick on you?"
he asked through his teeth.

"Try and see!" said Don Camillo. "No one's ever tried so
far!"

Twenty hands dragged Peppone back.

"Don't do anything rash," they said. "The Mayor mustn't
get into trouble."

The gang of Reds closed in on Don Camillo and began to
shout. Don Camillo felt an urge to create some fresh air
about him and a bench was the first fan that came into his
hand. With his steam up and a bench in his grasp, Don
Camillo was a cyclone. In a second there was an empty space
around him, but since the square was packed with people and
market-stands, an empty space at one point meant increased

149

density at some other. A chicken cage was trampled, a horse reared, and there was a chorus of shouts, moos and whinnies. The Red gang was routed, but Peppone, who was squashed into the entrance of the Town Hall by people who didn't want him to get into trouble, managed to seize a bench in his turn. And Peppone, too, when his motor was running at high speed and he had a bench in his grasp, was a tornado that knew neither friend nor foe. The crowd stepped back, while Peppone slowly and fatefully advanced towards Don Camillo, who stood his ground, bench in hand. The crowd had retreated to the periphery of the square, and only Smilzo kept his head and threw himself in Peppone's way.

"Forget it, Chief! Don't behave like a donkey!"

But Peppone implacably advanced towards the centre of the square, and Smilzo had to back away as he delivered his warning. Suddenly he found himself between the two benches, but he stood firm and awaited the shock of the earthquake. The crowd was silent. The most desperate of the Reds had grouped themselves behind Peppone, and Don Camillo was backed up by a group of old peasants, who had a nostalgic longing for the blackjack, and now shook their stout cherry sticks at their opponents. There seemed to be a tacit agreement between both sides. As soon as Peppone and Don Camillo let go with their benches, there would be a free-for-all fight. There was a moment of deathly silence while the two protagonists brandished their weapons, and then something extraordinary happened. The old clock and the new both started to strike eleven, and their strokes were in perfect synchronization.

The benches fell, and the empty middle of the square filled up with people. As if they were coming out of a dream, Don Camillo and Peppone found themselves in a busy market-place, where vendors were crying their wares. Peppone went off to the Town Hall and Don Camillo to the presbytery. Smilzo was left alone in the middle of the square, trying to puzzle out what had happened. Finally he gave up his attempt to understand, and since all the Reds had melted away he went over to a nearby stand and drank a Coca-cola.

RHADAMES

RHADAMES WAS the son of Badile, the locksmith, whose real name was Hernani Gniffa. Obviously an operatic family. Badile had a good ear, and when he had tucked away a bottle or two of wine he sang with a powerful voice that was a pleasure to hear. When Badile's son, Rhadames, was six years old, his father brought him to Don Camillo and asked to have him taken into the choir. Don Camillo tested the boy's voice and then said:

"The only thing I can do is set him to blowing the organ bellows." For Rhadames had a voice as hard and cutting as a splinter of stone.

"He's my son," said Badile, "so he must have a voice. It's still tight, that's all. What it needs is loosening up."

To say no would have meant giving Badile the worst disappointment of his life, and so the priest sighed and said, "I'll do my best."

Don Camillo did everything he could, but after two years Rhadames' voice was worse than ever. Besides being even harsher than before, it stuck in his throat. Rhadames had a magnificent chest, and to hear a miserable squeak come out of it was really infuriating. One day Don Camillo lost patience, got up from the organ and gave Rhadames a kick that landed him against the wall. Where singing is concerned, a kick may be more effective than three years' study of harmony: Rhadames went back to the choir and produced a voice that seemed to come straight from La Scala. When people heard him they said that it would be a crime for him to discontinue his studies.

This is the way they are in a village. If a fellow is disagreeable and unattractive they'll let him die of starvation. But if they take a liking to a fellow, they'll put together the money to get him singing lessons. In this case, they collected enough to send Rhadames to the city. Not to live like a gentleman—that couldn't be expected—but with his singing lessons paid for. And for the rest, Rhadames had to earn his board and keep by sawing wood, delivering parcels, and so on. Every now and then Badile went to see him and brought back the news: "He's not doing too badly. He's making progress."

Then the war came along and Rhadames was lost from sight. One day when it was all over he turned up in the village. Peppone was Mayor and, when Don Camillo told him that Rhadames' musical education must go on, he found the money to send him back to the city. A year or two later, Rhadames turned up again.

"They're letting me sing in *Aïda*," he said.

Things were tense in the village for political reasons, and violence was in the air, but because of this news hostilities were suspended. Peppone held a meeting at the Town Hall, and Don Camillo attended it. The first question that came up was how to raise funds.

"The honour of the village is at stake," Peppone explained. "Rhadames mustn't cut a poor figure before those big shots in the city."

And the committee agreed.

"If anyone can get money out of those that have it," said Peppone, "I can guarantee the support of the common people."

Don Camillo understood that this was a gentle hint, and answered. "Somebody will do it."

Then Rhadames gave a detailed account of his needs, which was found quite satisfactory.

"Here there's no question of corruption or special favours," Peppone said proudly. "This is definitely a proletarian victory."

Don Camillo turned to Rhadames.

"What is your stage name?" he asked him.

"His stage name?" shouted Peppone. "His own, of course! Do you want him to assume yours?"

Don Camillo did not lose his temper.

"Rhadames Gniffa isn't the kind of name you can put on an opera programme. It's a most unfortunate name, because it's bound to make people laugh."

Then Rhadames' father came into the discussion.

"My name is Hernani Gniffa, and I've borne it for sixty-five years without anyone's laughing!"

"That's all very well, but you're a locksmith, not a tenor!" Don Camillo answered. "Around here nobody cares, but in the theatrical world it's a different matter. There you need a name that sounds well and is sure to be popular."

"How ridiculous!" exclaimed Peppone. "Middle-class stupidity!"

Don Camillo looked at him hard.

"If Giuseppe Verdi had been called Rhadames Gniffa, do you think he would have won such fame as a composer?"

Peppone stopped to think, and Don Camillo gave him another example. "If Joseph Stalin had happened to be called Euripides Bergnocioni, would he have left the same mark on history?"

"The very idea!" stammered Peppone. "Think of Stalin under the name of Bergnocioni! Impossible!"

The committee sat until late at night, and finally made a unanimous choice of the name Franco Santalba.

"It's a queer world!" they all said.

Rhadames shrugged his shoulders. "Whatever you decide suits me all right," he said.

The great day came at last, and the committee met in the village square to read the announcement of the opera in the newspaper that had just arrived from the city. Rhadames' photograph was there, and under it the caption: "Franco Santalba, tenor." They couldn't resist going to hear him.

"There's room in the truck for all of us," said Peppone. "And we'd better make an early start in order to get seats. We'll meet here in the square at four o'clock."

"Somebody must tell the priest," one of the men observed. "He won't be able to come, but he ought to know about it."

"Priests don't interest me," said Peppone.

But they went to the presbytery in a body.

"I can't go, you know that," Don Camillo said sadly. "It

wouldn't do for a priest to go to the opera, especially on the opening night. You'll have to tell me all about it."

When the committee had gone, Don Camillo went to confide his sorrow to Christ on the altar.

"I'm distressed that I can't go," he said with a sigh. "Rhadames is almost like a son to us all. But of course duty is duty. My place is here, and not amid the worldly frivolities of a theatre...."

"Quite right, Don Camillo. One of those small sacrifices that you must accept cheerfully."

"Yes, of course from a general or absolute point of view, it's a small sacrifice," said Don Camillo. "But to the person concerned, it's a large one. Of course, the greater the sacrifice, the more cheerfully it should be accepted. Complaints take all the value of a sacrifice away. In fact, if a sacrifice brings out a complaint, it doesn't count as a sacrifice at all."

"Naturally," the Lord answered.

Don Camillo paced up and down the empty church.

"I developed the boy's voice," he explained, stopping in front of the altar. "He came not much higher than my knees, and he couldn't sing; he squeaked like a rusty chain. And now he's singing in *Aïda*. Rhadames in *Aïda*! And I can't hear him. Surely that's a tremendous sacrifice. But I'm bearing up very cheerfully."

"Certainly you are," the Lord whispered gently.

Peppone and his gang sat in the front row of the gallery with their heads whirling. To gain admission to the gallery, it's not sufficient to pay for a ticket; one has to fight for a seat as well. And when *Aïda's* on the boards, the gallery is a madhouse. That evening, however, a burly man made his way through the crowd at the last minute and came in just behind Peppone. He was wearing a green coat, and Peppone seemed to know him, because he squeezed over on the bench and made a place for him.

"If Rhadames loses his nerve, he's out of luck," Peppone mumbled. "This is a merciless crowd."

"Here's hoping," said the burly man in the green coat.

"If they hiss him, I'll kill somebody," said Peppone excitedly, and the man in the green coat motioned to him to keep his head.

But they didn't whistle; they were kind enough simply to snigger. Towards the end of the first act, things got worse and

154

worse. Rhadames grew really scared and sang off key. The gallery howled, vigorously enough to make the curtain tremble. Peppone clenched his teeth, and his stalwarts were ready to sow murder round them. But the burly man took Peppone by the collar and dragged him outside. They walked up and down in the fresh air, and, when they heard a howl, they knew that Rhadames had hit still another false note. Then at the sound of the triumphal march the audience began to calm down. Shortly before the third act, the burly man said to Peppone: "Let's go."

The attendants didn't want to admit them behind the scenes. But before two strapping men with the combined strength of an armoured division, there was nothing to do. They found Rhadames waiting in terror to be howled off the stage for the third and last time. When he saw the two men, his jaw fell open. The man in the green coat went behind and gave him a kick powerful enough to launch a Caruso.

Rhadames practically sailed through the air on to the stage, but he was completely transformed when he got there. When he sang the great aria *"Io son disonorato!"* the theatre almost broke down under the applause.

"You've got to know a singer down to the bottom," the burly man said triumphantly to the hysterical Peppone.

"Yes, Don . . ." Peppone started to reply, but at one look from the burly man he broke his sentence off in the middle.

THE STUFF FROM AMERICA

THE PARTY delegate was one of those gloomy, tight-lipped persons who seem to have been just made for wearing a red scarf round the neck and a tommy-gun slung from one shoulder. The reason for his visit to the village was to *galvanize* and *activate* the local section of the Party. He made endless speeches to the cell leaders, for when these gloomy, tight-lipped fellows start talking politics they are as long-winded as the late Adolf Hitler. He stayed three whole days, and on the morning of the third day, when he had finished laying down the latest Party line, he said to Peppone:

"On Saturday you're to call a meeting of the village Council and announce that you're resigning from the post of Mayor."

"Have I done so badly?" stammered Peppone.

"No, Comrade; you've done so well that you're to be promoted. You're to run for Parliament on the People's Front programme."

"Me run for Parliament?"

"Yes, that's what I said."

"But I haven't any education . . ."

"You know how to obey, Comrade, don't you? All a deputy to Parliament needs to know is how to obey Party orders. And you're sure to attract votes. You're known all over the province for the way you hustle round and get things done."

Peppone threw out his arms.

"But what about my own village?"

"Do you care more for the community than for Communism?"

Peppone bowed his head.

"Of course you'll have to make some campaign speeches. But we'll send you those, don't worry. You can just learn them by heart."

While the delegate was giving him further instructions as to how to conduct his campaign, Smilzo burst breathlessly into the room.

"The stuff from America is here!" he shouted. "I mean the foodstuff. There are posters up to announce that the needy can call at the presbytery for relief parcels. Spaghetti, tinned milk, preserves, butter and sugar. The posters have created quite a sensation."

"What's the exact wording of the announcement?" the delegate asked him.

"*The fatherly heart of His Holiness . . . etc. . . . etc. . . . parcels which all the needy are entitled to receive upon application to the parish priest, Don Camillo . . . etc. . . . etc. . . .*"

"*All* the needy, did you say."

"Yes, all of them, without distinction."

Peppone clenched his fists.

"I knew that devil was cooking up something," he said. "They speculate in human misery, the filthy cowards. We'll have to deal with it somehow."

"Yes, Comrade, deal with it!" the delegate ordered. "Call a meeting of the cell leaders."

When the cell leaders had hastened to answer the call, Peppone told them of the latest reactionary manoeuvre.

"Within half an hour the comrades must hear that if one of them accept so much as a safety-pin I'll strangle him for it. Smilzo, you stand guard in front of the presbytery. Keep your eyes peeled every minute and take down the names of all those who go to pick up parcels."

"Well spoken," the delegate said approvingly. "A case like this requires decisive action."

All day long there was a line in front of the presbytery. The priest was jubilant, because the parcels were plentiful and well filled and people were happy to get them.

"Tell me if the so-called People's Party gives you anything better," he said, laughing.

"They give nothing but tall talk," everyone answered.

157

Some of the Reds were needy enough, but they didn't come. This was the only fly in the priest's ointment, because he had prepared a special homily for their benefit. "You haven't any right to this, since you have Stalin to look after you. But take a parcel just the same, Comrade, and here's luck to you!" When none of the Reds put in an appearance and the priest was told that Smilzo was standing behind a bush, taking down the name of everyone that went away with a parcel, he realized that he would have to keep his homily to himself. By six o'clock in the evening all the "regular" needy had been taken care of and there were left only the parcels meant for "special cases." Don Camillo went into the church to talk to the Lord.

"See here, Lord, what do You think of that?"

"I see, Don Camillo, and I must admit I find it touching. Those people are just as poor as the rest, but they're putting Party loyalty above their hunger. And so Don Camillo has lost a chance to deliver some sarcastic remarks at their expense."

Don Camillo lowered his head.

"Christian charity doesn't mean giving the crumbs from your table to the poor; it means dividing with them something that you need yourself. When Saint Martin divided his cloak with a beggar, that was Christian charity. And even when you share your last crust of bread with a beggar, you mustn't behave as if you were throwing a bone to a dog. You must give humbly, and thank him for allowing you to have a part in his hunger. To-day you simply aped the part of an altruist and the crumbs you distributed were from someone's else's table. You had no merit. And instead of being humble, you had poison in your heart."

Don Camillo shook his head. "Lord," he whispered, "just send some of those poor Reds to me. I won't say a thing. I don't think I'd really have said anything before, either. You'd have shown me the light before I could say it."

Then he went back to the presbytery and waited. After an hour had gone by, he closed the door and the front window. But after another hour he heard a knock at the door. The priest ran to open it, and there was Straziami, one of Peppone's most loyal followers, looking just as frowning and glum as ever. He stood silently at the entrance for a moment and then said:

"I don't think any better of you and your friends, and I

intend to vote as I please. So don't pretend I misled you."

The priest barely nodded. Then he took one of the remaining parcels out of the cupboard and handed it to him. Straziami took it and tucked it away under his coat.

"Tell me the truth, Father," he said ironically. "You might very well make a good joke out of the sight of Comrade Straziami sneaking in for a relief parcel from America."

"Go out through the garden," was all the priest said in reply, and he lit the butt of his cigar.

Peppone and the Party delegate were having supper when Smilzo came to report.

"It's a quarter past eight, and the priest has gone to bed."

"Is everything in good order?" asked Peppone.

"On the whole, yes," Smilzo said with some hesitation.

"Speak up, Comrade," said the delegate harshly. "Tell us the entire story."

"Well, all day long there was just the usual crowd, and I got all the names. Then just a quarter of an hour ago, a latecomer went into the rectory and it was too dark for me to see who he was."

Peppone clenched his fists.

"Out with it, Smilzo! Who was he?"

"It looked like one of our people to me . . ."

"Which one?"

"It looked like Straziami. But I can't swear to it."

They finished their supper in silence, and then the delegate stood up. "Let's investigate," he said. "Such things need prompt attention."

Straziami's little boy was pale and thin, with big eyes and hair that tumbled over his forehead. Small for his age, he looked a lot and said little. Now he sat at the kitchen table and stared with wide-open eyes at his father, who was glumly opening a jar of fruit.

"That's for dessert," said his mother. "First have your spaghetti and tinned milk."

She brought the bowl to the table and stirred its steaming contents, while Straziami went to sit down by the wall, between the fireplace and the cupboard. From this vantage-point he gazed with a kind of wonder at his son, whose eyes roved in bewilderment from his mother's hands to the jar of fruit and then to the tin of milk on the table.

"Aren't you coming to supper?" the woman said to Straziami.

"I don't want anything to eat," he mumbled.

She sat down opposite the boy and was just about to fill his plate with spaghetti when Peppone and the Party delegate threw open the door. The delegate looked at the spaghetti and examined the label on the milk and the jar of fruit.

"Where did you get this stuff?" he said harshly to Straziami, who had risen hesitatingly to his feet.

He waited in vain for an answer. Then he calmly gathered the four corners of the tablecloth into his hand, picked it up and threw it out of the window. The little boy trembled, holding both hands in front of his mouth and staring at the delegate with terror. The woman had taken refuge against the wall and Straziami stood in the middle of the room with his arms hanging at his sides, as if he had been turned into stone. The delegate closed the window, walked over to Straziami and struck him across the face. A thread of blood trickled out of one corner of Straziami's mouth, but he did not move. The delegate went to the door and then turned round to say:

"That's Communism for you, Comrade. And if you don't like it, you can leave it."

His voice aroused Peppone, who had been gaping from one corner of the room as if the whole thing were a dream. They walked away in silence through the dark countryside, and Peppone could hardly wait to get home. In front of the inn the delegate held out his hand.

"I'm leaving at five o'clock to-morrow morning," he said. "You've got everything straight, haven't you? On Saturday you resign and put Brusco in your place. You're to make your first speech at Castellino, and to-morrow you'll receive the main body of the text. You can insert references to local conditions in the blank spaces. Good night, Comrade."

"Good night."

Peppone went straight to Smilzo's.

"I'll beat him up," he said to himself, but when he reached the door he hesitated and retraced his steps. He found himself in front of the presbytery, but there he did not linger either.

"That's Communism for you, Comrade. And if you don't like it, you can leave it." The delegate's words were im-

160

printed on his mind. At home he found his own son still awake in his crib, smiling and holding out his arms.

"Go to sleep," Peppone said brusquely. He spoke in so harsh and threatening a voice that no one, not even he himself, could have suspected that he was thinking of the wide-open eyes of Straziami's son.

In the room at the inn the Party delegate's mind was quite empty. He was fast asleep, satisfied with both himself and his Communism. But there was still a frown on his face, because Communists are on duty even when they are sleeping.

A MATTER OF CONSCIENCE

FOR SOME time Peppone had been bringing the hammer down on the anvil, but no matter how accursedly hard he struck it, he could not get a certain tormenting thought out of his mind.

"The fool!" he mumbled to himself. "He's going to make things worse!"

Just then he raised his eyes and saw the fool standing before him.

"You scared my boy," Straziami said gloomily. "He was restless all night long, and now he's in bed with fever."

"It's your own fault," said Peppone, hammering away, with his eyes on his work.

"Is it my fault that I'm poor?"

"You had orders, and Party orders have to be obeyed without discussion."

"Hungry children come before the Party."

"No, the Party comes before everything."

Straziami took something out of his pocket and laid it on the anvil.

"I'm turning in my card. It doesn't stand for Party membership any more; it just means that I'm under special surveillance."

"Straziami, I don't like your way of talking."

"I'll talk as I choose. I won my freedom at the risk of my own skin, and I'm not going to give it up so lightly."

Peppone put down the hammer and wiped his forehead with the back of one hand. Straziami was one of the old guard; they had fought side by side, sharing the same hunger and hope and despair.

"You're betraying the cause," said Peppone.

"Isn't the cause freedom? If I give up my freedom, then I'm betraying the cause."

"We'll have to throw you out, you know. You're not allowed to resign. If you turn in your card, you'll be thrown out."

"I know it. And anyone that cheats too much is thrown out three months before he does it. To think that we have the face to call other people hypocrites! So long, Peppone. I'm sorry that you'll have to consider me your enemy when I'll still look on you as a friend."

Peppone watched Straziami walk away. Then he took hold of himself, threw the hammer into the corner with a loud curse, and went to sit in the garden at the back of the workshop. He couldn't get used to the idea that Straziami had to be thrown out of the Party. Finally he jumped to his feet.

"It's all the fault of that damned priest," he decided. "Here's where I get him."

The "damned priest" was in the presbytery leafing through some old papers, when Peppone came in.

"I hope you're happy!" Peppone said angrily. "At last you've managed to hurt one of our people."

Don Camillo shot him a curious glance.

"Is the election affecting your mind?" he asked.

"Proud of yourself, aren't you? Just to have ruined a fellow's reputation, when this social system of yours has given him nothing but trouble."

"Comrade Mayor, I still don't understand."

"You'll understand well enough when I tell you that it's all your fault if Straziami is thrown out of the Party. You took advantage of the fact that he's so poor and lured him to accept a filthy food parcel from America. Our Party delegate got wind of it and caught him at his own house, red-handed. He threw the food out of the window and struck him across the face."

It was clear that Peppone was highly excited.

"Calm yourself, Peppone," said the priest.

"Calm yourself, my foot! If you'd seen Straziami's boy

when the food was practically taken off his plate and he watched his father being struck, you wouldn't be calm. That is, not if you had any feelings."

Don Camillo turned pale and got up. He asked Peppone to tell him again exactly what the Party delegate had done. Then Don Camillo shook an accusing finger in Peppone's face.

"You swindler!" he exclaimed.

"Swindler yourself, for trying to take advantage of poor people's hunger and get them to vote for you!"

Don Camillo picked up an iron poker standing in one corner of the fireplace.

"If you open your mouth again, I'll slaughter you!" he shouted. "I haven't speculated on anybody's starvation. I have food parcels to distribute and I haven't denied them to anyone. I'm interested in poor people's hunger, not their votes. You're the swindler! Because you have nothing to give away except printed papers full of lies, you won't let anyone have anything else. When somebody gives people things they need, you accuse him of trying to buy votes, and if one of your followers accepts, you brand him as a traitor to the people. You're the traitor, I say, because you take away what someone else has given. So I was playing politics, was I? Making propaganda? Straziami's boy and the children of your other poor comrades who haven't the courage to come for food parcels don't know that they come from America. These children don't even know that there is such a place. All they know is that you're cheating them of the food they need. You'd say that if a man sees that his children are hungry he's entitled to steal a crust of bread for them to eat, but you wouldn't let him take it from America. And all because the prestige of Russia might suffer! But tell me, what does Straziami's boy know about America and Russia? He was just about to tuck away the first square meal he's seen for some time when you snatched it out of his mouth. I say that you're the swindler."

"I didn't say or do a thing."

"You let another man do it. And then you stood by while he did something even worse, while he struck a father in the presence of his child. A child has complete confidence in his father; he thinks of him as all-powerful and untouchable. And you let that double-faced delegate destroy the only treasure of Straziami's unfortunate boy. How would you like it if I were to come to your house this evening and beat you in front of your son?"

Peppone shrugged his shoulders. "You may as well get it out of your system," he said.

"I will!" shouted Don Camillo, livid with rage. "I'll get it out of my system, all right." He grasped both ends of the poker, clenched his teeth and with a roar like a lion's bent it double.

"I can throw a noose around you and your friend Stalin as well," he shouted. "And after I've got you in it, I can pull it tight, too."

Peppone watched him with considerable concern and made no comment. Then Don Camillo opened the cupboard and took out of it a parcel which he handed to Peppone.

"If you're not a complete idiot, take this to him. It doesn't come from America, or England, or even Portugal, for that matter. It's a gift of Divine Providence, which doesn't need anybody's vote to rule over the universe. If you want to, you can send for the rest of the parcels and distribute them yourself."

"All right. I'll send Smilzo with the truck," muttered Peppone, hiding the parcel under his coat. When he reached the door he turned round, laid the parcel on a chair, picked up the bent poker and tried to straighten it out.

"If you can do it, I'll vote for the 'People's Front,'" leered Don Camillo.

Peppone's effort made him red as a tomato. The bar would not return to its original shape, and he threw it down on the floor.

"We don't need your vote to win," he said, picking up the parcel and going out.

Straziami was sitting in front of the fire reading the paper, with his little boy crouched beside him. Peppone walked in, put the parcel on the table and untied it.

"This is for you," he said to the boy, "straight from the Almighty." Then he handed something to Straziami: "And here's something that belongs to you," he added. "You left it on my anvil."

Straziami took his Party membership card and put it into his wallet.

"Is that from the Almighty too?" he asked.

"The Almighty sends us everything," muttered Peppone,

"the good along with the bad. You can't ever tell who's going to get what. This time we're lucky."

The little boy had jumped to his feet and was admiring the profusion of good things spilled out on the table.

"Don't worry; no one will take it away from you," Peppone said reassuringly.

Smilzo came with the truck in the afternoon.

"The chief sent me to pick up some stuff," he said to Don Camillo, who pointed out the parcels waiting stacked up for him in the hall.

When Smilzo came to pick up the last lot of them, Don Camillo followed him as he staggered under his loads and gave him a kick so hearty that both Smilzo and half of his parcels landed in the truck.

"Make a note of this along with the list of names you gave to the Party delegate," Don Camillo explained.

"We'll settle with you on election day," said Smilzo, extricating himself from the confusion. "Your name is at the head of another list of ours."

"Anything more I can do for you?"

"No. But I still don't understand. I've had the same treatment from Peppone and Straziami already. And all because I carried out an order."

"Wrong orders shouldn't be carried out," Don Camillo warned him.

"Right. But how can one know ahead of time that they're wrong?" asked Smilzo with a sigh.

166

WAR TO THE KNIFE

Don Camillo had something on his mind that would give him no peace. It all began the day he met the "live corpse," a young man who had supposedly died after fighting in the mountains with Peppone and his men during the Resistance. Don Camillo himself had officiated at the funeral and followed the coffin to the cemetery. Then one day in the city after the war was over, Don Camillo caught a glimpse of this same young man who was far from being dead as mutton.

But it wasn't the walking corpse that bothered Don Camillo. He discovered that the coffin had contained, not a dead body, but a collection of loot seized from the Germans. He also knew that Peppone and his men had used the loot to finance the building of their People's Palace; and just because he had run across this useful bit of information, as well as the walking corpse, he had been able to persuade Peppone and his followers to make a modest contribution to the building of a Recreation Centre for the children of the village. And there the matter rested. The People's Palace was built and the Recreation Centre had a swing which was the delight of the children—especially Peppone's son, who played on it by the hour, chirping joyfully like a fledgling. But the question that troubled Don Camillo was how Peppone's men had managed to smuggle the coffin containing the loot out of the cemetery in the first place without attracting attention.

The cemetery served the whole township and was therefore fairly large. It lay outside the village and was built on the conventional plan—that is, enclosed by four walls, one of which had an entrance gate. These walls were bare and plain on the outside, while on the inside they formed an arcade over rows of tombs.

In order to solve the mystery, Don Camillo took upon himself the role of Sherlock Holmes. He went to examine the cemetery. Halfway down the left-hand arcade, in the second row, he found the famous niche, bearing a marble tablet on which was carved the fake name of the fake corpse. He turned his back on the niche and proceeded to walk straight through the grassy plot, studded with crosses, until he came to the central aisle. There he wheeled round in the direction of the gate and counted the number of steps it took him to reach it. The next day he walked inconspicuously along the path running parallel to the outside of the left wall, once more counting his steps, and when he had counted enough of them he stopped to light the butt of a cigar. The wall was overgrown with vines, but an attentive eye could see that about three feet above the ground, at a point corresponding to the niche the priest had inspected the day before, there was a section of plaster of a lighter colour than the rest. And Don Camillo's eye was an attentive one.

"This is the way the treasure came out, and where one object came out another can go in. The thing about holes is that they allow two-way traffic."

He continued his walk, stopping in front of the police station to chat with the sergeant. That night the police quietly made a hole in the cemetery wall, at the point where Don Camillo had noticed the different shade of plaster, and out of the niche they took one machine-gun, thirty-eight tommy-guns, and twenty-three pistols, all of them so shiny and carefully oiled that they would have tempted any hothead to launch the "second phase of the revolution" then and there. The news created quite a stir and even got into the big-city papers, but no one came to claim the guns. At that point the story had seemed to fizzle out, because Don Camillo took care to make no reference to anything that had happened.

"When God gives you an inch, don't take a mile," he said to the police sergeant, when the latter tried to get something more out of him. "You ought to be glad you've got the guns."

"I can't be so easily satisfied. Now that I've found them I

feel I must find the dead man whose place they were taking."

"I understand, but I wouldn't worry about him, Sergeant," Don Camillo advised him. "The guns are more important. After all, they can shoot, and that's more than a dead man can do."

Peppone, of course, had no comment to make, but he was about as easy in his mind as a man who has swallowed a mouse.

"*He* must have done it," he shouted to Brusco. "No one would dig a hole in a tomb unless he was sure there was nobody in it. But I'll make him pay."

He, of course, was Don Camillo, who continued to be extremely discreet. All he did was to plaster the walls of the "People's Palace" and Peppone's workshop with signs reading:

FOUND

Near the local cemetery, the corpse of the "second phase of the Revolution." Claimants apply to the police.

Five days later the village woke up to find itself covered with big yellow posters bearing the following notice:

LOST

Six hundred pounds of dried foods and tinned groceries consigned by the Regional Relief Committee to the priest, Don Camillo, for distribution to the needy. If Don Camillo finds these goods, will he please turn them over to the rightful owners.

Signed: *The Village Needy.*

Death to all thieves!

Don Camillo rushed indignantly to the police station.

"I'll report them!" he shouted. "I'll report and accuse them, every one! This is an outrage!"

"Who's to be accused?" asked the sergeant. "The notice is signed 'the village needy'."

"'Needy' indeed! The village riffraff! Peppone and his gang are at the bottom of this."

"That may be. But we have only your word for it. Go ahead and file your complaint, and then we'll investigate."

Don Camillo started to go home, but in the square he

pulled down the first poster that caught his eye and tore it into small pieces.

"Go on! Tear it up!" a man shouted to him from a bicycle. "But truth will out!"

And a ragged and dishevelled woman added her cries to his:

"Look at the priest's bulk!" she jeered. "He's grown fat on the food he stole from the poor!"

Don Camillo went his way, and a little farther on he met Filotti.

"Do you see what I see, Signor Filotti?" he asked him.

"Yes, I see," answered Filotti calmly. "But you mustn't let it bother you. I'm sure you can clear yourself. If I were you, I'd put up a poster reproducing your receipts for the groceries and the list of the persons to whom you distributed them."

"What receipts? What groceries?"

"The groceries from the Regional Relief Committee."

"But I didn't receive anything!" Don Camillo shouted. "And I didn't know such a committee existed!"

"Good Heavens! Is that possible?"

"It's more than possible; it's the literal truth! I never received a single thing!"

"How's that? It's unbelievable that anyone should make up a story of the kind. But if you say so, it must be true . . ."

Farther along the way Don Camillo ran into Signor Borghetti, who was reading the poster through spectacles perched on the end of his nose.

"This is a wicked world, Don Camillo," he said, shaking his head.

Old Barchini, the printer, was standing at the door of his shop.

"I didn't print it," he explained. "If they'd given me the job, I'd have told you about it. What about these groceries, Don Camillo? Are these the goods we were supposed to get from the Bishop?"

Just then Peppone's truck went by with Smilzo at the wheel.

"Here's a good appetite to you!" he called out, and everyone laughed.

Don Camillo ate no lunch. At three o'clock he was still lying on his bed and staring up at the beams of the ceiling. At four o'clock an infernal clamour rose from the church square and he looked out to see what was happening. There was an enormous crowd below, and, as might have been expected, the front ranks were filled by women. Don Camillo found most of their faces unfamiliar, and he thought of Smilzo and the truck.

"They've picked up roughnecks from all the surrounding villages," he said to himself. "They know how to organize. I'll grant them that."

"We want our groceries!" the women and children shouted. "Down with the exploiters of the people!"

"I've nothing to give you," shouted back Don Camillo from the window. "Because no one gave anything to me. It's a miserable lie!"

"We want to see for ourselves," a woman shouted, shaking her fists at him. "If you have nothing to hide, let us see!"

The crowd surged against the presbytery door, and Don Camillo withdrew from the window and took his shotgun down from the wall. Then he laid it on the bed and went to look again. The police sergeant and six of his men were standing guard at the presbytery door. But the crowd seemed to have gone wild and was still clamouring to get in. At this point Peppone stepped forward.

"Quiet," he shouted. "I have something to say."

The crowd kept silence, and Peppone looked up at the window.

"Don Camillo," said Peppone, "I am speaking as Mayor. This is no time to argue about whether what the poster says is false or true. These people feel that they have been cheated and they are justified in protesting. In order to avoid bloodshed, you must allow a committee to inspect the presbytery. The committee will include myself and the village Council and also the police sergeant with his men."

"Bravo!" shouted the crowd.

Don Camillo shook his head.

"There's nothing to see," he said. "This is my house, and I won't have it invaded. The poster was a lie from beginning to end; I'll swear to that on the Gospel."

"Swear to it on the cupboard where you've stowed away six hundred pounds of our groceries!" the crowd shouted. "You're not going to get away with it so easily."

Don Camillo shrugged his shoulders and stepped back. The crowd threw itself against the policemen and threatened to engulf them. But the sergeant kept his presence of mind and fired a shot into the air. The crowd retreated far enough for the police to pull themselves together and take a new position of defence.

"Stay where you are, or I'll have to use force of arms!" shouted the sergeant.

The crowd hesitated, then moved slowly but resolutely forward. The policemen paled, clenched their teeth and loaded their guns. Just as it looked as if events might take a tragic turn, Don Camillo raised his hand.

"Stop!" he shouted. "I'm coming to open the door."

When he came to open it the committee was ready. There were thirty members in all—Peppone and his Councillors and the police sergeant with four of his men. They made a mercilessly thorough search, opening every chest of drawers and cupboard and cabinet, tapping the walls and floors, sounding every bottle and barrel in the cellar and exploring under the eaves, up the chimney, and in the woodshed. Even if anything so small as a needle had been the object of their search, they would surely have found it. All the food they discovered in the kitchen amounted to three eggs, a loaf of bread, and a rind of cheese. And in the cellar, two salami sausages and two gourds full of lard hung from the ceiling. Don Camillo stood by with folded arms and an indifferent air. After they had fingered the mattresses they said they wanted to examine the bell tower and the church. The sergeant turned pale, but Don Camillo led the way, and let the committee look into the sacristy and the confessionals and under the altar. They did not touch anything, but insisted upon nosing everywhere. Finally, with nothing to show for their pains, they left the house, with their heads hanging. They conferred for a while with the crowd, and finally the latter melted away.

Don Camillo ate no supper either. He lay for a while on his bed, gazing up at the beams of the ceiling, then when he could see them no longer he went into the church and knelt before the altar.

"Lord, I thank you," he murmured.

But there was no reply. Now whenever this happened Don Camillo acquired a fever and went on a diet of bread and water for days and days, until the Lord felt sorry for him and said: "Enough." But this time he hadn't had even bread and water so he went back to his room. There were two

172

windows in this room; one looked out on the village square and the other on the presbytery garden. The latter was still wide open, and hanging out of it was a blanket that had been put there to dry earlier in the day. He pulled the blanket in, revealing three nails in the outside wall of the house, each one with a tommy-gun strung to it. He pulled in the guns and put them in a sack. Then he went to the cellar and took down one of the two sausages and the gourds. Only one of the sausages was stuffed with pork, and both gourds contained heavy yellow grease with cartridges embedded in it. He added a sausage and both gourds to his sack, climbed over the garden hedge and walked across the fields until he came to the river. There he got into a boat, rowed out past that spit of land known locally as the Island and threw the sack into the water. After that, he went back to kneel in front of the altar.

"I thank You, Lord," he whispered again. "I thank You for not having let them find the things I have just thrown away. Those are what they were after. They wanted to make a sensational story out of their discovery. I thank You not for my sake, but for having saved the reputation of the Church."

"Very well, Don Camillo. But I told you many times before to throw those things away."

Don Camillo sighed.

"Here I am, stripped of everything, with only an old shotgun that would scare nothing bigger than an owl for a weapon. How am I to defend myself?"

"With your honesty, Don Camillo."

"No," said the priest. "You saw to-day for Yourself that honesty is no defence. Peppone and his gang knew what they were really looking for, but the others shouted against me just because of a false accusation intended to persuade them that I was a thief. My honesty was no help at all. And it won't do any good in the future. They don't know I've got rid of the guns, and because they were thwarted in their plan to disgrace me they'll continue their war to the knife against me. But I'll . . ."

He threw out his chest and clenched his big fists. Then he relaxed, lowered his head and bowed low.

"I'll do nothing at all. The lie has been sown by now, and I'm known as 'the priest who grows fat on the food of the poor'."

As he said this, the thought came to him that he hadn't eaten all day and so he closed the church for the night and went to the presbytery cellar. There he reached for the sausage with the intention of eating a slice or two for a late supper. But his knife struck something hard.

"I threw the good salami away with the guns, and here I am with one full of cartridges," he said to himself with a melancholy smile.

After a sad meal consisting of a rind of cheese he went to bed. Meanwhile, in the darkness of his own room, Peppone was thinking of the meagre contents of Don Camillo's cupboard: three eggs, a loaf of bread, and a piece of cheese. He turned over and over in his bed, unable to close his eyes. Then he remembered the two sausages hanging in the cellar. "Well, he'll have a bite of sausage," he muttered to himself, and went to sleep with an easy conscience.

THE POLAR PACT

THOSE WERE the days when there was a great deal of argument about that piece of international political machinery known as the "Atlantic Pact," which may have owed its name to the fact that between words and deeds there lies the breadth of an ocean. Peppone took the whole proposition as a personal insult. He was so thoroughly incensed by the American "saboteurs of peace" that if it had been within his power he would have declared war upon the United States without an instant's delay. He was in this state of boiling frenzy when he saw Don Camillo pass by with his nose in his breviary, and from the workshop door threw at him an oath enough to make anyone's hair stand up on end.

Don Camillo stopped and raised his eyes. "Did you call me?" he asked mildly.

"I was speaking to God," said Peppone threateningly. "Do you think you are the Deity in person?"

"No, I don't. But since God hasn't time to listen to you, say what you have to say to me."

Although Peppone could hardly wait to declare war on the United States, he didn't want to open hostilities with an attack upon Don Camillo, who stood all too close by and held in one hand a piece of steel cable he had just picked up from the ground. There was no point in being blessed by a priest who wielded an aspergillum like that, and so he contented himself with shrugging his shoulders. Fortunately, at this very moment, a tractor clanked up and came to a halt between them, and Peppone turned his attention to the driver's tale of woe.

"There's something wrong," said the driver. "The motor spits and kicks back. It must be the timing."

Now Peppone, in addition to being Mayor, was the village mechanic—in fact he was the best mechanic within miles. He could work wonders with machinery of all kinds, but in this case the tractor was a Fordson and Peppone looked at it with distaste, pointing the handle of his hammer at the plate bearing the words "Made in U.S.A."

"The U.S.A. and I are through with each other," he said. "If you want to get this piece of junk fixed, go and see the priest. He's the one that's in with the Americans."

Don Camillo had just resumed his walk, but he turned back slowly. He peeled off his overcoat and gave it, along with his hat and breviary, to the driver. Then he rolled up his sleeves and began to tinker with the motor.

"Give me a pair of pincers," he said and the driver got one out of his tool-box. Don Camillo worked for a few minutes longer and then stood up straight. "Start it going," he said.

The man stepped on the starter.

"Like clockwork," he said happily. "How much do I owe you, Father, for your trouble?"

"Not a penny," said Don Camillo. "It's included in the Marshall Plan!"

A moment later the tractor pulled away. Peppone was left gaping and Don Camillo opened his breviary under his nose.

"Read this and tell me what it means," he said, pointing to a sentence on the page.

Peppone shrugged his shoulder.

"My Latin won't take me that far," he mumbled.

"Then you're a donkey," Don Camillo said calmly, continuing his walk. He had got grease up his nose, but he was proud of it.

This incident was a trifling matter, but it put Peppone in a very bad humour. That evening, when he had gathered his stalwarts together in the People's Palace, he shouted that something must be done to show the indignation of the masses over the signing of the infamous Atlantic Pact.

"We must take over and occupy some important place," he exclaimed in conclusion. "It's got to be a spectacular protest."

"Chief," said Smilzo, "we already occupy the People's Palace and the Town Hall. Our children occupy the school and our dead the cemetery. All that's left for us to occupy is the church."

"Thanks!" said Peppone. "And if we occupy it, what do we do next? Say Masses to compete with those of the Vatican? No, we must occupy a place that will benefit the whole people. Brusco, do you get what I mean?"

Brusco caught on at once.

"Good," he said. "When do we start moving?"

"Right away. Before midnight all our people must be put on the alert. They must move in waves, beginning at two o'clock, and by five the whole Island must be ours."

Just at the village the river broadened to such an extent that it seemed like a patch of sea, and there lay the place known as the Island. It was not an island, really, but a strip of land fifty feet offshore running parallel for about half a mile to the mainland, and attached to it at the lower end by a spit or tongue of muddy earth almost submerged by water. The Island was not cultivated, but was given over to a grove of poplars. That is, the poplars grew of their own accord, and every now and then the owner, Signor Bresca, came to mark with a knife those which were to be cut down and sold.

Peppone and his followers had said for some time that this was a typical example of abandoned and neglected private property and that it ought to be turned over to the workers for development as a co-operative farm. Its occupation had been put off from one day to another, but now the time had come.

"We'll oppose the 'Atlantic Pact' with a 'Polar Pact' of our own!" Peppone exclaimed on the evening of this historic decision.

It seems that, in spite of appearances, the word "Polar" in this case was derived from the River Po. It was a strictly local and proletarian term, with no reactionary Latin pedigree. Surely it was time to do away with Julius Caesar, and the ancient Romans, who together with the clergy used Latin to pull the wool over the people's eyes. At least, this was Peppone's answer to someone who objected on etymological grounds to his idea of giving a Party newspaper the name of "The Polar Call."

"The days of etymology are over," Peppone told him. "Every word is making a fresh start."

In any case, the "Polar Pact" was put into action, and at seven o'clock the next morning Don Camillo was warned that Peppone and his men had occupied the Island. The "men" were actually for the most part women, but, be that as it may, they were cutting down poplars as fast as they could, one after another. One tree, higher than the rest, had been plucked like a chicken neck and now served as a pole from which the Red Flag fluttered happily in the April breeze.

"There's going to be trouble," the messenger told Don Camillo. "Someone's called for special police from the city. Peppone has started to cut the connecting spit of land and says he'll hold out there indefinitely. If you don't do something there's no telling where the trouble will end."

Don Camillo pulled on a pair of rough twill trousers, rubber boots and a hunter's jacket, for he knew that the Island was a sea of mud.

Peppone was on the spot, standing with his legs far apart, directing the cutting of the channel. At first he failed to recognize Don Camillo; then he pretended not to; but in the end he couldn't help bursting out with: "Did you disguise yourself so as to spy on the enemy's camp?"

Don Camillo came down from the river bank, plunged halfway up his legs into the mud, crossed the channel and arrived in front of Peppone.

"Drop all that, Peppone," he pleaded; "the police are on their way from the city."

"Let them come!" Peppone answered. "If they want to get over here, they'll have to borrow the United States Navy!"

"Peppone, it's only fifteen yards from the shore to the Island, and bullets can travel."

"It's only fifteen yards from the Island to the shore, for that matter," said Peppone sombrely, "and we have bullets too."

Peppone was really in a bad fix, and Don Camillo knew it.

"Listen," he said, pulling him to one side, "you have a right to be a fool and behave like one if you want to. But you have no right to involve these other poor devils in your folly. If you want to be sent to prison, stand your ground and shoot. But you can't compel the rest of them to be sent along with you."

Peppone thought for a minute or two and then shouted:

"The others can do as they please. I'm not forcing anybody. Those who want to stick it out can stay."

The men who were digging the channel stopped and leaned on their shovels. They could hear a roar of motors from the main road.

"The jeeps of the special police," Don Camillo said in a loud voice. And the men looked at Peppone.

"Do as you please," Peppone muttered. "Democracy allows every man to follow his own will. And here on the Island we have democracy!"

Just then Smilzo and the other Comrades arrived upon the scene. Smilzo shot a curious glance at Don Camillo.

"Is the Vatican sticking its nose into things again?" he asked. "You'd better make yourself scarce, Father; it's going to be hot around here."

"Heat doesn't bother me," Don Camillo answered.

A cloud of dust rose from the road.

"They're here," said the shovellers. With which they threw down their shovels and made their way ashore. Peppone looked at them with scorn.

There were six jeeps in all, and the police inspector stood up and called out to the men who were hacking at the underbrush on the Island: "Move on!"

They went on hacking, and the inspector turned to one of his aides.

"Perhaps they didn't hear," he said. "Play some music!"

His aide fired a volley of shots into the air, and the Islanders raised their heads.

"Get moving!" the inspector shouted.

Peppone and his henchmen grouped themselves at one end of the channel. Some of the men who had been working behind them crossed over. When they reached the shore they scattered to right and left, skirting the jeeps that were in their way. About a dozen die-hards continued to cut down the underbrush. Peppone and his men fell into line, forming a wall along the channel, and stood there with folded arms, waiting.

"Move on! Clear out!" came a shout from the bank.

No one budged, and the police got out of their jeeps and started down the river bank.

The veins of Peppone's neck were swollen and his jaw was set. "The first one to lay hands on me will get strangled," he said darkly.

179

Don Camillo was still there beside him, forming part of the living wall.

"For the love of God, Peppone," he murmured, "don't do anything rash."

"What are you doing here?" Peppone asked him, startled.

"Doing my duty. I'm here to remind you that you're a thinking being and therefore have got to think things out clearly. Come on, let's go!"

"Go ahead! I've never run away in my life, and I never will."

"But this is the law!"

"It's your law, not mine. Go on and obey it."

The police were down beside the river, just opposite the Island.

"Clear out!" they shouted.

Don Camillo tugged at Peppone's sleeve.

"Let's go!"

"I won't move out of here alive. And the first one to lay hands on me gets his skull cracked!"

The police repeated their injunction and then began walking through the mud. When they came up against the wall of men they repeated it again, but no one moved or gave any answer.

A sergeant grabbed hold of Peppone's jacket and would have come to a very bad end if Don Camillo hadn't pinned Peppone's arms down from behind.

"Let go!" he muttered between his clenched teeth.

Don Camillo had on the same sort of trousers and boots and jacket as the rest, and when the police started laying about them he got one of the first blows and was sorely tempted to let Peppone go, and to pitch some of the attackers into the water. Instead, he took it without batting an eyelash. More blows fell on his head and on those of Smilzo and the others. But no one said a word. They held on to each other and took it in silence. Finally, they had to be hauled away like rocks, but none of them had opened his mouth or moved a finger in revolt.

"They're crazy in this village," the inspector grumbled. By now the Island was empty, because the few men who were left had escaped in boats. The police got into their jeeps and drove away.

Don Camillo, Peppone, and the others sat silently on the

shore, gazing into the water and at the Red Flag waving from the plucked poplar.

"Father, you've got a bump as big as a walnut on your forehead," said Smilzo.

"You don't need to tell me," said Don Camillo. "I can feel it."

They got up and went back to the village, and that was the end of the "Polar Pact."

THE PETITION

DON CAMILLO was walking quietly along the Low Road towards the village, smoking his usual cigar when, just round a curve, he came upon Peppone's gang. There were five of them, and Smilzo was in charge. Don Camillo looked at them with frank curiosity.

"Are you planning to attack me?" he asked them. "Or have you some better plan in mind?"

"Don't you dare incite us to violence!" said Smilzo, taking a sheet of paper out of an envelope and unfolding it before him.

"Is this for the last wishes of the condemned man?"

"It's for everyone to sign who wants peace," said Smilzo. "If you don't sign, then you don't want peace. From now on, honest men and warmongers are going to be clearly divided."

Don Camillo examined the dove printed at the top of the paper.

"I'm an honest man," he said, "but I'm not signing. A man who wants peace doesn't have to testify to it with his signature."

Smilzo turned to Gigo, who was standing beside him.

"He thinks this is a political move," he said. "According to him, everything we do is tied up with politics."

"Look, there's no politics in this," put in Gigo. "It's just a question of preserving peace. Peace is good for all political parties. It will take plenty of signatures to get us out of the

Atlantic Pact, and if we don't get out, it's going to land us in war, as sure as shooting."

Don Camillo shook the ashes off the end of his cigar.

"You'd better make yourselves busy," he said. "If I'm not mistaken, you haven't even started."

"Of course not. We wanted you to have the honour of being the first name on the list. That's only natural. When peace is at stake, the clergy ought to take the lead."

Don Camillo threw out his arms. "It can be taken for granted that the clergy's in favour of peace, so it's just as if my signature were there."

"Then you're not going to sign?"

Don Camillo shook his head and walked away.

"If we're saddled with a clergy of this kind, then we'll have to fight not one war, but two," Smilzo said bitterly, putting the paper back in the envelope.

A little later, Peppone arrived at the presbytery door.

"No politics involved," he declared. "I'm here in the capacities of Mayor, citizen, father of a family, Christian, and honest man."

"Too many people!" exclaimed Don Camillo. "To big a crowd! Come in just as Peppone, and leave the rest outside."

Peppone came in and sat down.

"We've come to the ragged edge," he began. "If honest men don't stick together, the world's headed for a smash-up."

"Sorry to hear it," Don Camillo answered seriously. "Is there anything new?"

"Only that if we don't safeguard peace, everything's going to ruin. Let's leave politics and parties out of it and all get together."

Don Camillo nodded. "That's the way I like to hear you talk," he said. "It's about time you cut loose from that brood of Satan."

"I said we'd leave politics out of it," retorted Peppone. "This is a time for thinking in world-wide terms."

Don Camillo looked at him with astonishment, for he had never heard him mouth such big ideas.

"Do you want peace or don't you?" asked Peppone. "Are you with Jesus Christ or against Him?"

"You know the answer."

Out of his pocket Peppone took the envelope and paper that Don Camillo had seen earlier in the day.

"When it comes to fighting for peace, the clergy must be in the front line," he asserted.

Don Camillo shook his head. "You're changing the rules of the game. Didn't you say politics weren't in it?"

"I'm here as a plain citizen," Peppone insisted.

"Very well then, as one citizen to another, I tell you I'm not caught." And as Peppone started to rise excitedly to his feet, he added: "You know very well that if I sign your paper, a lot of other signatures will follow. Without me, you can only hope for those of your own people, and many of them can't write their own names. Since you see that I'm not to be taken in, put that pigeon back in your pocket and hand me two glasses from the sideboard. Otherwise, you and your pigeon and your cause of peace may as well all go back where you came from."

Peppone tucked the paper away.

"Since you're giving yourself such airs," he said proudly, "I'll show you that I can get all the signatures I want without yours as an attraction."

Smilzo and the rest of the "peace gang" were waiting outside.

"Start making the rounds," said Peppone. "But go to our people last. Everyone's got to sign. Peace must be defended; with blows if necessary."

"Chief, if I go to jail, what will happen?" Smilzo asked him.

"Nothing will happen. A man can serve the cause perfectly well in jail."

These words were not exactly comforting. But Smilzo set out, with the gang at his heels, strengthened by some reinforcements from the People's Palace.

Now when people have haystacks and vineyards and fields, it's almost impossible for them to say no to a fellow who asks them to sign for peace and swears that politics don't enter into it. And in a village the first five or six signatures are what count. It took several evenings to cover the whole area. But there were no arguments, except from Tonini, who shook his head when they showed him the paper.

"Don't you want peace?"

"No," said Tonini, who was a fellow with hands as big as shovels. "I happen to like war. It kills off a lot of rascals and clears the air."

Here Smilzo made a very sensible observation.

"Still you know, of course, that more honest men are killed off than rascals."

"But I care even less for honest men."

"And what if you get killed yourself?"

"I'd rather be killed than sign a paper. At least, when you die, you know where you're going."

The gang started to come forward, but Tonini picked up his shotgun, and Smilzo said he needn't bother.

Everything else went smoothly, and when Peppone saw the sheets full of signatures, he was so happy that he brought his fist down on the table hard enough to make the People's Palace tremble. He compared the peace list with the village census and found that they tallied. The mayors of the neighbouring villages complained that they couldn't get people to sign because the reactionaries obstructed them. There had been shooting at Castelina and fisticuffs at Fossa for a whole day. And to think that Smilzo, after taking an hour to persuade each of the first five or six signatories, had won over the rest without a murmur.

"It's the prestige I enjoy as Mayor," said Peppone, and he gathered together the papers and went to savour his triumph.

Don Camillo was reading a book when Peppone appeared before him.

"The power of the clergy is on the decline!" Peppone announced to him. "I thank you in the name of the world's democracies for not having signed. Your signature wouldn't have brought in half as many others. It's too bad for the Pope, that's all." And he added, spreading his papers out on the table, "America's done for! The Atlantic Pact is no good, because we have a totality of votes against it. And everywhere else it's going to go the same way."

Don Camillo scrutinized the lists carefully. Then he threw out his arms. "I'm sorry to tell you, but one signature is missing. Tonini's. So you can't claim a 'totality.'"

Peppone laughed.

"I have all the rest," he said. "What's one against eight hundred?"

Don Camillo opened a drawer, took out some papers, and scattered them in front of Peppone.

"You have signatures against the Pact and I have signatures in its favour."

Peppone opened his eyes wide.

"Russia's done for," said Don Camillo. "Because I have Tonini's signature along with the rest."

Peppone scratched his head.

"There's nothing so remarkable about it," Don Camillo pointed out. "I worked by day, and your men went around by night, when people were already softened up. As a matter of fact, they were glad to sign for you, because that cancelled their signing for me. The only one who didn't like it was Tonini, because I had to knock his head against a wall. But I advise you not to go after him, because he says that before he'll sign another petition he'll shoot to kill."

Peppone took his papers away. And so it was that in Don Camillo's village America triumphed by a majority of one, all on account of Tonini.

A SOLOMON COMES TO JUDGMENT

ONE DAY, after Don Camillo and Peppone had settled a slight misunderstanding to the mutual satisfaction of both, the Mayor turned to the priest and said, "There's no sense in turning everything in life into a tragedy. If we reason things out, we can always compromise."

"Right you are," said Don Camillo warmly. "Why did God give us brains if He didn't expect us to reason?"

The two men parted on this note, and a few days later something happened in the valley which clearly proves that man is a reasoning creature, especially when it comes to living peacefully with his neighbour. First, however, you need to know the local geography of the little world or you won't understand a thing about it.

The Po River rolls on its mighty way without so much as an if-you-please and on either side it is fed by countless streams and tributaries. The Tincone is one of these little streams. Now the Molinetto road, running parallel to the Po, connects the tiny communities of Pieve and La Rocca. At a certain point the road crosses the Tincone. Here there is a bridge; it is, in fact, a structure of some size because at this point the Tincone is fairly wide, being only a mile or so away from where it flows into the big river. Pieve and La Rocca are each about three miles from the bridge over the Tincone, which is, indeed, the boundary line between them.

This is the topography of the story, and its point of departure is the problem of public education. The school that served both communities was at La Rocca, and for the people of Pieve this was a serious matter. Every day their children had to travel six miles, and six miles are thirty thousand feet, even in the flat river valley. Children can't resist taking short-cuts, and since the road they travelled was straight as an arrow, the short-cuts always led them a longer way round.

One day a committee of women from Pieve came to the Mayor of the whole township, Peppone, and announced that unless they were given a schoolhouse of their own they wouldn't send their children to school. Now the township was about as rich as a travelling rabbit and a new school would have entailed not only building costs, but double the amount of teachers' salaries as well. So, having by hook or crook raised some funds, Peppone decided to build the new schoolhouse at the bridge over the Tincone, halfway between Pieve and La Rocca, and send the children from both communities there. But at this point the problem became thorny.

"That's all very well," they said at La Rocca, "as long as it's on our side of the bridge."

"All well and good," they said at Pieve, "but of course it must be on our side."

To be exact, both of them were in the wrong (or in the right, as you prefer), because the real halfway point was not on either side of the bridge, but in the middle.

"You don't want the school built on the bridge, do you?" Peppone shouted, after a long discussion with committees from both villages.

"You're the Mayor," they answered, "and it's up to you to find a fair solution."

"The only real solution would be to lead you all to the bridge, tie millstones round your necks and throw you into the water," said Peppone. And he wasn't so wrong either.

"It's not a question of a hundred yards one way or the other," they told him. "Social justice is at stake." And that silenced the Mayor very effectively, because whenever he heard the phrase "social justice," Peppone drew himself up as if he were witnessing the miracle of creation.

Meanwhile trouble began to brew. Some boys from La Rocca went by night to the bridge and painted a red line across the middle. Then they announced that anyone from Pieve would find it healthier to stay on his own side. The next evening, boys from Pieve painted a green line parallel to the red one and intimated that anyone from La Rocca would be better off at home. The third evening, boys from both villages arrived at the middle of the bridge at the same time. One of those from La Rocca spat over the green line and one of those from Pieve spat over the red one. A quarter of an hour later, three boys were in the river and five had severe wounds on the head. The worst of it was that of the three boys in the river, two were from Pieve and only one was from La Rocca, so to even up the score another boy from La Rocca would have to be thrown in. And of the five boys with head wounds, three were from La Rocca and two from Pieve and so another boy from Pieve needed a beating. All, of course, for the sake of social justice.

The number of head wounds and boys thrown into the river increased daily, and soon the numbers were swelled by grown men, both old and young. Then one day Smilzo, who hung about the bridge as an observer, brought Peppone a piece of really bad news.

"There's been a fist fight between a woman from Pieve and a woman from La Rocca."

Now when women get mixed up in an affair of this kind, the trouble really starts. Women are always the ones to stick a gun into the hand of husband, brother, lover, father or son. Women are the plague of politics and alas, politics are about ninety-five per cent of the world's occupation. So it was that knives were drawn and shots began to fly.

"Something's got to be done," said Peppone, "or else we shan't need a school, but a cemetery."

Apart from the fact that there's more to be learned in the cool grave than in a schoolroom, this was no joking matter, and Peppone handled it in masterful fashion. Out on the Po there had lain for years an old floating water mill, made of two big hulks with the millwheel between and a cabin bridging them over. Peppone had these towed under the central arch of the bridge across the Tincone. He chained them to the supporting columns and then remodelled them in such a way as to make them into one, joined by gang-planks to both banks of the river. So it was that one day there was a solemn opening of the new floating school. A large crowd was present, including a group of newspapermen from the big city.

The only accident ever recorded took place when Beletti, a boy who had to repeat the third grade for six years in succession, threw his teacher into the water. But this did not upset Peppone.

"Italy is in the middle of the Mediterranean," he said, "and everybody must know how to swim."

THUNDER ON THE RIGHT

PEPPONE'S PASSION to show moving-pictures was inherited
straight from his father. His father, too, was mechanically
minded, and he had brought the first threshing-machine to
the Valley, as all the old inhabitants remembered very well.
Young people may laugh because they fail to see any connection between moving-pictures and a threshing-machine.
But the young people of to-day are benighted creatures born
with their telephone numbers imprinted on their brains, and
where passion is concerned they have about as much grace as
a pig in a cornfield.

In the old days electric power was a luxury confined to the
city, and since a moving-picture projector has to be run
electrically, country people had no chance to see any pictures.
But Peppone's father mounted a dynamo on the steam
engine that powered the thresher, and when his machine
wasn't needed in the fields he hitched two oxen to it and
went from village to village, giving picture shows. So many
years have gone by that the young people of to-day can't
possibly visualize a steam engine drawn by two oxen. It was
painted green with magnificent bands of shiny brass around
it and had an enormous fly-wheel and a tall chimney, which
was lowered while it was travelling from one place to
another. It didn't smell or make any noise, and it had a very
wonderful whistle.

So Peppone's ambition to show moving-pictures was quite
legitimately in his blood. As soon as the auditorium of the
newly built "People's Palace" was at his disposal, this was the

first thing that came into his mind. One fine morning the village awoke to find itself plastered with posters announcing the opening of the moving-picture season at the People's Palace the next Sunday.

Now Don Camillo's father had never even thought about going round the countryside to show moving-pictures, but for some time Don Camillo had been set upon the idea of acquiring a projector for his Recreation Centre and Peppone's announcement made his stomach turn over. He was somewhat consoled on Sunday by a fierce storm and a flood-like downpour of rain. At ten o'clock in the evening he was still waiting to hear what had happened when his friend Barchini, dripping but happy, appeared at the door.

"There were only a few waifs and strays at the People's Palace," Barchini told him. "The rain kept the people from the outskirts away. What's more, the lights kept going on and off, and finally they had to stop the show. Peppone was fit to burst."

Don Camillo went to kneel before the Lord on the altar.

"Lord, I thank You . . ." he began.

"What for, Don Camillo?"

"For sending a storm and disrupting the electric current."

"Don Camillo, I had nothing to do with the lights going off. I'm a carpenter, not an electrician. And as for the storm, do you really think that Almighty God would inconvenience winds, clouds, lightning and thunder simply in order to prevent Peppone from showing his pictures?"

Don Camillo lowered his head.

"No, I don't really think so," he stammered. "We men have a way of thanking God for anything that falls in with our plans, as if it had come to pass just for our pleasure."

At midnight the storm died down, but at three o'clock in the morning it came back more fiercely than before, and an unearthly noise awakened Don Camillo. He had never heard a crash so loud and so close, and when he reached the window and looked out he was left gaping. The spire of the church tower had been struck by lightning and cleft with jagged rents. It was just as simple as all that, but to Don Camillo it was so incredible that he rushed to tell the Lord about it.

"Lord," he said in a voice shaky with emotion, "the church spire has been struck by lightning."

"I understand, Don Camillo," the Lord answered calmly.

"Buildings are often struck that way in the course of a storm."

"But this was the church!" Don Camillo insisted.

"I heard you, Don Camillo."

Don Camillo looked up at the crucified Christ and threw out his arms in dismay.

"Why did it have to happen?" he asked bitterly.

"A church spire has been struck by lightning in the course of a storm," said the Lord. "Does God have to justify Himself for this in your sight? A short time ago you thanked Him for sending a storm that damaged your neighbour, and now you reproach Him because the same storm has damaged you."

"It hasn't damaged me," said Don Camillo. "It has damaged the house of God."

"The house of God is infinite and eternal. Even if every planet in the universe were to be reduced to dust, the house of God would still stand. A church spire has been struck by lightning; that is all anyone is entitled to think or say. The lightning had to strike somewhere."

Don Camillo was talking to the Lord, but during the conversation the thought of the mutilated tower was uppermost in his mind.

"Surely that particular stroke could have stayed away," he said. And the Lord took pity on his sorrow and continued to reason gently with him:

"Calm yourself, Don Camillo, and think it out clearly. God created the universe, and the universe is a perfect and harmonious system, in which every element is indissolubly bound, whether directly or indirectly, to all the rest. Everything that happens in the universe is necessary and fore-ordained, and if this stroke of lightning had not fallen exactly where and when it did, the harmony of the universe would have been troubled. This harmony is perfect, and if the lightning struck at this time and place, then it is a meet and right thing and we must thank God for it. We must thank Him for everything that takes place in the universe, for everything is a proof of His infallibility and the perfection of His creation. The stroke of lightning had to fall just where it did and not an inch in any other direction. The fault is man's, for having chosen to build the tower in that place. He could quite as well have built it a couple of yards farther off."

Don Camillo thought of his mutilated tower and there was bitterness in his heart.

"If everything that happens in the universe is fore-ordained and a manifestation of God's will, and otherwise the system would not be perfect, then the church tower had to be built where it is and not a couple of yards farther off."

"Yes, it could have been built a couple of yards farther off," the Lord assured him, "but then man would unconsciously have violated God's law. And that God didn't allow."

"Then there's no free will," protested Don Camillo.

The Lord continued to speak with great gentleness.

"Woe to the man who out of anger or grief or sensual excitement forgets those things that deep down inside he cannot help but know. God points out the right way, but man has a choice of whether to follow it or not. In His infinite kindness, God leaves man free to choose the wrong way and yet, by repentance and recognition of his mistake, to save his soul. A church spire has been struck by lightning in the course of a storm. The lightning had to strike there, and so the man who built the tower is to blame. Yet the tower had to be built where it is and man must thank God for it."

Don Camillo sighed.

"Lord, I thank You. But if with Your help I manage to put up another spire, I am going to arm it with a lightning conductor."

"Yes, Don Camillo, if it is fore-ordained that you are to put a lightning conductor on the tower, then you will surely do so."

Don Camillo bowed his head. Then in the first light of dawn he climbed up to examine the damaged tower more closely.

"Exactly," he said to himself at last. "The tower had to be built just where it is!"

Soon people began to crowd into the square to see the tower. They stood there in the torrential rain and looked at it in bewilderment, without speaking. When the square was full, Peppone and his crew appeared on the scene. He pushed his way to the front of the crowd and stood there for some time staring at the sight. Then he solemnly pointed one finger to the sky.

"Here is a proof of God's wrath!" he exclaimed. "This is God's answer to your boycott. Lightning strikes where God wills, and God wills it to accomplish a purpose."

Don Camillo listened from the presbytery window. Peppone spied him there and pointed him out to the crowd.

"The priest is silent," he shouted, "because the lightning struck his church. If it had struck our People's Palace, he'd have plenty to say."

Smilzo looked up at Don Camillo too.

"This is God's answer to the warmongers!" he shouted. "Hurrah for Mao Tse-tung!"

"Hurrah for peace and the Confederation of Labour!" chorused his followers.

Don Camillo counted to fifty-two before saying what was boiling up inside him. Then he said nothing. He took a half-smoked cigar out of his pocket and lit it.

"Look at that!" shouted Peppone. "Nero fiddling while Carthage burns!"

With which slightly garbled historical reference, he and his gang stalked proudly away.

Toward evening Don Camillo took his bitterness to the altar.

"Lord," he said at the end of his prayer, "what maddens me is to hear those scoundrels speak of Your divine wrath. I wouldn't dream of destroying the harmony of the universe, but after the blasphemous things they said this morning it would serve them right if lightning were to strike their People's Palace. Their blasphemies were enough to provoke divine wrath in earnest!"

"You're indulging in somewhat loose talk yourself, Don Camillo," said the Lord mildly. "Have you the face to inconvenience God in all His majesty just in order to knock down the four walls of a village shack? You must respect your God more than that, Don Camillo!"

Don Camillo went back to the presbytery. The distance was a short one, but at night, even within the space of a few steps, there's no telling what may happen. It was still raining, and at midnight the rain was coming down harder than ever. At one o'clock the stormy cacophony of the night before was repeated, and at two a clap of thunder aroused the whole village. By 2.10 everyone was awake, because a building in the square was afire, and the building was the People's Palace. When Don Camillo arrived the square was crowded with people, but Smilzo and his followers had already extinguished the flames. The roof had caved in, most of the framework was destroyed and the rest was a heap of smouldering ashes. Don Camillo edged up as if by accident to Peppone.

"A neat job," he observed casually. "Lightning seems to have a conscience."

Peppone wheeled around.

"Have half a cigar?" said Don Camillo.

"I don't smoke," answered Peppone darkly.

"You're quite right. The People's Palace is doing enough smoking. But I'm sorry. If you don't smoke, how can I say 'Nero fiddling while Carthage burns'? Only, for your information, it wasn't Carthage, it was Rome."

"That's good news! With every priest in it, I trust!"

Don Camillo shook his head and said gravely and in a loud voice: "You mustn't provoke God's wrath. Don't you see what you've brought upon yourself with the sacrilegious words you uttered this morning?"

Peppone almost jumped out of his skin with rage.

"Don't lose your temper," Don Camillo advised him. "The Marshall Plan might help you out."

Peppone stood face to face with Don Camillo, his fists clenched.

"The roof will be repaired in a few days," he shouted. "We don't need any plans; we'll take care of it ourselves."

"Good for you, Mr. Mayor," said Don Camillo, dropping his voice. "That way you can kill two birds with one stone. When you get the Council to appropriate money for the People's Palace, you can allot something for the repair of the church tower as well."

"Over my dead body!" said Peppone. "Ask your Americans for that. The People's Palace is a public utility, and the church is a private corporation."

Don Camillo lit the butt of his cigar.

"It was a fine stroke of lightning," he observed; "much more powerful than mine. It made a magnificent noise and did quite a bit of damage. Someone really ought to study it from a scientific point of view. I think I'll speak to the police sergeant about it."

"Keep your nose in your own dirty business," said Peppone.

"My business is to get you to repair the church tower."

Peppone shot him a sombre look.

"All right," he said between clenched teeth. "But some day I'll settle accounts with you."

Don Camillo started back to the presbytery. There was nothing more to see or to say. He meant to go straight home, but he knew that the Lord was waiting for him.

"Don Camillo," said the Lord severely, when the priest stood before him in the half-dark church. "Aren't you going to thank Me because the People's Palace was struck by lightning?"

"No," said Don Camillo, with his head hanging. "A stroke of lightning is part of the natural order created by God. Surely God wouldn't inconvenience winds, clouds, lightning and thunder simply in order to please a poor devil of a country priest and knock down the walls of a village shack."

"Exactly," said the Lord. "And how could God take advantage of a storm to throw a bomb on to the roof of the People's Palace? Only a poor devil of a country priest could think of a thing like that."

Don Camillo held out his arms.

"Yes, Lord, but even in this shameful deed there is evidence of God's mercy. If the poor devil of a country priest, tempted by Satan himself, hadn't tossed a bomb on to the roof of the People's Palace, then the case of dynamite hidden in the Palace attic wouldn't have exploded, and its presence there was a menace. Now the menace has been eliminated and the poor devil of a country priest has found a way to have the spire of his church tower properly replaced. Moreover, an individual who took the Lord's name in vain has received the punishment he deserved."

"Don Camillo," said the Lord, "are you sure you did the right thing?"

"No," Don Camillo replied. "God leaves man free to choose between right and wrong. I did wrong, I admit it, and I shall repent."

"Aren't you repentant already?"

"No, Lord," whispered Don Camillo. "It's still too early. I must ask for an extension."

The Lord sighed, and Don Camillo went off to bed. In spite of his guilty conscience, he slept like a log and dreamed that there was a gleaming gold spire on the church tower. When he woke up, he thought happily of his dream. But he realized that he had forgotten one very important thing. So he dropped off to sleep again and dreamed that on the gleaming spire there was a wonderful lightning conductor.

RED-LETTER DAY

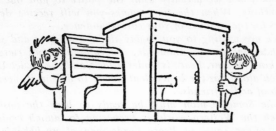

BARCHINI, THE village printer and stationer, had been ill for some time, and there was no one to replace him in the shop, for his was the sort of business where "boss" and "workers" are combined in one and the same person. So it was that Don Camillo had to hire someone in the city to print his parish magazine, and when he went back to read the proofs he amused himself by poking about among the machines.

The devil is a rascal who has no respect for anything or anybody, and plays his tricks not only in night-clubs and other so-called resorts of perdition, but also in places where honest men are at work. In this case, the devil was lurking near the machine where a man was printing letterheads, and when Don Camillo got out to the street he found himself in a pretty pickle. Since the flesh is notoriously weak and even the most honourable of parish priests has some flesh and blood in his make-up, what was Don Camillo to do when, upon his return to the village, he found his pockets stuffed with five or six sheets of writing paper bearing the address of the provincial headquarters of a certain political party?

A few days later Peppone was surprised to receive a registered letter with a city postmark and on the back the name Franchini, which he had never heard before. Inside, there was a letterhead which made him instinctively draw himself to attention.

Dear Comrade,—Of course, you are already acquainted with the latest American betrayal, a secret clause in the nefarious

Atlantic Pact which compels the other conspiring nations to watch over their democratic parties and sabotage any efforts on behalf of peace. Since we are under watch by the police, it is folly to put our Party name on our envelopes, that is, except when we actually want the police to find out about something. When the time comes you will receive detailed rules for the conduct of your correspondence.

We are writing to you to-day about a delicate and strictly confidential matter. Comrade, the capitalists and clergy are working for war. Peace is under attack, and the Soviet Union, which alone has the benevolent power to defend it, needs the help of active friends.

The Soviet Union must be ready to bear the onslaught which the Western world is preparing to launch against it. The sacred cause of Peace needs men of unshakable faith and professional ability, ready to discipline themselves for action. We are so sure of you, Comrade, that the Special Committee for Political Action has unanimously decided to admit you to the inner sanctum. Here is a piece of news that should fill you with pride and joy: you are to be sent to the Soviet Union, where your mechanical talents will be put to work in the cause of Peace.

The Socialist Homeland will accord to the members of the Peace Brigade the rights and privileges of a Soviet citizen. We call this to your attention as one more sign of our Soviet comrades' generosity.

Instructions as to the day of departure and the equipment you should take with you will follow. You will travel by air. In view of the delicacy of this matter, we order you to destroy this letter and to send your reply to the comrade whose name and address are on the envelope. Take good care. To-day, more than ever, the sacred cause of Peace is in your hands. In the expectation of a prompt reply . . .

For the first time in his life Peppone disobeyed a Party order. He did not burn the letter. "This is the most eloquent testimonial I have ever received from the Party," he said to himself. "I can't part with an historical document of this kind. If some fool should ever question my merits I'll wave this in his face and make him bite the dust. There's nothing more powerful than the printed word."

He read the letter over any number of times, and when he knew it by heart he added: "I've worked hard, certainly, but this is a great reward!" His only regret was that he could not exhibit the letter. "Now," he said, "I must write an answer in equally historic terms, an answer that will bring tears to their eyes. I'll show them what kind of feelings I have in my heart, even if I never went past the third grade in school." That evening he sat down in the cellar to work over his reply.

Comrade,—I overflow with pride to be chosen for the Peace Brigade and awate further Party orders. Let me anser with the Socialist cry, "I obey!" like the red-shirt Garibaldi, even if my first impulze is to go rite away. I never asked a favor befor, but now I ask to be alowed to be the first to go.

Peppone read this over and saw that it needed a bit of polish and punctuation. But for a first draft it would do very well. There would be time enough to make a second draft the next day. No need to hurry. It was more important to write the kind of a letter that would be published in the Party papers with a note from the Editor above it. And he calculated that three drafts would do the job.

As Don Camillo was smoking his cigar and admiring the beauties of spring one evening on the road that led to the mill, he found Peppone in his path. They talked about the time of day and the weather, but it was obvious that there was something Peppone wanted to get off his chest and finally he came out with it.

"Look here, I'd like to talk to you for a minute as man to man instead of as man to priest."

Don Camillo stopped and look at him hard.

"You've made an unhappy start," he observed, "by talking like a donkey!"

Peppone made an impatient gesture.

"Don't let's talk politics," he said. "I'd like you to tell me, as man to man, what you think of Russia."

"I've told you that eighty thousand times," said Don Camillo.

"We're quite alone, and no one can overhear us," Peppone insisted. "For once you can be sincere and leave political propaganda out of it. What's it like in Russia, anyhow?"

Don Camillo shrugged his shoulders.

"How should I know, Peppone?" he said. "I've never been there. All I know is what I've read about it. In order to tell you anything more, I'd have to go and see for myself. But you ought to know better than I."

"Of course I do," Peppone retorted. "Everyone's well off in Russia; everyone has a job. The Government is run by the people, and there's no exploitation of the poor. Anything the reactionaries say to the contrary is a lie."

Don Camillo looked at him sharply.

"If you know all that, why do you ask me about it?"

"Just to get your man-to-man opinion. So far I've always heard you talk strictly as a priest."

"And I've always heard you talk as a *comrade*. May I hear your man-to-man opinion as well?"

"To be a comrade means to be a man. And I think as a man just the same that I think as a comrade."

They walked on for a while, and then Peppone returned to the attack.

"In short, you'd say a fellow's just about as well off in Russia as he is here."

"I said nothing of the sort, but since you say it, I'll admit that's more or less my opinion. Except, of course, for the religious angle."

Peppone nodded.

"We agree then," he said. "But why do you suppose people speak and write so much against it?"

Don Camillo threw out his arms. "Politics . . ."

"Politics! . . . Politics! . . ." muttered Peppone. "America is all mixed up with politics in the same way. But no one talks about America quite so violently as about Russia."

"Well, the fact is that people can go to see America for themselves, while very few of them have ever set foot in Russia."

Peppone explained that Russia had to be careful. Then he grasped Don Camillo's sleeve and stopped him.

"Listen . . . as man to man, of course. If a fellow had a chance to take a good job in Russia, what would you advise him to do?"

"Peppone, you're asking me quite a hard . . ."

"Man to man, Father. . . . I'm sure you have the courage to be frank."

Don Camillo shook his head.

"To be frank, then, I'll say that if it were a question of taking a good job I might advise him to go."

Life is a queer sort of proposition. Logically, Peppone

ought to have leaped into the air with joy. But Don Camillo's reply did not make him at all happy. He touched his hat and started to go away. After he had taken a few steps he turned round.

"How can you conscientiously advise a fellow to go to a place where you've never been yourself?" he asked.

"I know more about it than you think," Don Camillo said. "You may not realize it, but I read your newspapers. And some of the people that write for them have been to Russia."

Peppone wheeled abruptly.

"Oh, the newspapers! . . ." he grunted as he walked away.

Don Camillo was jubilant and he hurried back to the church to tell the Lord the whole story.

"Lord, he's got himself into a real tangle! He'd like to say he won't go, but in view of his position he doesn't dare to refuse the honour. And he came to me in the hope that I'd bolster up his resistance. Now he's caught worse than ever and doesn't see how he can get out of it. I shouldn't like to be in his shoes, I can tell you!"

"And I shouldn't like to be in yours—that is, if God would allow it," the Lord answered. "For they're the shoes of a wicked man."

Don Camillo's mouth dropped open.

"I played a good joke on him, that's all," he stammeringly protested.

"A joke's a joke only so long as it doesn't cause or rejoice in pain," the Lord rebuked him.

Don Camillo hung his head and left the church. Two days later Peppone received another letter.

Dear Comrade,—We are sorry to say that, on account of unexpected complications, neither you nor any of the others chosen as members of the Peace Brigade will be able to go to the Soviet Union at this time. Forgive us for causing you this disappointment, but for the moment you can best serve the cause of Peace by staying where you are.

No one ever knew who it was that brought an enormous candle into the church under the cover of darkness that evening. But Don Camillo found it burning near the crucifix when he went that night to say his prayers.

THE STRIKE

DON CAMILLO walked into Peppone's workshop and found the owner sitting in a corner, reading his paper.

"Labour ennobles man," Don Camillo observed. "Take care not to overdo it."

Peppone raised his eyes, turned his head to one side in order to spit, and went on with his reading. Don Camillo sat down on a box, took off his hat, wiped the perspiration away from his forehead and remarked calmly: "Good sportsmanship is all that really matters."

Just then Smilzo came in, out of breath from having ridden his racing bicycle so fast. At the sight of Don Camillo, he raised a finger to his cap.

"Greetings, Your Eminence," he said. "The influence exercised by the clergy upon minds still beclouded by the Dark Ages is a brake upon social progress."

Peppone did not stir, and Don Camillo continued to fan himself with his handkerchief, only imperceptibly turning his head so as to look at Smilzo out of the corner of one eye.

Smilzo sat down on the floor, leaned up against the wall, and said no more. A few minutes later, Straziami came in with his jacket over one shoulder and his hat pushed back on his head. Taking in the situation at a glance, he stood against the door-post and gazed at the world outside. The next to arrive was Lungo, who pushed some tools to one side of the work-bench and sat down on it. Ten minutes went by, and the only sign of life among the five of them was the fanning motion of Don Camillo's hand. Suddenly Peppone crumpled up his paper and threw it away.

"Devil take it!" he exclaimed angrily. "Hasn't anyone got a cigarette?"

Nobody moved, except for Don Camillo, who went on fanning.

"Haven't *you* one?" Peppone asked him maliciously. "I haven't smoked since early this morning."

"And I haven't even smelled tobacco for two whole days," Don Camillo answered. "I was counting on *you*."

"You asked for it," Peppone shouted. "I hope you're enjoying your De Gasperi Government."

"If you were to work instead of reading your paper, you'd have some cigarette money," Don Camillo said calmly.

Peppone threw his cap on the ground.

"Work! Work!" he shouted. "How can I work if no one brings me anything to do? Instead of having their mowers repaired, people are cutting their hay with a scythe. And my truck hasn't been called out for two months. How am I supposed to get along?"

"Nationalize your business," Don Camillo said calmly.

Smilzo raised a finger.

"The Marshall Plan is the enemy of the people," he began gravely. "And the proletariat needs social reforms, not just a lot of talk."

Peppone got up and stood with his legs wide apart in front of Don Camillo.

"Stop raising a breeze with that damned handkerchief, will you?" he shouted. "And tell us what that Government of your choice is doing about the general strike."

"Don't ask me," said Don Camillo. "I can't fit newspapers into my budget. This last month I haven't read anything but my missal."

Peppone shrugged his shoulders.

"It suits you not to know what's going on," he said. "The fact is that you've betrayed the people."

Don Camillo stopped fanning.

"Do you mean me?" he asked gently.

Peppone scratched his head and went back to sit in his corner with his face buried in his hands. In the half-dark workshop silence once more reigned. Each returned to his thoughts on the general strike which had been called from the national headquarters of the Party. Bulletins had been issued, pamphlets distributed and posters put up to explain what the Party leaders were accomplishing for the people, with the result that in the little world of Don Camillo the people were hungry and life in the village was at a standstill. As the days seemed to grow longer and the tempers shorter, Don Camillo had begun to worry.

"To think that on the other side of the river there are people who might work and choose to strike instead!" Don Camillo exclaimed. "At a time like this, I call that a crime!"

He had diplomatically referred to the neighbouring township, which was outside Peppone's jurisdiction. It was an important agricultural centre and there, as everywhere in the valley, the farmers, unable to get labour, were forced to tighten their belts and watch their harvests rot.

Peppone raised his head.

"The strike is the workers' only weapon," he shouted. "Do you want to take it away? What did we fight for in the Resistance movement?"

"To lose the war faster."

So they began to discuss who should pay for the war, and that argument took a long time. Then they emptied some tins of petrol into the tank of Lungo's motorcycle, and Smilzo and Lungo rode away, while Don Camillo returned to the presbytery.

At midnight a boat shot silently out over the river. In it were five men in overalls, with grease all over their faces, looking like mechanics of some kind; three of them were fellows with especially broad shoulders. They landed on the opposite bank, quite a long way downstream, and after walking a mile through empty fields found a truck waiting to take them to a big commercial farm. They proceeded to clean the stable and then to milk the cows. Although there were only five of them, they worked liked a whole battalion. Just as they were finishing with the cows, someone breathlessly spread the alarm: "The squad!"

The five barely had time to get out of the stable by one door before the squad appeared at another, where cans of milk were lined up ready for delivery. The squad leader kicked over one of the cans and said: "I'll give you a lesson in making butter!" Then, turning to his followers, he added: "Some of you take care of the rest of the cans, and the others come with me to give a lesson to the strike-breakers."

He advanced threateningly towards the five, but the iron bars wielded by the three with the broad shoulders did the work of eight, and their two smaller companions were as slippery as eels and gave just as much trouble. Before long the squad retired, licking its wounds. But, three hours later, a veritable army came to reinforce it. The five picked up pitchforks and awaited the attack, while their new enemies stopped some sixty feet away.

"We don't want to hurt you," shouted their leader. "We're after the farmer that got you out from the city. You go on about your business, and we'll settle accounts with him."

The women of the family began to cry, and the farmer and his two sons were white with fear.

"No, we can't let you do that," mumbled one of the five, and they held their ground, while the others, waving sticks, advanced towards them.

"Look out!" said one of the giants. And he threw the pitchfork in the direction of the advancing enemy, who drew back while the pitchfork went into the vacated ground. Then he ran into the stable and reappeared just in time to face the enemy's regrouped forces with a tommy-gun in his hand.

A tommy-gun is no laughing matter, but what is even more frightening is the face of the man who bears it, which reveals from the start whether he intends to shoot or not. In this instance the bearer's face made it very clear that if the enemy didn't desist and retire, he would mow them down. They made another attempt late at night to besiege the stable, but a volley of shots decided them to keep their distance. The strike-breakers stayed on the job twelve days, until it was all over, and when they went away they were loaded down with foodstuffs and money.

No one ever knew exactly who the strike-breakers were. But for some time Peppone, Smilzo, Lungo, and Straziami were very quiet. When Don Camillo discussed the matter at the altar, the Lord reproached him for having carried a tommy-gun, but Don Camillo insisted it had been Peppone. Finally, however, he threw out his arms and gave in.

"What do you expect, Lord?" he said. "How can I explain it to You? We were so alike that no one could say which was me and which Peppone. All strike-breakers look the same by night."

And when the Lord insisted that the tommy-gun had been carried by broad daylight, Don Camillo only threw out his arms again and said: "There are circumstances that cause a man to lose all notion of time!"

THUNDER

Two DAYS before the opening of the hunting season, Lightning died. He was as old as the hills and had every reason to be sick and tired of playing the part of a hunting dog when he wasn't born one. Don Camillo could do nothing but dig a deep hole beside the acacia tree, toss in the body and heave a long sigh. For a whole fortnight he was depressed, but finally he got over it, and one morning he found himself out in the fields with a shotgun in his hands A quail rose out of a nearby meadow, and Don Camillo shot at him, but the quail flew on as calmly as before. Don Camillo nearly yelled, "You wretched dog!" but he remembered that Lightning wasn't there, and felt depressed all over again. He wandered about the fields, over the river bank and under grape arbours, discharged as many volleys as a machine-gun, but never made a single hit. Who could be lucky without a dog beside him?

With the one cartridge he had left, he aimed at a quail flying low over a hedge. He couldn't have missed, but there was no way to be sure. The quail might have fallen either into the hedge or into the field on the other side. But to search for it would be like looking for a needle in a haystack. Better give the whole thing up. He blew into the barrels of his gun and was looking round to see where he was and which was the shortest way to go home when a rustle made him turn his head. Out of the hedge jumped a dog, holding a hare in his mouth, which he proceeded to drop at Don Camillo's feet.

"Heaven help us!" Don Camillo exclaimed. "I shoot a quail, and this dog brings me a hare!"

He picked the hare up and found that it was soaking wet, and so was the dog. Obviously he had swum across from the opposite side of the river. Don Camillo slipped the hare into his bag and started home, with the dog following. When he reached the presbytery, the dog crouched outside the door. Don Camillo had never seen a dog like him. He was a fine animal and seemed to be in the pink of condition. Perhaps he was a dog with a pedigree like that of a count or a marquis, but he had no identification papers on him. He wore a handsome collar, but there was no plate or tag attached to it.

"If he doesn't come from another world but has a rightful owner in this one, surely someone will turn up to look for him," Don Camillo thought to himself. And he let the dog in. That evening before going to bed, he thought about the dog and finally put his conscience at rest by saying to himself: "I'll mention him in church on Sunday." The next morning, when he got up to say Mass, he forgot all about the dog until he found him at the church door.

"Stay there and wait for me," Don Camillo shouted.

And the dog curled up in front of the sacristy door, where after Mass he gave the priest an enthusiastic greeting. They breakfasted together, and when the dog saw Don Camillo take his shotgun out of the corner where he had left it and hang it on a nail, he barked, ran to the door, returned to see if Don Camillo were following and, in short, would give him no peace until Don Camillo slung the gun over his shoulder and made for the fields. He was an extraordinary dog, one of the kind that puts a hunter on his mettle and makes him think: "If I miss my aim, *I'm* a dirty dog." Don Camillo concentrated as if he were under examination and showed himself to be a worthy master. On his way home with a bag full of game, he said to himself: "I'll call him Thunder." Now that the dog had done his work, he was amusing himself by chasing butterflies in a meadow.

"Thunder!" Don Camillo shouted.

It seemed as if from the far side of the meadow someone had launched a torpedo. The dog streaked along with his belly close to the ground, leaving the long grass parted in his wake. He arrived in front of Don Camillo with six inches of tongue hanging out, ready for orders.

"Good dog!" said Don Camillo, and Thunder danced and

barked with such joy that Don Camillo thought: "If he doesn't leave off, I'll find myself dancing and barking."

Two days went by, and Satan tagged at Don Camillo's heels, whispering to him that he should forget to say anything about the dog in church on Sunday. On the afternoon of the third day, when Don Camillo was on his way home with a bag of game and Thunder frisking ahead of him, he ran into Peppone. Peppone was in a gloomy mood; he had been hunting, too, but his bag was empty. Now he looked at Thunder, took a newspaper out of his pocket and opened it.

"That's funny," he said. "He looks just like the dog they've advertised as lost."

Don Camillo took the paper from him and found what he had hoped he would not find. Someone from the city was offering a reward to anyone who found a hunting dog with such and such marks upon him, lost three days before along the river.

"Very well, then," said Don Camillo. "I needn't make any announcement in church. Let me keep this paper. I'll give it back to you later."

"It's really too bad," said Peppone. "Everyone says he's an extraordinary dog. And they must be right, because when you had Lightning you never brought home a haul like that one. If I were in your shoes . . ."

"And if I were in yours . . ." Don Camillo interrupted. "But I happen to be in my own, and as an honest man I must restore the dog to his rightful owner."

When they reached the village Don Camillo sent a telegram to the man in the city. Satan had been working out a new argument to use on Don Camillo, but he was too slow, because he had counted on Don Camillo's sending a letter rather than a telegram. That would have taken fifteen or twenty minutes, time enough for anyone so persuasive as Satan to win a point reluctantly defended. But a five-word telegram was so quickly despatched that Satan was left at a standstill. Don Camillo went home with his conscience in good order, but with a feeling of deep depression. And he sighed even more deeply than when he had buried Lightning.

The city man drove up the next day in a low-slung sports model. He was vain and unpleasant, as might have been expected from his flashy taste in cars; what is called a city slicker.

"Where is my dog?" he asked.

"A dog has been found that must belong to somebody," said Don Camillo. "But you'll have to prove your owner-ship."

The man described the dog from stem to stern.

"Is that enough?" he asked. "Or do I have to describe his insides as well?"

"That's enough," said Don Camillo glumly, opening the cellar door.

The dog lay on the floor without moving.

"Thunder!" called the city slicker.

"Is that really his name?" asked Don Camillo.

"Yes."

"That's funny."

Still the dog did not move and the man called again:

"Thunder!"

The dog growled and there was an ugly look in his eyes.

"He doesn't seem to be yours," observed Don Camillo.

The claimant went and took the dog by the collar in order to drag him up from the cellar. Then he turned the collar inside out, revealing a brass plate with a name on it.

"Just read this, Father. Here are my name and address and telephone number. Appearances to the contrary, the dog is mine."

Then he pointed to the car.

"Get in!" he ordered.

The dog obeyed, with his head hanging low and his tail between his legs, and curled up on the back seat. His owner held out a five-thousand lire note.

"Here's for your trouble," he said.

"It's no trouble to restore something lost to its rightful owner," said Don Camillo, proudly pushing the money away.

"I'm truly grateful," said the city slicker. "He's a very expensive dog, a thoroughbred from one of the best English kennels, with three international blue ribbons to his credit. I'm an impulsive sort of fellow, and the other day, when he caused me to miss a hare, I gave him a kick. And he resented it."

"He's a dog with professional dignity," said Don Camillo. "And you didn't miss the hare, because he brought it to me."

"Oh well, he'll get over it," said the city slicker, climbing back into his car.

Don Camillo spent a restless night, and when he got up to say Mass the next morning he was immersed in gloom. It was windy and pouring rain, but Thunder was there. He was covered with mud and soaked like a sponge, but he lay in front of the sacristy door and gave Don Camillo a welcome worthy of the last act of an opera. Don Camillo went in and spoke to the Lord.

"Lord, Your enemies are going to say that Christians are afraid of wind and water, because not a single one of them has come to church this morning. But if You let Thunder in, they'll be confounded."

Thunder was admitted to the sacristy, where he waited patiently, except when he stuck his nose through the door near the altar, causing Don Camillo to stumble over his prayers. They went back to the presbytery together, and the priest sank into his former melancholy.

"No use fooling myself," he said with a sigh. "He knows the way, and he'll come back for you."

The dog growled as if he had understood. He let Don Camillo brush him and then sat down by the fire to dry. The owner returned in the afternoon. He was in a very bad humour, because he had got his car muddy. There was no need for explanations; he walked into the presbytery and found Thunder in front of the spent fire.

"Sorry to have given you more trouble," he said, "but it won't happen again. I'll take him to a place of mine in the next province, and he couldn't find his way back from there even if he were a carrier pigeon."

When his master called this time, Thunder gave an angry bark. He would not get into the car of his own accord, but had to be lifted on to the seat. He tried to escape, and when the door was closed he scratched and barked without ceasing.

The next morning Don Camillo left the presbytery with his heart pounding. Thunder was not there either that day or the next, and little by little the priest resigned himself to his absence. A fortnight went by, and on the fifteenth night, at about one o'clock, Don Camillo heard a cry from below and knew that it was Thunder. He ran downstairs and out on the church square, quite forgetting that he was in his nightshirt. Thunder was in a very bad condition: starved, dirty, and so tired that he could not hold up his tail. It took three days to restore him to normal, but on the fourth day, after Mass, Thunder pulled him by his cassock to where the shotgun was hanging and made such a scene that Don

Camillo took his gun, bag and cartridge belt and set out for the fields. There followed a rare and wonderful week, when Don Camillo's catches made the most seasoned hunters green with envy. Every now and then someone came to see the dog, and Don Camillo explained:

"He's not mine. A man from the city left him here to be trained to chase hares."

One fine morning Peppone came to admire him. He stared at him for some time in silence.

"I'm not going to hunt this morning," said Don Camillo. "Do you want to try him?"

"Will he come?" said Peppone incredulously.

"I think he will. After all, he doesn't know you're a Communist. Seeing you in my company, he probably takes you for a perfectly respectable person."

Peppone was so absorbed by the prospect of trying the dog that he did not answer. Don Camillo turned his gun and bag and cartridge-belt over to Peppone. Thunder had been excited to see Don Camillo take down his gun, but now he seemed taken aback.

"Go along with the Mayor," said Don Camillo. "I'm busy to-day."

Peppone put on the belt and hung the gun and bag over his shoulder. Thunder looked first at one man and then at the other.

"Go on," Don Camillo encouraged him. "He's ugly, but he doesn't bite."

Thunder started to follow Peppone, but then he stopped in perplexed fashion and turned round.

"Go on," Don Camillo repeated. "Only watch out that he doesn't enlist you in the Party."

Thunder went along. If Don Camillo had turned over his hunting equipment to this man, he must be a friend. Two hours later he bounded back into the presbytery and laid a magnificent hare at Don Camillo's feet. Soon, panting like a locomotive, Peppone arrived upon the scene.

"Devil take you and your dog!" he exclaimed. "He's a perfect wonder, but he eats the game. He stole a hare a yard long. After he had brought me the quails and the partridges, he had to steal a hare."

Don Camillo picked up the hare and held it out to Peppone.

"He's a thinking dog," he answered. "He thought that if

the gun and the cartridges were mine, I was entitled to part of the kill."

It was plain that Thunder had acted in good faith, because he did not run away from Peppone, but greeted him with affection.

"He's an extraordinary animal," said Peppone, "and I wouldn't give him back to that man even if he came with a regiment of militia."

Don Camillo sighed.

The owner turned up a week later. He wore a hunting outfit and carried a feather-weight Belgian shotgun.

"Well, he got away from up there, too. I've come to see whether he landed here again."

"He arrived yesterday morning," said Don Camillo glumly. "Take him away."

Thunder looked at his master and growled.

"I'll settle accounts with you this time," said the city slicker to the dog.

Thunder growled again, and the city slicker lost his head and gave him a kick.

"You cur! I'll teach you! Lie down!"

The dog lay down, growling, and Don Camillo stepped in.

"He's a thoroughbred, and you can't handle him with violence. Let him quieten down while you drink a glass of wine."

The man took a seat, and Don Camillo went down to get a bottle from the cellar. While he was there he found time to scribble a note which he gave to the bell-ringer's son.

"Take it to Peppone at his workshop, and hurry."

The note contained only a few words: *The fellow's here again. Lend me twenty thousand lire so that I can try to buy the dog. And get them here fast.*

The city slicker drank several glasses of wine, talked idly to Don Camillo, then looked at his watch and stood up.

"I'm sorry, but I must go. Friends are expecting me for the hunt, and I've just time to get there."

Thunder was still crouching in a corner, and as soon as he saw his master looking at him he began to growl. He growled louder when the man came near. Just then there came the roar of a motorcycle and Don Camillo saw Peppone dismount from it. He made an interrogative gesture and Peppone nodded an affirmative answer. He held up two open hands, then one, and finally one finger. Then with his right hand he made a horizontal cut through the air. Which signified that he had sixteen thousand five hundred lire. Don Camillo sighed with relief.

"Sir," he said to the visitor. "You can see that the dog has taken a dislike to you. Thoroughbreds don't forget, and you'll never make him put it behind him. Why don't you sell him to me?"

Then he made a mental calculation of all his resources.

"I can pay you eighteen thousand eight hundred lire. That's all I possess."

The city slicker sneered.

"Father, you must be joking. The dog cost me eighty thousand and I wouldn't sell him for a hundred. He may have taken a dislike to me, but I'll make him get over it."

Heedless of Thunder's growling, he seized him by the collar and dragged him over to the car. As he tried to lift him in, the struggling dog clawed some paint off the mudguard. The city slicker lost his head and with his free hand beat him over the back. The dog continued to struggle, caught the hand that held his collar and bit it. The owner let go, and the dog went to lie against the presbytery wall, still growling. Don Camillo and Peppone stared from where they stood and did not have time to say a word. The city slicker, as pale as a corpse, pulled his shotgun out of the car and aimed it at the animal.

"You bastard!" he said between his teeth as he fired.

The wall of the rectory was stained with blood. After a piercing howl, Thunder lay motionless on the ground. The city slicker got into his car and drove off at top speed. Don Camillo took no heed of his departure and did not notice that Peppone had followed on his motorcycle. He knelt beside the dog, with all his attention concentrated upon him. The dog groaned as Don Camillo stroked his head, and then suddenly licked his hand. Then he got up and barked happily.

After twenty minutes, Peppone returned. He was red in the face and his fists were clenched.

"I caught up with him at Fiumaccio, where he had to stop at the level crossing. I dragged him out of the car and boxed his ears until his head was as big as a water-melon. He reached for his gun, and I broke it over his back."

They were in the hall, and now a howl came from farther inside.

"Isn't he dead yet?" asked Peppone.

"Only his flank was grazed," said Don Camillo. "In a week he'll be livelier than ever."

Peppone ran a big hand doubtfully over his chin.

"Morally speaking," said Don Camillo, "he killed the dog. When he shot that was his intention. If Saint Anthony deflected his aim, that doesn't take away from the vileness of the deed. You were wrong to box his ears, because violence is never a good thing. But in any case . . ."

"In any case . . . he won't show his face here again," said Peppone, "and you have acquired a dog."

"Half a dog," declared Don Camillo. "Because I'm morally indebted to you for the money you were ready to lend me. So half the dog is yours."

Peppone scratched his head.

"Well, by all that's wonderful!" he exclaimed. "An honest priest, and one that doesn't defraud the people!"

Don Camillo gave him a threatening look.

"Listen, if you bring politics into it, I'll change my mind and keep the dog to myself!"

"Consider it unsaid!" exclaimed Peppone, who underneath it all was a man and a hunter and cared more for Thunder's esteem than for that of Marx, Lenin and company. And Thunder, with a bandage around his hips, came barking in to seal the pact of non-aggression.

THE WALL

PEOPLE CALLED it Manasca's Garden, but it was just a quarter of an acre of underbrush, with weeds as tall as poplars, surrounded by a ten-foot wall. A forgotten plot with a hundred and fifty feet of frontage on the square and ninety feet on the tree-lined street leading into it. Because it was the only vacant site in the square, old Manasca had been offered any amount of money for it but he had never been willing to sell. For years and years it lay there, just as fallow and uncultivated as its owner, until finally the old man died and it was inherited by his son, together with a pile of thousand-lire notes and other pieces of property here and there on both sides of the river. Young Manasca thought it was a shame not to put the plot to use, and finally he went to see the Mayor.

"Men are starving because they can't find work," he said very directly, "but you proletarians, as you call yourselves, with all your red kerchiefs, are such a filthy bunch that it's a sin to give you anything to do."

"We're not as filthy as you fine gentlemen," Peppone answered peacefully. "The best of you deserves to be strung up on a rope made of the guts of the most miserable of us."

Young Manasca and Peppone had had a fist-fight every day until they were twenty; as a result they were very good friends and understood one another perfectly. So now Peppone asked what he was driving at.

"If you promise you won't trip me up with trade unions, Party, vice-Party, victims of the Resistance movement, social justice, rightful claims, sympathy strikes and all the rest of your revolutionary paraphernalia, I'll provide work for half the men in the village," Manasca told him.

Peppone put his fists on his hips.

"Do you want me to help you to exploit the worker? To convince him he ought to toil for a dish of spaghetti and a kick in the pants?"

"I don't intend to cheat anybody. I'll pay regular wages and old-age insurance and give you a barrel of wine into the bargain if you promise me that those stupid fools won't walk out in the middle of the job and try to blackmail me. It's a big project, and if it doesn't come off I'm a ruined man."

Peppone told him to lay his cards on the table.

"I propose to put up a five-storey building in the garden," said Manasca. "Big-city stuff, with a hundred-foot arcade on to the square, shops, a café, a restaurant with rooms to let above it, a garage, a petrol pump and so on. If all goes well, I'll let you run the petrol pump. However much of a nuisance you are, you know how to get things done. With a building like that we'll make this into an important market centre and turn our yokels into sophisticates."

Peppone had never laid eyes on Paris or London or New York, but he imagined the new building as equal to any of theirs. And he could see a red-and-yellow petrol pump in front of his workshop, with a pump for compressed air as well.

"A complete filling-station needs a hydraulic machine to lift cars up for greasing," he murmured.

"There'll be a hydraulic machine and all the other gadgets you can think of," said Manasca. "But you've got to make me a promise."

"What if I'm not re-elected Mayor?" Peppone said anxiously.

"So much the better! The new Mayor will be afraid of you and your gang. And that's more than you can say for yourself!"

Peppone brought a fist down on his desk.

"That's a bargain! And I'll kill the first man that gives you trouble. The future of the village is concerned, and anyone that doesn't do a good job will get a swift kick. Tell me what you need and I'll find you the right people."

"Let's have a clear understanding," said Manasca. "You're not to hire only people from your own Party. I want men that are willing to work and have the know-how."

"That's right; all men are equal when they're hungry," Peppone said sententiously.

And that evening, with due solemnity, he gave the news to to his Party stalwarts.

"Tell people that, while others chatter, we actually do something. We're building a skyscraper."

A week later, a crew of wreckers began to tear down the wall. And then it was that trouble began. The wall was a mass of stones and rubble and mortar, at least three hundred years old, which was easy enough to smash; but there was something on the wall that everyone had forgotten. On the street side, just a yard before the corner, there was a niche, with a rusty grating over it to protect a Madonna painted inside.

The Madonna was a thing of no artistic value, painted by some poor devil two or three hundred years before, but everyone knew her; everyone had greeted her a thousand times and stopped to put a flower in the tin can at her feet. And if the wall around her were torn down, the Madonna would fall to pieces. Manasca sent for an expert from the city, one of those fellows who can peel a painting off a wall. But after studying the situation he declared that there was nothing to do.

"If we so much as touch the painting, it will crumble into dust."

Meanwhile the wreckers were advancing, and when they were a couple of yards away on either side, they stopped. Peppone came to look at the Madonna clinging to the last bit of wall and shook his head.

"Nonsense!" he said. "This isn't religion; it's superstition. There's no intention of hurting anybody's feelings. For the sake of this painting, are we to give up a plan that's providing work for a lot of people and doing something for the village as well?"

The wreckers were tough fellows, who would just as soon have demolished their own mothers. And there they stood in front of the remaining scrap of wall. Their chief, Bago, spat out a cigarette butt and shook his head.

"I wouldn't destroy it even on orders from the Pope!" he exclaimed, and the others looked as if they felt as he did.

"No one said anything about destroying it," shouted Peppone. "That's all sentimentality, traditionalism, childishness and so on. There's only one thing to do, to tear down as much of the wall as possible, then to prop up and protect what's left, lift it away and put it somewhere else. In Russia they move fifteen-storey buildings from one street to another, and no matter how far we may be behind them, we ought to be able to pull off a trick like this one."

Bago shrugged his shoulders.

"In Russia they may move buildings, but they haven't any Madonnas to move," he mumbled.

Brusco took a good look and then threw out his arms in despair.

"There's a crack at the back of the niche, and it's a miracle that the whole thing hasn't fallen apart years ago. The wall's made of mud and stones, and if you try to lift a piece of it out you'll be left with a fistful of sand."

Peppone strode up and down, and half the village gathered to look on.

"Well then, what have you got to say, all of you?" Peppone snarled. "You can see the situation for yourselves. Are we to stop work or not? Say something, or may God strike you dead!"

"We'd better go and see the priest about it," was their conclusion.

Peppone jammed his cap down on his head.

"All right. Since the future of the village is at stake, I suppose we'll have to call upon the priest."

Don Camillo was transplanting some vegetables in his garden when Peppone and the rest of them looked over the hedge. Manasca explained the problem, and Peppone put the question:

"What shall we do?"

Don Camillo asked for further details and prolonged the discussion. Of course, he already knew what it was all about and only wanted to gain time.

"It's late now," he said at last. "We'll decide to-morrow."

"In the city I've seen any number of churches that have been de-consecrated and taken over by coal merchants or cabinet-makers," said Peppone. "If a church can be transformed in that way, why can't we do the same thing with a picture painted on a wall?"

"The very fact that you've come to consult me shows that there are some difficulties in your minds." said Don Camillo.

That night the priest could not sleep for worry. But the next morning, when Peppone and his gang appeared before him, he had a solution.

"If you are quite sure in your consciences that there is no way of saving the picture, then go ahead and tear down the wall. It's for the good of the whole community, and a poor old painted Madonna wouldn't want to take bread out of men's mouths and stand in the way of progress. God be with you! But go at it gently."

"Very well," said Peppone, touching his cap, and marching off with his men to the square.

When they reached the Madonna he turned and said to Bago:

"You heard what the priest told us, didn't you? We're not giving offence to anyone."

Bago twisted the visor of his cap to one side of his head, spat into his hands and grasped the handle of his pick. He raised the pick in the air, left it suspended there for several minutes, and then said: "Not me! I'll not be the one to do it."

Peppone stormed and shouted, but none of the men was willing to deliver the fatal blow. Finally he seized the pick himself and advanced towards the wall. He raised it above his head, but when through the grating he saw the Madonna's eyes upon him, he threw it down on the ground.

"Devil take it!" he exclaimed. "Why should this be the Mayor's job? What has a Mayor to do with the Madonna? The priest ought to be good for something. Let him do it! Everyone to his own trade, I say."

And he went angrily back to the presbytery.

"All done?" Don Camillo asked him.

"The devil it's done!" shouted Peppone. "It's no use."

"Why?"

"Because the Madonna and saints are your racket. I've never called on you to smash a bust of Marx or Lenin, have I?"

"No, but if you want me to, I'd be glad to oblige," said Don Camillo.

Peppone clenched his fists.

"Do what you see fit," said Peppone. "But remember that as long as the Madonna's there, we can't go on with the work, and you'll be responsible for the resulting unemployment. I'm a Mayor by profession, not a destroyer of Madonnas. And I don't want to be told that we're a bunch of sacrilegious Reds, smashing up saints wherever we find them."

"Very well, then," said Don Camillo. "The rest of you can go along, while I talk to the Mayor."

When the two men were left alone together, they said nothing for several minutes. Then Don Camillo broke the silence.

"Peppone, it's no good, I can't tear it down."

"Neither can I," said Peppone. "If you, who specialize in saints, haven't got the nerve...."

"It's not a question of nerve," said Don Camillo. "It's like it was with the angel in the bell tower, that for hundreds of years had looked down on the village. The eyes of this Madonna have seen all our beloved dead, they have reflected the hope and despair, the joys and sorrows of centuries past. Do you remember, Peppone, when we came back from the war in 1918? I gave the Madonna flowers, and you put them in your tin cup."

Peppone grunted, and Don Camillo ran his hand over his chin. Then he threw his coat around him and put on his hat. When they arrived in front of the Madonna, they found half the village waiting there. There was a stranger also, a young man who had come in a car, and from the manner in which Peppone ran to greet him, it was clear that he was a Party bigwig from the city. Now he stepped forward and looked at the Madonna.

"Well," he said, "if things are as you tell me and the priest agrees that you can't give up a project that's so good for the community and the working-man, then I'll be the one to cut through your middle-class sentimentality. I'll do the job myself."

He took a pick and started over to the wall. But Don Camillo laid a hand on his shoulder and pulled him back.

"It's not necessary," he said roughly.

There was a deep silence, while everyone looked expectantly at the wall. Suddenly the wall quivered and then slowly cracked open. The wall did not fall to the ground; it crumbled into a heap of stones and plaster. On top of the heap, free of the rusty grating and the shadows of the niche in which it had dwelt for so long, stood the Madonna, completely unscathed. Although she had been painted two or three hundred years before, she was as fresh as a rose.

"She can go back to the same place in the new wall," said Manasca.

"Motion carried by unanimous applause!" shouted Peppone. And he thought of his old Army tin cup, with the offering of flowers from Don Camillo.

THE SUN ALSO RISES

ONE AFTERNOON an old woman by the name of Maria Barchini came to confession. Don Camillo listened to her quietly, but toward the end he was startled almost out of his skin to hear her say hesitantly: "Father, I'm going to vote for the Communists."

He came out of the confessional and said to her: "Come along over to the presbytery." And when they had sat down in his study, he asked if there were anything wrong with her head. "I thought I'd explained all these things any number of times," he told her. "Didn't you understand me?"

"Yes, I understood," said the old woman. "I'm willing to do whatever penance you prescribe, to fast or make a pilgrimage to the Sanctuary. . . . But I'm voting for the Communists."

"There's no use in my wasting breath to explain something you say you already understand," Don Camillo said brusquely. "If you vote for those people, I can't give you absolution."

She spread out her arms in a gesture of resignation.

"God will forgive me," she said, "and I'll pay whatever the price may be. The main thing is for my boy to come home. A mother must be ready to sacrifice herself for her son."

Don Camillo looked at her in bewilderment and asked her what her son had to do with the election.

"Two ladies came from the city the other day," she explained, "and promised that if I voted for the right candidates my boy would be sent back from Russia. These people are friendly to the Russians, and if they win they'll bring back the prisoners of war. They took down my name and put it high on their list. And I gave them the boy's picture. I can understand why you can't give me absolution, but I still say a mother must sacrifice herself for her child."

Don Camillo shook his head.

"I see," he muttered. "But you've got to be sure your boy will really come."

"I had lost all hope until they gave it back to me. When you're drowning, you know, you'll clutch at any straw."

"I see," said Don Camillo. "But what if the Communists don't win?"

"Ah well . . ." the old woman sighed. "I have to do all I can. They put his name at the head of the list. I saw them write it down. And they were respectable people, educated people. They said they knew how things are, but a mother has to do everything she can for her son. I'll have to vote for the 'People's Front.'"

Don Camillo stood up and traced a cross in the air.

"*Ego te absolvo,*" he said. "Say four Our Fathers, four Hail Marys and four Glorias for penance. And God be praised."

And when from his window he saw the old woman leave the church, he went to talk to the Lord on the altar.

"Lord," Don Camillo said impetuously, "if a woman is willing to sacrifice herself in the hope of saving her son, Don Camillo has no right to take her hope away. If I had refused her absolution it would have been like saying: 'You're willing to make any sacrifice for your boy, but God is against you.' And that would have been a wicked thing to say, for even when hope is based on material things, its origin is divine. In Your divine wisdom You know how to turn evil means to a good end, and You choose to speak through sacrilegious mouths in order to restore hope to a mother's heart. To refuse her absolution would have meant telling her she had no right to hope, and to deny hope means to deny You."

223

The Lord smiled.

"What have you in mind, Don Camillo?" he asked. "Do you want me to vote for the 'People's Front'?"

"I merely wanted to explain why I gave old Maria Barchini absolution in spite of the fact that she's voting for the Communists."

"And why must you explain, Don Camillo? Did I ask for any explanation? Aren't you at peace with your own conscience?"

"I'm not, Lord, that's just the trouble. I should have taken away from Your enemies the vote they have extorted from that poor woman."

"But her illusions have been turned into hope, and you have just said that hope is divine, Don Camillo."

Don Camillo ran his big hands over his face.

"That's equally true," he admitted. "What's to be done?"

"I can't tell you," the Lord said. "I don't go in for politics."

Peppone was in his workshop, busy repainting a mudguard on his truck, when Don Camillo accosted him.

"Some of your filthy propagandists are going round telling poor people whose boys are still in Russia that if they vote for the Communists the Russians will send all the prisoners home."

"I don't believe it," muttered Peppone. "Give me the names of some of the people."

"That would be violating the secrecy of the confessional. But I swear to you it's true."

Peppone shrugged his shoulders.

"I didn't send anybody out on such a mission. It must be an idea from the city. Anyhow, we're at war, aren't we? And each side must use whatever cards he has in his hand."

"Exactly," said Don Camillo gloomily.

"You have a trick up your sleeve, for that matter. If someone votes for us, you won't grant him absolution."

"I shan't refuse absolution to anyone who's been given the false hope of recovering a son. But when the time comes, God will refuse absolution to you. You're damning your own soul!"

Don Camillo spoke very calmly and then went away. Peppone stared after him, open-mouthed, for he had never heard Don Camillo speak just like that before, in a cold, far-away voice that seemed to come from another world. He thought of it several times both that day and the next. Then posters appeared on the walls announcing a meeting of the Socialist Unity Party and, in accordance with directives from headquarters, he had to organize a counter-demonstration. On Sunday the village was packed with people.

"In the front row, just below the platform, put the comrades from Molinetto and Torricella," ordered Peppone. "At the first slip made by one of the Socialist speakers they're to go into action. Our own people are all going to Molinetto and Torricella to do the same job at the Christian Democrat and Nationalist rallies. Brusco and I and the rest of the local leaders will stay in the Town Hall. We're not to appear on the scene unless there's trouble."

The Socialist speaker was about thirty-five years old, a well-bred man and a born orator. As soon as Peppone heard the voice he jumped up on a chair and peered out of the window.

"It's him!" he stammered. And Brusco and Bigio and Smilzo and all the rest agreed that it was he indeed and had nothing more to say.

A few minutes later, the nuisance squad went into action. The speaker made telling answers to their insults and accusations, and finally they lost control of themselves and made a rush for the platform. Peppone signalled to them from the window, but it was too late. The crowd gathered in front of the house where the speaker had been rushed to safety. Peppone and his seconds made their way through to the door. The speaker was sitting on a sofa inside, while a woman bandaged his hand. He had blood on his face because someone had struck him with a key across the forehead. Peppone looked at him, gaping.

"Hello there, Peppone," said the wounded man, raising his head. "Did you organize this little party?"

Peppone did not answer, and the wounded man smiled again.

"Ah, so Brusco's here, and Smilzo, and Straziami, and Lungo. Well, I'm here too. Our old group is together again, all except for Rosso and Giacomino, who died in our mountain encampment. Who could have imagined that Peppone was going to organize a party like this for his old commander? . . ."

Peppone spread out his arms.

"Chief, I didn't know . . . ." he stammered.

"Oh, don't let that bother you," the wounded man interrupted him. "We're at war, and everyone plays the cards he can. I quite see your point of view." The bandage was finished, and he got up to go. "So long, Comrade Peppone," he said with a smile. "We saved our skins from the Germans; now let's hope we can save them from the Communists, too. Rosso and Giacomino are lucky to have died when they did, up in the mountains."

He got into a waiting car, and Peppone heard the hooting and shouting that accompanied its departure. When the "chief" had spoken that last sentence, his voice had been as cold and far-away and other-worldly as Don Camillo's when he had said: "You're damning your own soul!"

That evening, the leaders of the squads that had done a job at Molinetto and Torricella came to report. At Molinetto the Christian Democrat speaker had been forced to stop half-way through his address, and nothing serious had happened. At Torricella the Nationalist had received a slap in the face. Peppone knew them both. The first was a university professor and the second had been in a German labour camp.

"They gave them an even rougher time in the city," the leader of the Molinetto squad was saying. "They trampled down some students and gave a police sergeant a black eye."

"Good," said Peppone, getting up to leave the room.

The sun was setting as he walked slowly along the road leading down to the river. On the bank someone was smoking a cigar and looking into the water. It was Don Camillo. They said nothing for a while, until Peppone observed that it was a fine evening.

"Very fine," Don Camillo answered.

Peppone lit the butt of a cigar, inhaled a few mouthfuls of smoke, then put it out with his shoe. He spat angrily.

"Everybody's against us," he said glumly. "Even my old Partisan commander. Everybody, including God."

Don Camillo went on quietly smoking. "Everybody's not against you. You're against everybody, God included."

Peppone crossed his arms on his chest. "Why did you say I was damning my own soul? Just because old Maria Barchini's going to give us her vote?"

"Maria Barchini? Who's she?"

"I went yesterday to see all the families whose boys are prisoners in Russia, and she told me that two women had called upon her on behalf of the People's Front. I told her that they were fakers and that even if she were to vote as they said she'd never see her son again."

Don Camillo threw away his cigar.

"And what did she say?"

"She asked how she was to vote in order to get back her son. I told her I didn't know, and she said if no party could bring him back there was no use in voting at all."

"You're an idiot," said Don Camillo.

He said it solemnly, but not in that cold far-away voice. Peppone felt better. When he thought of the blood on his former commander's face and the slap given to the former labour-camp inmate at Molinetto and the old professor at Torricella who couldn't finish his address because of the shouts, he felt like crying. But he took hold of himself and called out fiercely:

"We're going to win!"

"No," Don Camillo said calmly but firmly.

For a moment they just stood there silently, each one looking straight ahead. The valley stretched out peacefully under the evening sky and the river was just the same as it had been a hundred thousand years before. And so was the sun. It was about to set, but the next morning it would rise again from the opposite direction. Peppone—who can say why?—found himself thinking of this extraordinary fact and privately came to the conclusion that, to tell the truth, God knows His business.

TECHNIQUE OF THE *COUP D'ÉTAT*

AT TEN o'clock on Tuesday evening the village square was swept with wind and rain, but a crowd had been gathered there for three or four hours to listen to the election news coming out of a radio loudspeaker. Suddenly the lights went out and everything was plunged into darkness. Someone went to the control box but came back saying there was nothing to be done. The trouble must be up the line or at the power plant, miles away. People hung around for a half-hour or so, and then, as the rain began to come down even harder than before, they scattered to their homes, leaving the village silent and deserted. Peppone shut himself up in the People's Palace, along with Lungo, Brusco, Straziami and Gigio, the lame leader of the "Red Wing" squad from Molinetto. They sat around uneasily by the light of a candle stump and cursed the power and light monopoly as an enemy of the people, until Smilzo burst in. He had gone to Roccaverde on his motorcycle to see if anyone had news, and now his eyes were popping out of his head and he was waving a sheet of paper.

"The Front has won!" he panted. "Fifty-two seats out of a hundred in the Senate and fifty-one in the Chamber. The other side is done for. We must get hold of our people and have a celebration. If there's no light, we can set fire to a couple of haystacks nearby."

"Hurrah!" shouted Peppone. But Gigio grabbed hold of Smilzo's jacket.

"Keep quiet and stay where you are!" he said grimly. "It's too early for anyone to be told. Let's take care of our little list."

"List? What list?" asked Peppone in astonishment.

"The list of reactionaries who are to be executed first thing. Let's see now . . ."

Peppone stammered that he had made no such list, but the other only laughed.

"That doesn't matter. I've a very complete one here all ready. Let's look at it together, and once we've decided, we can get to work."

Gigio pulled a sheet of paper with some twenty names on it out of his pocket and laid it on the table.

"Looks to me as if all the reactionary pigs were here," he said. "I put down the worst of them, and we can attend to the rest later."

Peppone scanned the names and scratched his head.

"Well, what do you say?" Gigio asked him.

"Generally speaking, we agree," said Peppone. "But what's the hurry? We have plenty of time to do things in the proper style."

Gigio brought his fist down on the table.

"We haven't a minute to lose, that's what I say," he shouted harshly. "This is the time to put our hands on them, before they suspect us. If we wait until to-morrow, they may get wind of something and disappear."

At this point Brusco came into the discussion.

"You must be crazy," he said. "You can't start out to kill people before you think it over."

"I'm not crazy, and you're a very poor Communist, that's what you are! These are all reactionary pigs; no one can dispute that, and if you don't take advantage of this golden opportunity then you're a traitor to the Party!"

Brusco shook his head.

"Don't you believe it! It's jackasses that are traitors to the Party! And you'll be a jackass if you make mistakes and slaughter innocent people."

Gigio raised a threatening finger.

"It's better to eliminate ten innocents than to spare one individual who may be dangerous to the cause. Dead men can do the Party no harm. You're a very poor Communist, as I've said before. In fact, you never were a good one. You're as weak as a snowball in Hell, I say; you're just a *bourgeois* in disguise!"

Brusco grew pale, and Peppone intervened.

"That's enough," he said. "Comrade Gigio has the right

229

idea, and nobody can deny it. It's part of the groundwork of Communist philosophy. Communism gives us the goal at which to aim and democratic discussion must be confined to the choice of the quickest and surest ways to attain it."

Gigio nodded his head in satisfaction, while Peppone continued: "Once it's been decided that these persons are or may be dangerous to the cause and therefore we must eliminate them, the next thing is to work out the best method of elimination. Because if by our carelessness we were to allow a single reactionary to escape, then we should indeed be traitors to the Party. Is that clear?"

"Absolutely," the others said in chorus. "You're dead right."

"There are six of us," Peppone went on, "and twenty names on the list, among them Filotti, who has a whole regiment in his house and a cache of arms in the cellar. If we were to attack these people one by one, at the first shot the rest would run away. We must call our forces together, and divide them up into twenty squads, each one equipped to deal with a particular objective."

"Very good," said Gigio.

"Good, my foot!" shouted Peppone. "That's not the half of it! We need a twenty-first squad, equipped even better than the rest, to hold off the police. And mobile squads to cover the roads and the river. If a fellow rushes into action in the way you proposed, without proper precautions, running the risk of botching it completely, then he's not a good Communist, he's just a damned fool."

It was Gigio's turn to pale now, and he bit his lip in anger while Peppone proceeded to give orders. Smilzo was to transmit word to the cell leaders in the outlying settlements, and these were to call their men together. A green rocket would give the signal to meet in appointed places, where Falchetto, Brusco and Straziami would form the squads and assign the targets. A red rocket would bid them go into action. Smilzo went off on his motorcycle, while Lungo, Brusco, Straziami, and Gigio discussed the composition of the squads.

"You must do a faultless job," Peppone told them. "I shall hold you personally responsible for its success. Meanwhile, I'll see if the police are suspicious and find some way to put them off."

Don Camillo, later waiting in vain for the lights to go

on and the radio to resume its mumble, decided to get ready for bed. Suddenly he heard a knock at the door, and when he drew it open cautiously, he found Peppone before him.

"Get out of here in a hurry!" Peppone panted. "Pack a bag and go! Put on an ordinary suit of clothes, take your boat and row down the river."

Don Camillo stared at him with curiosity.

"Comrade Mayor, have you been drinking?"

"Hurry!" said Peppone. "The People's Front has won, and the squads are getting ready. There's a list of people to be executed, and your name is the first one!"

Don Camillo bowed.

"An unexpected honour, Mr. Mayor! But I must say I never expected you to be the sort of rascal that draws up lists for murder."

"Don't be silly," said Peppone impatiently. "I don't want to murder anybody."

"Well then?"

"Gigio, the lame fellow from Molinetto, came out with the list and secret Party orders."

"You're the chief, Peppone. You could have sent him and his list to blazes."

Peppone rubbed his perspiring face.

"You don't understand these things. The Party always has the last word, and he was speaking for the Party. If I'd stood out against him he'd have added my name to the list, above yours."

"That's a good one! Comrade Peppone and the reactionary priest, Don Camillo, strung up together!"

"Hurry, will you?" Peppone repeated. "You can afford to joke because you're all alone in the world, but I have a mother, a wife, a son and a whole lot of other dependants. Move fast if you want to save your skin!"

Don Camillo shook his head.

"Why should I be saved? What about the others?"

"I can't very well go to warn them, can I? You'll have to do that yourself. Drop in on one or two of them on your way to the river, and tell them to pass on the alarm. And they'd better look lively! Here, take down the names."

"Very well," said Don Camillo when he'd taken them down. "I'll send the sexton's boy to call the Filotti family, and there are so many of them that they can take care of the rest. I'm staying here."

"But you've got to go, I tell you!"

"This is my place, and I won't budge, even if Stalin comes in person."

"You're crazy!" said Peppone, but before he could say anything else, there was a knock at the door and he had to run and hide in the next room.

The next arrival was Brusco, but he had barely time to say: "Don Camillo, get out of here in a hurry!" before someone knocked at the door again. Brusco, too, ran to hide, and a minute later Lungo burst in.

"Don Camillo," said Lungo, "I've only just been able to sneak away for a minute. Things are hotting up, and you'd better get out. Here are the names of the other people you ought to take with you."

And he rushed to hide, because there was another knock at the door. This time it was Straziami, as glum and pugnacious as ever. He had hardly stepped in, when Lungo, Brusco, and Peppone emerged to meet him.

"It's beginning to look like one of those old-fashioned comedies," said Don Camillo, laughing. "As soon as Gigio comes, the whole cast will be on the stage."

"He's not coming," muttered Peppone.

Then with a sigh, he slapped Brusco on the back.

"Notice anything?" he said reminiscently. "Here we are again, the way we were up in the mountains in the old days of the Resistance. And we can still get along together."

The others nodded.

"If Smilzo were only here the old guard would be complete," sighed Peppone.

"He is here," said Don Camillo. "In fact, he was the first to come."

"Good," said Peppone approvingly. "And now you'd better hustle."

But Don Camillo was a stubborn man.

"I told you once that my place is here," he said. "I'm quite happy enough to know that you're not against me."

Peppone lost patience. He twisted his hat about and then jammed it down on his head in the way that he did when he was ready to come to blows.

"You two take his shoulders, and I'll take his legs," he ordered. "It's too late to go by boat. We'll tie him to the seat of his cart and send him away. Straziami, go and harness the horse."

But before they could raise their arms the lights went on, and they stood there, dazzled. A moment later the radio began to mumble.

"Here are the results of the election of Deputies to Parliament, with 41,000 out of 41,168 electoral districts heard from: Christian Democrats, 12,000,257 votes; People's Front, 7,547,468 . . ."

They all listened in silence until the announcement was over. Then Peppone looked gloomily at Don Camillo.

"Some weeds are so tough that they overrun everything," he said angrily. "You had a lucky escape, that's all I can say."

"You had a lucky escape yourself," Don Camillo answered calmly, "for which God be praised."

One man didn't escape and that was Gigio. He was proudly waiting for orders to set off the green rocket and, instead, he got a volley of kicks that left him black and blue all over.

BENEFIT OF CLERGY

THE TIME has come to speak of Smilzo, official messenger at
the Town Hall and head of the "flying squad" of the local
Communist Party, and to brand him for what he was, an
example of flagrant immorality, a man without any sense of
shame, because a man must be shameless to live openly with
a woman to whom he is not married in a village of the Po
Valley. And the woman who shared his bed and board was
just as shameless as he.

People called Moretta a "kept woman," but in reality she
was a girl quite capable of keeping herself. She was big-boned
and as strong as any man, and farmers hired her to run a
tractor, which she manoeuvred just as skilfully as Peppone.
Although the women of the village referred to her as "that
hussy," no man but Smilzo had ever made advances to her
without getting a slap in the face that left him groggy.
Nevertheless, it was a village scandal to see him carry her on
the handlebars of his bicycle, which was where she rode when
she didn't occupy the saddle and carry him.

Don Camillo had come into the world with a constitutional preference for calling a spade a spade and so it was
that he spoke from the pulpit of "certain women who rode
around on racing bicycles, flaunting their flanks as freely as
their faces." From then on, Moretta wore blue dungarees and
a red kerchief around her neck, which left the village even
more shocked than before. Once Don Camillo managed to
catch hold of Smilzo and say something to him about
"legalizing the situation," but Smilzo only jeered in his face.

"There's nothing to 'legalize' about it. We do nothing more and nothing less than people who are idiotic enough to get married."

"Than decent men and women . . ." Don Camillo sputtered.

"Than idiots who spoil the beauty of affinity between two united souls by dragging a clumsy oaf of a mayor or a priest reeking of tobacco into it."

Don Camillo swallowed the aspersion on his tobacco and came back to the main point of what he was saying. But Smilzo continued to jeer at him.

"If God Almighty had intended men and women to be joined in matrimony, He'd have put a priest with Adam and Eve in the Garden of Eden! Love was born free and free it ought to remain! The day is coming when people will understand that marriage is like a jail sentence, and they'll get along without benefit of clergy. And when that day comes there'll be dancing in the churches."

Don Camillo found only a brick handy. He picked this up and threw it, but Smilzo had learned during the period of the Resistance movement to slip between one volley of machine-gun fire and another, and so the brick was wasted. But Don Camillo was not discouraged, and one day he lured Moretta to the presbytery. She came in her blue dungarees, with the red kerchief around her neck, and lit a cigarette as soon as she sat down before him. Don Camillo refrained from scolding her and spoke in the mildest tone of voice he could manage.

"You're a hard-working girl and a good housekeeper," he told her. "I know that you don't gossip or waste money. And I know too that you love your husband . . ."

"He isn't my husband," Moretta interrupted.

"That you love Smilzo, then," said Don Camillo patiently. "And so, although you've never come to confession, I'm convinced that you're a decent sort of woman. Why do you have to behave in such a way that people brand you as indecent?"

" 'People' can go straight to . . . where they belong," Moretta retorted.

Don Camillo was growing red in the face, but he went ahead with his plan and murmured something about getting married. But Moretta interrupted him.

"If God Almighty had intended men and women to be joined in matrimony. . . ."

"Never mind," said Don Camillo, interrupting her in his turn. "I know the rest already."

"Love was born free and free it ought to remain!" Moretta concluded gravely. "Marriage is the opium of love."

The village gossips did not give up so easily. They formed a committee and went to tell the Mayor that the affair was bringing shame upon the village and for the sake of public morals he must do something about it.

"I'm married myself," said Peppone, "and I have a right to perform a civil marriage, but I can't force people to marry when they don't want to. That's the law. Perhaps when the Pope comes into power things will be different."

But the old crones insisted.

"If you can't do anything as Mayor, then as head of the local section of the Party you can bring pressure on them. They're a disgrace to the Party, too."

"I'll try," said Peppone, and so he did.

"I'd rather join the *Socialist* Party than marry," was Smilzo's answer.

That was all there was to it, and with the passage of time the scandal abated, or rather politics took its place. But one day it came to the fore again and in a clamorous manner. For some time Comrade Moretta was not seen about, and then all of a sudden there was a startling piece of news. There were no longer two Comrades, but three, because, as the midwife told it, a little girl had been born to them, and one far prettier than they deserved. The old crones of the village began to wag their tongues again, and those who were politically-minded said:

"There are Communist morals for you. It's a hundred to one these godless parents will never have the child baptized."

The news and the comment reached Peppone's ears, and he rushed to the godless parents' home.

Don Camillo was reading when Smilzo came in.

"There's a baptizing job for you to do," Smilzo said abruptly.

"A fine job indeed," muttered Don Camillo.

"Must one obtain a *nihil obstat* before having a baby?" Smilzo asked him.

"The *nihil obstat* of your own conscience," said Don Camillo. "But that's strictly your affair. Only if Moretta

236

arrives dressed in her blue dungarees, I'll chase you all away. You can come twenty minutes from now."

Moretta came with the baby in her arms and Smilzo at her side. Don Camillo received them along with Peppone and his wife at the door to the church.

"Take all that red stuff off," he said, without even looking to see if they really were wearing anything red. "This is the House of God and not the People's Palace."

"There's nothing red around here except the fog in your brain," muttered Peppone.

They went into the church and over to the baptismal font, where Don Camillo began the ceremony.

"What's the name?" he asked.

"Rita Palmira Valeria," the mother stated firmly.

There was a dead silence as the three names—every one of them of internationally famous Communists—echoed in the little church. Don Camillo replaced the cover on the font and was just about to say "then go and get her baptized in Russia" when he saw the Lord looking down at him from the Cross. So he just took a deep breath and counted to ten instead.

"Rita is for my mother, Palmira for his and Valeria for my grandmother," Moretta pointed out.

"That's their bad luck," said Don Camillo dryly. "I say Emilia Rosa Antonietta."

Peppone pawed the ground, while Smilzo sighed and shook his head, but Moretta seemed secretly pleased.

Afterwards they went to the presbytery to sign the register.

"Under the Christian Democrat Government, is Palmira a forbidden name?" Peppone asked sarcastically.

Don Camillo did not answer, but motioned to him and his wife to go home. Smilzo, Moretta and the baby were left standing in front of the table.

"*Enciclica rerarum novium,*" said Smilzo more cleverly than correctly, with the look of a man resigned to his fate.

"No. I'm not making a speech," Don Camillo said coldly. "I just want to give you a warning. By not getting married you are not hurting the Church. You're just two cockroaches trying to gnaw at one of the columns of Saint Peter's. Neither you nor your offspring are of the slightest interest to me."

At this moment the bundle in Moretta's arms stirred, and the "offspring" opened her eyes wide and smiled at Don Camillo. She had such a pink little face that Don Camillo paused and then his blood began to boil and he lost his temper.

"Miserable creatures!" he shouted. "You have no right to visit your foolish sins upon the head of this innocent baby. She's going to grow up to be a beautiful girl and when people are envious of her beauty they'll throw mud at her by calling her a 'kept woman's child.' If you weren't such wretches you wouldn't expose your daughter to people's jealous hypocrisy. You may not care what people say about you, but if on your account they slander her . . ."

Don Camillo had raised his fist and thrown out his chest so that he looked even taller and bigger than he was, and the two parents had taken refuge in a corner.

"Get married, you criminals!" the priest shouted.

Pale and perspiring, Smilzo shook his head.

"No; that would be the end of everything for us. We couldn't face people."

The baby seemed to enjoy the scene. She waved her hands and laughed, and Don Camillo was taken aback.

"Please, I'm begging you!" he exclaimed. "She's too beautiful!"

Strange things can happen in this world. A man may try with a crowbar to force a door open and not move it a single inch. Then when he is dead tired and hangs his hat on the knob in order to wipe the sweat off his brow, click, the door opens. Moretta was a stubborn woman, but when she saw that Don Camillo's anger was dying down as he looked at her baby, she threw herself on to a chair and began to cry.

"No, no," she sobbed. "We can't marry because we're married already. We did it three years ago, only nobody knows, because we chose somewhere far away. We've always liked free love. And so we've never told a soul."

Smilzo nodded.

"Marriage is the opium of love," he began. "Love was born free, and if God Almighty . . ."

Don Camillo went to douse his face in cold water. When he came back, Smilzo and his wife were quite calm, and Moretta was holding out a paper which was a marriage certificate.

"Under the secrecy of the confessional," she whispered.

Don Camillo nodded.

"So you've registered with your employer as 'single,' " he

238

said to Smilzo, "and you don't get any of the benefits of being a family man."

"Exactly," said Smilzo. "There's nothing I wouldn't do for my ideals."

Don Camillo handed back the certificate.

"You're two donkeys," he said calmly. Then, when the baby smiled, he corrected himself: "Two donkeys and a half."

Smilzo turned round at the door and raised a clenched fist in salute.

"There'll always be a place on the gallows for those who run down the people," he said gravely.

"You'd better hang your hat on it then, so as to reserve a place for yourself!" answered Don Camillo.

"The election we lost was just a passing phase," said Smilzo. "We have come from very far and we still have far to go. Farewell, citizen priest."

OUT OF THE NIGHT

FOR SOME unknown reason Don Camillo had fallen into the habit of waking up in the middle of the night. He could hear nothing out of the ordinary, and yet he felt sure that there was something wrong. Finally, one night he heard a scuffling noise outside and, looking out of the window, he saw a shadow moving about near the small side door of the church, below the tower. He must have made a noise, for the shadow slipped away. But the next night Don Camillo was better prepared. He left the window slightly open and laid his shotgun on the sill. Then at the last minute he gave up this plan.

"If it's someone trying to break into the church, then he isn't after me. That is, unless he's trying to place a time bomb inside."

This was a possibility, but one shouldn't impugn a stranger's intentions, even in the valley. And so Don Camillo finally decided to keep watch in the church. For three nights he played sentry in vain, and on the fourth night, when he was just about to give the whole thing up, he heard someone scraping at the lock of the side door. He kept perfectly still, and in a few minutes the lock sprang and the door slowly opened. There was no light in the church other than that given by a feeble sanctuary lamp, but Don Camillo made out the hesitant figure of a skinny young man. The man looked about him, found a ladder and cautiously raised it against the wall to the right of the altar. High along this wall were many offerings, in the form of silver hearts

240

mounted in frames and hung as tokens of gratitude for some mark of divine favour. "So that's what you're after?" Don Camillo said to himself.

He let the intruder climb halfway up the ladder before he came out of ambush, but Don Camillo was a big man and about as graceful in his movements as a division of armoured cars so he made a tremendous racket. The man leaped down and tried to reach the door, but Don Camillo seized him by the nape of the neck. Then, in order to get a better hold, he let go of the neck, caught the arms and raised them up in the air to make sure the fellow didn't carry a gun. The fellow had crumpled up completely, and even if he had had a revolver on him he wouldn't have had the strength to pull the trigger. Don Camillo carried his catch into the sacristy, where he switched on the light and looked him in the face. When he saw who it was, he let him drop like a bundle of rags to the floor and sat down in front of him.

"Smilzo, you're no good as a thief, either!"

Smilzo shrugged his shoulders.

"It's not my trade," he answered. "I didn't mean to steal."

Don Camillo laughed.

"I don't suppose it was in order to say your prayers that you let yourself into the church with a pass-key in the middle of the night and started climbing up a ladder."

"Everyone prays in his own way," Smilzo protested.

"Well, you can explain it to the police," said Don Camillo.

This last word caused Smilzo to leap up, but Don Camillo simply stretched out one paw and put him down.

"Don't you get me into trouble," said Smilzo. "Here everything is tied up with politics, and that means a mess."

"Don't worry," Don Camillo reassured him. "This is a strictly criminal affair, and the charge will be attempted burglary."

Then he yanked the limp Smilzo to his feet and searched his pockets.

"Actual burglary!" he corrected himself. "This is the real thing!" And he held up what he had found.

"It isn't burglary at all," said Smilzo. "That belongs to me, and I paid for it with my own money."

The object was a votive offering, a frame with a silver heart inside. Obviously it was brand new, but Don Camillo found it difficult to believe Smilzo's story and dragged him over to the wall where the ladder was still standing. Sure enough, nothing was missing. The offerings formed a perfect rectangle and the absence of even a single one would have been noticed. Don Camillo examined the offering he had found in Smilzo's pocket. The heart was of sterling silver and carefully framed.

"Well then, what's it all about?" he asked. "How can you explain?"

Smilzo shrugged his shoulders.

"Gratitude is a good thing, but politics are filthy. I promised that if a certain deal came off, I'd offer one of these things to God. But since the Party and the Vatican are at swords' points, I couldn't afford to be seen. People might talk, because everyone knows you priests start them talking. Yes, when you warmongers . . ."

"Drop that," Don Camillo interrupted. "I know that whole rigmarole by heart. Let's stick to our present business. If you didn't want to be seen, you could have sent somebody. Why did you turn it into a detective story?"

Smilzo puffed up his chest.

"We who come from the people always keep our word, even in matters of religion. I had promised to offer this thing in person and so I brought it. Now I shall hand it over to you."

In the valley close to the shore of the river they're all a little queer in the head, and after a few moments of reflection, Don Camillo gave up and threw out his arms.

"Very well," he said, "here's a receipt, and let's forget about it."

Smilzo slipped away from the foot Don Camillo had ready for him and called from the door:

"If you priests get through another year without being swept away by the rising tide of the people's revolution, you can thank God with one of these things ten feet square!"

Don Camillo was left with the silver heart in his hand, and took it to the altar to show to the Lord.

"Lord, these people require understanding," he said. "They're less complex than one might think. They're simple, primitive souls, and even when they do something good they have to be violent about it. There are many things which we must forgive them."

"We must forgive them, indeed, Don Camillo," said the Lord with a sigh.

Don Camillo was sleepy.

"I'll hang this up and not think about it any more until tomorrow," he said to himself. And he climbed up on the ladder and hung it just under the bottom row. Then he pulled out the nail he had just driven in and changed the location. "I'd better place it beside the one given by his wife. Whom God has joined together let no man put asunder, either in God's house or the Devil's."

Three months before, Smilzo's wife, Moretta, had been very ill, and since it seemed that the Party couldn't heal her, she had turned to God. After an almost miraculous cure, she had brought an offering. Now Don Camillo leaned back and admired the two identical hearts.

"There's the same sinful soul in both bodies," he mumbled, shaking his head. After he had come down from the ladder he started to leave the church, but did not get as far as the door. He stopped short and went back to the altar.

"Lord, a man breaks into a church at two o'clock in the morning in order to hang up a votive offering. It simply doesn't make sense."

He paced up and down for a few minutes, then climbed up on the ladder again. He took down the two framed hearts and examined them under the light. Then he raised his head.

"We must indeed forgive them," commented the Lord.

Smilzo appeared at the presbytery the next evening.

"I'm here about the same old story," he said with an indifferent air. "My wife's got it into her head that she must add two silver flowers to the offering she made three months ago. If you give it to me, I'll bring it back tomorrow."

"That's a good idea," said Don Camillo. "I actually have it here. Last night, when I was hanging yours beside it, I saw that some dust had got under the glass and I took it down to clean it."

He opened a drawer of his desk and took out the offering given by Smilzo's wife. Then he reached for something else and showed it to Smilzo.

"Between the wooden frame and the velvet lining I found this object. I can't imagine how it got there. Is it yours?"

The object was Smilzo's Party membership card. Smilzo put out his hand, but Don Camillo slipped it back into the drawer.

"Well, what's the game?"

"It's not so funny," said Smilzo. "Moretta was about to die. She vowed she would give a silver heart and I promised a proletarian one. When she got well I put my Party card in with her offering, but at the last minute I didn't dare to get out of the Party, so I stayed in. Now Peppone wants to check all our cards. And it's no joking matter, as it would be in Church or big business circles, where anything can be condoned for a little bribe. I'd be in serious trouble. So that's why I've got to get my card back."

Don Camillo slowly lit his cigar.

"Now the story makes sense," he said. "You had an exact duplicate of Moretta's offering made and sneaked into the church like a thief in order to switch them and rescue your Party card."

Smilzo shrugged his shoulders.

"I planned to return the offering the next day to take the place of the card, so you end up with two offerings instead of one," he said. "What use is a Party card to God, anyhow?"

Don Camillo raised his finger.

"A vow is a solemn obligation, and you vowed . . ." he said.

"I'll fulfil it when the time comes," said Smilzo. "But I can't do it just now."

He seemed to be the same limp bundle of rags as the night before. Don Camillo took out the card and gave it to him.

"This filthy thing has no place in church," he said with scorn.

Smilzo put the card carefully into his wallet.

"Render unto Caesar that which is Caesar's, unto God that which is God's, and unto the people that which is the people's," he said as a parting shot.

"And unto Smilzo that which is Smilzo's!" added Don Camillo, giving him a hearty kick in the pants.

Smilzo took it with dignity.

"Come the revolution, those who have lifted a hand against the defenceless people will be paid back with interest," he proclaimed, "even when the hand happens to be a foot!"

Don Camillo went to hang up the hearts and as he passed the altar he threw out his arms. The Lord smiled upon him.

"There are many things which we must forgive them, Don

Camillo," he said. "On the Judgment Day none of them will carry a Party card."

Meanwhile Smilzo was walking proudly toward the People's Palace with his card in his pocket, feeling at peace with both God and man. Perhaps because what he had called his "proletarian heart" wasn't in his wallet, as he imagined, but in the votive offering to the right of the altar.

Camillo, he said. "On the Judgement Day none of them will
carry a Paty card.
Meanwhile Smilzo was walking proudly toward the
People's Palace ... ... feeling at peace
with both God and man. Perhaps because what he had called
his proletarian heart ... ... in his wallet, as he imagined,
but in the voice of his ... ... heart of the altar ...

THE BICYCLE

IN THIS slice of land between the river and the highway it is
hard to imagine a time when the bicycle did not exist. Here,
in the valley, everyone from five years old to eighty rides a
bicycle. Little boys make remarkable riders because they support themselves on bent legs in the middle of the frame, and
their bicycles move in anything but a straight line, but they
do move just the same. The peasants for the most part use
women's models, and the paunchy landowners trundle along
on old-fashioned contraptions with a high seat which they
reach by means of a little step screwed on to the rear
axle.

City people's bicycles are utterly laughable. With gleaming metal gadgets, electric batteries, gears, baskets, chain-
guards, speedometers and so on, they are mere toys and leg-
exercisers. A genuine bicycle should weigh at least sixty-five
pounds; it should have lost most of its paint and at least one
pedal. All that should be left of the remaining pedal is the
shaft, rubbed smooth and shiny by the sole of the rider's
shoe. Indeed, this should be its only shiny feature. The
handlebars (with no rubber tips to them) should not be at the
conventional right angle to the wheels, but inclined at least
twelve degrees one way or the other. A genuine bicycle has
no mudguard over the rear wheel, and hanging before the
front mudguard there should be a piece of automobile tyre,
preferably red, to ward off splashes of water. A rear mudguard may be allowed when the rider is excessively disturbed
by the streak of mud that accumulates on his back during a
rainstorm. But in this case the mudguard must be split open

in such a way that the rider can brake in so-called "American style," that is by pressing his trouser turn-up against the rear wheel.

A Po Valley bicycle has no mechanical brakes and its tyres wear conspicuous patches, so protuberant as to impart to the wheels a spirited, jumping motion. In the little world a bicycle blends with the landscape; it would never try to be showy, and beside it, those dressed-up racing models are like third-rate chorus girls next to a substantial housewife. City people can't be expected to understand these things; where sentiments are concerned they are about as delicate as cows in clover. They live quite contentedly in their civic corruption, and never refer to their female poodles as bitches. They have what they call their "toilets" or "lavatories" right in the middle of the house, whereas every self-respecting country-man puts his honestly named "water-closet" in an outhouse at the far end of the courtyard. To locate this convenience next to one's eating or sleeping quarters is supposed to be a symbol of "Progress," but to leave it outdoors, where it is out of reach and lacking tiled walls and pavement, is to my mind cleaner and more truly civilized.

In the valley a bicycle is just as necessary as a pair of shoes, in fact more so. Because even if a man hasn't any shoes he can still ride a bicycle, whereas if he hasn't a bicycle he must surely travel on foot. This may hold true in the city as well, but in the city there are trams, while in the valley there are no rails of any kind, but only bicycle, motorcycle, and wagon tracks, cut every now and then by the trail of a snake that has slithered from one ditch to another.

Don Camillo had never been in business, unless it is business to buy a pound of beef or a couple of black cigars and the accompanying box of what are locally called "lightning bolts," that is, sulphur matches to be struck on the soles of one's shoes or the seat of one's trousers. But if Don Camillo had never been in business he enjoyed seeing it go on, and whenever Saturday was a fine day he mounted his bicycle and went to the weekly market at La Villa. He was interested in livestock, farm machinery, fertilizers, and sprays, and when he could buy a bag of copper sulphate with which to protect the grapevines behind the presbytery he felt just about as happy as Farmer Bidazzi with all his acres. There were all kinds of amusement stands in the market-place and the holiday atmosphere and bustling activity never failed to put him in a good humour.

On this particular Saturday, then, Don Camillo got on his old bicycle and gaily ate up the seven miles to La Villa. The market was unusually crowded and Don Camillo got more fun out of it than if it had been the yearly fair at Milan. At half-past eleven he went to get his bicycle from the spot where he had left it. He pulled it out by the handlebars and, working his way through all the confusion, started towards the narrow street leading to the open country. Here the Devil came into the picture, because Don Camillo stopped at a shop to buy some trifle, and when he came out his bicycle, which he had left leaning against the wall, had disappeared.

Don Camillo was equipped with outsize bones and muscles. From his toes to the top of his head he was as tall as an ordinary man standing on a stool, and from the top of his head to his toes he was a hand's breadth taller, which means that although other people saw him as of one height he saw himself as of another; that is, his courage was a hand's breadth greater than his considerable physical stature. Even if someone were to have pulled a shotgun on him, his blood-pressure wouldn't have gone up a single degree. But if he stumbled over a stone in the road or someone played a trick upon him, he was unnerved by the humiliation. At such times he felt almost sorry for himself and positively melancholy.

Now, with his bicycle gone, he did not make a row. He asked an old man standing near by if he had seen anyone ride off on a woman's bicycle with a green basket. And when the man said no, he touched his hat and went away. He walked by the police station, but never thought of going in. The fact that a country priest, with twenty-five lire in his pocket, had been robbed of a bicycle was a private and moral problem, and not one to be introduced into the public domain. Your rich man, to whom it is all a matter of money, may rush to report a theft. But to the poor it is a personal injustice, in the same class as striking a cripple or knocking his crutch out from under him.

Don Camillo pulled his hat down over his eyes and started to walk home. Every time he heard a cart or wagon behind him, he ducked down at the side of the road. He wanted to go home under his own steam without having to talk to anybody. And he wanted to cover the whole seven miles on foot in order to underline the thief's guilt and his own sense of injury. He walked alone through the dust and heat for a solid hour without pause, brooding over the misfortunes of a Don Camillo who seemed to him to exist quite apart from himself. At a certain point a side road came into the one along which he travelled, and he stopped to lean on the wall of a small brick bridge. Leaning up against the same wall was his bicycle. He knew every inch of it, and there was no chance of any mistake. Immediately he looked round, but no one was in sight. He touched the bicycle and tapped the handlebars with his knuckles. Yes, they were of solid metal. The nearest house was at least half a mile away and the bushes were not yet covered with enough leaves to provide a hiding-place. Finally, he looked over the wall of the bridge and saw a man sitting in the dried-up bed of the stream. The man stared up at him enquiringly.

"This bicycle is mine," Don Camillo said with a little hesitation.

"What bicycle?"

"The one here against the wall of the bridge."

"Good," said the man. "If there's a bicycle on the bridge and it's your bicycle, that's not my business."

"I was just telling you," Don Camillo said with considerable perplexity. "I didn't want there to be any muddle about it."

"Are you sure it's yours?" the man asked.

"I should say I am! It was stolen from me while I was in a shop at La Villa an hour ago. I don't know how it got here."

The man laughed.

"It must have got bored waiting and gone on ahead of you," he said.

Don Camillo threw out his arms in uncertainty.

"Are you, as a priest, able to keep a secret?" the man asked him.

"Certainly."

"Then I can tell you how the bicycle got here, because I brought it here myself."

Don Camillo opened his eyes wide.

"Did you find it?"

"Yes, I found it in front of the shop. And I took it."

"Was that your idea of a joke?" asked Don Camillo, after another moment of hesitation.

"Don't be silly!" the man protested. "Do you think that at my age I go around joking? I meant to take it for keeps. Then

249

I thought better of it and pedalled after you. I followed you up to about a mile back, then I took a short-cut, got here before you and put it right under your nose."

Don Camillo sat down on the wall and looked at the fellow below him.

"Why did you take a bicycle that wasn't yours?" he asked.

"Everyone to his own trade. You deal in souls and I deal in bicycles."

"Has that been your trade for long?"

"No; just for the last two or three months. I operate at markets and fairs, and I usually do pretty well, because a lot of these peasants have stone jars full of banknotes. This morning I had no luck, and so I took your bicycle. Then I saw you come out of the shop and go your way without telling anybody. I began to be sorry and followed you, I still don't understand exactly why. Why did you duck down every time a wagon caught up with you? Did you know I was behind you?"

"No."

"Well, I was. And if you'd accepted a lift, I'd have turned back. But since you kept on walking I had to follow."

Don Camillo shook his head. "Where are you going now?" he asked.

"Back to see if there's anything doing at La Villa."

"To see if you can lay hands on another bicycle."

"Of course."

"Then keep this one."

The man looked up at him.

"Not on your life, Father. Not even if it were made of solid gold. It would be on my conscience and ruin my career. I prefer to stay clear of the clergy."

Don Camillo asked if he had had anything to eat, and the man said no.

"Then come and eat something with me."

A wagon came by, and in it rode a peasant called Brelli.

"Come along, you wretch!" said Don Camillo. "You take the bicycle and I'll go in the wagon."

Then he stopped Brelli and told him that he had a pain in his leg. The man came up from below the bridge. He was so angry that he threw his cap on the ground and cursed a large number of saints before he got on the bicycle.

Don Camillo had had the meal ready for ten minutes

by the time the bicycle thief arrived at the presbytery.

"There's only bread, sausage, cheese, and a drop of wine," said the priest. "I hope that's enough for you."

"Don't worry, Father," said the man. "I've taken care of that." And he put a chicken on the table.

"The creature was crossing the road and I accidentally ran over it," he explained. "I didn't want to leave it to die there, and so I put an end to its pain. . . . Don't look at me like that, Father. I'm sure that if you cook it properly, God will forgive you."

Don Camillo cooked the chicken and brought out a bottle of special wine. After an hour or so, the man said he must be about his business, but there was a worried look on his face.

"I don't know how I can go back to stealing bicycles," he sighed. "You've demoralized me completely."

"Have you a family?" Don Camillo asked him.

"No, I'm all alone."

"Then I'll take you on as a bell-ringer. Mine just went away two days ago."

"But I don't know how to ring bells."

"A man who knows how to steal bicycles won't find that hard to learn."

And he was bell-ringer from that day on.

THE PRODIGAL SON

ONE DAY Don Camillo was in the church talking things over
with the Lord, and at a certain point he said:

"Lord, too many things in this world are out of joint."

"I don't see it in that way," the Lord answered. "Man may
be out of joint, but the rest of the universe works pretty
well."

Don Camillo paced up and down and then stopped again
in front of the altar.

"Lord," he said, "if I were to start counting: one, two,
three, four, five, six, seven, and count for a million years,
should I ever come to a point where there were no more
numbers?"

"Never," said the Lord. "You remind me of the man who
drew a big circle on the ground and began to walk round it,
saying: 'I want to see how long it will take me to get to the
end.' So I must tell you: 'No, you'd never come to such a
point.'"

In his imagination, Don Camillo was walking round the
circle and feeling the breathlessness that must stem from a
first glance into infinity.

"I still say that numbers must be finite," he insisted.
"Only God is infinite and eternal, and numbers can't claim
to have the attributes of God."

"What have you got against numbers?" the Lord asked
him.

"Why, that numbers are what have put men out of joint.
Having discovered numbers, they've proceeded to deify
them."

When Don Camillo got an idea into his head, there was no easy exit for it. He locked the main door of the church for the night, paced up and down again, and then came back to the altar.

"Perhaps, Lord, men's reliance upon the magic of numbers is just a desperate attempt to justify their existence as thinking beings." He remained uneasily silent for a minute and then went on: "Lord, are ideas finite? Are there new ideas in reserve or have men thought of everything there is to be thought?"

"Don Camillo, what do you mean by ideas?"

"As a poor country priest, all I can say is that ideas are lamps shining through the night of human ignorance and lighting up some new aspect of the greatness of the Creator."

The Lord was touched.

"Poor country priest," He said, "you're not so far from right. Once a hundred men were shut into an enormous dark room, each one of them with an unlit lamp. One of them managed to light his lamp, and so they could all see one another and get to know one another. As the rest lit their lamps, more and more of the objects around them came into view, until finally everything in the room stood out as good and beautiful. Now, follow me closely, Don Camillo. There were a hundred lamps, only one idea: yet it took the light of all the lamps to reveal the details of everything in the room. Every flame was the hundredth part of one great idea, one great light, the idea of the existence and majesty of the Creator. It was as if a man had broken a statuette into a hundred pieces and given one piece to each of a hundred men. The hundred men groped for one another and tried to fit the fragments together, making thousands of misshapen figures until at last they joined them properly. I repeat, Don Camillo, that every man lit his own lamp and the light of the hundred lamps together was Truth and Revelation. This should have satisfied them. But each man thought that the beauty of the objects he saw around him was due to the light of his own lamp, which had brought them out of the darkness. Some men stopped to worship their own lamps, and others wandered off in various directions, until the great light was broken up into a hundred flames, each one of which could illuminate only a fraction of the truth. And so you see, Don Camillo, that the hundred lamps must come together again in order to find the true light. To-day men wander mistrustfully about, each one in the light of his own lamp, with an area of melancholy darkness all around him, clinging to the slightest detail of whatever object he can illuminate by himself. And so I say that ideas do not exist; there is only one Idea, one Truth with a hundred facets. Ideas are neither finite nor finished, because there is only this one and eternal Idea. But men must join their fellows again like those in the enormous room."

Don Camillo threw out his arms.

"There's no going back," he sighed. "To-day men use the oil of their lamps to grease their filthy machines and machine guns."

"In the Kingdom of Heaven," the Lord said, "oil is so bountiful it runs in rivers."

In the presbytery Don Camillo found Brusco waiting. Brusco was Peppone's right-hand man, a big fellow who opened his mouth only when he had something important to say. His daily average of spoken words was perhaps the lowest in the village.

"Somebody must be dead. Who is it?" Don Camillo asked him.

"Nobody. But I'm in trouble."

"Did you kill somebody by mistake?"

"No, it's about my son."

"Which one? Giuseppe?"

"No, none of the eight that are here at home. The one that's been in Sicily all these years."

Don Camillo remembered that in 1938 one of Brusco's sisters, who had married a man with land holdings in Sicily, had come to visit him. Before going home she had lined up Brusco's nine children.

"Can I have one?" she asked him.

"Take whichever one you like best."

"I'll take the least dirty of the lot."

And her choice fell upon Cecotto, who happened to have just washed his face. He was about eight years old and somehow different from the rest.

"Let's be quite frank if we want to stay friends," said Brusco's sister. "I'll take him and bring him up and you'll never see him again."

Brusco's wife had just died, and to be relieved of responsibility for one of his nine children was a blessing from

Heaven. He nodded assent and only when his sister was at the door did he tug at her sleeve and say:

"Do you mind taking Giuseppe instead?"

"I wouldn't have him even as a gift," she answered, as if she had paid hard cash for Cecotto.

Don Camillo remembered the whole story.

"Well then?" he asked.

"I haven't seen him for twelve years," said Brusco, "but he's always written to me, and now he says he's coming home for a visit."

Don Camillo looked at him hard.

"Brusco, has the Five-year Plan gone to your head? Is it such a misfortune to see your son? Are you Reds ashamed of your own children?"

"No, I'm not ashamed even of Giuseppe, who's one of the biggest cowards I've ever known. It's my fault, not his, if he's turned out the way he has. This is an entirely different matter. In Sicily they're all reactionaries of one kind or another: barons, landowners, priests and so on. Of course, a son's a son, no matter what he does. But if he comes here I'll fall into disgrace with the Party. I should have let the Party know about the whole situation. . . ."

Don Camillo could hold himself back no longer.

"Come on and let the cat out of the bag!" he exclaimed. "What has the poor fellow done?"

Brusco lowered his head.

"They sent him to school . . ." he muttered.

"Well, you're not ashamed of him for that, are you?"

"No, but he's studying for the priesthood."

Don Camillo couldn't help laughing.

"So your son's a priest! That's a good one! A priest!"

"Pretty nearly one. . . . But you needn't rub it in."

Don Camillo had never heard Brusco speak in just this tone of voice. He waited to hear more.

"If he comes here, and Peppone catches on, he'll kill me. And since the boy's a priest, or nearly, I don't want him to know that I'm on the other side. You priests understand one another. And if you can't think of something, I'm done for. He's arriving at eight o'clock to-morrow."

"All right. Let me sleep on it."

Brusco had never thanked anyone in his life.

"I'll make it up to you," he muttered. And he added, from

the door: "I have the worst luck! With all the reactionaries there are around, why did I have to have a priest for a son?"

Don Camillo was not in the least discomfited.

"With all the rogues there are available, why should a poor priest be cursed with a Communist father?"

Brusco shook his head.

"Everyone has his own troubles," he said with a bitter sigh.

SHOTGUN WEDDING

Whenever Don Camillo saw old man Rocchi come to the church or the presbytery he grumbled to himself: "Here's the commissar." For old man Rocchi was the leader of the watchdogs who appoint themselves in every parish to scrutinize the conduct of the priest, in church and out of it, and to write letters of protest to the bishop when they find it shocking or even improper. Of course the old man never missed a single service, and since he and his family occupied one of the front pews he followed everything Don Camillo said and did, and would turn to his wife in the middle of Mass with: "He's skipped something," or: "To-day he's not got his wits about him," or: "Don Camillo isn't what he used to be." And he would go to the presbytery afterwards to comment upon the sermon and give Don Camillo some sound advice.

Don Camillo wasn't the type to worry about such things, but it was a nuisance to feel old Rocchi's eyes constantly upon him, and whenever he had to blow his nose in the middle of Mass he raised his eyes to Christ on the cross above the altar and silently prayed: "Lord, help me blow my nose in a manner that will not cause a scandal!" For Rocchi was a great stickler for form. More than once he had remarked: "When the priest at Treville has to blow his nose in the middle of Mass, nobody knows it, but this one sounds like a trumpet call to the Last Judgment."

That is the kind of a man Rocchi was, and if such men

exist in the world it must mean that they have a place to fill in it. He had three sons and one daughter, Paolina, who was the most virtuous and most beautiful girl in the village. And it was Paolina who startled Don Camillo almost out of his wits one day in the confessional.

"I can't grant you absolution before you do what you are supposed to," he told her.

"I know," said the girl.

This is the sort of thing that happens in every village, and in order to understand it one really has to have lived in one of the low houses in the broad valley and to have seen the moon rise like a great red ball over the bank of the river. There is no visible movement in the valley and a stranger may have the idea that nothing ever happens along the deserted river banks, that nothing *could* happen in the red and blue houses. Yet more things happen there than up in the mountains or in the big city. For the blazing summer sun gets into people's veins, and that big red moon is utterly unlike the pale satellite they see in other places; it blazes just like the sun, inflaming the imaginations of the living and the bones of the dead. Even in winter, when the valley is filled with cold and fog, the heat stored up during the summer is so great that people's imaginations aren't cooled off sufficiently to see things as they actually are. That is why every now and then a shotgun peeps out of a thicket or a girl does something she ought not to.

Paolina went home, and when the family had finished saying the evening rosary she stepped up to her father.

"Father, I must have a talk with you," she said.

The others went their various ways and Paolina and her father were left beside the fire.

"What's it all about?" asked the old man suspiciously.

"It's time to think about my getting married."

"Don't you bother your head about that. When the time comes, we'll find the right sort of fellow."

"The time has already come, Father, and I've found him."

The old man opened his eyes wide.

"Go straight to bed, and don't let me hear you talk of such things again!" he ordered.

"Very well," said the girl, "but you'll hear other people talking about them."

258

"Have you given some cause for scandal?" asked the horrified father.

"No, but the scandal will come out. It's not something that can be concealed."

Rocchi took hold of the first thing that came to hand, which happened to be a broken broomstick. The girl crouched in a corner, hiding her head, and received a rain of blows upon her back. Luckily, the broomstick broke again and her father quietened down.

"If you're so unlucky as to be still alive, get up," he told her. "Does anyone know about it?"

"*He* knows . . ." murmured the girl, causing the old man to lose his head again and start to beat her with a stick taken from a bundle of faggots by the fire. "And so does Don Camillo," she added. "He wouldn't grant me absolution." Again the old man took it out on her. Finally she got in another word: "If you kill me, it will be an even worse scandal," she said, and that calmed him.

"Who's the man?" he asked.

"Falchetto," she answered.

She would have produced less of an effect if she had named Beelzebub in person. Falchetto was the nickname of Gigi Bariga, one of the most stalwart of Peppone's henchmen. He was the intellectual member of the gang, the one who wrote speeches, organized rallies and explained the Party directives. Because he understood more than the others, he was the unholiest of them all. The girl had taken so much punishment by now that the old man pushed her on to a couch and sat down beside her.

"You've beaten me enough," she said. "If you touch me again, I'll call for help and tell everybody. I have to protect the life of my child."

At eleven o'clock that night the old man gave in to his fatigue.

"I can't kill you, and in the state you're in, you can't very well enter a convent," he said. "Marry, then, and be damned, both of you."

When Falchetto saw the effects of Paolina's beating his jaw dropped.

"We must get married," she said, "or this will be the death of me."

"Of course!" said Falchetto. "That's what I've been asking

259

you all along. Any moment, if you give the word, Paolina."

It was no use thinking of marriage at a quarter to one in the morning, but words exchanged at the garden gate, before the fields covered with snow, had a certain value and significance.

"Have you told your father everything?" Falchetto asked.

She did not answer, and Falchetto realized that it was a stupid question.

"I'll take my tommy-gun and shoot your entire family," he exclaimed. "I'll . . ."

"There's no need to shoot. All we have to do is to go and get the priest's permission."

Falchetto stepped back.

"You know I can't do that," he said. "Just think of my position. We can go to the Mayor."

The girl pulled her shawl around her

"No, never," she said. "I don't care about what may happen. Either we are married like Christians or else I'll never see you again."

"Paolina! . . ." Falchetto implored her, but she had already slipped through the gate in the opposite direction from that which she had so often taken before.

Paolina stayed in bed for two days, and on the third day her father came up to her room.

"You saw him the other evening," he said. "I happen to know."

"So do I."

"Well, then?"

"There's no way out. He won't have a Christian wedding. And I say a Christian wedding or nothing at all."

The old man shouted and stamped his feet. Then he left his daughter, threw his overcoat over his shoulders and went out. And a few minutes later Don Camillo had a difficult problem before him.

"Father, you already know the story," said Rocchi.

"I do. Children need looking after. It's a parent's job to give them some moral principles."

Rocchi was properly put in his place, and he would gladly have strangled Don Camillo.

"I've consented to the marriage, but the rascal won't have anything to do with the Church."

"That doesn't surprise me."

"I've come to ask you this: is it more scandalous for a girl in my daughter's condition to marry outside the Church or not to marry at all?"

Don Camillo shook his head.

"This isn't a question of scandal. It's a question of good or evil. We must consider the unborn child."

"All I care about is to get them married and let them be damned!" said Rocchi.

"Then why do you ask for my advice? If all you care about is to get them married, let them marry as they please."

"But she says if she can't have a church wedding she'll have none at all," groaned the unhappy father.

Don Camillo smiled.

"You ought to be proud of your daughter. Two wrongs don't make a right. I say she has a head on her shoulders and you ought to be proud of her."

"I'll have to kill her, that's all," Rocchi shouted as he left the presbytery.

"You don't expect me to argue the girl out of a church wedding, do you?" Don Camillo shouted back after him.

During the night Paolina heard a hail of pebbles against her window and finally her resistance was overcome and she went down. Falchetto was waiting, and when she saw his face she burst into tears.

"I've left the Party," he told her. "To-morrow they'll get out an announcement of my expulsion. Peppone wanted me to write it myself."

The girl went closer to him.

"Did he beat you?" she asked.

"I thought he'd never stop," Falchetto admitted. "When are we going to get married?"

"Any moment, if you give the word," she said. And her impulse was just as foolish as his, because it was almost one o'clock in the morning and poor Falchetto had one eye as black as a lump of coal.

"I'll talk to the priest about it to-morrow," he said. "But I won't go near the Town Hall. I don't want to see Peppone."

He touched his black eye and Paolina put a hand on his shoulder.

"We'll go to the Mayor, too," she said. "I'll be there to stick up for you."

Paolina went early the next morning to Don Camillo.

"You can grant me absolution," she told him. "I didn't do any of the things I confessed to you. My only sin is to have told you a big lie."

Don Camillo was puzzled, but she quickly explained.

"If I hadn't made up that story, my father would never have let me marry Falchetto."

Don Camillo shook his head.

"Don't tell him the truth at this point," he advised her, secretly thinking that old man Rocchi had earned it.

"No, I won't tell him, not even after we're married," said the girl. "He beat me just as hard as if what I told him had been true."

"That's what I say," chimed in Don Camillo. "Such a beating shouldn't be given in vain."

As he passed by the altar, the Lord frowned down at him.

"Lord," said Don Camillo, "Whosoever shall exalt himself shall be humbled and he that shall humble himself shall be exalted."

"Don Camillo," said the Lord, "for some time now you've been skating on thin ice."

"With God's help, no ice is too thin," said Don Camillo. "This wedding will be worth a dozen of the usual kind."

And so it was.

SEEDS OF HATE

PEPPONE POPPED up in front of Don Camillo without any warning, followed by Smilzo, Bigio, Brusco, and Lungo. It looked like revenge or intimidation, and Don Camillo's first thought was of Falchetto, who had left the Party to marry Rocchi's daughter. "They're furious because they imagine I had something to do with it," he said to himself. But the gang wasn't thinking of Falchetto at all.

"There's no God in this, and no politics either," said Peppone, puffing like a steam engine on the Mulino Nuovo hill. "This is a patriotic matter. I'm here in my capacity of citizen Mayor and you in your capacity of citizen priest."

Don Camillo threw out his arms in welcome.

"Speak, citizen Mayor! The citizen priest is all ears."

Peppone stood in front of the table where Don Camillo was sitting, while his followers silently lined up behind him with their legs wide apart and their arms crossed over their chests.

"The Nemesis of History . . ." Peppone began, somewhat to Don Camillo's alarm, ". . . and not only the Nemesis of History but the Nemesis of Geography as well, and if that isn't enough. . . ."

"I think it *is* enough," said Don Camillo, feeling reassured by the addition of Geography. "Just tell me what's it's all about."

Peppone turned toward his followers with an indignant and ironical smile.

"They claim independence and home rule," he said, "and yet they don't know what's going on a mere fifty yards away."

"They're still living in the egotistical Middle Ages," said Smilzo unctuously. "*Cicero pro domo sua* and let the people eat cake!"

Don Camillo looked up at him.

"Are they teaching you Latin now?" he asked.

"Why not?" Smilzo retorted. "Do you think you have a monopoly on culture?"

But Peppone interrupted this exchange.

"They're a bunch of unpatriotic scoundrels, who want to usurp the sacred rights of the people by setting up an utterly unfounded claim to independence. I'm speaking of those wretched citizens of Fontanile, who want to secede from our township and set up a village administration of their own. We must nip their attempt in the bud by a manifesto outlining from A to Z the historical and geographical Nemesis which makes this town their capital city and their miserable village a mere suburb or dependency. . . ."

The discovery of what Peppone meant by "historical and geographical Nemesis" was not completely reassuring after all. Don Camillo knew his river valley and was aware of the fact that when two of its communities started to bicker, even on the basis of such a big word as "Nemesis," it was no laughing matter. Between these two in particular there were several old unsettled grudges. And for some time the inhabitants of Fontanile had had this home-rule bee in their bonnets. They had struck the first blow in 1902, when three or four groups of four houses each had put together the money to erect a public building, complete with arcade, sweeping stairway, clock tower and coat-of-arms over the door. This was to be the Town Hall. Then there was such high feeling about it that the police were called in and several citizens went to jail. That was as far as they got then. But the building remained and it was never put to any other use. They tried again in 1920, just after the First World War, but with no more success. And this was a third attempt. Don Camillo proceeded to feel his way cautiously.

"Have you tried talking to them about it?" he asked.

"Me talk to them?" shouted Peppone. "The only language I can make them understand is the tommy-gun."

"It doesn't seem as if negotiations would get very far on that basis," observed Don Camillo.

Peppone couldn't have been any angrier if his status had been lowered to that of a feudal serf.

"We'll act in strictly democratic fashion," he said with painful deliberation. "We'll draw up a statement explaining the historical and geographical Nemesis, and if they're too dense to understand it...."

Here Peppone paused, and Bigio, who was the best balanced of the gang, put in sombrely: "If they don't understand, we'll teach them a real lesson."

When the slow-going Bigio spoke in these terms, it meant that things were close to the boiling-point. Don Camillo tried another tack.

"If they want to secede, why not let them do it? What do you care?"

"It doesn't matter to me personally," shouted Peppone, "but it's an attack on the sovereignty of the people. This is the seat of the township. If we lose Fontanile and some of the territory beyond La Rocchetta, what's left? What sort of a one-horse place would this be? Are you by any chance unpatriotic?"

Don Camillo sighed.

"Why turn it into a tragedy? Fontanile has never been allowed to set itself up as an independent village, has it? Why should the authorities allow it to do so now? There's no change in the situation."

Peppone brought his fist down on the table.

"That's what *you* say!" he shouted ironically. "There's a political factor involved. Our Party is entrenched in the Town Hall and over at Fontanile they're all reactionaries. So the national Government would be glad to see some of our land and our people fall under a different administration!"

Don Camillo looked at him hard.

"You're the citizen Mayor and in politics up to your ears, so you ought to know. As a mere citizen priest, I'm in the dark."

Smilzo came forward and pointed an accusing finger at him. "You hireling of the Americans!" he said cuttingly.

Don Camillo shrugged his shoulders.

"Well, what are we going to do?" he asked Peppone.

"The first thing is to draw up a manifesto embodying our historical, geographical and economic arguments."

"And where am I to find them?" asked Don Camillo.

"That's up to you. Didn't they teach you anything at the seminary except how to make propaganda for America? . . . After that we'll see. If they drop their plan, all right; if they don't, we'll send them an *intimatum* to the effect that either they drop it or else . . . or else the will of the people shall decide!"

"God's will, you mean," Don Camillo corrected him.

"God doesn't come into this; we've said that already," replied Peppone. "But I'll take care of the *intimatum,* anyhow."

Don Camillo spent half the night putting together a manifesto of the reasons why Fontanile should not set itself up as an independent village. The hardest part was to reconcile the conflicting points of view and not to tread on anybody's toes. Finally, the manifesto was sent to the printer and then a group of young men went to paste it up at Fontanile.

At noon the next day a box was delivered to Peppone at the Town Hall. It contained one of the posters that had been pasted up at Fontanile the night before, and rolled up inside was something extremely unpleasant. Peppone wrapped it up again and hurried over to the presbytery, where he unfolded it in front of Don Camillo.

"Here is the answer from Fontanile," he said.

"Very well," said Don Camillo. "I wrote the statement, so that's meant for me. Leave it here and don't think about it any more."

Peppone shook his head. He folded it up again and started to go silently away. But at the door he turned round.

"Citizen priest," he said, "you'll soon have plenty of work to do."

Don Camillo was so taken aback that he could find nothing to answer. Peppone's words had transfixed him with fear.

"Lord," he said to the Lord at the altar. "Haven't war and politics put enough hate into these men's hearts?"

"Unfortunately, they can always find room for more," sighed the Lord.

WAR OF SECESSION

MESSENGERS WERE coming and going at the Town Hall all day long, and Don Camillo could not guess what those devils were up to, especially as everybody claimed not to know. But towards nine o'clock in the evening, when he was preparing to go to bed, someone knocked at the shutter of the window on the church square. It was Smilzo, who said at once: "You've got to come to the Town Hall immediately. Hurry up, because the people have no time to wait upon the convenience of the clergy."

Smilzo was even more peremptory than usual. He felt that he could be so quite safely with the grating of the window between Don Camillo and himself, and furthermore his tone of voice made plain that he believed that he was entrusted with an unusually important mission.

"What do you mean by the people?" Don Camillo asked him. "People like yourself?"

"I didn't come here for a political discussion. If you're afraid to come out of your lair, that's another matter."

Don Camillo threw on his coat and picked up an umbrella, because just for a change it was raining.

"May I be told what's going on?" he asked on the way.

"It's not something that can be discussed in the street," said Smilzo. "That's just as if I were to ask you about the latest secret instructions sent you by the Pope."

"Leave the Pope alone," said Don Camillo, "or I'll break this umbrella over your head. The Pope has nothing to do with it."

"Whether he does or doesn't is something that we shall see about later, come the revolution," said Smilzo. "But never mind about that just now. You'll see what's going on when we reach the Town Hall."

Before they arrived a sentry halted them.

"Give the password," said a voice.

"*Venezia,*" said Smilzo.

"*Milano,*" came the reply.

Once they were past, Don Camillo asked what was the meaning of all this nonsense, but Smilzo said that it wasn't nonsense at all.

"It's war," he maintained.

When they walked into the Council room, Don Camillo was very much surprised. The place was full of people, and not people to be dismissed as unimportant, either. All the notables of the village were there, representing all shades of political opinion, with nobody missing. There was a sepulchral silence, and evidently they were waiting for Don Camillo, for when he came in they made way before him. Then Peppone stood up and gave an explanation.

"Father," he said, "at this tragic time, when our country is in danger, you see here before you our most representative citizens, without distinction of party; farmers, workers, landowners, and shopkeepers, all joined in one faith. The attempt of an irresponsible group to trespass on our sacred rights must be defeated at any cost whatsoever . . . and so far I believe we all agree."

"Good," was the crowd's unanimous reply.

"In order to do away with any suspicion of party intrigue, the representatives of every faction have decided to choose someone who shall impartially pass opinion upon every decision made by the Committee for Public Safety for the defence of the village. By a secret ballot you were elected, and so, overcoming our political differences, we call upon you to be a member of the Committee in the role of neutral observer."

"I accept," said Don Camillo, looking around him, and the crowd applauded him loudly.

"We welcome your help. Here, then, is the situation. The people of Fontanile have answered our statement, duly approved by the representative of the Vatican here present, in an insulting and anti-democratic manner. In short, they have defied their capital city."

An angry murmur arose from the audience.

"Yes!" shouted Peppone. "On historical, geographical, and economic grounds we may call our village the spiritual 'capital' of the whole township, a capital one and indivisible forever."

"Well spoken!" called the crowd.

Peppone had now swung into top gear and was going full speed ahead:

"Strengthened by this gathering's lofty spirit of concord and comprehension, we say that we will not tolerate the 'home-rulers' of Fontanile in their attempt to secede from our township and set up a village administration of their own. We suggest sending them an *intimatum* to say: Either drop the idea or we'll make you drop it. Because democracy is all very well, but when you're dealing with a bunch of people like those at Fontanile...."

Peppone was so swollen with rage that he looked even bigger and stronger than usual and his audience stared at him in fascination. Unfortunately, with the word "Fontanile" his vocabulary suddenly gave out and he could not find another word to say. He was standing on a two-inch-thick telephone book, and he seized upon this and slowly twisted it in his hands until it was torn in two. In the river valley an argument of this kind is invariably decisive. The assembly let out a yell of enthusiasm, and when Peppone threw the two parts of the book on the table before him, crying: "And this is our *intimatum*!" the applause threatened to bring down the ceiling. When quiet once more prevailed, Peppone turned to Don Camillo.

"Will the neutral observer give us the benefit of his opinion?"

Don Camillo got up and said calmly but in a loud voice: "My opinion is that you're all crazy."

His words were like an icy wind, and a heavy silence fell over the gathering.

"You've lost all sense of reality and proportion," Don Camillo continued. "It's as if you were building a skyscraper on a six-inch foundation, with the result that the whole thing will topple down on you. It isn't a question of sending ultimatums or tearing telephone books in two. We must use our heads, and if we do so it is clear that there's no use in even discussing the matter until the authorities give Fontanile permission to secede."

"But we're the authorities," shouted Peppone. "This is a matter for our concern."

Looking at the assembly, Don Camillo saw old man Rocchi rise from his seat in the front row.

"We agree, Father," said Rocchi, "that we should act calmly and not dramatize the situation. But if we wait for the authorities to give their permission, then our protest will be a revolt against the Government. We must, in orderly fashion, of course, prevent Fontanile from putting in any request for home rule. I think the Mayor is wrong to speak of using force, but the substance of what he says is right."

"Good!" came voices from the assembly. "The Mayor has the right idea, even if we belong to different political parties. Politics don't come into this at all; it's the welfare of the village that's at stake. And let's be frank. We know what sort of people they are in Fontanile, and this is something we can't endure."

Peppone shot a triumphant glance at Don Camillo and Don Camillo threw out his arms in dismay.

"It's a sad fact," he said, "but people seem to agree only when it comes to doing something very foolish. But before carrying things too far, the two parties to the dispute must have a discussion. We must send a committee over to Fontanile."

"Of course," said Rocchi, and all the others nodded assent.

Peppone had no more telephone books to which he could give a "twister," but he took something out of the drawer of the table. This was the famous and insulting answer from Fontanile.

"How can you 'discuss' anything with people like these?" he asked.

At that the crowd became very restless.

"Even an *intimatum* would be too good for the likes of them," said Farmer Sacchini, shaking his big stick. "This is the only language they can understand."

Don Camillo felt himself entirely alone.

"It's no use my asking God to illuminate your minds," he cried, "because it's plain you haven't any. But I say that you simply can't do any of these things you proposed."

"Who'll stop us?" asked Peppone.

"I will," said Don Camillo. He went resolutely to the door and then turned round while he put up his umbrella. "I'm

270

going straight to the police sergeant," he said. "That may change your plans."

"You spy!" Peppone shouted, pointing an accusing finger at him from the platform. The crowd formed a wall between Don Camillo and Peppone, and the priest had no alternative but to go straight to the police station.

The forces of the law, consisting of the sergeant and four men, were put on watch, half at Fontanile and half in the "capital city." The sergeant, since he could not be split in two, rode on his bicycle to reinforce first one squad and then the other. Three days went by and nothing happened.

"It's clear that they've thought better of it," the sergeant said to Don Camillo. "They seem to have calmed down."

"Here's hoping God gave them minds and then illuminated them," Don Camillo replied without much conviction.

But on the afternoon of the fourth day an ugly incident took place at a big farm known as Case Nuove. A group of unemployed farm labourers swarmed over the place on bicycles, saying that they must be given work. Among other things, their claim was a stupid one, for it had rained for ten days in succession and the only work anyone could do in the fields was to walk a couple of yards and then sink up to the hips in mud. Obviously it was a trouble-making political manoeuvre. But for fear the farmer or some of his family might pull out a shotgun, the sergeant had to dispatch his men to the spot. Toward evening Don Camillo went to look the situation over. The farm had been cleared of intruders, and these were wandering about in small groups not far away.

"If we leave, they'll be back in five minutes and start more trouble," said the sergeant. "Night is coming, and that's a tricky time where something like this is concerned."

Don Camillo ran into one of the groups on his way home and recognized among it the tailor from Molinetto.

"Have you changed your trade," the priest asked him, "and turned into an unemployed farm labourer?"

"If people weren't so inquisitive, it would be a very fine thing," grumbled the tailor.

A little farther on Don Camillo met the old postman riding a bicycle, with a tool-box slung round his shoulder, which served him for his supplementary job as linesman for the telephone and telegraph systems. The priest was surprised to see him out so late, but the old man explained:

"I'm having a look round. The storm must have brought down a wire somewhere. Neither the telephone nor the telegraph is working."

Instead of going back to the presbytery, Don Camillo went to Brelli's house. He wrote a hurried note and gave it to the youngest boy to deliver.

"Take your motorcycle and get this to the parish priest at Villetta as fast as you can. It's a matter of life and death."

The boy was off like a flash. An hour later he came back to report:

"The priest said he'd telephone right away."

The river was swollen with rain and pressing against its banks. So were all the tributaries that poured into it across the plain. In normal weather these streams are ridiculous affairs. Either their beds are completely dry or else they contain only a few spoonfuls of water and one wonders why people with any sense should throw away money building up banks on either side. But they are not only ridiculous; they are unpredictable as well, like an ordinarily temperate man who once in a while goes out and gets . . . well, dead drunk is too mild a phrase for it. When these valley streams rise, they are so many Mississippis, with the water surging halfway up their banks and over. Now, after the prolonged storm, even the tiniest streams were frighteningly high and people went along the banks measuring their height with a stick. And the water continued to rise.

Fontanile was divided from the "capital" by just such a stream, and for twenty years no one had seen so much water in it. Night had fallen, but Don Camillo paced nervously up and down the road leading along the bank. His nervousness did not pass until he heard the brakes of a big car. The car was full of policemen, and with their arrival Don Camillo went back to the presbytery and hung his shotgun on the wall. After supper Peppone came to see him, looking very glum.

"Did you call the police?" he asked Don Camillo.

"Of course I did, after you staged that diversion at Case Nuove in order to have a free hand for your other mischief; yes, and after you cut the telephone and telegraph wires, too."

Peppone looked at him scornfully.

"You're a traitor!" he said. "You asked for foreign aid. A man without a country, that's what you are!"

This was such a wild accusation that Don Camillo was left gaping. But Peppone had still more to say.

"You're positively Godless!" he exclaimed. "But your police won't get anywhere. In two minutes God's justice will triumph!"

Don Camillo leaped to his feet, but before he could say a word there was a loud roar in the distance.

"The bank at Fontanile has given way," Peppone explained. "A concealed wire attached to a mine did the job. Now that Fontanile is flooded, they can found a little Venice if they want to!"

Don Camillo grabbed Peppone by the neck, but before he could squeeze it there came another roar, followed by a splash of water. A moment later the presbytery was flooded. When the water had reached the two men's belts it stopped rising.

"Do you see what murderers they are?" Peppone shouted. "So this was their little plan!"

Don Camillo looked sadly at the liquid mess, then shook his head and sighed.

"Dear God, if this is the beginning of the Great Flood, then I bless You for wiping this idiotic human race off the face of the globe."

But Peppone didn't see it the same way.

"*Navigare necessariorum est!*" he shouted, wading toward the door. "Italy's manifest destiny is on the seven seas!"

"Then all we have to do is wait for low tide," concluded Don Camillo philosophically.

There were three feet of water in the church, and when the candles were lit on the altar they cast the reflection of their flames into the water.

"Lord," said Don Camillo to the crucified Christ, "I beg your forgiveness, but if I were to kneel down, I'd be up to my neck in water."

"Then remain standing, Don Camillo," the Lord answered, smiling.

BIANCO

Nowadays the people of the Po River Valley go to the city by bus, in one of those cursed modern machines where a human being travels like a trunk, and even if he is sick at his stomach he cannot budge from his seat. And during the winter, when there is a heavy fog or a treacherous coating of ice on the roads, he risks, at the very least, ending up in a ditch.

And to think that once upon a time there was a real steam train—even though it was only a very small one, with no more than a couple of carriages—which ran smoothly along its track through fog and ice! Until one fine day a city slicker discovered that it was out of date and substituted for its fidelity the fickleness of a vehicle supposedly more modern.

The steam train used to transport not only people, but sand, gravel, bricks, coal, wood, and vegetables as well. It was eminently practical and at the same time full of poetry. Then, one day, a dozen workmen wearing municipal badges appeared upon the scene and proceeded to tear up the tracks. And nobody protested; in fact, the general comment was: "It's about time." Because nowadays even old women who go to the city no more than once a year and spend the rest of their days just waiting for time to go by are in a hurry.

The train ran from the city to the river, and no farther, although this was not the end of the line. The largest villages of the region are strung out along the highway followed by the train, except for a particularly important one, two or three miles away, which it could not have reached except by making a long detour among the canals. On the road which linked this village to the highway, a special horse-drawn car carried passengers to and fro.

Bianco, the last horse to perform this service, was the handsomest of the lot, a beast so noble that he seemed to have stepped down from some public monument. On the village road the ties between the two rails of the line had been covered with tightly packed dirt and along this path Bianco trotted six times a day. A few minutes before the car came to a stop, that is, as soon as he heard the brake grinding, Bianco stepped out from between the rails and trotted alongside them. Then, as soon as the driver called: "Whoa!" he slowed down, without any danger of the car's bumping into his hindquarters.

Bianco was on the job for a number of years and knew it thoroughly. He had extraordinarily keen ears and could hear the train's steam whistle long before anyone knew that it was coming. He heard the whistle announcing the train's arrival at Trecaselli and pawed the stable floor to signify that it was time to hitch him to his car, pick up the village passengers, and start for the highway, in order to reach it with five minutes to spare. The first day that the whistle failed to sound because the train was no longer running, Bianco seemed to be bewitched. He stood tensely, with his ears sticking straight up into the air, and waited. For a whole week he behaved in the same way, until finally he set his mind at rest.

Yes, Bianco was a fine creature, and when he was put up at auction everyone wanted to buy him. Barchini was the highest bidder, and he hitched Bianco to a brand-new red wagon. Even between the wagon shafts, Bianco cut a handsome figure. The first time that he was hitched to the wagon, Bianco almost upset his new master, who was sitting on top of a load of beets. For when Barchini called out: "Whoa!" and pulled the reins, Bianco stepped to one side so abruptly that Barchini almost toppled over. But this was the only time that Bianco's memory tricked him; he caught on at once to the fact that the wagon was very different from a car running on rails. He had a touch of nostalgia every time he went along the road between the village and the highway. On the way out, nothing happened, but when he started home Bianco had a way of walking on the extreme left-hand

275

side of the road, beside the ditch where the track had formerly been laid. The years went by, but, as he grew older, Bianco was such a good fellow that Barchini considered him one of the family, and even when he was no longer of much use no one dreamed of getting rid of him. He was given light work, and one day when Barchini caught a hired man beating him he went for him with a pitchfork, and if the fellow hadn't run up into the hayloft he would have found himself speared.

With the passage of the years, Bianco became increasingly weary and indifferent. There came a time when he did not swish his tail to scare off the flies, and he never had to be tied up because there was no likelihood that he would move from the place where anyone left him. He stood stock-still, with his head hanging, like a stuffed horse instead of a real one.

One Saturday afternoon Bianco was hitched to a light cart to take a bag of flour to Don Camillo. While the driver carried the bag into the presbytery on his shoulder, Bianco waited outside with his head hanging. All of a sudden he raised his head and pricked up his ears. The sight was so unexpected that Don Camillo, who was standing at the door lighting a cigar, let the match drop from his hand. Bianco stood tautly on the alert for several minutes, and then, wonder of wonders, bolted away. He galloped across the square, and it was sheer luck that nobody was run down. Then he turned into the road leading to the highway and disappeared, leaving a cloud of dust in his wake.

"Bianco's gone crazy," people shouted.

Peppone came by on his motorcycle, and Don Camillo tucked up his cassock and mounted behind him.

"Fast!" Don Camillo shouted, and Peppone threw out the clutch and went like the wind.

Bianco galloped down the road, with the cart swaying behind as if it were tossed on a stormy sea. If it didn't smash to pieces, it must have been because the patron saint of carts had his eye on it. Peppone drove his motorcycle at full speed, and half-way up the road the horse was overtaken.

"Run along beside him," said Don Camillo, "and I'll try to catch the rein near the bit."

Peppone steered close, and Don Camillo stretched out his hand toward the rein. For a moment Bianco seemed to remember that he was a very old nag and consented to being

276

caught; then suddenly he speeded up and Don Camillo had to let go.

"Let him run!" Don Camillo shouted into Peppone's ear. "Go faster, and we'll wait for him at the highway."

The motorcycle shot ahead. When they reached the highway, Peppone braked. He tried to say something, but Don Camillo motioned to him to be silent. A few seconds later Bianco galloped into sight. Soon he threatened to join the highway traffic and Peppone had an impulse to give the alarm. But he didn't move in time, and then, after all, it turned out to be unnecessary. When Bianco reached the highway he came to a halt and dropped down on one side. He lay there sprawling in the dust, while the cart fell, with its shafts broken, into the ditch. Along the highway came the steam-roller, which was flattening out a coat of macadam. As the steam-roller passed by it whistled and then from the bag of bones—which was all that was left of Bianco—came a whinny. That was the end; now Bianco was a bag of bones indeed. Peppone stood looking down at the carcass, then he tore off his cap and threw it down on the ground.

"Just like the State!" he shouted.

"What do you mean, the State?" asked Don Camillo.

Peppone turned round with a fierce look on his face.

"The State! A man may say he's against it, but when the whistle calls him, he comes forward, and there he is."

"Where is he?" asked Don Camillo.

"Here! There! Everywhere!" shouted Peppone. "With his helmet on his head, his gun in hand and a knapsack over his shoulder. . . . And then it turns out that the call came not from the train, but from a steam-roller. But meanwhile he's a dead duck!"

Peppone wanted to say a great many things, but he didn't know where to begin. He picked up his cap, put it on his head and then lifted it again in salutation.

"A salute to the People!" he exclaimed.

Others began to arrive, in carts and on bicycles, and among them was Barchini.

"He heard the whistle of the steam-roller," Don Camillo explained, "and believed it was the train. That was plain from the way he stopped at the highway."

Barchini nodded. "The main thing is that he should have died believing," he said.

THE UGLY MADONNA

DON CAMILLO had a thorn in the flesh, one that had annoyed
him intensely for a very long time. Once a year it was
particularly painful, and that was during the procession in
honour of the Assumption. For three hundred and sixty-four
days the dim, shadowy chapel afforded concealment, but
under the pitiless sun of August fifteenth the true state of
affairs was visible to everybody. And it was a serious matter.

She was known as the "ugly Madonna," a phrase which
smacked of collective blasphemy. But actually no disrespect
towards the Mother of God was intended; this was merely an
accurate description of the statue which was the cause of Don
Camillo's pain. The statue was a six-foot-tall terracotta
affair, as heavy as lead, and painted in colours so offensive
as to give anyone an eye-ache. The sculptor—God rest his
soul!—appeared to have been one of the most miserable
cheats the world has ever known. If an ignorant but honest
man had done the job, no one would have called it ugly.
Ignorance is not detrimental to a work of art, because a
simple-minded craftsman may put his heart and soul into
it and these count for infinitely more than his technical
ability. But in this case the sculptor was obviously able and
had turned all his skill to the creation of something ugly.

On that day long ago when Don Camillo set foot in the
church for the first time, he was shocked by the statue's
ugliness and he determined then and there to replace it with
some more fitting image of God's Mother. He declared this
intention on the spot, and was told to forget it. It was

278

pointed out to him that the statue dated from 1693, and there was a date on the pedestal to prove it.

"I don't care about the date," Don Camillo objected. "It's downright ugly."

"Ugly, but venerably antique," they insisted.

"Venerably antique, but ugly," retorted Don Camillo.

"Historical, Father," they said, insisting upon having the last word.

For several years Don Camillo struggled in vain. If the statue had such historical importance, then it could be sent to a museum and replaced by one with a decent face. Or, if this wouldn't do, it could be moved into the sacristy and thus make way for a more suitable successor. Of course the purchase of another statue would require money. When Don Camillo started to make the rounds with fund-raising in view, he came upon more opposition.

"Replace the ugly Madonna? That statue is historical, and nothing can take its place. It wouldn't be right. Whoever heard of crowding out history?"

Don Camillo gave the project up, but the statue remained a thorn in his flesh, and every now and then he exploded to the Lord at the main altar about it.

"Lord, why don't You help me? Aren't You personally offended by the sight of Your Mother in such an unworthy guise? How can you bear it that people call her the 'ugly Madonna'?"

"Don Camillo," the Lord answered, "true beauty does not reside in the face. That, as we all know, must one day return to the dust from which it sprang. True beauty is eternal and does not die with the flesh. And the beauty of the Mother of God is in her soul and hence incorruptible. Why should I take offence because someone has carved a woman with an ugly face and set her up as a Madonna? Those who kneel before her aren't praying to a statue, but to the Mother of God in Heaven."

"Amen," said Don Camillo.

There was no other answer, but it still troubled him to hear people refer to the "ugly Madonna." He became accustomed to the thorn in his flesh, but every August fifteenth, when the statue was taken down and carried in the procession, the pain was more than he could bear. Once removed from the kindly shadows of the chapel and exposed to the sunlight, the face stood out all too clearly. It was not

279

only an ugly face, but an evil one as well; the features were heavy and vulgar, and the eyes expressionless rather than ecstatic. And the Infant Jesus in the Madonna's arms was just a bundle of rags with an empty doll's head sticking out of them. Don Camillo had tried to mask the ugliness of the statue with a crown and necklace and veil, but these had served only to accentuate it. Finally, he removed all extraneous ornaments and let the vile colouring show for exactly what it was.

Then war came to the river valley, leaving in its wake death and destruction. Bombs fell upon churches and thieving, sacrilegious hands plundered their altars as they passed by. Don Camillo didn't dare admit it but he secretly hoped that someone would "liberate" him from the "ugly Madonna." When foreign soldiers first appeared upon the scene Don Camillo hurried to the proper authorities to say:

"Our ugly Madonna is a masterpiece dating from 1693, an object of both historical and artistic importance. Shouldn't it be evacuated to a safe place of storage for the duration?"

But they told him to set his mind at rest. Historically and artistically important as the Madonna might be, the fact remained that she was ugly, and this was her best defence. If she hadn't been ugly, she would never have stayed in place for so many years.

The war came to an end, and the first post-war years went by, and then a time came when the thorn in Don Camillo's flesh troubled him most acutely. He had painted the church walls, varnished the imitation marble columns and the wooden railings, and gilded the candlesticks on the various altars. As a result, the "ugly Madonna" simply didn't belong. A dark spot on a grey background is not too conspicuous, but on a white one it stands out like a black eye.

"Lord," said Don Camillo, on his knees before the Lord. "This time You simply must help me. I've spent all the money I had and some I didn't have on doing up the church. In order to pay my debts, I've rationed my food and given up cigars. And I rejoice not so much in the beauty of the church as in the God-given strength to sacrifice a few of my comforts. Now, won't You deliver me from the thorn in my flesh? Won't You do something to stop people from calling Don Camillo's church the 'Church of the Ugly Madonna'?"

"Don Camillo, do I have to tell you the same thing over

and over?" the Lord answered. "Do I have to tell you again that true beauty does not reside in the face, that true beauty cannot be seen, because it is a thing of the spirit, which defies the erosion of time and does not return to the dust whence the body sprang?"

Don Camillo lowered his head without answering. And this was a bad sign.

The feast of the Assumption was drawing near, and one day Don Camillo summoned those who would carry the statue in the procession.

"This year the route followed by the procession will be longer than usual," he told them, "because we must go as far as the newly built houses along the south road."

It was a steaming hot August, and the idea of walking an extra mile over a freshly gravelled road was enough to make even a strong man flinch.

"We might carry the statue in two shifts," suggested old Giarola, who was in charge of arrangements.

"That's dangerous," said Don Camillo. "The sun beats down and the bearers' hands get sweaty and may slip just at the moment of changing. No I think we might rig up Rebecci's small truck. As a matter of fact, that would add to the dignity of the whole thing, and I don't see any real objections."

In a way the bearers were half sorry, but when they thought of the length of the route and the heat of the sun, they felt relieved and gave their assent. Rebecci was glad to lend his truck, and the next day he brought it to the shed at the back of the presbytery. Don Camillo insisted on decorating it in person, and for a whole week he worked so hard that all over the village they could hear the sound of his hammer. He had built a platform on the back of the truck and then covered it with draperies and flowers, producing a truly magnificent effect. When Sunday came, the "ugly Madonna" was brought out of the church and hoisted up on to the platform. The pedestal was tied down with strong ropes and these were covered with garlands of flowers.

"You don't have to worry about the driving," Don Camillo said to Rebecci, "Even if you go at fifty miles an hour, I guarantee that it will hold fast."

"With all those decorations the Madonna is very nearly beautiful," people said when the truck started.

The procession began to wind its way towards the south road, with the truck moving at the speed of a man's walk. The freshly laid gravel was bumpy and suddenly the clutch went wrong, which jolted the truck so hard that if Don Camillo hadn't tied the pedestal securely to the platform the "ugly Madonna" would have been out of luck. Don Camillo saw that something was wrong and knew that Rebecci must be worried about it, so when they reached the south road he decided to change the route.

"The truck can't go so slowly over the gravel," he said, "so we'll cut across the fields to the highway. Rebecci will drive back at normal speed and wait for us at the bridge. There we'll re-form the procession and march on a smooth surface all the way back to the centre of the village."

Rebecci went dutifully back, and the "ugly Madonna" made the most uncomfortable trip of her long life. The procession re-formed at the bridge and moved smoothly along the paved road, although occasionally Rebecci's clutch caused the truck to leap forward as if someone had given it a kick from behind. The village was all decked out, especially the main street, with the arcades on either side, where every house was covered with streamers and people threw handfuls of flowers out of the windows. Unfortunately, this street was paved with cobble-stones, and because the truck had hard tyres as well as a broken clutch, it bounced up and down as if it had St. Vitus's dance. But the "ugly Madonna" seemed to be glued to the platform, through Don Camillo's particular merit. Halfway down the main street, however, there was an especially rough bit of paving, punctuated by holes left from the construction of a sewer running below it.

"Once they're over that, there's no more danger," people said. Although they had complete faith in Don Camillo, they left a considerable space between themselves and the bouncing truck.

But the "ugly Madonna" did not get through the danger zone. She didn't fall, because Don Camillo's ropes held her fast, but on a particularly rough bump she just crumbled into pieces. The statue was not made of terracotta after all; it was some infernal mixture of brick dust or plaster or who knows what, and after two or three thousand death-dealing jars such as it had just received, an inevitable fate overtook it. But the shout which rose from the bystanders was not occasioned by the crumbling of the "ugly Madonna." It was a salute to the "fair Madonna," which as if by a miracle took its place.

On the pedestal, which was still roped securely to the truck, there emerged, like a butterfly coming out of its cocoon, a somewhat smaller statue of solid silver. Don Camillo stared at it in astonishment, and into his mind came the Lord's words: "True beauty does not reside in the face. . . . True beauty cannot be seen, because it is a thing of the spirit, which defies the erosion of time and does not return to the dust whence the body sprang. . . ." Then he turned round because an old woman was shouting:

"A miracle! A miracle!"

He shouted her down and then stooped over to pick up a fragment of the "ugly Madonna," a piece of one of the expressionless eyes which had once so annoyed him.

"We'll put you together again, piece by piece," he said in a loud voice, "even if it takes us ten years; yes, I'll do it myself, you poor 'ugly Madonna.' You concealed and saved this silver statue from one of the many barbarian invasions of the last three hundred years. Whoever hurriedly threw you together to cloak the Silver Madonna made you ugly on purpose. And so you did not attract an invader already on the march against this village or some distant city from which you may have originally come. When we have put you together, piece by piece, you shall stand side by side with your silver sister. Quite involuntarily, I brought you to this miserable end."

Don Camillo was telling the most shameless lie of his life. But he could not, in the face of his assembled parish, explain that he had chosen a roundabout and rocky route for the procession, blown up the truck tyres to the bursting-point, sabotaged the clutch and even abetted the destructive power of holes and gravel by driving a pointed tool into the terracotta and starting to crack it open, which last effort he had abandoned when he had seen that the material of which the ugly statue was made would crumble of its own accord. He meant to confess it to the Lord, who of course already knew about it. Meanwhile, he went on with his peroration.

"Poor 'ugly Madonna,' you saved the silver statue from one of the many waves of barbarian invaders. But who will save the silver Madonna from the barbarians of to-day as they press at our frontiers and eye with hatred the citadel of Christ? Is your appearance an omen? Does it mean that the new barbarians will not invade our valleys, or that if they do our strong faith and powerful arms will defend you?..."

Peppone, who was standing in the front row, in order to "observe the phenomenon more closely," turned to his lieutenant, Smilzo: "What's he mean by the 'new barbarians'?" he asked him.

Smilzo shrugged his shoulders. "Just a bit of unbridled clerical imagination."

There was a moment of silence and then the procession continued.

THE FLYING SQUAD

THAT YEAR as usual the time came round for "Party Paper Promotion Day." Peppone himself was supposed to go about hawking papers in order to give a good example, but he didn't want to be made a fool of, and so three or four days beforehand he stopped Don Camillo, who was coming back from a parochial call he had made on his bicycle.

"Once is enough, Father, but twice is too much," Peppone said solemnly.

"What do you mean?" asked Don Camillo, putting one foot on the ground.

"Sunday is Party Paper Promotion Day, and I won't stand any of your joking. You stick to your business and I'll stick to mine. An insult to me is an insult to the Party."

Don Camillo shook his head.

"If I meet you on the street, I can at least buy a paper, can't I?"

"No; if a reactionary in uniform approaches the local leader of the People's Party to buy the People's Party paper, it's an attempt to provoke violence. It's almost as bad as if I were to force a paper on you. Each one of us should stick to his own job: you dish out propaganda for the Pope and I dish it out for the Party.

"Good," said Don Camillo. "Then you admit that dishing out propaganda for the Pope is within my rights."

"Of course, as long as you don't do it in an aggressive and provocative fashion. Within your own province you

285

can dish out propaganda for anything you damn well please."

"That's a bargain!"

When Sunday morning came, Peppone had mapped out his strategy.

"We won't show our faces, because rather than buy a paper these people are capable of staying away from Mass. Of course, their staying away is a Party triumph, because it rescues them for once from the domination of the clergy. But the Party paper doesn't profit. We'll spread word that we've gone to Castelletto, and that way they'll be tricked into going to Mass. When they all come out at noon, we'll blockade the square and see who has the nerve to refuse the paper!"

The plan worked well. People went to Mass, and a few minutes before noon every street leading away from the square was covered. But when twelve o'clock came nobody left the church.

"He's caught on to the trick and is dragging out the Mass so as to keep them there longer," said Peppone. "But a lot of good that will do him!"

A few minutes later, they did pour out, but instead of scattering they stood compactly together.

"What are those devils up to?" mumbled Peppone. "They must be waiting for someone."

Just then there came a loud noise from the top of the church tower.

"He's set up a loud-speaker," Peppone shouted. "But if he makes a political speech there'll be hell to pay."

The noise from the loud-speaker increased, and became recognizable as the applause of a crowd. Then came a clear, powerful voice, that of the Pope speaking to two hundred and fifty thousand citizens of Rome. He spoke succinctly of the cardinal imprisoned by the Reds of Hungary, and when the loud-speaker had spilled the last wave of shouting and cheering down from the church tower, the village square was filled with people. They had come out of their houses, even the oldest and most infirm among them, from every direction, and Peppone's gang was disrupted and drowned in their surge. Some people were hurrying home, others talking excitedly to one another and feeling braced up by the two hundred and fifty thousand Romans gathered in St. Peter's Square. When the transcribed broadcast from Rome was over, Don Camillo turned on the gramophone, and a flood of music and singing kept the villagers' spirits high.

In the end, Peppone's gang found themselves still holding their papers in the middle of a deserted square. Smilzo tried offering them to a few stragglers, but they paid him no attention. Peppone was the last one to regain his self-control. He had such confusion in his head and such convulsions of rage in his stomach that he didn't know his left hand from his right. He began to see straight only when Don Camillo appeared at the church's open door. With lowered head, Peppone advanced toward him, and when he had come close he stood his ground and clenched his teeth. Don Camillo looked at him with a smile.

"As you see, I kept my part of our bargain," he said. "You advertised the Party and I advertised the Pope."

When you have a whole dictionary full of swear-words in your mind, it is useless even to begin to come out with them, so Peppone merely drew a sigh that had the volume of a cyclone. He stood there, with lowered head, wishing that he had horns like a bull and could disembowel Don Camillo and the whole of Christianity as well.

"Give me a copy of your paper," said a voice, and fifteen lire floated into Peppone's field of vision. Mechanically he held out the paper and took the money, but before slipping it into his pocket he remembered something, raised his head and saw Don Camillo standing there with the Communist paper in his hand. Then he really lost control. He raised the pile of papers above his head and threw them down to the ground with every ounce of strength the Creator had put into his muscles. It was a lovely crash. Then he wheeled about and walked away, while Smilzo picked up the papers and started to follow. But after he had gone a few feet, he turned to throw over his shoulder:

"When Stalin speaks from St. Peter's Square, then you'll hear something!"

Don Camillo showed considerable interest.

"Does your paper say when that's going to be?" he asked.

"No, it doesn't," Smilzo grudgingly admitted.

"Well, for a Russian paper, it's singularly ill-informed," Don Camillo said in a loud voice.

Peppone heard him, and wheeling about again he came back and stood in front of Don Camillo.

"Does the Vatican news-sheet say when the Pope will speak in Moscow's Red Square?" he asked him.

"No," said Don Camillo.

"Then we're even," Peppone shouted.

Don Camillo threw out his arms in mock despair.

"If that's so, why do you lose your temper so easily?" he asked.

"Because it's not so. And I'd like to see you and that Pope of yours hanging up there where you put the loudspeaker."

"Peppone, you know His Holiness can't travel so far from Rome."

"Then I'll take you there," shouted Peppone. "All I want is to see you swinging from the same gallows."

"You pay me too much honour, Peppone. I'm tempted to buy another copy of your informative paper."

At that Peppone walked away. He had a family and couldn't afford to get into real trouble.

It was a stormy February evening and the valley was full of melancholy and mud. Don Camillo was sitting in front of the fire, looking at some old newspapers, when he got news that something serious had happened. He threw down the papers, put on his black coat and hurried into the church.

"Lord," he said, "there's more trouble with that devil's son."

"Whose son do you mean?" asked the Lord.

"Peppone's. God the Father must have turned His back on him. . . ."

"How do you know, Don Camillo? Does God let you look into His books? And how can you intimate that He loves one human being less than another? God is the same for all men."

Don Camillo went behind the altar to search for something in a cabinet.

"Lord, I don't know anything," he said. "The fact is that Peppone's little boy is badly hurt and they've called me to give him Extreme Unction. A rusty nail did it . . . apparently just a trifle. . . . And now he's at death's door."

Having found what he was searching for, Don Camillo passed hastily in front of the altar, genuflected and started to hurry away. But he had only gone half the length of the church when he stopped and came back.

"Lord," he said, when he came to the altar, "I have a lot to say, but no time to say it. I'll explain to You on the way. Meanwhile, I'm not taking the Holy Oil with me. I'm leaving it here on the railing."

He walked hurriedly through the rain, and only when he arrived at Peppone's door did he realize that he was holding his hat in his hand. He wiped his head with his coat and knocked. A woman opened and led him down the hall until she stopped in front of a door to whisper something. The door was thrown open with a loud shout, and there was Peppone. Peppone's eyes were startled and bloodshot, and he raised his fists threateningly.

"Get out of here!" he shouted. "Go away!"

Don Camillo did not move. Peppone's wife and his mother were hanging on to him, but Peppone seemed half-mad and threw himself upon Don Camillo, grabbing hold of his chest.

"Get out! What do you want here? Did you come to liquidate him? Get out, or I'll strangle you!"

He shouted an oath strong enough to make the sky tremble, but Don Camillo did not blench. Pushing Peppone aside, he walked into the child's room.

"No!" shouted Peppone. "No Holy Oil! If you give him that it means he's done for."

"What Holy Oil are you talking about? I didn't bring any Holy Oil with me."

"Do you swear it?"

"I swear."

Then Peppone grew calm.

"You mean you really didn't bring the Holy Oil?"

"No. Why should I?"

Peppone looked at the doctor, then at Don Camillo and then at the child.

"What is the trouble?" Don Camillo asked the doctor.

"Father," the doctor answered, "only streptomycin can save him."

Don Camillo clenched his fists.

"Only streptomycin?" he shouted. "And what about God? Can't God do anything?"

The doctor shrugged his shoulders.

"I'm not a priest. I'm a doctor."

"I'm disgusted with you," said Don Camillo.

"Good," chimed in Peppone.

289

"And where is this streptomycin?" Don Camillo asked, beside himself.

"In the city," the doctor answered.

"Then we'll go and get it."

"It's too late, Father. It's only a matter of minutes now. And there's no way of reaching the city. The telephone and the telegraph are both cut off because of the storm. There's nothing we can do."

Don Camillo picked up the little boy and wrapped him in a blanket with a rubber sheet over it.

"Come on, you idiot," he shouted to Peppone. "Call out your squad!"

The squad was waiting in Peppone's workshop. It consisted for the moment of Smilzo and a few young loafers.

"There are half a dozen motorcycles in the village. I'll get Breschi's racer, and you round up the rest. If they won't give them to you, shoot."

Then all of them went off in various directions.

"If you don't lend me your motorcycle, this child is going to die," Don Camillo said to Breschi. "And if he dies, I'll wring your neck."

Breschi was speechless, although deep-down inside he wept at the idea of his brand-new machine being rattled about on a wet night. Ten minutes later the motorcycle squad was complete. A few of the owners had been knocked down, but Don Camillo said that didn't matter.

"With six of us starting, surely one will get to the city," said Don Camillo. He himself was astride the shining red racer and held the child to him under his coat.

Two ahead, two behind, with Don Camillo in the middle and Peppone ahead of them all on Brusco's big motorcycle, this was the formation of the "flying squad" as it shot along the deserted valley roads under the rain. The roads were slippery and every curve an unexpected menace. Skirting hedges and ditches, the "flying squad" went through gravel and mud to the paved highway. There the motors began to roar, and they raced in dead earnest. All of a sudden Don Camillo heard a pitiful moan from the bundle he pressed to him. He must go even faster.

"Lord," he implored through clenched teeth, "give me more speed! And you, you filthy machine, let's see if you have any real guts in you!" The racer seemed to leap ahead, passing all the rest, including Peppone, who didn't have Don Camillo's Lord to give him more speed!

Don Camillo could not remember the details of his arrival. They told him that he charged in with a child in his arms, took the hospital doorman by the neck, thrust a door open with one shoulder and threatened to strangle a doctor. The "flying squad" went home, leaving Peppone's boy in the hospital to recover. Don Camillo returned to the village blowing his horn like the last trump, and covered with glorious mud.

HORSES OF A DIFFERENT COLOUR

THEY CALLED him Romagnolo, simply because he came from
the province of Romagna. He had come to the village years
ago, but he was still *romagnolo* to the core. And to explain
what this means I must tell you that this man had the nickname of "Civil-and-with-the-band." In the course of a
political rally, the platform under him gave way and he
started to fall to the ground. Upon which he called out with
alacrity: "Civil, and with the band!" to signify that he
wanted a civil burial, and not a Church one, with the band
playing the Hymn of Garibaldi in slow tempo for a funeral
march. When they start a new town in Romagna, they first
throw up a monument to Garibaldi and then build a church,
because there's no fun in a civil funeral unless it spites the
parish priest. The whole history of the province is concerned
with spite of this kind.

Now, Romagnolo was a man with the gift of gab and one
who spoke with the big words that can be read in revolutionary papers. The fact that there was no more king had
knocked the props from under his pet subject for an argument, so he had to concentrate his heavy artillery upon the
clergy. He finished every speech with the sentence:

"When I die, I want a civil funeral and the band playing."

Don Camillo was acquainted with the whole story, but had
never paid it any attention. And so one day Romagnolo
button-holed him in order to say:

"For your information, remember that after having
steered clear of you my whole life long, I intend to steer clear

of you when I'm dead. I don't want any priest at my funeral."

"Very well," said Don Camillo calmly. "Only you're barking up the wrong tree. You ought to go to the veterinary surgeon. I look after Christian souls, not animals."

Romagnolo started to make a speech.

"When that Pope of yours . . ."

"Don't bother anyone so far away. Let's stick to present company. I'll have to pray God to grant you a long life so that you'll have plenty of time to think better of it."

When Romagnolo celebrated his ninetieth birthday the whole village turned out for the festivities, including Don Camillo, who walked up to him with a smile and said: "Congratulations!"

Romagnolo shot him a resentful look and shouted:

"You'd better pray to your God again. Some day or other He'll have to let me die. And then it will be my turn to laugh."

The strange business of the horses took place in the following year.

The business of the horses took place in a village on the other side of the river.

A seventy-four-year-old Red had died, and they held a civil funeral, with red flags, red carnations, red kerchiefs, and in short red everything. The coffin was placed on the hearse carriage, the band began to play the "Red Flag" in funeral tempo, and the horses started forward with their heads hanging low as they always did on such occasions. Behind them came the procession, with red flags flying. But when they reached the church, the horses came to a stop and no one could make them budge. Several men pulled them by their bridles and others pushed the hearse from behind, but the horses stood their ground. When someone took a whip and began to beat them over the back, the horses reared up and then fell on to their knees. Finally, they were set on their feet and walked along for a short distance, but when they got to the cemetery they reared up again and started to go backward.

The old man himself hadn't refused to have a religious funeral, the newspapers explained; his sons had imposed their ideas upon him. The story travelled all over the countryside, and anyone who wanted to test the truth of it had only to cross the river to hear it first-hand. Whenever a little knot of people gathered to discuss it, Romagnolo would descend upon them, shouting: "Middle Ages. That's stuff for the Middle Ages!"

And he went on to say that there was nothing miraculous about it; there was a perfectly rational explanation. For years immemorial the horses had stopped in front of the church, and so they had followed their usual habit this time as well. People were impressed by this version of the story and went to Don Camillo about it.

"What do you say?"

Don Camillo threw out his arms.

"Divine Providence knows no limits, and may well choose the humblest flower or tree or stone to teach a lesson to men. The sad part of it is that men pay so little attention to those of their fellows whose job it is to explain God's word, and choose rather to heed the example given them by a horse or a dog."

Many people were disappointed with this way of speaking and some of Don Camillo's most important parishioners brought their complaints to the presbytery.

"Father, this thing has created quite a sensation. Instead of dismissing it so lightly, you ought to interpret it and bring out its moral teaching."

"I can't say anything more than what I said before," answered Don Camillo. "When God decided to give men the Ten Commandments he did it, not through a horse, but through a man. Do you think that God is so badly off as to call upon horses? You know the facts; let each one of you take from them what lesson he may. If you don't like what I have said, go to the Bishop and tell him to put a horse in my place."

Meanwhile, Romagnolo was sputtering with rage, because people shrugged their shoulders at his explanation.

"That's all very well," they said, "there's nothing extraordinary or miraculous involved, but . . ."

So it was that Romagnolo button-holed Don Camillo again.

"Father, you're just the man I wanted to see. What is the official interpretation of the horse story?"

"Barking up the wrong tree, as usual," Don Camillo replied with a smile. "Horses aren't my line. You ought to go to the vet."

Romagnolo made a long speech to explain the horses'
behaviour, and at the end Don Camillo simply threw out his
arms.

"I can see that the thing has made quite an impression
upon you. If it has caused you to stop and think, then I say
thank God for it."

Romagnolo raised a threatening skinny finger.

"I can tell you one thing," he said, "and that is, the horses
won't stop when my coffin passes by!"

Don Camillo went to talk to the Lord on the altar.

"Lord, the foolish things he says are not meant to hurt
You; they're just barbs directed at me. When he comes up
for Judgment, remember that he hails from Romagna. The
trouble is that he's over ninety, and anyone could knock him
over with a feather. If he were in his prime, it would be a
different matter. I'd get after him."

"Don Camillo, the system of teaching Christian charity by
knocking people over the head is one that doesn't appeal to
me," the Lord answered severely.

"I don't approve of it myself," said Don Camillo humbly.
"But the fact is that often the ideas people have in their
heads aren't so bad; it's just that they're in bad order. And
sometimes a good shaking-up will cause them to fall into
place."

Romagnolo went to Peppone's office and declared with no
preamble: "Take this piece of legal paper, call two of
your jumping-jacks to bear witness, and write down what I
say."

He threw the piece of paper on the Mayor's desk and sat
down.

"Put the date on top and write clearly: 'I, the undersigned Libero Martelli, ninety-one years old, by profession a
free-thinker, in full possession of all my faculties, desire that
upon my death all my property and possessions be transferred to this township for the purpose of buying a motor
hearse to take the place of the present horse-drawn
vehicle. . . .'"

Peppone stopped writing.

"Well?" said Romagnolo. "Do you want me to leave all
my worldly goods to the priest?"

"I accept, of course," Peppone stuttered. "But how are we
to buy a motor hearse so soon? It would cost at least a million
and a half liras, and we . . ."

"I have two millions in the bank. Just go ahead and buy it, and I'll pay."

Romagnolo came out of the Town Hall glowing with satisfaction and for the first time in his life went deliberately to the church square.

"Everything's settled, Father!" he shouted. "When I go by in my coffin, the horses won't stop. I've taken care of priests and horses alike."

Romagnolo got too excited, and drank more than was good for him. Not that wine hurt him, after having been good for him all his life long. Water was his downfall. Coming home one night full to the gills with wine, he was so over-poweringly sleepy that he lay down in a ditch. At over ninety years of age, spending the night in a puddle of water isn't exactly healthy. Romagnolo caught pneumonia and died. But before closing his eyes he summoned Peppone.

"Is everything agreed?" he asked him.

"Yes. Your wishes will be faithfully observed."

Romagnolo was the motor hearse's first customer. And the whole village turned out to see its inauguration. The band struck up, and the hearse moved slowly and steadily along. But in front of the church it came to a sudden stop. The driver wriggled the gear lever frantically, but all in vain. He looked under the hood, but found the plugs, carburettor and points all in perfect order and the tank full of petrol. The church door was closed, but Don Camillo was looking through a crack. He saw men milling about the hearse, and the hearse standing, obviously stuck, among them. The band had stopped playing and the bystanders had fallen into an astonished silence. The minutes dragged by, until Don Camillo ran to the sacristy and pulled the bell rope.

"God have mercy on you," he panted; "God have mercy on you. . . ."

And the bells tolled out in the silent air. People shook themselves and the driver shifted the gear. The motor started and the motor hearse pulled away. No one could follow it any longer, because the driver put it into second and then into third gear, and it disappeared in a cloud of dust in the direction of the cemetery.

BLUE SUNDAY

OLD MAN Grolini turned up at the presbytery to show Don Camillo a letter. Under the watchful eye of his dog Thunder, Don Camillo was greasing cartridges for his shotgun. Even before he read the letter he threw a questioning look at Grolini.

"The usual thing," Grolini sputtered. "That little wretch is in hot water again."

The Headmaster of young Grolini's boarding-school was thoroughly dissatisfied with him and wanted his father to do something about it.

"You'd better go in my place," Grolini said. "If I go, I'm likely to hit him over the head. When you see him, Father, tell him that if he doesn't behave I'll kick him out of the house."

Don Camillo shook his head.

"That would be even more stupid than hitting him over the head," he muttered. "How can anyone kick a boy out of the house when he's only eleven years old?"

"If I can't kick him out of the house, then I'll send him to the reformatory," shouted Grolini. "I don't want to see him again!"

Seeing that the father was not to be appeased, Don Camillo finally said: "I'll go and talk to him on Sunday afternoon."

"Then I authorize you to kick him about the school grounds," Grolini shouted. "The worse you treat him the better pleased I'll be."

After Grolini had gone, Don Camillo turned the letter over and over in his hands. The matter troubled him, because he had been the one to advise Grolini to encourage the boy in his studies and send him away to school. Grolini was a rich man. He tilled the soil, but the soil was his own. Moreover, it was fertile soil, and he had livestock in his stable and as many tractors and other agricultural machines as he could desire. Giacomino, his youngest son, was a quick-witted fellow who had always done well at school, and his father was attracted by the idea of having a university graduate in the family. Not to mention his wife, who gave herself very great airs. So it was that as soon as Giacomino finished elementary school he was bundled off to the city. Don Camillo had filled in his application papers and escorted him there in person. Giacomino was one of the mildest and best boys Don Camillo had ever known. He had been an acolyte for years and never got himself into the least trouble. So now the priest could not understand why he had turned out so badly.

When Sunday came, Don Camillo appeared at the boarding-school at the visitors' hour. When the Headmaster heard the name of Grolini he held his head in his hands. Don Camillo threw out his arms in a gesture of hopelessness.

"I'm amazed," he said with mortification. "I always knew him to be a good, obedient boy. I can't understand why he should be so wild."

" 'Wild' isn't exactly the word for it," the Headmaster put in. "His conduct doesn't give us any worry. But we're more concerned about him than about the worst boys in the school."

He took an envelope out of his desk drawer and drew forth a sheet of paper.

"Look at this composition," he said.

Don Camillo found himself looking at a clean paper, bearing on it in neat writing: *Giacomino Grolini. Class IB. Theme: My favourite book. Exposition.*

Turning the page, he came upon a perfect blank.

"There you are," said the Headmaster, holding out the entire envelope to him. "All his class work follows the same pattern. He neatly puts down the theme subject or problem, then sits back with folded arms and waits for the time to

298

go by. When he's asked a question, he makes no answer. At first we thought he must be a perfect idiot. But we've watched him and heard him talk to his companions, and we find that he isn't an idiot at all. Quite the contrary."

"I'll talk to him," said Don Camillo. "I'll take him to some quiet place outside, and, if necessary, I'll give him a proper dressing-down."

The Headmaster looked at Don Camillo's big hands.

"If you can't bring him round that way, I'm afraid there's nothing more to do," he mumbled. "He has no right to leave the premises after the way he's behaved, but I'll give him permission to stay out with you until five o'clock."

When Giacomino arrived on the scene a few minutes later, Don Camillo did not even recognize him. Quite apart from his school uniform and closely clipped hair, there was something entirely new in his manner.

"Have no fear," Don Camillo said to the Headmaster. "I'll work on him."

They walked in silence through the empty streets, typical of a tedious Sunday afternoon, and beside the bulky priest Giacomino looked smaller and skinnier than ever. When they had reached the outskirts, Don Camillo looked round for a place where they could talk freely. He turned on to a thoroughfare leading out into the country and then fifty yards later on to an unprepared road running beside a canal. The sun was shining, and although the trees were bare the landscape was pleasant to the eye. Finally, Don Camillo sat down on a tree trunk. He had in mind the speech he intended to make to the boy, and it was ferocious enough to make an elephant quiver. Giacomino stood in front of him and suddenly said:

"May I have a run?"

"A run?" said Don Camillo severely. "Can't you run during recreation at school?"

"Yes, but not very far," the boy answered. "There's always a wall in the way."

Don Camillo looked at the boy's pale face and clipped hair.

"Have your run, then," he said, "and then come here. I want to talk to you."

Giacomino was off like a bolt of lightning, and Don Camillo saw him cross the field, duck under a fence and run parallel to it under some bare grapevines. A few minutes later he came back, with his eyes and cheeks glowing.

"Rest a minute and then we'll talk," mumbled Don Camillo.

The boy sat down, but a minute later he jumped to his feet and ran over to an elm near by. He climbed it like a squirrel and made for a vine among its top branches. He explored among the red leaves and then came down with something in his hand.

"Grapes!" he exclaimed to Don Camillo, showing him a cluster that had survived the autumn picking. He proceeded to eat the grapes one by one and when he had finished he sat down beside the trunk.

"May I throw a stone?" he asked.

Don Camillo continued to lie low. "Go ahead and amuse yourself," he was thinking, "and we'll talk business later."

The boy rose, picked up a stone, brushed the dirt off it and threw it with all his strength. Don Camillo had a feeling that the stone had flown behind the clouds, never to return. A cold wind had blown up, and Don Camillo began to think they had better repair to some quiet café, where he wouldn't have to shout in order to make the boy hear him. As they walked away Giacomino asked permission to race ahead, and found another cluster of grapes left from the autumn.

"That's just a small part of what there must have been on the vine!" he murmured as he ate them. "At home now, they must have hung up the grapes to dry. . . ."

"Never mind about the grapes," Don Camillo mumbled.

The outskirts of the city were squalid and melancholy. As they walked along they met a man selling roast chestnuts and peanuts. Giacomino opened his eyes wide.

"Silly stuff," said Don Camillo ill-humouredly. "I'll get you a piece of cake when we sit down."

"No thanks," said the boy in a tone of voice that set Don Camillo's nerves on edge.

The nut-vendor knew his business and had stopped a few yards behind them. And the proof of his astuteness was that Don Camillo turned round and grudgingly tossed him a hundred-lire note.

"Mixed, Father?"

"Yes, mixed."

Don Camillo put the bag of silly stuff into the boy's hand,

and they continued to walk along the deserted thoroughfare. The priest held out as long as he could, and then finally stuck his hand into the bag. The taste of the nuts called up memories of the melancholy Sunday afternoons of his own youth, and filled him with a sudden sadness. A church bell rang, and when Don Camillo pulled out his heavy gold watch he saw that it was twenty minutes to five.

"Hurry," he said to the boy. "You must be back promptly on the hour."

They quickened their pace, as the sun sank below the houses around them. When they arrived, without a minute to spare, the boy held the bag out to Don Camillo.

"When you come back from outside they take everything like this away," he explained in a low voice.

Don Camillo put the bag into his pocket.

"That's where I sleep," said the boy, pointing to a barred second-storey window with a box-like protuberance under it that blocked the sight of the ground below. Then he hesitated for a moment before pointing to a window on the ground floor, barred in the same way but affording a view of the world outside.

"In that hall are the cupboards where we hang our clothes," he said. "I'll try to walk along it on my way upstairs and in that way I'll be able to wave goodbye."

Don Camillo went with him to the heavy front door; then he came back and waited on the pavement outside the ground-floor window, which gave on to a side street. Nervously he lit a cigar. After what seemed like an endless time, he heard a whisper. Giacomino had opened a window and was waving to him from behind the bars. Don Camillo walked over and handed him the bag of nuts. Then he started to walk away, but something made him turn back. He could see nothing of Giacomino but a pair of eyes, but these were so filled with tears that Don Camillo broke out into a cold perspiration. By some mysterious process his dangerously powerful hands found themselves twisting the iron bars, and the iron bars bent and gave way. When the opening was large enough, Don Camillo stretched out an arm, grasped the boy's collar and pulled him through. It was dark by now, and no one saw anything strange in the sight of a priest and a schoolboy walking together.

"Wait for me," Don Camillo said, "while I get my motor-cycle."

301

By eight o'clock they were back in the village, and Giacomino had eaten all the nuts on the way.

"Come into the presbytery by the back door," Don Camillo told him as they got off the motorcycle, "and don't let anyone see you."

By nine o'clock Giacomino was sleeping on a couch in the hall while Don Camillo finished his supper in the kitchen. At a quarter past nine Grolini turned up, waving a telegram in one hand.

"That rascal has run away from school," he shouted. "If I lay my hands on him, I'll kill him for sure."

"Then I hope you don't lay hands on him," Don Camillo murmured.

Grolini was beside himself with anger.

"At least you gave him a good scolding this afternoon," he added.

Don Camillo shook his head.

"No, not I. That boy was made to follow in your footsteps and live on the land. He simply can't stay away from the country. A good little fellow, too. . . . But perhaps he's dead by now."

"Dead?" Grolini shouted.

Don Camillo sighed.

"I found him in a very bad state of mind, and he talked to me in a most alarming way. . . . You'd more or less given him up for lost, hadn't you? I told him what you said, that rather than see his face again you'd send him to the reformatory."

Grolini sank on to a chair and finally managed to say:

"Father, if God brings him home safe and sound I'll foot the bill for repairs to the bell tower."

"That's not necessary," said Don Camillo gently. "God will be satisfied with your grief. Go back home, and don't lose heart. I'll go and look for your boy."

Giacomino came home the next day, and Don Camillo was with him. His family were gathered in the yard, but no one said a word. Only Flick, the old dog, barked and jumped like a kangaroo because he was so happy. Giacomino threw him his school cap and Flick ran off, holding it between his teeth with Giacomino running after him.

"The Headmaster called me up this morning," said old man Grolini. "He can't understand how the boy could have twisted two heavy iron bars."

"He's an able boy, I tell you," said Don Camillo. "He'll make a very good farmer. And it's better to farm for love than to study for fear of a beating."

And Don Camillo went away very fast, because he had just felt a peanut in his pocket and couldn't wait to eat it.

DON CAMILLO GETS INTO TROUBLE

SAINT MARTIN'S Summer brought some strangers to the village, among them a certain Marasca, who might better have stayed away. Marasca had a little boy and when he took him to school for the first time he said to the teacher:

"I hear that the priest comes every Wednesday to give religious instruction. When he arrives, will you kindly send my boy home?"

And since the teacher told him that was impossible, every Wednesday Marasca kept the boy away from school. Don Camillo stayed out of it as long as he could, then one Wednesday afternoon he went to Olmetto, the farm where Marasca was a tenant. He meant to make a joke of it rather than to stir up trouble, but at first sight Marasca showed signs of resentment at his visit.

"This is my land," he said. "You must have crossed the wrong bridge."

"No; I didn't cross the wrong bridge," said Don Camillo. "I hear that on Wednesdays your boy can't come to school, and so I thought I'd give him a little religious instruction at home."

Marasca came out with an oath that was really more than Don Camillo deserved.

"I see you need a little religious instruction yourself," said the priest, "and I'm ready to give it to you."

Marasca's brother came out of the house and looked threateningly at the visitor.

"Get out of here and don't let me see you again, you cursed black crow!" shouted Marasca.

Don Camillo did not say a word. He retraced his steps, and when he was across the bridge and back on the road, he called out.

"Now I'm off your land," he said. "But you'll have to come and repeat your words, because I don't understand you."

The two brothers looked at one another; then they crossed the bridge and planted themselves defiantly in front of Don Camillo. And there they found that the priest had quite a bag of tricks up his sleeve. While he was slapping the dust off the face of the first Marasca, the brother, who had already had a taste of the same medicine, ran back to the yard and returned with a pitchfork. The pitchfork was of an ordinary kind, and had a handle. But this was where the trouble began, for in Don Camillo's powerful hands the handle turned into a regular earthquake. The two Marascas found this out to their sorrow, because the handle was broken on their backs.

The whole village was turned upside down, and the Communist newspaper sent a special correspondent who painted Don Camillo as a dangerously aggressive and violent man. As a result, Don Camillo was called up before the old Bishop, and before he could say any more than: "Self-defence . . ." the Bishop interrupted him gently.

"Monterana is without a priest. Go up there this evening and stay until the return of the regular incumbent."

"But the regular incumbent is dead," Don Camillo stammered.

"Exactly," said the Bishop, making a gesture which indicated that he had nothing more to say.

Don Camillo bowed his head and went to pack his bag.

Monterana was one of the most forsaken spots on the surface of the globe: half a dozen huts made of mud and stones, one of which was the church, but distinguishable from the others only because of the bell tower at its side. The road to Monterana was a stony ditch, called by courtesy a mule-track, but no mule would ever have ventured upon it. Don Camillo arrived at the top with his heart in his throat and gazed round. When he went into the presbytery the walls were so low that they seemed to crush him. A scrawny old woman came out of a hole and looked at him through half-open eyes.

"Who are you?" Don Camillo asked, but she threw out her arms as if to say that she had forgotten.

The main beam of the kitchen ceiling was supported by a tree trunk in the middle of the room, and Don Camillo was tempted to play the part of Samson and pull the whole place down around him. Then he realized that another priest, a man like himself, had spent a lifetime amid these same squalid surroundings, and this caused him to recover some of his calm. He went into the church, and the miserable condition of it brought tears to his eyes. He knelt on the step before the altar and raised his eyes to the cross.

"Lord . . ." he began, and then he stopped, because the cross was of crudely cut wood, black and peeling; it was completely bare. Don Camillo felt very nearly afraid. "Lord," he sorrowfully exclaimed, "You are everywhere in the universe, and I need no image of You to tell me that You are near, but here I feel as if You had abandoned me. . . . My faith must be a very poor thing, if I feel so terribly alone."

He went back to the presbytery, and there he found a cloth on the table, a loaf of bread and a piece of cheese. The old woman was just bringing in a jug of water.

"Where did these things come from?" Don Camillo asked.

She threw out her arms and looked up to Heaven. Plainly, she didn't know. With the old priest it had always been like this, and now the miracle was repeating itself. Don Camillo made the sign of the cross, and involuntarily thought of the bare, black wooden cross he had just seen on the altar. He shivered, and reproached himself for being afraid. But indeed he had a fever, sent to him by Divine Providence, like the bread and the cheese and the water. He stayed in bed for three days, and on the fourth day he received written orders from the Bishop.

> *"You are not to leave your new post, for any reason whatsoever. Don't show your face in the village, for the people there must forget that they ever had a priest so unworthy. May God strengthen and protect you. . . ."*

Don Camillo got up, with his head still reeling. He went

306

over to the window and found that it was chilly outside with a premonition of fog in the air.

"Winter will be here any minute," he said to himself with terror, "and I shall be snowbound and all alone. . . ."

It was five o'clock in the afternoon, and he must not let night overtake him. He rolled rather than walked down the mule-track and reached the road just in time to catch a bus to the city. There he went to several garages, until he found someone who would take him by car to the crossroad at Gaggiola. From the crossroad, Don Camillo cut over the fields and at ten o'clock he was in Peppone's garden.

Peppone stared at him with a worried air.

"I must transport some things to Monterana," said Don Camillo. "Can I hire your truck?"

Peppone shrugged his shoulders.

"Did you have to wake me up for that?" he asked. "We can discuss that to-morrow morning."

"We're going to discuss it right away," the priest insisted. "I need your truck to-night."

"Are you mad?" Peppone asked him.

"Yes," Don Camillo answered.

Upon receiving such a logical reply, Peppone could only scratch his head.

"Let's hurry," said Don Camillo. "How much will it cost?"

Peppone took the stub of a pencil and made some calculations.

"Forty miles there and forty miles back, that makes eighty. Sixty-five hundred lire-worth of petrol and oil. Then there's the charge for my services, which are higher paid at night. But since it's to help you get out of this village, and I'm happy to see you go. . . ."

"Come on," said Don Camillo. "How much is it?"

"Ten thousand for the whole job."

Don Camillo agreed, and Peppone stretched out his hand.

"Cash will do it," he muttered.

Ten thousand lire represented Don Camillo's savings of years.

"Get your truck going, and meet me halfway down the Boschetto road."

"What in Heaven's name can you be loading there?"

"That's none of your business, and not a word to a soul."

Peppone muttered something to the effect that in the

307

woods at midnight he probably wouldn't find many people with whom to exchange conversation. Don Camillo's fever excited rather than tired him. He made a detour through the fields and approached the church from the orchard. Or rather he bumped straight into it, because there was a thick fog all around. He had his keys in his pocket and went in by the tower door. He had to go out by the main entrance, but no one saw him.

Peppone had a bright idea. When he saw the fog and thought of Don Camillo trying to make his way through it with all his bags and baggage, he decided to blow his horn to guide him. Led by the horn and the excitement of his fever, Don Camillo arrived panting at the meeting-place. Peppone started to get down from the truck to help him, but the priest said:

"I don't need any help. Start up your motor and be ready to go when I give the word."

When he had loaded everything on to the truck, Don Camillo went to sit beside Peppone, and off they went. The fog pursued them for the first twenty miles, but they made the second half of the trip as fast as if they were flying. At two o'clock in the morning Peppone brought his truck to a halt at the beginning of the famous mule-track leading to Monterana. Don Camillo once more refused Peppone's help in unloading. Peppone heard him scuffling about at the back of the truck and then, when he saw him in the glare of the headlights, his eyes opened wide.

"The Crucified Christ from the altar!"

Don Camillo started the painful ascent of the mule-track, and Peppone had pity and overtook him.

"Father, can I give you a hand?"

"Hands off!" shouted Don Camillo. "Go home, and think twice before you spread any gossip!"

"Here's wishing you a safe arrival!" said Peppone.

And so it was that Don Camillo's Stations of the Cross began.

The crucifix was large and heavy, made out of solid oak. And the figure of the Crucified Christ was carved out of equally heavy, hard wood. The mule-track was steep and its stony surface was bathed by the rain. Never had Don Camillo carried such a weight on his shoulders. His bones creaked, and after half an hour he had to drag the crucifix. The crucifix became heavier and heavier and Don Camillo was more and more tired, but still he did not give up. He slipped and fell on a sharp stone, and felt the blood trickling down from one knee, but still he did not stop. A branch carried away his hat and scratched his forehead, thorns ripped his cassock, but on he climbed, with his face bent low, near to that of the Crucified Christ. Even a gushing spring did not tempt him to linger. One, two, three hours went by.

It took him four hours to reach the village. The church was the building farthest away, and to reach it he had to climb up a path which was less rocky, but filled with mud. Everyone was still in bed and he toiled on quite alone, borne up by the hope that is born of despair. He entered the empty church, but his task was not yet over. He still had to dismount the bare, black cross and install his own crucifix on the altar. After one last struggle, his mission was accomplished. Then he collapsed on the floor. But when the bell rang he jumped up, went to wash his hands in the sacristy and said his first Mass. He lit the candles himself; there were only two of them, but they seemed to shed a very great light.

Only two people came to Mass, but Don Camillo had the sensation of a multitude, because one of the two was the old woman who had forgotten her name, and the other was Peppone. He had been too tired to drive his truck back and had followed Don Camillo step by step up the mountain. Although he did not have the cross on his shoulders, he had felt the priest's weariness as if it were his own. As he went by the poor-box in the church he slipped into it the ten-thousand lire note given him by Don Camillo.

"Lord," whispered Don Camillo raising his eyes to the Crucified Christ. "I hope you don't mind my having brought You to this wretched place."

"No, Don Camillo," said the Lord. "The place is wonderful." And He smiled.

WHEN THE RAINS CAME

EVERYONE was waiting for the arrival of the new priest, but
nobody came except old Don Anselmo, who for years had
had the parish of Torretta, two miles away. Since the two
villages were so close, he had obviously been asked to fill in
until a replacement was found for Don Camillo.

Don Anselmo looked round during his first Mass, and
saw that there were only two people in the church, himself
and his acolyte. And the acolyte was there only because Don
Anselmo had called for him at his own house. Things went
on in this way for some time, until Don Anselmo went to talk
to the Bishop.

"Monsignore," he concluded, "that's not all. It's a serious
business. They behave as if neither church nor priest were
there. No one comes to confession. 'I'll go when Don Camillo
comes home,' they say. When babies are born, they don't
bring them to be baptized. 'That can wait for Don Camillo,'
is still the refrain. And they get married in the Town Hall
and say they'll wait for Don Camillo to perform a church
wedding. So far no one has died, and I suppose there'll
be no necessity for a funeral until Don Camillo comes
for it."

The Bishop threw out his arms in despair.

"That blessed Don Camillo is fated to be a thorn in my
flesh even when he's not there!" he sighed. "But people must
get it into their heads that he made a mistake and has to pay
for it."

Don Anselmo shrugged his shoulders.

"It is my duty to report on everything I know," he said. "And I may as well tell you that many people don't think it was a mistake for Don Camillo to snatch the pitchfork away from someone who was trying to stick it into his stomach."

"Quite right," the Bishop agreed. "It wasn't a mistake to snatch it away; the mistake was to hit those two fellows over the head with the handle."

"Even then, some people think that Don Camillo had right on his side," Don Anselmo said in a respectful manner. "It is my further duty to inform you that under the circumstances I should have done the same thing myself."

The Bishop raised his eyes to Heaven.

"Lord, forgive this old madman!" he exclaimed. "He doesn't know what he is saying."

Don Anselmo was not just an impulsive boy; he was well on towards eighty, and now he hung his head in embarrassment but continued to be of the same opinion. The Bishop delivered a long and very wise sermon, and ended up by saying: "Now go on house-to-house visits, to explain to the people that Don Camillo made a mistake and must be punished for it. It's your plain duty to make them see reason."

Don Anselmo went from house to house, and everywhere he received the same answer:

"If he did make a mistake, then it's only right that he should pay. We're waiting for him to finish paying and come back, that's all."

Meanwhile the Reds were beside themselves with joy. They had got Don Camillo out of the way and no one was going to church. One evening Peppone accosted Don Anselmo.

"It's sad to see an old racket like the Vatican closing down," he sighed. "If we weren't excommunicated, we'd come to your Mass ourselves! Anyhow, if you decide to lease the premises, give me an option on them."

Don Anselmo did not let himself be perturbed.

"I can't even ask you to lease me your brain in return!" he retorted. "You leased that out a long time ago. I only hope you didn't let your soul go with it."

Then it began to rain. It rained on the mountains and in the valleys. Old oak trees were shattered by lightning, the sea foamed up in a storm, the rivers began to swell, and as the rain continued, they overflowed their banks and flooded whole towns with their muddy waters. Most dangerous of all, the mighty Po was rising, pressing harder and harder against its embankments. During the war, the embankment was bombed at a point called La Pioppa, and they had neglected to mend it until within the last two years. Everyone looked fearfully at La Pioppa, feeling sure that if the pressure became too great this was the point where the embankment would give way. The earth hadn't had time to pack solidly, and whereas the rest of the bank would hold just as it had always held before, La Pioppa would crumble.

Meanwhile it continued to rain, night and day, and after each momentary respite it came down harder than before. The papers were filled with news of squalls, floods and landslides, but the village people thought only of their own danger. Already a lot of old crones were saying:

"Ever since Don Camillo went away, taking the altar crucifix with him, there's been trouble brewing."

The crucifix had a long-standing association with the river. Every year the people of the village carried it in a procession to the banks, where the priest gave the waters his blessing. The old crones shook their heads.

"As long as he was here, we were protected. But now he's gone away."

As the river rose, they spoke more and more of the crucifix, and even the wisest among them lost their heads. One morning the Bishop found a village delegation waiting upon him.

"Give us back our crucifix," they implored. "We must form a procession at once and hold a blessing of the waters. Otherwise the village will be swept away."

The Bishop sighed.

"Brethren, have you so little faith?" he asked them. "God seems to be not within your souls but extraneous to them, if you pin all your trust to a wooden image, and without its help fall into despair."

Some of the men of the delegation hung their heads. And one of them, old Bonesti, stepped forward to say:

"We have faith in God, but we have lost faith in ourselves. All of us love our country, but when we go into battle, we need to see our regimental flag. The flag keeps us fighting for the country whose love is within us. That crucifix was our flag, and Don Camillo our flag-bearer. If we can have our flag back, we shall face our troubles more courageously."

Don Camillo came back during the night, when no one was expecting him. But he had no sooner walked from the presbytery to the church the next morning than the whole village knew it. They crowded to hear his first Mass, and afterwards they gathered round him to say:

"We want a procession!"

"The Lord has gone back to His altar, and there He stays," said Don Camillo severely. "He will not move until we hold the regular procession next year. This year, the waters have been blessed already."

"Yes, but the river is rising."

"He knows that," said Don Camillo. "No one needs to refresh His memory. All I can do is pray that the Lord will give us strength to bear our sufferings serenely."

The people were obsessed with fear, and when they insisted on a procession Don Camillo had to speak to them even more sternly than before.

"Have a procession, then, but rather than carry a wooden cross about the streets, carry Christ in your hearts! Let every one of you hold a private procession of this kind. Have faith in God, and not in graven images. And then God will help you."

But the people's fear continued to rise, along with the river. Engineers came to inspect La Pioppa and declared it would hold, but they advised the villagers to get their belongings together and be prepared for evacuation. The engineers went away at ten o'clock in the morning, and at eleven the water was still rising. Then fear turned into terror.

"There's no time to save anything," someone was saying. "The only thing to do is to cross the river and cut an opening in the embankment on the other side."

No one knew who was the first person to suggest this blasphemy, but very soon everyone was repeating it. Eighty people out of a hundred were trying to work out the best way to cross the river and make a cut that would channel the overflow to the opposite shore. Sooner or later someone might have actually done it. But all of a sudden the rain ceased, and hope returned to their hearts. The church bells called them to the square, and there Don Camillo addressed them.

"There's only one thing to do, and that is to carry our most important belongings to safety."

Just then the rain began to fall again.

"There's no time!" the people shouted. "La Pioppa won't hold."

"Yes, it will," said Don Camillo firmly.

"That's what you say!" they shouted.

"That's the word left by the engineers," said Don Camillo.

"It's only a word!" someone shouted.

"It's a fact, I say!" Don Camillo retorted. "I'm so sure it will hold that I'll go and stand on the weakest point of the embankment. If I'm mistaken, then I'll pay!"

Don Camillo raised his big umbrella and walked towards the river, with a crowd following after him. They followed him along the embankment until he came to the newly built stretch at La Pioppa. There Don Camillo turned round.

"Let everyone go and pack up his things calmly," he called out. "I'll wait at La Pioppa for you to finish."

He walked on, and fifty yards farther he came to the exact point where everyone thought there would be a break. The crowd looked in bewilderment first at the priest and then at the raging water.

"I'm coming to keep you company," a voice shouted, and out of the crowd stepped Peppone, with all eyes upon him.

"The embankment will hold," Peppone shouted; "there's no danger. Don't do anything silly, but prepare to evacuate in good order, under the chief councillor's direction. To prove my confidence in the embankment, I'll stay here."

When they saw the priest and the Mayor at the point of what they thought was the greatest danger, the people hurried to get their livestock out of the stables and load their household goods on trucks and wagons. The rain continued to come down and the river to rise, and the village population made ready. Meanwhile, Don Camillo and Peppone sat on two big stones under the umbrella.

"You'd be better off if you were still exiled in the mountains, Father," said Peppone.

"Oh, I don't know about that," Don Camillo answered.

Peppone was silent for a few minutes and then clapped his hand to his hip.

"If this thing were to break while people are still loading

their things and we're sitting here, that would be a pretty mess! We'd be done for and so would they."

"It would be a great deal worse if we'd saved ourselves by cutting the embankment, dealing out death and destruction on the other side. You must admit there's a difference between misfortune and crime."

Peppone shrugged his shoulders.

"I've got the better of you, in any case."

Towards evening the rain paused and the river fell. The village had been completely evacuated, and Don Camillo and Peppone left the embankment and went home. As they crossed the church square, Don Camillo said:

"You might thank God for saving your skin. You owe that good luck to Him."

"True enough," said Peppone. "But He saved your skin too, and that's enough bad luck to make us even!"

THE BELL

THE RIVER embankment did not give way, even where everyone said it was sure to crack, and so the next morning many
people went back to the village, which lay below the water-
level, in order to fetch more of their belongings. But towards
nine o'clock something unexpected happened. The water
had risen higher, and although it did not penetrate the
main embankment it found a weak spot elsewhere.

About a mile east of the village, the road running along
the embankment went over a bridge across the Fossone, a
tributary which poured at this point into the Po. The
Fossone had solid banks of its own, but because the Po was so
high, it had reversed its course and was running away from
instead of into the river. Just below the bridge, where the
banks of the Fossone joined those of the river, the water
tunnelled underneath and then came up in a jet, making the
hole larger and larger. There was no way of holding it, and
the villagers soon returned with wagons and trucks to seek
safety.

Don Camillo had worked all alone until three o'clock in
the morning, carrying things to the second floor and attic of
the presbytery. Then he was so tired that he fell into a dead
sleep. At half-past nine in the morning he was awakened by
the shouts of people running to take refuge on the embankment. Soon the noise died away, and he got up to look out of
the window at the deserted church square. He went down to

explore further and then climbed up into the bell tower. From this vantage point he could see that the water had already crept up on the lower part of the village and was slowly creeping higher. It had encircled the isolated hut of old Merola, and when it reached the ground-floor windows the whole thing crumbled. Don Camillo sighed. The old man had not wanted to leave, and it was by sheer force that they had taken him away. Now the pace of the advancing water was faster; the rain had left the earth so thoroughly soaked that it could not absorb a drop. It was up to the higher part of the village, which lay stretched out perfectly flat before it. Hearing a crash in the distance, he looked through his field-glasses and saw that a hundred and fifty feet of one bank of the Fossone had given way. Then, going over to another window, he noticed a crowd of people on the main embankment gazing in the direction of the village.

Those who had gone with their trucks and wagons for a second load of their belongings had been forced back. Now they stood with evacuees from other villages, who had brought their livestock and household goods with them, looking down at the newly flooded area, half a mile away. No one spoke, and old women shed silent tears. Their village seemed to be dying there before them, and they began to think of it as already dead.

"There is no God!" said an old man gloomily.

But just at that moment the church bell rang. There was no mistaking the sound, even if the tone was somewhat different from usual. All eyes were fixed on the church tower.

After Don Camillo had seen the crowd on the embankment he went back to the ground. The water had climbed the three steps leading to the church door and was running into the nave.

"Lord, forgive me for forgetting that it is Sunday," said Don Camillo, kneeling in front of the altar.

Before going to prepare himself in the sacristy, Don Camillo stepped into the little room at the base of the bell tower, whose floor was lower than that of the church and already covered with eight or ten inches of water. He tugged at a rope, hoping that it was the right one. It was, and when the crowd on the embankment heard it ring, they said:

"Eleven o'clock Mass!"

The women joined their hands in prayer and the men took off their hats.

Don Camillo lit the candles and began to say Mass. The water was climbing the altar steps and soon it touched his vestments. It was muddy and cold, but Don Camillo paid no attention. His congregation was dry and safe on the embankment. And when it was time for the sermon, he did not mind the fact that the church was empty, but preached to his parishioners just as if they were there before him. There were three feet of water in the nave, and pews and confessionals had overturned and were floating at random. The door was wide open, and beyond it he could see the submerged houses on the square and the lowering clouds on the horizon.

"Brethren," he said, "the waters have boiled up from the river bed and now are sweeping everything before them. But one day they will be calmed and return to their rightful place and the sun will shine again. Even if you lose everything you have, you can still be rich in your faith in God. Only those who doubt God's mercy and justice will be impoverished, even if their possessions are intact."

And he went on at considerable length in the flooded church, while from the embankment people continued to stare at the tower. When the bell sounded for the elevation, the women knelt down on the damp ground and the men bowed their heads. Then the bell rang again for the final blessing. The Mass was over, and people moved about freely and talked in a low tone of voice, hoping to hear the bell again. Soon afterwards it rang out gaily once more, and the men took out their watches and said:

"Noon! It's time to go for dinner."

They got into whatever vehicles they had with them and went to the improvised canteens and shelters. And looking back over their shoulders at the village, which seemed to be afloat in a sea of mud, they were obviously thinking:

"As long as Don Camillo's there, everything's all right."

Before Don Camillo went back to the presbytery he looked up at the Lord above the altar.

"Forgive me, Lord, for not kneeling. If I were to kneel, I'd be in water up to the neck."

His head was bent and he could not be sure that the Lord

318

had smiled. But he was almost sure that He had, for there was a glow in his heart that made him forget the fact that he was soaked to the waist. He got over to the presbytery, seizing on the way a floating ladder, with whose help he managed to climb into a second-storey window. He changed his clothes, had something to eat and went to bed. Towards three in the afternoon there was a knock at the window.

"Come in," said Don Camillo, and there was Peppone.

"If you'll come down, there's a boat rowed by some of my boys waiting for you," Peppone mumbled.

When a man is lying in bed, or even sitting up in it, he is in no position to come out with a phrase that will go down in history. So Don Camillo leapt to his feet and shouted:

"The old guard dies, but it never surrenders!"

Although he was on his feet, he had nothing on but his drawers, and this detracted from the solemnity of the occasion. But Peppone was in no mood to notice.

"Then devil take you," he said angrily. "You may not get another chance to escape so soon!"

The rescue squad rowed on. When the boat passed in front of the open church door, Peppone shouted to the rowers to watch out on the left. While they were looking in the other direction, he had time to take off his cap and put it back without being observed. For the rest of the way he cudgelled his brain to know what Don Camillo had meant about the old guard that dies but never surrenders. Even if the water stood eight feet high, the flood seemed to him to have abated since he knew that Don Camillo was at his post.

EVERYONE AT HIS POST

MAROLI WAS as old as sin, and all skin and bones, but at times he could be as hard-headed as a young man of twenty-five. When the flood became really serious, his two sons loaded all their belongings on to wagons and prepared to take their families away, but the old man refused to budge. He said as much to his daughters-in-law when they came to carry him down from the bed to which he had been invalided for some time. And the two women told their husbands to do something about it themselves, because there was no use arguing with a madman. The sons and two grandsons went upstairs to try to persuade him, but they received the same answer:

"Here is my home, and here I stay."

His sons explained that the whole village was being evacuated because at any moment the river might overflow its banks, but Maroli only shook his head.

"I'm a sick man and I can't stand the exposure. I'm staying here."

The daughters-in-law came up again to tell their husbands to hurry. And one of them said:

"Don't be silly. No sick people are being left outside in the bad weather. They're all sheltered and taken care of."

Maroli sat up in bed and pointed a rheumatic finger at her.

"I see now. You want to get me away from here and into an institution. For a long time you've been looking for a way to get rid of me. But I don't want to go to the hospital and die there, alone, like a dog. I'll die here, among my own things, even if I am in your way. Here, in this bed where my wife died, I intend to breathe my last. And you must bury me beside her."

All of them together tried to persuade him, but he held fast. Finally his elder son came close to the bed.

"That's enough talking," he shouted. "You take his other shoulder, and you two women hold his feet. We'll carry him down on the mattress."

"Go away, the lot of you," the old man protested.

But they were all around him, holding on to the mattress. A minute more, and they would have lifted it up without the least difficulty, because the old man was light as a feather. He took hold of the shirt-front of his elder son and tried to push him away, but the son was beside himself with exasperation and tore himself loose. He threw the old man back on the bed and held him down.

"Stop this crazy stuff, or I'll bash your head in!" he shouted.

The old man tried to free himself, but it was as if a stone were bearing down on his chest and he could do nothing but suffer.

"Rosa! . . . Rosa! . . ." he called.

But what was a twelve-year-old girl to do?

She threw herself like an angry cat at the man who was pinning him to the bed, but a dozen hands caught hold of her, pushed her aside and slapped her.

"Keep out of this, you stupid girl! Are you crazy?"

The old man was breathless with rage.

"You're crazy!" he shouted. "And chicken-hearted too! If her father were alive, you wouldn't dare treat me this way."

But Rosa's father was dead and buried, and so was her mother. The father was Maroli's favourite and most promising son, and his death had broken the old man's heart.

"We're all you've got now," said his eldest, jeeringly, "and you'll have to do what we say. Let's hurry."

A dozen impatient arms raised up the mattress, while the heavy hands of the eldest son kept the old man still. Just then they heard Rosa's voice:

"Let him go, or I'll shoot!"

A shotgun in the hands of a young girl is more terrifying than a tommy-gun in those of a man. And Rosa was not only a young girl, but not quite right in the head as well, so that naturally enough the owners of the dozen hands (two men, two women and two boys) agreed to let the old man go. They put down the mattress and the eldest son withdrew his hands.

"Go away, or I'll fire!" said the girl.

They backed out of the door and when they were gone the girl chained it.

"I'll send the police and a male nurse after you," shouted the eldest son from the stairs.

The old man was undaunted.

"Better mind your own business, because if anyone comes near I'll burn the house down," he retorted.

As in all the peasant houses of the region, there was a direct connection between the living quarters and the stable. The old man's room was just above this, and next door to the hayloft. He had chosen this room, formerly used to store wheat, because he could look through a hole in the floor and see the animals in the stable below as well as the movements of the men who took care of them. The hayloft was full of hay, and with a piece of tow on the end of a stick he could easily have set it on fire. For this reason his threat threw the rest of the family into a cold perspiration. The old man had a shotgun, a kerosene lamp, a can of kerosene and a mad girl at his disposal.

"We'll leave you alone," they called back from the stair.

"You'd better!" he said mockingly.

When they got out into the yard one of the daughters-in-law had a bright idea and called up to the old man's window:

"If you choose to stay, that's your own business. But let the girl go. You have no right to expose her to danger. Let her come along with us."

The old man was momentarily taken aback.

"Rosa," he said, "the water's rising and there may be danger. If you want to be safe, go along."

The girl shook her head and closed the shutters.

"God blast the two of them!" said the bright daughter-in-law.

And the grandsons observed that if both the old man and the girl were to perish, it would be a gain to everybody, themselves included. Maroli's two sons maintained a gloomy silence. But when they and their possessions had reached safety they looked in the direction of the house and the elder one said angrily:

"This won't last for ever. And when we go back, we'll have to put things in order. He must be sent to a hospital and she to an asylum."

"Yes," said his brother approvingly. "They can't get away with it any longer."

The old man and the girl remained alone in the house and no one knew that they were there. When she was sure that the last of the family had gone, she went downstairs, locked the doors and bolted the windows. There was plenty to eat in the kitchen and the old man told her what to bring upstairs. Finally he told her to put an empty barrel in his room and gradually fill it with buckets of water from the pump below. When evening came she was dead tired and lay down on a mattress on the floor.

"That blessed family may come back," the old man grumbled. "You go ahead and sleep and I'll watch out for them. If I hear anything I'll call you."

He sat on the edge of his bed, shotgun in hand, but nobody came. The next morning the river overflowed its banks and the water rose to within two feet of the downstairs ceiling.

"Now we can set our minds at rest," said the old man.

Toward eleven o'clock they heard a bell ringing and the old man sent the girl to look out of the attic window. She came down after some time and said:

"The church door is open and there's water everywhere. And there's a crowd of people up on the embankment."

At three o'clock she went up to look again and ran down to report:

"There's a boat going round from one house to another."

"Rosa, if you want to go, go," the old man sighed.

"If they come for us we'll set fire to the hayloft," she answered.

The boat came through their yard, and the girl looked out at it through a crack in the shutters.

"There's that big mechanic who always wears a red kerchief," she said to the old man.

And a minute later Peppone called out:

"Is there anyone here?"

The old man and the girl held their breath, and the boat went away.

"The family must have been scared to say anything about

323

us," muttered the old man. "Now we can have some peace and quiet."

Don Camillo awakened suddenly and found himself in the dark. He was so tired that he had fallen asleep in the afternoon, and now evening had overtaken him. When he threw open the window he looked out over an expanse of water as wide as the sea, and saw on the horizon a red fringe left by the sunset. The silence was oppressive, and the memory of cheerfully lighted houses seemed very far away. Now the houses were all blacked out and the water came to within two feet of the ground-floor ceilings. The distant howl of a dog reminded him of his own Thunder. Where was Thunder now? Where had the flood surprised him? The howling continued, and now it seemed to come from directly below and filled him with a mixture of anxiety and fear. He lit the lamp, took a piece of iron and prised up a piece of the floor. There was Thunder, floating on a raft. And the raft was the downstairs table.

Thunder must have been caught by the flood away from home, and God only knows how he had been saved. When the first wave had subsided he must have swum back and in through the front door Here he would have been a prisoner had not the table left downstairs by Don Camillo provided him with a perch and safety. The water had stopped rising and Thunder waited for help from above, until help actually did come from the ceiling. Don Camillo pulled him through the hole, and Thunder shook himself so joyfully that his master was splashed all over.

It was time to ring the Ave Maria bell. Don Camillo was of the school which believes that the old guard dies but never surrenders, and as a corollary to this he believed that the old guard should not resort to swimming for transportation. With four empty petrol tins and a big washing-board he had built himself a raft, upon which he now made his way to the church to talk on his knees to the Lord on the Cross above the submerged altar.

"Lord, forgive me for bringing Thunder to Your house, but he is the only living creature in the village and I couldn't leave him behind. As a matter of fact, You've seen many a church-goer that's more of a dog than Thunder. . . . And forgive me for attaching my old army field altar to the bell tower and saying Mass over there. A flood is something

324

like a war, and I feel as if I had been called to combat duty."

The Lord sighed.

"Don Camillo, what are you doing here?" He asked. "Shouldn't you be with your people?"

"My people are here," Don Camillo answered. "Their bodies may be far away, but they are here in their hearts."

"But, Don Camillo, your strong arms are inactive and useless, instead of bringing help to those who are weaker than yourself."

"I can best help them by ringing the familiar bell to keep up their hope and faith while they are gone. And then, Lord, when Thunder was lost he came to look for me at home rather than among the evacuees. Which means that my post is here."

"It's a pretty poor fellow that looks to an animal for a rule of conduct rather than to his own powers of reason. God gave you a brain to think with, not a dog."

"But God gave me a heart, too. The heart may not reason, but sometimes it is more powerful than the brain. Forgive my heart and Thunder...."

Don Camillo tied up his raft below his bedroom window and went to sleep. Because of the oppressive silence, he slept for a very long time. He was awakened by the barking of Thunder, who was jumping up at the window. Don Camillo took his shotgun and without lighting the lamp peered out between the closed shutters. Someone called him, and he played his flashlight over the water below. He saw a big vat with a bundle of rags stirring at the bottom.

"Who's there?" he called.

"Rosa Maroli," said the bundle of rags. "Grandfather wants to see you."

"Grandfather?"

"He's sick, and wants to die like a Christian."

Don Camillo put the girl on his raft and pushed off with a long pole in his hand.

"What in Heaven's name are you doing here?" he asked her.

"Grandfather wanted to stay and I want to keep him company."

"Haven't you been scared?"

325

"No. Grandfather was there. And we could see a light in the presbytery and hear the church bell."

Old Maroli had not much longer to live.

"They wanted to send me to the hospital to die like a dog," he said. "But I want to die a Christian death in my own house. . . . And they said I was crazy . . . yes, and that she was crazy too."

The girl stared at him dumbly.

"Rosa," he panted, "is it true that you're crazy?"

She shook her head.

"Sometimes my head aches and I can't seem to understand," she said timidly.

"Her head aches, do you hear?" said the old man. "She fell on a stone when she was little, and there's a bone pressing on her brain. The doctor told me that himself. He told me they could cure her with an operation. Then I fell ill, and the others wouldn't spend the money. . . . They want to send her to the asylum, because it hurts their conscience to see her."

"Calm yourself; I'm here," said Don Camillo, trying to check the old man's growing excitement.

"You must arrange for that operation . . ." said the old man. "Now, just pull my bed out a little. . . . There on the wall. . . . Lift out that striped brick. . . ."

Don Camillo moved the brick and found a heavy bag behind it.

"Gold!" panted the old man. "Gold coins. . . . All mine, and all for her! Have her operated on, and send her to stay with someone who can give her an education. We'll show them how crazy we are, Rosa, won't we?"

The girl nodded.

"I want to die like a Christian," panted the old man.

When Don Camillo rose from his knees, it was dawn. Old man Maroli had died like a Christian, and the girl was staring with wide-open eyes at his motionless body.

"Come with me," said Don Camillo gently. "No one will upset your grandfather any more. And no one will upset you, either."

He took hold of a chair and with his enormous hands broke a leg in two as easily as if it were a breadstick.

"That's what I'll do to anyone who touches you."

Thunder waited for them, barking, at Don Camillo's

window. The priest poled up to it and told the girl to go through.

"Lie down on the first bed you find," he said, "and have a good sleep."

Then he went over to the church and stopped in front of the altar.

"Lord," he said, "now you see what I meant. She said herself that she wasn't afraid because she could see my light and hear the church bell ring. . . . And she isn't crazy. She had a bad fall as a child. The operation will cure that."

"You must have had a bad fall as a child, too," said the Lord gently. "But there's nothing can cure you. You'll always listen to your heart rather than your brain . . . may God keep that heart of yours whole!"

Thunder kept watch at the foot of the bed where Rosa lay sleeping. The bell tolled for old man Maroli's death, but no one heard it, because the wind carried the sound away.

At last the big river returned to its bed and the people were busy putting their land and homes in order. A thick autumn fog hung over the drenched valley, but everybody felt the danger had passed and that, above the mist, the sky was serene. Once more Don Camillo was able to celebrate Mass in his little church. The organ notes vibrated in thanksgiving, and from the towers of church and Town Hall the chimes echoed through the valley while the golden wings of the great angel seemed to spread over the little world.

DON CAMILLO'S DILEMMA

translated by
FRANCES FRENAYE

ELECTIONEERING IN THE HOME

PEPPONE HAD hardly gobbled down the last mouthful of his supper when, as usual, he started to jump up from the table and go out for the rest of the evening. But this time his wife didn't let him get away.

"I want to have a talk with you."

"I haven't time," said Peppone. "They're waiting for me at headquarters."

"Let them wait! After all, you're not married to them. For months we haven't been able to exchange a word."

"Don't harass me," said Peppone, breathing hard. "You know I'm not going out for fun. Elections are coming. Just a few days more, and then here's hoping we've seen the last of them for another five years."

"Good. But if we don't discuss it now, when election day does come around, I'll find myself with a ballot in my hand and not a thought in my head. What am I supposed to do? For whom should I vote?"

"That's the limit!" exclaimed Peppone. "You want me to tell you how to vote!"

"Where should I go to ask? To the priest? You're supposed to tell me what's what."

"But things are exactly the way they were before."

"Then I vote again for you?"

"No, when you voted for me, it was a local election. This is a nation-wide affair, the way it was in 1948."

"I see. Then I should vote for the Garibaldi ticket."

331

"No, silly! The Garibaldi ticket's a thing of the past. Every party has a symbol of its own. Do you at least know the symbols?"

"Yes, I do."

"Then all you have to do is make an X over the symbol of the party you have chosen. I don't see what else there is to explain. Nothing has changed."

She shook her head in perplexity.

"Even now that he's dead, is the Party just the same?"

"Just the same, only more so!" shouted Peppone, bringing a fist down on the table. "Men may pass, but ideas are eternal!"

"But this Malenkov doesn't seem to me as powerful as Stalin. He looks more like a compromiser."

"Don't listen to foolish gossip! Just give Malenkov a chance and you'll see! He employs different tactics, but the goal is still the same."

"Then you think we're still moving toward the proletarian revolution?"

"It's closer than ever!" Peppone declared. "Present tactics are designed to allay the enemy's suspicions. Then, when the time comes, we'll put one over."

She did not appear to be altogether convinced.

"You say the situation's the same as it was in 1948. . . ."

"Where Communism's concerned, it's a hundred per cent better. In 1948 Communism was terrific, and now it's tremendous. Stalin may be dead, but his spirit marches on, at the head of the victorious armies of liberation."

"So it isn't true that the Russians want peace, the way they say they do, is that it?"

"Of course it's true! They want peace, but as long as there are warmongers, peace is impossible. In order to obtain peace, the western warmongers must be eliminated. And that means America, the Vatican, big businessmen, priests, landowners, reactionaries, fascists, royalists, liberals, social-democrats, imperialists, nationalists, militarists and intellectuals. It will take an enormous blood-bath to cleanse the world of this medieval residue. We must destroy a rotten old world in order to build up one that's healthy and new. Don't listen to gossip, I tell you. The Garibaldi ticket has been replaced by one that bears our own symbol, but the situation is just what it was before. You can go right ahead, without any misgivings, and vote as you did in 1948."

"All right, Chief," she said, not mentioning the fact that in 1948 she voted for the Christian Democrats.

"Anyhow," Peppone said as he got up, "I'm not imposing my choice upon you. You're free to do as you please, and I shan't even ask what is your decision. Even as a husband, I'm genuinely democratic."

"Oh, I'm not changing my mind," she protested. "I chose, once and for all, last time."

"Good," said Peppone, starting toward the door. "And would you get my gun out of the drawer this evening so I can clean it when I come home? If we win, then we're to start shooting. That's orders."

After Peppone had gone, his wife stared for a long time at the door. Then she raised her eyes to heaven and prayed:

"Lord, make them lose!"

Meanwhile, as Peppone passed by the church on his way to the People's Palace, he mumbled to himself:

"Lord, please let us win. But without my wife's vote, if you don't mind!"

IN THE village and its surroundings there were quite a lot of people who started as early as February to lay aside money for the pre-Lenten Carnival. There were twelve rival clubs, five in the village and seven in the countryside, and every Saturday the members contributed part of their pay to the decoration of the floats which each one entered in the parade. In short, the brief Carnival season was a very important affair.

The floats came into being bit by bit in farmyards scattered over the plain. Each club chose the farmyard most suitable for the purpose and with poles, sticks, reed mats and blinds, strips of canvas and tarred paper built a shed which housed the construction. Only members of the club were allowed to look in until the great day came. Then the shed was joyfully torn down and the float emerged, for all the world like a chick newly hatched from the shell. There were sizable prizes to be won, and individual floats and costumed figures came from nearby townships and even from the city. For three whole days the village was crowded.

The Carnival was a serious affair, not only because it drew so many people in a spending mood to the village, but also because it brought with it a complete truce to all political activities. For this reason Don Camillo never made it the butt of any of his sermons.

"Lord," he explained to Christ over the main altar, "we've come to a point where men behave themselves only when they're silly. Let's allow them their fun: *Semel in anno licet insanire."*

As for Mayor Peppone, he frowned upon the Carnival because it irritated him to see that men couldn't pull together for any cause other than a frivolous one.

"They'll all come across with the money to decorate one of those stupid floats," he protested. "But just try to put over something worth while, such as the People's Revolution, and every last one of them is a skinflint."

Peppone spoke against the Carnival for six months of the year. For the other six months he worked overtime organizing the parade and helping to build his own club's float. Incidentally, he put up considerable money. And if a local float failed to win the first prize, he took it as a personal insult.

That year everything smiled upon the Carnival, because it came in a period of exceptionally fine weather and people came from far and wide to see it. Competing floats and wearers of fancy dress arrived from a widespread area, and no one had ever witnessed so long a parade, which as usual wound its way around the village three times. From his post in the grandstand Peppone looked down at the first round with general satisfaction, finding it worthy of the population gathered in such large numbers to acclaim it. As a result his deportment seemed to be modelled upon that of the Lord Mayor of London.

When the parade came around for the second time, he began to look more closely at the various entries in order to determine whether those of the village were likely to carry away the first prize, or at least the second, third, fourth and fifth prizes. In other words, he was transformed from Lord Mayor of London into mayor of his own town. And among the single competitors for a fancy-dress prize his eyes fell upon a Red Indian riding a motorcycle. After the fellow had gone by, he wondered exactly what had drawn his attention, for the costume had nothing extraordinary about it, being composed chiefly of a big cardboard nose and a band of chicken feathers around the head. He concluded that it must have reminded him of something from times gone by, and sure enough, it came to him in a flash that it was the poster figure that used to advertise "Indian Motorcycles."

During the third round Peppone ascertained that there was indeed a basis for his conclusion. This was the "Indian Motorcycle" figure, and no mistake about it. Only the figure

335

wasn't riding an "Indian" at all; he was astride an old B.S.A. model. Where motorcycles and their engines were concerned, Peppone was like one of those musical quiz experts, who no sooner hear a few notes from a piece than they can tell you its title and composer. And there was a further reason why he could make no mistake: this particular motorcycle had been in his hands for repairs at least a hundred times. Only one question remained in Peppone's mind: Who was riding in Indian costume on Dario Camoni's old B.S.A.?

He left the grandstand, having momentarily lost all interest in the parade. This was a matter that had nothing to do with the mayoralty; it was of a strictly private character. He made his way with difficulty through the crowd, trying to keep up with the Indian, and during a brief pause, the latter turned his head and looked at him. Peppone's doubts vanished. The rider of Dario Camoni's old B.S.A. was Dario Camoni. Even behind a cardboard mask, those were unmistakably his eyes.

Peppone continued to follow the parade, step by step, and nothing in the world could have stopped his implacable *Panzer* pursuit. When the parade had gone around for the third time it drew up in the open space between the village and the river and disbanded. There was such an array of floats, lorries and farm wagons that the Indian could not possibly escape. The only opening in the crowd was on to the street that had led them away from the central square. He was aware that Peppone had been following him and did not hesitate to turn around in this direction, even at the risk of running down a pedestrian. But after he had gone a few yards an enormous float blocked the street and he had to dart into an alley on the right, with Peppone practically panting down his neck from behind.

The smaller square in front of the church was deserted, and the redskin sped up the alley with this destination in view. A few seconds later, he braked his machine abruptly in order not to run down Don Camillo, who was smoking a cigar butt in front of the rectory. Once upon a time this alley had made a right-angle turn just in front of the rectory and gone into the road leading to the river, but for the last ten years it had been blocked off.

Don Camillo was stunned by the abruptness of the motorcycle's arrival. His impulse was to grab the fellow by the chest and knock his head against the wall for his reckless folly. But

336

he was too late. The motorcyclist had dropped his machine on the street and dashed through the rectory's open door. A second later Peppone rushed upon the scene, and without so much as a glance at the priest, followed the fugitive's example. But Don Camillo's powerful body stood in the way.

"What the devil?" Don Camillo shouted. "What in the world are you doing? First an Indian nearly runs me down with a motorcycle and then a mayor bumps into me on foot. Is it all part of some symbolical charade?"

"Look, you've got to let me in," panted Peppone, reluctantly drawing back. "I have a score to settle with Dario Camoni."

"Camoni? How does he come into the picture?"

"That Indian is Camoni!" said Peppone between clenched teeth.

Don Camillo pushed Peppone back, went into the rectory and fastened the door behind him with a chain. The Indian was sitting in the study, and the first thing Don Camillo did was to pull off his cardboard nose.

"Well, it's me, all right," said the Indian, rising from his chair. "What are you going to do about it?"

Don Camillo sat down at his desk and relighted his cigar.

"Nothing at all," he answered, after he had blown several puffs of smoke into the air. "But you'd be better off if you really were an Indian."

Back in 1922 the river country of the little world was still in a state of political ferment, even although elsewhere the Fascists had consolidated their governmental position. The land had something to do with it, and so did the boiling-point of its people. Dario Camoni was seventeen years old, and he wanted to make up for the time when he was too young to take part in the Black-versus-Red battle. In 1919, when he was a mere fourteen years old, some Reds had beaten up his father for refusing to take part in a farm labour strike, right in front of his eyes. This explains, among other things, why three years later Dario was still in a combative mood, and ready to beat up any stray Red he could find for revenge.

Dario Camoni was a husky boy, and above all a hotheaded one. When he went into action his eyes blazed in a way that was more convincing than any amount of words. Peppone was several years older and stood head and shoulders above him, but those cursed eyes caused him to steer clear. One evening when Peppone was talking to his girl on the bridge in front of her house, Dario Camoni rode up on a motor-cycle.

"Sorry to intrude," he said, "but I've been given a job to do."

He took a glass and a bottle out of his pocket and proceeded to empty the contents of the bottle into the glass.

"The doctor says you have indigestion and a little laxative will do you good," he continued, advancing with the full glass in one hand and his other hand grasping a hard object in his pocket. "My advice to you is to take your medicine, because some of this castor oil dripped on to my revolver and I don't want the trigger to slip in my fingers. If the dose is too strong for you, you can share it with your girl. I'm going to count to three. One ... two ..."

Peppone took the glass and drained it to the last drop.

"Good for you!" said Dario Camoni, mounting his motor-cycle. "Be careful not to step on certain people's toes, or you may get something worse next time."

Although Peppone had managed to drink the castor oil, a form of punishment which the Fascists had brought into style, he could not swallow the insult, which was all the more grave because Dario had humiliated him in front of his girl. As it happened, he married the girl later on, but that made it worse rather than better. Every time that he raised his voice at home his wife taunted him:

"If the fellow who gave you the dose of castor oil that night were here, you wouldn't be up on such a high horse, would you?"

No, Peppone had never forgotten this dirty trick, and neither, for that matter, had Don Camillo. In that far-away 1922, Don Camillo was a greenhorn priest, just out of the seminary, but he was nobody's fool and preached a sermon against violence in general, and in particular against the bullies who were going around forcing unsavoury drinks upon other people. For this reason, one night he was called downstairs because someone was fatally ill and needed Extreme Unction. When he came down, there was Dario Camoni, with a Mauser in one hand and a glass of castor oil in the other.

"You're the one that needs the oil, Father, even if it's unholy. This will make your motor hum. And because I owe you particular respect as a member of the clergy, I'll count to four instead of to three."

338

And Don Camillo drank his ration down.

"There, Father," said Dario Camoni, "you'll see how much more clearly your brain will function tomorrow. And if you really want to be reduced to a condition where you'll need holy oil rather than unholy, just go on sticking your nose into our business."

"The Church's business extends to everything that concerns good Christian people," objected Don Camillo.

"If we'd used Christian behaviour toward the Reds, your church would be a Red headquarters and seat of the Consumers' Co-operative today! Anyhow, whenever you need to change the oil in your motor, just whistle!"

Like Peppone, Don Camillo had found it easier to swallow the oil than the insult.

"Lord," he said several times to Christ over the altar. "If he'd beaten me up, it would be different. But castor oil is too much. You can kill a priest, but you have no right to make him ridiculous with a dose of castor oil!"

Years went by, and Dario Camoni remained an active Fascist as long as there was strong-arm work to be done. Then he retired from politics altogether. But he had oiled and beaten up too many people in his time to be forgotten. When the régime was overturned, in 1945, he found things too hot for him and went away. And Peppone sent word after him to say that if he showed his face in the village it would be at the risk of his skin. More years passed, without news of Dario Camoni. And now he had returned, in the disguise of a Red Indian.

"I'd like to know what got into your head to think up something like this," Don Camillo said to Dario Camoni.

"I've been away from home for six years," murmured the Indian, "and I wanted like anything to come back. The only way I could do it was in disguise. Seems to me it wasn't such a bad idea."

"Poor Camoni!" Don Camillo said with a sigh. "You're so comical in your Indian dress that I'm inclined to be sorry for you. An Indian on a motorcycle, who takes refuge in the priest's house from a mayor who is chasing him on foot. It's almost as melodramatic as the comics. Well, you may as well take it easy. You're almost a hundred per cent safe. If there weren't that glass of castor oil between us, I'd say a hundred per cent with no reservations."

339

"Is that silly business still on your mind?" asked the Indian, who was still panting from the chase. "That was thirty years ago and childish."

Don Camillo was about to embark upon a long harangue when the study door swung open and Peppone appeared on the scene.

"Excuse me, Father, for coming through the window," he said, "but I had no other choice, since I couldn't come through the door."

The Indian had leaped to his feet, for the expression on Peppone's face wasn't exactly pretty. Moreover, Peppone had an iron bar in his hand and looked as if he intended to put it to use. Don Camillo stepped between them.

"Don't let's have a tragedy in the middle of the Carnival," he interposed. "We must all be calm."

"I'm perfectly calm," said Peppone, "and I have no intention of causing a tragedy. I have a job to do, that's all."

He took two glasses out of one pocket, then, without taking his eyes off the Indian, a bottle out of the other and divided its contents between them.

"There," he said, standing back against the door. "The doctor says you have indigestion and a little laxative will do you good. Hurry up, because the oil has greased my iron bar and I'm afraid it may slip and fall on to your head. Drink down both glassfuls, one to my health and the other to the health of Don Camillo. I'm happy to pay my respects to him in this way."

The Indian turned pale as he backed up against the wall, and Peppone was truly fear-inspiring.

"Drink them down, I tell you!" he shouted, raising the iron bar.

"No, I won't," answered the Indian.

Peppone rushed forward and grabbed him by the neck.

"I'll make you drink!" he shouted.

But the Indian's neck and face were covered with greasepaint and he managed to free himself. He leaped behind the table, and as Peppone and Don Camillo noticed too late for their own good, he took down the shotgun hanging on the wall and pointed it straight at Peppone.

"Don't do anything crazy," shouted Don Camillo, drawing over to one side, "that thing is loaded."

The Indian advanced on his enemy.

"Throw down that bar," he said sternly, and his eyes were

340

as blazing as they had been thirty years before. Peppone and Don Camillo both remembered them distinctly, and knew that Dario Camoni was quite capable of shooting. Peppone let the bar fall to the floor.

"Now *you* drink," the Indian said between clenched teeth to Peppone. "I'll count to three. One . . . two . . ."

Yes, he had the same wild eyes and the same voice as long ago. Peppone gulped down the contents of one of the glasses.

"And now go back where you came from," the Indian commanded.

Peppone went away, and the Indian barred the study door.

"He can send his police if he wants to," he said, "but if I'm killed, I won't go to Hell alone."

Don Camillo relit his cigar.

"That's enough of your horseplay," he said quietly. "Put down that gun and go away."

"Go away yourself," said the Indian coldly. "I'm waiting for them here."

"Very unwise, Redskin," said the priest. "I don't believe the palefaces will come, but if they do, how can you defend yourself with an empty gun?"

"That's an old joke and a poor one," laughed the Indian. "I wasn't born yesterday, for your information!"

Don Camillo went to sit down on the other side of the room.

"Just look and see," he suggested.

The suspicious Camoni peered into the gun and his face whitened. The gun was not loaded.

"Put the gun down," said Don Camillo quietly; "take off your costume, leave the rectory on the garden side and cut through the fields. If you hurry, you'll catch the bus at Fontanile. I'll put your motorcycle in safe-keeping, and you can either let me know where to send it or else come and fetch it in person."

The Indian laid the gun on the desk.

"No use looking for the cartridges," Don Camillo told him. He had put on his glasses and was reading the paper. "The cartridges are in the cupboard and the key to the cupboard is in my pocket. I warn you that unless you get out of here in double-quick time, I'll be reminded of that drink you pressed upon me long ago."

The Indian tore off the remains of his costume and wiped

341

the grease-paint off his face. He took a cap out of his pocket and jammed it down over his head. Dario Camoni started to leave the room, but he lingered at the door and turned hesitantly around.

"Let's even the score," he said, and picking up the second glass of castor oil, he drained it.

"Quits?" he said interrogatively.

"Quits," answered Don Camillo, without even raising his head.

And the Indian disappeared.

Peppone came back later, looking green around the gills.

"I hope you won't sink so low as to go around telling what happened to me," he said gloomily.

"I should say not," Don Camillo answered with a sigh. "You had one glass, but that wretch made me drink the other."

"Has he gone away?" asked Peppone, sitting down.

"Gone with the wind."

Peppone stared at the floor and said nothing.

"Well, what can I say?" he finally mumbled. "It was a little like going back to the time when we were young, thirty years ago. . . ."

"True enough," said Don Camillo. "That Indian brought back a bit of our youth."

Peppone started to relapse into anger.

"Easy there, Peppone," Don Camillo advised him. "You don't want to endanger the dignity of your office."

Peppone went cautiously home, and Don Camillo made a report to the crucified Christ over the altar.

"Lord," he explained, "what else could I do? If I'd told Peppone the gun wasn't loaded he'd have killed the other fellow for sure. Those Camonis are too pig-headed to ever give in. As things are, there was no violence, and the Indian had a dose of oil, which You must chalk up to his credit. And by sacrificing my personal pride, I managed not to humiliate Peppone."

"Don Camillo," Christ answered, "when the Indian told Peppone to drink the oil, you knew the gun wasn't loaded and you could perfectly well have stepped in."

"Lord," said Don Camillo, throwing out his arms in resignation, "what if Peppone had found out that the gun wasn't loaded and failed to get that healthy drink?"

"Don Camillo," Christ said severely, "I ought to prescribe a drink of the same kind for you!"

It seems that as Don Camillo left the church he was muttering something to the effect that only Fascists could order any such prescription. But this is not altogether certain. In any case, when he hung the shotgun up on the wall, he placed the Indian bonnet as a trophy beside it, and every time he looked at it he reflected that there is perfectly good hunting to be found without benefit of a gun.

A SOUL FOR SALE

NERI, THE mason, had been hammering away for three hours without accomplishing much of anything. The wall seemed to be an unbreakable solid mass, and he had to smash every brick before he could get it out. He stopped for a minute to wipe the sweat off his forehead, and cursed when he saw how small a hole he had made with so much effort.

"It's going to take patience," said the voice of old Molotti, who had engaged him to do the work, behind him.

"Patience, my eye!" Neri exclaimed ill-humouredly. "This is no wall, it's a block of steel. It'll take something more than patience to pierce a door."

He started pounding again, but a few minutes later he dropped his hammer and chisel and let out another oath. He had given his left thumb a tremendous crack and it was bleeding.

"I told you to take it easy," said Molotti. "If you'd had a bit more patience you wouldn't have lost your temper and banged your own thumb."

Neri's only answer was another outburst of profanity.

Old Molotti shook his head.

"God Almighty has nothing to do with it," he said. "You can only blame the fellow who was wielding the hammer. And remember, you'll never get to Heaven without a lot of pain."

"It's painful enough to make a living," Neri retorted angrily. "I don't give a damn for your Heaven."

Neri was as Red as they make them, and one of Peppone's

344

most excitable followers, but although Molotti was over ninety years old, he wasn't going to let that upset him.

"I'd forgotten that you don't give a damn for our Heaven," he said. "You're one of the Reds, aren't you, and they promise some sort of heaven on earth."

"That's a lot more honest than promising it somewhere up in the sky," countered Neri. "We promise things you can see and touch with your own hands."

"Never fear!" said Molotti, raising an admonitory finger. "Some day you'll see and touch things that are now hidden from you."

Neri burst into loud laughter.

"When I'm dead, I'm dead, and that's the end of everything for me. Anything else is just priest's chatter."

"May God save your soul!" sighed old Molotti.

Neri resumed his hammering.

"Who could have believed that people would still go around preaching all that stuff and nonsense!" he muttered. "My soul, eh? A soul flapping through the air with a brand-new pair of wings, and receiving a prize for its good behaviour! You must take me for a complete idiot!"

"If I didn't think you were talking tough just to enjoy the sound of your own voice, when all the time you know better deep down inside, then I'd say you were crazy."

"You priests and landowners are crazy, to imagine you can still hand us out all that nonsense!"

Old Molotti shook his head. "Do you really think the soul dies with the body?" he asked.

"Just as sure as I am to be alive. There isn't such a thing as a soul!"

"And what have you got inside you?"

"Lungs, liver, spleen, brains, heart, stomach and intestines. We're flesh-and-blood machines, which run just as long as these organs are working. When one of them breaks down, the machine stops, and if the doctor can't repair it, then it's good-bye, machine."

Old Molotti threw out his arms in indignation.

"But you've forgotten the soul!" he shouted. "The soul is the breath of life!"

"Bunk!" said Neri. "Try taking out a man's lungs and you'll see what happens. If the soul were the breath of life, he ought to be able to get along without them."

"That's blasphemy!"

345

"No, I'm just using my reason. Anyone can see that life is linked to the internal organs. I've never seen a man die because they've taken his soul away. And if you say the soul's the breath of life, then chickens must have souls just like the rest of us, and go to the same Heaven, Purgatory and Hell."

Old Molotti saw that it was no use to argue further and so he walked away. But he hadn't given up the struggle and at noon, when Neri had stopped to eat his lunch, he came over to the shady spot where he was sitting.

"Look here," said Neri, "if you want to fight some more, you're wasting your time, I can tell you."

"I have no intention of fighting," said the old man. "I want to make you a strictly business proposition. You're perfectly sure, are you, that you have no soul?"

Neri's face clouded over, but Molotti did not give him time to protest.

"In that case, you may as well sell it to me," he continued. "I'm offering you five hundred liras."

Neri looked at the banknote in the old man's hand and burst out laughing.

"That's a good one! How can I sell you something I haven't got?"

"That's not your worry," Molotti insisted. "You're selling me your soul. If you actually don't possess such a thing, then I lose my money. But if you do have it, then it's mine."

Neri began to enjoy himself thoroughly. He thought the old man must have softening of the brain.

"Five hundred liras isn't much," he said gaily, "you might at least offer me a thousand."

"No," said Molotti. "A soul like yours isn't worth it."

"But I won't take less!"

"Very well, then, a thousand. Before you go home we'll put it in writing."

Neri hammered away, more cheerfully, until evening. When it was time to knock off, the old man brought him a fountain pen and a sheet of legal paper.

"Are you still willing?" he asked.

"Of course."

"Then sit down and write: 'I Francesco Neri, hereby legally bind myself, in return for the sum of one thousand liras, to sell my soul to Giuseppe Molotti. Having paid me this sum, Molotti enters from this day forth into possession

346

and can dispose of my soul as he sees fit. Signed: Francesco Neri.'"

Molotti handed Neri a thousand-lira note, and Neri made his signature with an appropriate flourish.

"Good!" said the old man. "The business is done, and that's all there is to it."

Neri laughed as he went away. Yes, Molotti was in his dotage, that was the only explanation. He only wished he'd asked for more money. But this thousand-lira note was so much gravy.

As he pedalled off on his broken-down bicycle, he couldn't get the strange contract off his mind. "If Molotti isn't in his dotage, as he seems to be, why would he give me a thousand liras?" he wondered. The rich old man was notoriously stingy, and he wouldn't part with his money for no purpose. All of a sudden Neri saw the whole thing clearly. He let out a volley of oaths and pedalled back as fast he could in order to make up for his stupidity. He found old Molotti in the yard and came out immediately with what was on his mind.

"Look here," he said gloomily. "I was a fool not to think of it before. But better late than never. I know your reactionary methods. You got that contract out of me for propaganda purposes. You're going to publish it in order to ridicule my Party. 'Here are the Communists,' you'll say, 'people that go around selling their souls for a thousand liras!'"

The old man shook his head.

"This is a strictly private affair," he answered. "But if you like, I'll add a guarantee to the contract: 'I swear never to show this document to anyone whatsoever.' Does that suit you?"

Molotti was an honourable man, and his solemn oath was to be respected. He went into his study, wrote down the codicil and signed it.

"You've nothing to worry about," he said. "But as far as that goes, you needn't have worried before. I didn't buy your soul for political purposes. I bought it for my own private use."

"That is, if you can lay your hands on it!" said Neri, who was restored to his good humour.

"Naturally," said Molotti. "And as far as I'm concerned it's good business. I'm quite sure you have a soul, and besides, this would be the first time in my life I'd failed to strike a good bargain."

347

Neri went home feeling completely reassured. Molotti had softening of the brain. At his age, that wasn't surprising. He wanted to tell his cronies the story, but he was afraid that if it got around, the reactionaries would use it to shock their public of churchgoing old ladies.

The alterations of Molotti's house lasted for over a week and Neri met the old man every day. But Molotti made no mention of the contract and entered into no political discussion. It seemed as if he had forgotten the whole thing. After the job was done, Neri had no further occasion to see him, and a whole year went by before the matter returned to his mind.

One evening Peppone called him to lend a hand in the workshop. He had forged the parts of a wrought-iron gate, and now it was a question of putting them together.

"It's an order from old man Molotti." Peppone told him, "and he wants it finished by tomorrow morning. The gate's for his family tomb. He says he wants to have it made before he dies, because none of the rest of them has enough sense to do the proper thing."

"Is he sick?" Neri asked.

"He's been in bed for a week with a bad cold that's gone down into his lungs. And at ninety-three years of age, that's no joke."

Neri began to work the bellows.

"Then there's one more reactionary swine gone," he muttered. "Even the family ought to be glad, because he's in his dotage."

"I wouldn't say that," put in Peppone. "Only a month ago he made a deal with the Trespiano farm which netted him at least fifteen million liras."

"Just disgusting good luck," said Neri. "I happen to know that he's been dotty for some time. Chief, shall I tell you a story?"

And he proceeded to tell how he had sold his soul to Molotti. Peppone listened attentively.

"Don't you think a man must be soft in the head to buy another man's soul for a thousand liras?" Neri concluded.

"Yes, I do, but the man that sells it is even softer."

"Well, of course I should have got much more money than that out of him," said Neri, shrugging his shoulders.

"I'm not speaking of the price," said Peppone.

Neri took his hand off the bellows.

"Chief, are you joining the Children of Mary? What in the world do you mean? Never mind the attitude of the Party and the policy of not making a frontal attack upon organized religion, but just between ourselves, don't you agree that the soul, Heaven, Hell and all the rest of that stuff are just priestly inventions?"

Peppone continued to hammer out the red-hot iron.

"Neri," he said, after a long pause, "that's irrelevant. I say that for a man to sell his soul for a thousand liras is non-productive and counter-revolutionary."

"Now, I understand, Chief," said Neri with relief. "But you needn't worry. In order to prevent him from turning the thing to political use, I had a codicil added, which stipulates that Molotti will never speak about it to anyone."

"Well, with that codicil, it's different," said Peppone. "That makes it your own private business, which is of no concern to the Party. As far as the Party goes, you're in perfectly good standing."

Peppone proceeded to talk of other matters, and Neri went home at midnight in an excellent humour.

"The main thing is to be in good standing with the Party," he said to himself before falling asleep. "Then everything else is in line, too."

Molotti got worse and worse every day. One evening, when Don Camillo was coming back from his bedside, he ran into Neri.

"Good evening," said Neri, and Don Camillo was so bowled over that he was moved to get off his bicycle and go and look him in the face.

"Extraordinary!" he exclaimed. "You're Neri, sure enough, and you said good evening to me. Are you sure you weren't making a mistake? Did you take me for a tax collector instead of the parish priest?"

Neri shrugged his shoulders.

"With you, it's hard to know how to behave. If we don't speak to you, you say we're godless Reds, and if we do, then you think we're crazy."

"You've got something there," said Don Camillo, throwing out his arms. "But that's not the whole story. Anyhow, good evening to you."

Neri stared for a minute at the handlebars of Don Camillo's bicycle. Finally he said:

"How's old man Molotti?"

"He's dying by slow degrees."

"Has he lost consciousness?"

"No, he's perfectly clear-headed and has been all along."

"Has he said anything to you?" asked Neri aggressively.

Don Camillo opened his eyes wide in astonishment.

"I don't understand. What should he say?"

"Hasn't he said anything about me and about a contract between us?"

"No," said Don Camillo, convincingly. "We've talked about practically everything, but not about you. And besides, I don't go to talk to a dying man about business matters. My concern is with souls."

This last word caused Neri to start, and Don Camillo nodded and smiled.

"Neri, I have no intention of preaching at you. I told you what it was my duty to tell when you were a little boy and came to hear. Now all I do is answer your questions. I've had no talk about any business contract with Molotti and I have no intention of bringing up any such subject. If you need help of that kind, consult a lawyer. But hurry, because Molotti has one foot in the next world, already."

"If I stopped you, it's because I needed a priest's help, not a lawyer's," Neri insisted. "It's just a small matter but you must give Molotti a thousand liras and ask him to return a certain legal paper."

"A legal paper? A thousand liras? That sounds to me very much like a lawyer's affair."

By this time they had come to the rectory, and after casting a suspicious eye about him, Neri followed Don Camillo in. The priest sat down at his desk and motioned Neri to a chair.

"If you think I can really help you, go ahead and tell me what it's all about."

Neri twisted his hat in his hands and finally said:

"Father, the fact is this. A year ago, in return for a thousand liras, I sold Molotti my soul."

Don Camillo started. Then he said threateningly:

"Listen, if you think that's a good joke, you've come to the wrong place. Get out of here!"

"It's no joke," Neri protested. "I was working in his house and we had a discussion about the soul. I said there was no such thing and he said: 'If you don't believe the soul exists, then you may as well sell yours to me for a thousand liras.' I accepted his offer and signed a contract."

"A contract?"

"Yes, an agreement written and signed by my hand, on legal paper."

He knew the terms of the contract by heart and recited them to Don Camillo. The priest could not help being persuaded of his sincerity.

"I see," he said, "but why do you want the paper? If you don't believe you have a soul, then why do you care whether or not you sold it?"

"It's not on account of the soul," Neri explained. "I don't want his heirs to find that paper and make political capital out of it. That might damage the Party."

Don Camillo got up and stood in front of Neri with his hands on his hips and his legs far apart.

"Listen to me," he said between clenched teeth. "Am I supposed to help you for the sake of your party? You must take me for the stupidest priest that ever was! Get along with you!"

Neri went slowly toward the door. But after a few steps he turned back.

"Never mind about the Party!" he exclaimed. "I want my paper!"

Don Camillo was standing with his hands on his hips, defiantly.

"I want my paper!" Neri repeated. "For six months I haven't had a decent night's sleep."

Don Camillo looked at the man's distraught face and eyes and the perspiration on his forehead.

"My paper!" he panted. "If the swine insists upon making money, even on his deathbed, then I'll pay something extra, whatever he asks. But I can't go to his house. They wouldn't let me in, and besides, I wouldn't know how to put it."

"Take it easy!" interrupted Don Camillo. "If it's not for the Party, what does it matter? The soul and the next world and all that sort of thing are priestly inventions——"

"The reason's not your affair," Neri shouted. "I want my paper, I tell you!"

"Very well, then," said Don Camillo resignedly, "I'll try to get it for you tomorrow morning."

"No, right now!" Neri insisted. "Tomorrow morning he may be dead. Take the thousand liras and go to him right away, while he's still alive. I'll wait for you outside. Hurry, Father, hurry!"

Don Camillo understood, but he still couldn't tolerate the miscreant's peremptory way of speaking. And so he continued to stand there with his hands on his hips, looking into Neri's distraught face.

"Father, go ahead and do your duty!" Neri shouted in exasperation.

All of a sudden Don Camillo was overtaken by the same impatience. He ran out, minus his hat, jumped on to his bicycle and rode away in the darkness.

An hour later Don Camillo returned and Neri once more followed him into the rectory.

"Here you are," said the priest, handing him a large sealed envelope. Inside were another envelope, closed with sealing-wax, and a short letter. The letter ran as follows: "The undersigned, Giuseppe Molotti, hereby declares null and void the contract he made with Francesco Neri and restores it to him." And there, in the smaller envelope, was the famous piece of legal paper.

"He didn't want the thousand liras," said Don Camillo. "Take them. He said to do with them whatever you liked."

Neri did not say a word, but went out with all his belongings in his hands. He thought of tearing up the contract, but on further reflection decided to burn it. The side door of the church was still open and he could see candles blazing. He went in and paused in front of the big candle behind the altar rail. Holding the paper in the flame, he watched it crumple, then squeezed it in his hand until it was reduced to ashes. Finally he opened his fingers and blew the ashes away. Just as he was about to leave, he remembered the thousand liras, took them out of the envelope and stuffed them in the poor-box. Then, quite unexpectedly, he took another thousand-lira note out of his pocket and put it in the same place. "For a blessing received," he thought to himself as he went home. His eyes were drowsy and he knew that this night he would sleep.

Shortly after this, Don Camillo went to lock up the church and bid good-night to the Christ over the altar.

"Lord," he asked, "who can possibly understand these people?"

"I can," the Crucified Christ answered, smiling.

BEAUTY AND THE BEAST

THEY HAD met dozens of times in the People's Palace, marched side by side in parade, gone out as a team to collect signatures for the Peace Crusade and other devilries of the same kind, and so it was natural enough that things should come spontaneously to a head one summer evening.

"It seems to me we two work pretty smoothly together," Marco said to the girl as they came out of the People's Palace.

"I think so too," Giulietta admitted.

They didn't say anything more, but the next evening Marco went over to Brusco's house to call for Giulietta. Then they went to sit together on the bridge that spanned the Po River. That was how it all began, and everyone found it the most logical thing in the world. Marco and Brusco's daughter did indeed seem to be made for one another. They were of the same age and had the same wild ideas, and if Giulietta was the prettiest girl in the village, Marco was certainly an up-and-coming young man. Both of them were so bitten by the political bug that they thought of practically nothing else.

"Marco," said Giulietta, "I like you because you're different from other boys. You talk to me as if I weren't just a mere woman."

"Giulietta," he answered, "what difference does it make if we're of opposite sexes, as long as our ideals are the same?"

They continued way into the autumn to meet four evenings a week on the bridge. Finally, one time when it was pouring with rain, Giulietta's mother met Marco at the door and said he and Giulietta might as well come on to the porch for shelter. And when winter came, she suggested that they'd better come into the house. Brusco's wife was a truly old-fashioned woman. She was completely absorbed in her home and thought of everything beyond the bridge as a foreign land, whose goings-on were of no interest to her. As far as she knew, this foreign land was just the same as it had been twenty or thirty years before. And so, when Marco came into the kitchen she pointed to a chair near the cupboard and said:

"Sit down."

After that she motioned her daughter into a matching chair on the other side of the cupboard and returned to the seat where she had been knitting, in front of the fire. Giulietta and Marco went quietly on with the conversation they had begun on the porch. Two hours later Marco went away and Giulietta took herself off to bed. Her mother didn't say a word, but she thought plenty, and when Brusco came home, she let off steam.

"That young man came to the house," she told him.

"Did he?" asked Brusco. "And what do you think of him?"

"He's a poor wretch, that's what I think."

"He's a good boy, a boy with his head on his shoulders," said Brusco. "I know him well."

"I say he's a wretched creature," his wife repeated. "For two whole hours they talked of nothing but politics: political parties, party papers, Russia, America and other such ridiculous things. And she lapped it up! Poor wretches, both of them, that's what I say."

"What do you expect them to talk about?" said Brusco. "That's what interests the youth of today."

"Chattering about politics doesn't lead anyone to get married. Marriage means starting a family, not a political party. No, I don't like the fellow at all."

"Well, you don't have to marry him," said Brusco, starting upstairs. "The main thing is that he's a thoroughly good boy."

"No one that belongs to your godless party, can be a good boy!"

"Well, your daughter belongs to my godless party, too," Brusco countered. "And isn't she a good girl?"

"She's not my daughter, she's yours!" answered his wife, throwing out her arms in despair.

354

As she thrashed about in her bed, trying vainly to sleep, a suspicion came into her mind. Perhaps they had talked about those ridiculous things simply because she was there. When they were alone, they might talk of something completely different.

She decided to put this suspicion to the test, and when Marco came to call she said she was dead tired and supposedly went up to bed. Once upstairs, she lifted up a board which she had previously loosened from the floor, and was able to hear everything they were saying below. Marco and Giulietta talked quietly for some ten minutes or so, and then Marco raised his voice to say:

"Now that your mother's gone to bed, we can talk more freely. I say that if we go on with the halfway methods of Peppone and your father, we'll never get anywhere. We've got to get tough with the landowners if we want results."

"I agree with you a hundred per cent," said Giulietta gravely. "Next time there's a meeting, we'll have to let Peppone know what's what. As for my father, I've been trying to put it over for some time, but it's no use. They're getting old, and you can't expect them to have any flexibility in their thinking."

Upstairs, the woman held her breath. This was even looser talk than that of the night before. But it was so boring that she couldn't keep her eyes open, and when Brusco came up he found her asleep, with her ear glued to the floor.

"Fine ideas they have, those two!" she exclaimed, pulling herself together. "If you want to know, your daughter told that wretched boy that you and Peppone are old fuddy-duddies and the landowners twist you around their fingers."

"These young people are full of enthusiasm," said Brusco, shaking his head, "but of course they carry everything to extremes. And as far as Peppone and myself are concerned, we're in perfect harmony with the Party."

Things went on in very much the same way, but Brusco's wife had lost all interest in Giulietta and her young man. Whenever he appeared upon the scene, she simply said:

"Here comes the committee!"

Finally something different did happen, and it was brought about by Giulietta. One evening she came late to supper, waving a magazine in her hand.

"Look at this!" she shouted, opening it up before them, "I'm in the finals!"

355

Brusco looked at the magazine and passed it over to his wife.

"Do you know who this is?" he asked, pointing to a photograph.

"It looks like her," his wife answered.

"It looks like me so much that it *is* me," said the girl, laughing. "And there's my name underneath to prove it."

Still her mother didn't understand.

"What's it all about?"

"It's the contest for 'Miss New Life.' I'm in the final round."

Her mother looked again at the magazine and shook her head uncomprehendingly.

"Anyone can see," said Giulietta. "*New Life* is our Party magazine and it runs a contest every year. Girls from all over the country send in their pictures and a jury decides among them. Those that last as far as the finals are called to Rome to be looked over in person, and then the winner is proclaimed 'Miss New Life.' Now I'm one of the eight called to Rome for the final selection."

There was still something her mother didn't understand.

"But what's the basis of the selection? What sort of a contest is it?"

"A beauty contest, of course!" Giulietta exclaimed. "The prettiest girl wins the title and a whole lot of prizes. It's a serious business, I tell you. The jury is made up of artists, moving-picture directors, newspapermen, and so on. And you can be sure it's conducted the way it should be since it's sponsored by the Party."

The woman turned to her husband. "Are you letting your daughter get her picture into print and then show herself off in Rome?"

"Don't turn it into a tragedy," said Brusco, shrugging his shoulders. "There are plenty of contests of this kind, and I don't see anything the matter with them. Haven't there been beauty queens as long as we can remember?"

"There've been no-good girls as long as we can remember, too," she said, "but that doesn't mean we have to encourage ours to be one."

"Don't be stupid, Mother!" cried Giulietta angrily.

The woman looked at her husband, but he went right on eating. Finally she got up and went over to the stairs. Brusco wolfed down the rest of his supper and hurried out, mumbling something about a meeting. Giulietta cleared the table, washed the dishes and sat down to wait for Marco. This was his regular evening, and he arrived promptly.

"Have you seen this?" she said at once, showing him the magazine.

"Yes, I have," he answered. "Your picture came out very well. I didn't know you'd sent it in."

Giulietta was still in a state of excitement. She leafed through the magazine pages.

"Look at the other girls in the finals," she said, "and tell me what you think."

"It's hard to judge from a print on cheap paper," he said, after a thorough examination.

"That's why they call us to Rome," said Giulietta. "There they'll look us over from head to toe. And all modesty aside, it seems to me I have a chance."

"When do you go to Rome?" he asked.

"On the twentieth, it says here. That's just four days away."

"It's a long trip," Marco observed.

"Four hundred miles! And all expenses paid. It's the opportunity of a lifetime to see the city."

Marco agreed that it was an opportunity.

"But this whole idea of a beauty contest has something terribly bourgeois about it," he added.

"Beauty isn't a bourgeois monopoly," laughed Giulietta. "Beauty's universal."

"Right," Marco admitted, "but you don't catch them holding beauty contests in Russia."

"Russia's different," she protested. "They don't have strikes or seizures of factories there, either. In Russia everything's done for the People. There's not a beastly bourgeoisie whose propaganda paints all Communists as monsters, as creatures with three nostrils and the like. *New Life's* contest will prove there are plenty of pretty girls in the Party, much prettier than your bourgeois young ladies. If the contest didn't have a serious purpose, the Party wouldn't permit it. The Party knows its business, after all."

Marco agreed that the Party was always right.

"But, personally, I'm a little sorry that you sent in your picture."

"Marco," she said severely, "what sort of silly talk is this? Are you giving in to ordinary masculine conventions?"

357

"You misunderstood me," answered Marco. "I've always admired you because you weren't like other women. You didn't seem to have their vanity and petty ambition . . . . now . . . your idea of going into this contest makes me wonder . . ."

Giulietta drew herself up proudly.

"If the Party's sponsoring it, that means it's beneficial to the Party. And if I can benefit a cause that benefits the Party, it's my obligation to do so."

"Forgive me, Giulietta," Marco said, blushing. "To tell the truth, I have feelings I've never had before. It bothers me to see your picture on display and it bothers me to think of your going to Rome."

Giulietta gave a sarcastic laugh.

"Control yourself, Comrade, or you'll turn into one of those idiots that lose their head every time they see a pretty girl. And I don't want you to disappoint me. After you've led me to believe you were different from other men and capable of a platonic friendship, please don't show yourself up as the kind that thinks only of putting over a fast one."

"Giulietta!" cried Marco, turning very pale. "Now you've hurt my feelings."

"No, Marco, you've hurt mine. And beside that, you've insulted my father. Because, remember, my father hasn't breathed a word of opposition."

"Don't take it so hard, Giulietta," said Marco throwing out his arms in despair. "I don't want to hurt or insult a soul. I'm only asking whether, for my sake, you're not willing to give up the trip to Rome. Why do you care about being the *New Life* beauty queen, when you're the queen of my heart?"

He spoke in a most unusually gentle voice, which caused Giulietta to stare at him in disgust.

"You fool!" she shouted.

Marco turned even more pale, and came towards her, attempting to grasp her hand.

"Go away, and don't hurry back!" shouted Giulietta, pushing him back roughly and pointing to the door.

Marco lowered his head and started to go. But he wasn't really such a fool; in fact, he was a young man of considerable character. So it was that he wheeled around and said sternly:

"Giulietta, I forbid you to go to Rome. I won't have you take part in a beauty contest or anything of the kind. Your father may be an idiot, but I'm not."

358

Giulietta planted herself in front of him with her hands on her hips.

"Forbid me?" she shouted. "What right have you to do that? Who do you think you are?"

"I'm somebody that loves you," said Marco, losing his usual self-possession. "I'm not the kind that puts his wife on public display."

Giulietta giggled, and after a minute or so Marco clenched his fists and said:

"You're not going to Rome, I tell you!"

Giulietta stopped giggling and looked him straight in the eye.

"Instead of waiting four days, I'm going tomorrow," she said defiantly, "and I'll appear before the jury in a bathing-suit. I have a new one right here in the drawer, if you want to see it, in two pieces . . ."

She could not finish because Marco tore the package out of her hands, threw the contents on the floor and stepped on them.

"There are plenty more where that came from," said Giulietta angrily. "You'll see my picture in a bathing-suit in all the papers. And now get out of my house! I'll send you a postcard from Rome."

Marco was beside himself with rage and despair, but there was nothing he could do. He looked around without knowing exactly what for, and saw a shotgun, with a hunting bag and cartridge belt hanging up on the wall beside it. And on the mantelpiece another sinister object was gleaming. Giulietta didn't have time to escape because Marco had reached out with one hand while with the other he grabbed Giulietta by the neck. His fingers were like iron bands, and Giulietta could barely breathe. Marco raised the weapon and brought it down on her head. The girl couldn't even cry out, because fright had caused her to faint away.

When Giulietta came to, she was sitting on the floor and Marco was watching over her. She didn't yet know what had happened, because her head felt quite empty. No wonder, for the object that Marco had taken from the mantelpiece was a pair of shears and with it he had shorn all the long, silky hair from her head. Now he threw the scissors at her feet and Giulietta began to realize what he had done.

"Go to Rome, if you like," said Marco fiercely. And he disappeared through the door.

Lying on the floor of their upstairs room, Brusco's wife had through the aperture left by the removed board followed every detail of the scene.

"I told you he was a good boy, didn't I?" murmured Brusco, who had sneaked home through the garden and in by the back door and was now on watch beside his wife.

The next day the whole village had heard about the shearing. There was no way of knowing who told the tale but in the river country of the little world everyone knows everyone else's business. And, of course, a girl friend came to see Giulietta in the afternoon and told her that the whole village was buzzing.

"Listen, Giulietta," her friend said through a crack in the door; "nobody's actually seen you. If I were you, I'd clear out and go to your uncle's up in the mountains for a couple of months. While you're there you can wear a little wig and tie a scarf around it. And meanwhile your hair will grow back."

"Thanks for the good advice," said Giulietta coldly.

She stayed at home all day, but after supper she went to sit on the side of the bridge. It was a magnificent August evening, with an enormous moon in the sky, and the first passer-by could see Giulietta's condition quite clearly. He ran to spread the news, and soon a whole procession of people came by. And at the end of the crowd came Marco. He stood there hesitatingly until Giulietta said:

"Well, aren't you coming to see the show?"

Marco swallowed hard and then said: "Giulietta, if you want your revenge, take it right away. But don't throw vitriol in my face. I'd rather you shot me."

"Shoot you?" said Giulietta in amazement. "If I shoot you while I'm in this condition, where can I find another fool ready to marry me right away?"

Giulietta wore a Party-approved grey tailored suit and a blouse with a black bow to the wedding, and when Don Camillo found this strange pair standing before him he looked in perplexity from one to the other, with his eyes coming to a pause on Giulietta's shorn head.

"Which one of you is the groom?" he asked.

"He is," sighed Giulietta, covering her baldness with a veil.

A COUNTRY PRIEST'S DIARY

GIUSEPPE VERDI

BRUSCO LOOKED at the wall and shrugged his shoulders.

"Well, what do you say?" asked Don Camillo.

"I don't know," Brusco answered.

"If a mason doesn't know whether or not he can make a door through a wall, then he'd better change trades!" exclaimed Don Camillo. "Perhaps I should call Neri."

"This wall is as old as the hills," Brusco explained, "and an old wall can be very tricky. Unless you let me knock off a bit of plaster and explore underneath, I can't give you any definite reply."

And so Don Camillo authorized him to make an exploration.

"Just remember you're in a sacristy," he admonished him; "try to do a neat job and not cover the place with litter."

Brusco took a hammer and chisel out of his bag and began to knock plaster off the wall.

"It looks bad," he said after two or three strokes of the hammer. "The wall's filled with clay and stones. If it were made of bricks, we could put a reinforced cement architrave in just at the point of the first break-through and then carry the break down to the floor. But this way, it looks like trouble."

Don Camillo borrowed the hammer and knocked some plaster off another part of the wall. But here, too, he came upon a conglomeration of stones and clay.

"Queer," he observed. "The outside walls of the church are all brick. Why should they have put stones inside?"

361

Brusco threw out his arms with a baffled air.

"They may have made the supporting columns and an outer layer of bricks," he said, "and then stuffed the rest with stones. But let's take it easy and explore a little deeper."

By means of a big nail he loosened the clay around an uncovered stone and pulled it out. Then he hammered at the clay behind it and came to another stone. While he was trying to dig this out too, it disappeared.

"There must be an empty space behind the stones, and I don't understand it. You'd expect the stones to go all the way to the brick outer wall."

Don Camillo widened the hole and soon they found an enormous wardrobe which the secondary wall had been built to conceal. Of course the priest was feverishly anxious to open it, and when they had come back down into the sacristy he said to Brusco:

"Thanks. I don't need you any more."

"I'm afraid you do," said Brusco calmly. "A wall fifteen feet long, nine feet high and eighteen inches thick makes a considerable mass of stones and clay. And if you want to open the wardrobe, the whole thing will have to come down."

"And what makes you think I'll tackle that wall?" Don Camillo asked. "I'm not totally mad."

"You're worse than that; you're Don Camillo!" Brusco retorted.

But when Don Camillo had thought twice about the dimensions of the wall he had to acknowledge that it was too much for him.

"Very well," he said. "Go and get enough men to tear it down and wagons to carry the debris away. But once the work is done, I want it understood that you will all go home. I want to open the wardrobe myself."

Ten minutes later most of the people of the village were on the church square and all of them for this reason:

"Don Camillo has discovered a hidden treasure in the sacristy."

They imagined pots and pans filled with gold ducats, paintings and all sorts of other objects of art, and so great was the excitement that everyone wanted to see. Brusco's eight helpers soon turned into eighty, and a long line of volunteers passed buckets full of debris from one hand to another. The wall came down very fast and the majestic wardrobe began

362

to stand out in all its mystery. Darkness fell, but no one thought of going away, and soon after the last bucketful of clay and stones was carried away. Don Camillo took up his stand right in front of the wardrobe and said to the crowd in the sacristy:

"Thanks for your help, and good night to you!"

"Open it up! Open it up! We want to see!" they shouted at him.

"It's not your personal property," said an angry woman. "A hidden treasure belongs to all of us together."

"You're not out in the public square," Don Camillo replied. "You're in the church. And I'm responsible for everything in the church to the ecclesiastical authorities."

The carabinieri and their sergeant lined up beside Don Camillo, but the people were so frenzied that no one could keep them from pushing forward.

"Very well," said Don Camillo; "step back and I'll open it up."

They stepped back, and Don Camillo opened the first door. The compartment was filled with books, every one of which bore a number. And there were more and more books in all the other compartments. Don Camillo pulled out a book at random and leafed it through.

"It *is* a treasure," he explained, "but not of the kind you imagined. These are birth, death and marriage registers of the two hundred and fifty years ending in 1753. I don't know what happened in that year, but apparently the priest was afraid they might be destroyed and walled them up here for safe-keeping."

Things had to be arranged in such a way that everyone could see with their own eyes the truth of what Don Camillo was saying, and only when they had all marched by the wardrobe could Don Camillo call it a day.

"Lord," he said when he was left alone in the church, "forgive me if through my fault Your house was turned into an encampment of sacrilegious gold-diggers. I repeat that the blame is not theirs but mine; I was the first one to be in an indecent hurry. When the shepherd acts like a madman, what can you expect of his flock?"

In the course of the following days Don Camillo was stricken with another madness; his impatience to examine all the registers at once. He looked at them quite at random, one after another, and this turned out to be a good idea, for along with the registers of 1650 he found a notebook in which the priest had written up all the events worthy of remark every day.

He threw himself eagerly upon this diary and discovered all sorts of curious things. But among the notes of May 6, 1650, he found two really remarkable items, the first one of which was concerned with Giosue Scozza, whose marble statue stood in the main square of the neighbouring village of Torricella on a pedestal marked with the following inscription:

GIOSUE SCOZZA

CREATOR OF DIVINE HARMONIES

BELOVED SON OF TORRICELLA

WHO WROTE ITS NAME AND HIS

OWN ON THE ROLLS OF GLORY

1650–1746

Torricella had dedicated to this favourite son not only this monument but also its main square, the theatre, the widest street, the primary school, the public orphanage and the local band. His name inevitably came out in every piece of writing or speech-making in these parts and even big-city newspapers and magazines always referred to Giosue Scozza as "the swan of Torricella."

For centuries there had been a feud between the two villages, and the compatriots of Don Camillo and Peppone could not bear to see or hear this name. Now, in the old diary, Don Camillo found a passage which, translated into contemporary language, ran:

> *"Today Geremia Scozza, blacksmith, moved away to enter the service of Count Sanvito of Torricella. With him went his wife, Geltrude, and his son, Giosue, born in this parish on June 8, 1647."*

The records of 1647 confirmed the fact that the great man had indeed been born in this parish, and those of preceding years made it clear that the same was true of his family. In short, Torricella had acquired its "swan" when he was three years old.

This item in the diary was preceded by another equally extraordinary:

> *"Today, May 6, 1647, Giuseppe Bottazzi, blacksmith,*

364

48 years old, was decapitated in the public square, having on April 8 made an armed attack and inflicted wounds upon Don Patini, rector of Vigolenzo for the purpose of stealing a bag of gold. Giuseppe Bottazzi, a skilled worker but a man of sacrilegious ideas, was not born here but came twenty years ago and married a local girl, Maria Gambazzi, who bore him a son baptized Antonio, now fifteen years old. Giuseppe Bottazzi has turned out to be the chief of a band of brigands who have committed thefts and murders in the land of Count Sanvito. Last December they surprised and murdered the men-at-arms of the Castello della Piana where Count Sanvito himself was in residence and managed to save his life only by fleeing through the secret underground passage."

Don Camillo took a look at the records of later years and clearly established the fact that the present-day Giuseppe Bottazzi, known as Peppone, mayor and Red leader, was a direct descendant of this blacksmith of the same name.

"When elections come around, I'll cook his goose," muttered Don Camillo. "I'll have this page of the diary photographed and plaster it up at every street corner, and under it the phrase: 'Blood will tell.' History repeats itself!"

This project was one that could not be carried out until the time was ripe, but its appeal was tremendous, for it meant killing two birds with one stone. Don Camillo planned to stake an indisputable claim to "the swan of Torricella" and strike a fatal blow at Peppone.

But the news about Giosue Scozza was so exciting that Don Camillo couldn't help dropping hints about it, and one day Peppone came to the rectory to see him.

"Father," he said, "there's a lot of talk about some of the things you've discovered in the famous books. Since it's no political matter, but one concerning the honour of the village, may I ask you to tell me the whole story?"

"What's this?" muttered Don Camillo, throwing out his arms. "It's just a bit of history, that's all."

"What do you mean by history?"

"I mean something in the nature of geography—geography is what makes history, you know."

"I don't get it," said Peppone, scratching his head. "Will you kindly explain?"

"I don't know whether it's really proper."

"I see. You're cooking up some of your usual reactionary

365

propaganda and planning to destroy somebody's reputation."

Don Camillo turned bright red.

"If I go in for propaganda, there's nothing false about it. I have documents to show that 'the swan of Torricella' was born not in Torricella, but right here, three years earlier than it's always been stated."

Peppone leaned forward.

"Either you're telling tall tales or else you're a man completely without honour. Because if you can demonstrate in private that Scozza came from here rather than from Torricella and refuse to do so openly, then you're depriving the village of a God-given right."

Don Camillo pulled out the diary and shoved it in front of Peppone's nose.

"Here's the whole truth for you; and there's other proof, besides."

"Then why don't you release it?"

Don Camillo lit his cigar butt and blew several mouthfuls of smoke up to the ceiling.

"The only way to release the news is to print a photograph of a whole page of the diary, or at least to be ready to show it to anyone who asks to see."

"Well, what's the matter with that?"

"I can't make up my mind to do anything so drastic. The note about Scozza is preceded by another one corroborating the date, which happens to bear *your* family name. So, in the last analysis, it's up to you."

"*My* family?" exclaimed Peppone, dumbfounded.

"Yes, the Giuseppe Bottazzi who fills the entry for 6 May, 1647 is the unfortunate ancestor of the tribe of Peppone. I've checked the whole thing, and it's indubitably correct."

Don Camillo pointed out the entry to Peppone and the latter proceeded to read it.

"Well," he said afterwards, "what have I got to do with a Bottazzi of 1647?"

"You know how people are. The original Giuseppi Bottazzi revealed to be a blacksmith, a priest-baiter and gang-leader, just like you! Your enemies would be able to put that to good use in their campaign. Just think it over."

Peppone read the two items several times and then gave the diary back to Don Camillo.

"I don't care what the reactionary swine may say. The important thing is to add Giosue Scozza to our village's glory. I put the village's reputation before my own. So go ahead and make the whole thing public."

Peppone started to go, then wheeled about and went over to the desk where Don Camillo was sitting.

"And do you know what?" he added. "I'm proud to have that Bottazzi for an ancestor. It means that Bottazzis had the right idea even in 1647; they knew that they must get rid of priests and land-owners, even at the cost of their own lives. And it's no use your smiling, Father. Your turn is coming!"

"Remember that my name's Don Camillo, not Don Patini!" said the priest in reply.

"Politics may divide us, but for the good of the village, we are as one," Peppone shot over his shoulder. "We'll talk of that later; meanwhile, let's get after Giosue Scozza!"

Don Camillo threw himself like a lion into the chase for "the swan of Torricella." Without dragging Peppone's ancestor into the picture, he placed devastating articles in the provincial paper. Eventually the big-city papers chimed in. The romantic discovery of the archives sealed into the church wall made a good story, and they spread it so widely that Torricella had to surrender. And when people of Torricella were convinced that Giosue Scozza belonged to their enemies, they turned against him. A "public safety committee" was formed, for the purpose of wiping out all traces of the interloper, beginning with the statue in the public square, which was to be replaced by a fountain. Thus the blot would be washed away.

At this point Peppone appealed to the Reds on the other side. He proposed to give Torricella a marble fountain in exchange for the marble statue of the great man. It was settled that the exchange of gifts should be made into a solemn occasion. A wagon drawn by white oxen would carry the fountain to the boundary-line of the village, and meet there a similar wagon, bearing the statue. The money for the fountain was quickly raised, and a month later the wagons set forth. Giosue Scozza arrived in the village nailed to his pedestal and tied with ropes to the sides of the wagon, but looking very proud indeed. And Peppone, who was waiting to receive him, with the rest of the persons in authority and the local band, pronounced a speech written for the occasion, which began:

"Greetings, illustrious brother, upon your return, after centuries of absence, to your native place. . . ."

It was all very moving. When the wagon from Torricella had taken over the fountain and gone away, Peppone took a hammer and chisel out of his pocket and knocked off the tablet which described Giosue Scozza as the "beloved son of Torricella." The smashed tablet was thrown outside the boundary line, and the little procession wound its way happily into the central square. There everything was ready: masons, marble-workers, a crane and a stone for the base. Soon the statue stood erect on its new foundation and a new tablet was fastened to the pedestal. A canvas had been thrown around it, and this was removed at just the right moment. Don Camillo pronounced a blessing and made a short speech on the theme of the return of the prodigal son. The welcoming committee, which was non-political in nature, had done things proud, and the festivities did not end until evening, when Peppone rose to explain the significance of the occasion.

"We have seen your face, dear long-lost brother," he said, "but we have not heard your voice, that divine voice which you raised to the heights of immortal glory. And so a string orchestra is to play a programme which will acquaint all of us with the greatest melodies of our own celebrated Giosue Scozza."

The square was crowded with people, and after Peppone had finished speaking there was a burst of applause, followed by a religious silence. The string orchestra, which had been brought from the city, was really first-class, and the first of the twelve pieces on the programme *The Andantino Number Six*, turned out to be a musical jewel. After this came the *Air in C sharp Minor* and the *Sonata in D*, which met with equal success. But when the fourth piece, *Ballet in F*, began, there was a chorus of voices shouting:

"Verdi, Verdi!"

Peppone and Don Camillo were sitting in the front seats, and the conductor looked beseechingly at Peppone. Peppone looked at Don Camillo and Don Camillo nodded. Then Peppone called peremptorily:

"Verdi!"

Everyone was wild with joy. The conductor held a whispered consultation with his musicians, tapped the music stand with his baton, and the crowd was silent. At the first notes of the prelude to *La Traviata*, people had difficulty restraining their applause and after it was finished it was almost overpowering.

"This is real music!" shouted Peppone.

"You can't beat Verdi," answered Don Camillo.

Verdi supplied all the rest of the programme, and at the end the orchestra conductor was carried off in triumph. As Smilzo passed in front of the statue of Giosue Scozza, "creator of divine harmonies," he observed:

"The climate of Torricella didn't do him any good."

"Exactly," said Bigio. "If he'd stayed here, he'd have written much better music."

"Historical things are beautiful even when they're ugly," put in Peppone severely. "Giosue Scozza belongs to history, and he'll go down as a very great man, don't you agree, Don Camillo?"

"Of course," Don Camillo answered. "You must always look at an artist against the background of his times."

"But Verdi . . ." objected Smilzo.

"What's Verdi got to do with it?" Peppone interrupted. "Verdi's no artist; he's just a man with a heart as big as this——"

And he threw out his arms so eloquently that they cut a wide swathe all around him. Don Camillo wasn't agile enough to get out of the way, and received a blow in the stomach. But out of respect for Verdi he said nothing.

REVENGE IS SWEET

THE PEOPLE of Torricella were furious over having lost their musical supremacy and were dead set on winning a championship in some other field. So one fine morning our villagers found posters stuck up all over the place, which read as follows:

> *If you have eleven young men*
> *who know the difference*
> *between a soccer ball*
> *and a tin of tomato sauce,*
> *Send them to the sports field at*
> *Torricella*
> *to see what's going on.*

As soon as Peppone had read this challenge he turned to his lieutenant, Smilzo, and said:

"Tell the Dynamo team to start training immediately and then go to Torricella to decide on a day for the match."

Smilzo got on his bicycle, rode off at full speed and came back an hour later. Peppone was waiting impatiently in his office, and before him were proofs of the poster to be plastered, by way of a reply, on the walls of Torricella.

"Well, is it all set?" he shot at Smilzo.

"Set, my eye!" Smilzo growled. "We missed the boat."

"What do you mean?"

"I mean that the priest's team got there ahead of us."

Without hesitation Peppone pulled his cap down over his eyes and marched on the rectory. He found Don Camillo in the square in front of the church and plunged right into the subject which was on his mind.

"If there's any team that has a right to defend the village honour, it's the Dynamos," he stated emphatically.

"Ditto for the Diehards," answered Don Camillo.

"The Diehards aren't a team, they're a deformation."

"The Dynamos aren't a team, they're a collection of chickens."

On these premises, there seemed to be no likely agreement, and the argument continued in such an excited key that it attracted nearly a hundred listeners. Finally, after Peppone and Don Camillo had reached so high a pitch that it seemed as if they could never climb down from it, the voice of reason intervened. The voice was that of the local chemist.

"There can be no real discussion here," he said. "The teams are neck and neck, and we must choose between two solutions. Either we toss a coin to see which one is to represent the village, or else we take the best men of both and weld them together."

"The Diehards have eleven best men," maintained Don Camillo.

"And the Dynamos twelve," retorted Peppone, "because I'm including the masseur, who may be lame but rates as high as any Diehard you care to mention."

But the idea of welding the best men of both teams into one was obviously sensible and eventually both Peppone and Don Camillo had to admit it.

"We'll talk about it another day," said Don Camillo, retiring to the rectory.

"Yes, another day," echoed Peppone, withdrawing to the People's Palace.

The next day the two men met on neutral ground, each of them accompanied by a group of backers.

"I don't want to be mixed up in this business," said Don Camillo. "My job is to be a priest, and so I've turned it over to this committee of experts."

"My job is to be mayor," echoed Peppone, "and so I've put it up to a committee too."

"Then let the two committees get together," concluded Don Camillo.

"Exactly," said Peppone, "I shall stay on merely as an

observer, and whatever the committees decide suits me. It should be easy enough to reach a decision, because after having made a dispassionate analysis of the Diehards, it's obvious that we should take their centre man and leave the rest of the places to the Dynamos."

"That's just what we thought after we had taken the Dynamos under careful consideration. Give us Smilzo, and we'll supply the other ten."

Peppone gritted his teeth.

"I don't want to influence the committees' decision, but one thing is sure: if you like it, then it's just as I say, and if you don't, then it's just as I say too. And you can thank God for the honour of having one of your men play with a team like ours."

"Smilzo will be a decided handicap to the Diehards," said Don Camillo, "but we want to show that on our side there's a real spirit of conciliation."

"Then you and your dummies can go to hell," Peppone shouted.

"If the committee have no more to say," said Don Camillo, "we may as well adjourn."

The head of the committee chosen by Don Camillo threw out his arms in despair. And so did the head of Peppone's committee. Then both parties went home.

Three days later a new challenge arrived from Torricella.

NOTICE

*In order to give a chance to the two teams
which we have challenged
Instead of beating them one after the other,
Our Torricella team has decided to take
them both on together.
Hence the Torricella Eleven will play the
Diehard-Dynamo twenty-two.*

The necessity of forming a single team was now more urgent than ever, and the chemist, together with the doctor, managed to form a committee to effect a liaison between the two already existing committees. This was a very complicated affair, but finally the two committees met for the purpose of making a final decision.

"I bow to the will of the joint committee," said Don Camillo, who was the first to take the floor. "But since it's inevitable that the committee make up a half-and-half team, I say that the Diehards will furnish six players and the Dynamos five."

"I agree," said Peppone, "Diehards five and Dynamos six."

For a moment Don Camillo respected the silence which followed upon this declaration. Then he said:

"Since this point is bound to hold up the committee's deliberations, why don't we settle it by drawing cards?"

A pack of cards was produced, and Don Camillo and Peppone drew a card each. Peppone won by a single point, and it was decided that the Dynamos should contribute six men to the team and the Diehards five.

"In that case," said Don Camillo, "it's only fair that a Diehard be the captain."

"Democracy has very definite regulations," retorted Peppone. "You may not know it, Father, but there you are. In a democratic system the majority rules. So we shall choose our own captain."

Don Camillo shook his head.

"That's Communism for you!" he exclaimed. "Once they've seized power, they install a dictatorship under a democratic label."

"Sport has nothing to do with politics," Peppone protested. "But in order to give the lie to your reactionary slander, let's settle it with another draw."

This time Don Camillo won, and the Diehards chose a captain for the team. The next day the mixed team met for a first practice. The game lasted exactly eight minutes, after which the two factions had a free-for-all fight. The next day brought considerable improvement, because the Dynamos and Diehards began rough-housing in the dressing-room long before the game. On the third day the players didn't fight either in the dressing-room or on the field. They fought outside the field, before they ever got there. On the fourth day, after they had exhausted all other possible dodges, they actually played a game, but with the saddest result imaginable. And the following day things went even worse. They couldn't muster any teamwork whatsoever, but seemed to be eleven savages who were making their first acquaintance with a ball and kicking it around at random.

Meanwhile, time was going by. The day of the match was drawing near, and still no progress had been made. Finally the last day came. After the final, eminently unsuccessful practice game, Don Camillo and Peppone found themselves going back to the village together.

"So," said Peppone, "we're going to reap the result of your stubbornness tomorrow. If you'd given in to me and let the Dynamos defend the honour of the village, we shouldn't be having any of this trouble."

"Peppone," said Don Camillo, "I know my boys, and I say that all our trouble is your fault. You used your usual obstructionist tactics to make us hand you over the controls. I said 'make us' because anyone with fine feelings and conscience will always yield a point, and that is exactly what we are going to do. Your bullying has met with success. The Diehards are withdrawing and your Dynamos will play. Don't pretend to make a fuss, because I know that the Dynamos have been holding a practice of their own every day, on the sly, and your pretence of training with us hasn't hurt your form."

Peppone did not bother to make a denial. He slipped away, and two hours later the village was plastered with big red posters.

The Diehards have withdrawn their men
because of admitted technical failings
and so tomorrow's match will be
played by an all-Dynamo team,
sole defender of the village's honour.

Before going to bed Don Camillo went to kneel before the Crucified Christ.

"Lord," he prayed, "don't let them lose the match tomorrow. Not for their sake, because they don't deserve to win, but for mine. Don't let them lose, that is, unless you want to lead me into the temptation of rejoicing over their defeat."

"Don Camillo," Christ answered, "you know that I have no dealings with sport!"

Peppone's men made a miserable showing and Torricella scored a large number of goals against them. Don Camillo was unable to resist temptation and inwardly rejoiced over their discomfiture. He rejoiced outwardly as well, and with the devil hot upon his trail challenged the Torricella team

374

to a match with the Diehards the following Sunday. The Diehards won. This victory seemed to call for a celebration and he called the Diehards together.

"Boys," he said, "I have three magnificent capons in my chicken coop. On Sunday evening we'll eat them and drink to the health of the Dynamos. This isn't top secret, so if you happen to say something about it, no harm is done."

Obviously several people did, quite accidentally, spread the good word, because almost immediately the whole village knew that on Sunday evening the rectory would be the scene of what was dubbed "the revenge supper."

In order to make the occasion more festive, the Diehards needed a song, and Don Camillo sat up most of one night in order to write the words and most of the next in order to set them to music on the church organ. On Thursday night, he emerged from the sacristy with words and music complete and plenty of time to teach his boys the song so that they could come out with it at the supper. The tune was simple, and if necessary they could always read the words. He was quite pleased with himself as he returned to the rectory for the night, and before going to bed, he decided to take a look at the three capons in his chicken coop. Alas, the capons were gone, and so were three hens. All that was left were one bedraggled chick and a scrawny rooster. To take the place of the missing capons, a sign was hung on the wall which said in dog-Latin: *Crescete et moltiplicorum.*

Increase and multiply, indeed! Don Camillo was breathless with indignation, and seizing the sign, he went to tell his troubles to the Christ over the main altar.

"Lord," he panted, "they've stolen my chickens!"

"I'm sorry to hear it," Christ answered with a smile. "But before making any such categorical statement you'd better make sure they didn't just run away."

Don Camillo held up the sign.

"I know what I'm talking about, Lord," he said. "Look what the thieves left behind! Isn't it disgusting?"

"You don't expect a petty thief to write good Latin, do you, Don Camillo?"

"I'm not talking about the Latin. I'm concerned with the impudence of his adding insult to injury. Lord, who in the world could it be?"

These words reminded Don Camillo of the real delinquent, his dog Thunder. Why hadn't Thunder barked and given the alarm? He went to look for the dog and found him lying peacefully in his kennel.

"You traitor!" the priest shouted. "You're in enemy pay!"

What angered him even more than the loss of the chickens were the disturbances of the festive supper. He was pacing up and down the church square, when a voice roused him from his ire.

"Have you insomnia, Father? What keeps you up so late?"

The speaker was the carabinieri sergeant, who was coming back from his evening rounds, together with one of his men.

"I've been robbed of my chickens!" Don Camillo exclaimed. "At ten o'clock, when I went into the sacristy, they were there, and when I came out at eleven, they had disappeared. I was playing the organ, and someone crept up, under cover of the music. . . ."

"Didn't your dog bark?"

"That's just what I mean. Perhaps he did bark, but I couldn't hear him."

"And do you suspect anyone in particular?"

Don Camillo threw out his arms.

Don Camillo shut himself up in the rectory and refused to see a soul. The whole village knew what had happened, and the Reds were rubbing their hands and laughing.

"It seems that the Sunday-night supper will be a paltry affair. Well, if they haven't the capons they can feed on their new song!"

The supper was cancelled, and that evening Don Camillo was in the depths of despair. At eight o'clock he whistled for Thunder to come and get a bowl of soup, but Thunder failed to respond. Don Camillo resolved to find him, and went out on the road leading away from the village. Ten minutes later he walked through Peppone's vegetable garden and into the dark hall of his house. From the kitchen there came the echoes of loud laughter, and Don Camillo turned the doorknob and went in. Peppone was sitting at the table, together with Smilzo, Brusco, Bigio and the rest of the gang, over a dish of roast chicken, and at the sight of Don Camillo they were positively petrified in their chairs.

"Excuse me, Peppone," said Don Camillo, "but I'm looking for my dog. Do you happen to have seen him?"

Peppone shook his head, but Don Camillo had keen eyes and knew better. He lifted up the edge of the table-cloth and saw Thunder crouching under the table with a heaping dish of chicken bones before him.

"He just dropped in," Peppone exclaimed lamely.

"I see," said Don Camillo.

Thunder flattened himself out on the floor in shame.

"If you'd care to join us, Father, please sit down," said Peppone.

"I've had my supper, thank you. Good evening."

Don Camillo walked out, and Thunder, after a questioning look at Peppone, followed the priest at a distance, dragging his tail. When they reached the rectory, the priest turned on him and said indignantly:

"You thief!"

And since this word seemed to make very little impression the priest added with utter scorn:

"You've sold out to the Russians!"

The next day the carabinieri sergeant received several anonymous letters, and the affair assumed a sudden importance. Six chickens don't amount to much, but when there is reason to think that the theft has been committed by the mayor, then there is a political angle to it. Peppone received an unexpected visit from the law.

"Sorry, Mr. Mayor, but I must do my duty. Can you tell me where you were between ten and eleven o'clock of last Thursday evening? You weren't at home, we know that. At five minutes past ten you were seen climbing over the fence around the rectory garden. There are three witnesses to that. And others saw you climb over your own fence three quarters of an hour later."

Peppone was as confused as a child.

"That's my business," he finally sputtered.

"And where did you get the five chickens you ate at your house Sunday night?"

"That's my business, too."

The sergeant received equally unsatisfactory replies to his other questions, and finally went away saying:

"You'll have to tell the court."

Now the affair took on really colossal proportions. Mayor Giuseppe Bottazzi was accused of being a vulgar chicken thief and summoned to appear before the magistrates' court in the nearest city. How had the mighty fallen, when the tamer of lions was laid low by a church mouse.

Don Camillo found himself in court, without knowing

exactly why. But there he was, and there in the dock, was Peppone. It looked very much like the end of his career.

"The accused has steadily refused to say where he spent the hour between ten and eleven o'clock, that is between the time when he was seen climbing the rectory fence and the time when he was seen sneaking back over his own. Has he, even at this late date, anything to say?"

The magistrate looked at Peppone and everyone in the courtroom turned their eyes in his direction. But Peppone helplessly threw out his arms.

"I can't say where I was," he answered in a low voice.

"Do you refuse, absolutely?"

"It isn't that I refuse, Judge. I simply can't do it."

At this point Don Camillo asked if he might be allowed to say a word.

"From ten to eleven o'clock, Mayor Bottazzi was with me in the sacristy," he stated.

"Why didn't you say so before?"

"Nobody asked me. And besides, before testifying, I had to secure my superiors' permission."

The magistrate shot him a questioning look.

"Excuse me, Father, but what brought him to the church at that hour, when you were playing the organ. Was it for a singing lesson?"

"The sound of the organ doesn't prevent one of the faithful from saying his prayers."

"I don't deny that, Father, but I don't see why the accused didn't give the law this explanation. No one need hesitate to use church-going as an alibi. If I'd spent my time in church I'd be glad to say so."

"But you're not a Communist Party leader and mayor of a village in a region where the Party is so strong," Don Camillo replied. "He comes to church at an hour when his Party comrades can't see him. If your Honour requires any further explanation . . ."

"No, nothing more," the magistrate interrupted, smiling broadly.

"Then just let me say this: Giuseppe Bottazzi is a good-hearted, hard-working, God-fearing fellow," concluded Don Camillo.

Don Camillo made the trip home on Peppone's motorcycle, but Peppone did not open his mouth the whole way. When they came to the rectory he gave a deep sigh.

378

"You made a laughing stock of me," he said plaintively. "The reactionary press will have a field-day with this story."

"They'd have treated you a good deal more roughly if you'd been convicted of being a chicken thief," said Don Camillo.

"But you've got me in hot water with the Party. If I tell the truth they'll bawl me out for being so stupid as to steal chickens. And if I stick to your version of events, then they'll brand me as even more of a fool."

"Never mind about the Party," grumbled Don Camillo. "I'm in hot water with Almighty God. Here I am, a priest, and I've given false testimony before a court of law! How shall I ever get up my nerve to go into church?"

Peppone jumped off his motorcycle and marched into the church and straight up to the main altar. He remained standing there for several minutes and then went back outside.

"You can go in now," he said. "I've fixed things up for you. I'd like to see you straighten things out for me with the Party in the same way!"

Don Camillo threw out his arms.

"Of course it's easier to deal with God than one of your Party bosses. They never forgive anything."

Exactly in what terms Peppone had "fixed things" up no one ever knew. But when, late that night, Don Camillo summoned up the nerve to go into church and kneel in front of the main altar, the Crucified Christ said:

"What in the world have you been up to now, Don Camillo?"

"I had the Bishop's permission," said Don Camillo in justification of his perjury.

"He's quite a fellow, too!" Christ sighed, half smiling.

379

THE MAN WITHOUT A HEAD

DON CAMILLO leaped to his feet and very nearly shouted, because the discovery was so sensational. Just then the sound of the clock in the church tower ringing three o'clock in the morning brought him around to the thought that the only sensible thing to do at that hour was to go to sleep. But before dozing off he read over the extraordinary bit of news he had just found in his predecessor's diary. "On November 8, 1752," the passage began, "something quite terrible happened . . ."

The eighteenth-century parish priest had explained the mystery of the black stone and at the same time provided Don Camillo with an excellent subject for his Sunday sermon. Now he closed the book and hurried to bed, because three hours of Sunday morning had already gone by.

"Brethren," Don Camillo began his sermon, "today I want to talk to you about the black stone, the one you have all seen in one corner of the cemetery with the mysterious inscription: *November 8, 1752. Here lies a man without face or name.* For years this stone has been the subject of research and discussion. Now at last the mystery has been made clear."

A murmur of amazement greeted these words. And Don Camillo continued:

"Every evening for the last few months I've been looking over the old books and registers which turned up in a forgotten wardrobe some time ago, and as you know I've found all sorts of interesting information. But just last night I came across the most extraordinary item of all, which I shall now translate into contemporary language for your benefit.

" 'On November 8, 1752, something quite terrible happened. For a whole year some marauders known as the "hole-in-the-wall gang" because of the method they used to break into respectable houses, had been wreaking havoc all over the countryside. None of them had ever been caught red-handed. But on the night of November 8, Giuseppe Folini, from Crocilone, a merchant by profession, was awakened by a suspicious noise and after he had got out of bed to go down to his cellar storeroom, he realized that the noise came from that part of the wall which bordered on the open fields and had no door or window of any kind. Obviously someone was boring his way into the cellar and such an enterprise could only be conducted by the "hole-in-the-wall" gang.

" 'A few minutes later, while Folini was still standing there, indecisively, a piece of plaster fell from a spot about six inches above the floor and the moonlight streaming in from a window across the way allowed him to see a brick moving. Soon the brick was lifted out and a gaunt white hand came through the hole and removed another brick beside it. Now that the hole was sufficiently widened, an arm came through, all the way up to the elbow, and began feeling the surface of the surrounding wall in order to ascertain whether anything hung there which might fall and spread the alarm.

" 'Folini, who is a big, strapping fellow, took hold of the wrist, determined not to let it go, and at the same time he shouted for help. Various members of the family arrived upon the scene and one of his sons tied a rope around the intruder's arm, thus making him a prisoner.

" 'Because Folini's house is in a lonely and isolated spot, they could not hope to arouse the village by giving the alarm. And for fear of falling into a trap set by the prisoner's accomplices, they did not dare set foot outside until morning. They had captured one member of the gang and when he was turned over to the police he would probably supply the names of the others.

" 'They ventured out at dawn and made their way cautiously toward the back of the house. But all they found was a headless body. The bandits had feared that the captured man might be compelled by torture to reveal their names, or that the knowledge of his name might lead to the discovery of the rest. And so, in order to cheat the law of any clue whatsoever they had chopped off his head and carried it away.

" 'Since nothing on the body permitted identification, I buried it by night in one corner of the cemetery and raised a stone over the grave with the inscription: *November 8, 1752. Here lies a man without face or name.*' "

Don Camillo closed the old diary, looked down for a moment at the confusion written upon his hearers' faces and concluded:

"And so, brethren, this terrible tale has cleared up a mystery. Under the black stone there sleeps a man without face or name. A terrible tale, indeed. But there is something far more terrible rampant among us at this very hour: the presence of a hundred headless men in this village of ours who are working night and day to bore a hole through the unguarded wall of our houses, steal the householders' brains away and leave in their place the propagandistic stuffing of an extreme left-wing party, which for obvious reasons I shall not call by name. . . ."

The story of the headless man made a great impression upon the village, and everyone felt an urge to go and look at the black stone. The old Folini house at Crocilone was still standing, but it served only as a barn and the foot of the wall on the side of the open fields was overgrown with weeds. Now these weeds were cut down and the hole mentioned in the story was exposed to view. All those who passed this way after dark pedalled their bicycles extra fast or accelerated their motorcycles because of the shiver that ran up and down their spines.

Then came the November mists, and the river took on a dark and mysterious air. One evening, as she walked along the embankment road, on her way back from Castellina, old Signora Gabini met a man without a head. She ran all the rest of the way home and arrived in such a state of collapse that she had to be put to bed. She asked for the priest, and the fellow who went to the village after Don Camillo stopped for a drink in the arcade café and told the whole story. It spread like wildfire through the village, and when Don Camillo returned from his visit to Signora Gabini he found a small crowd of people waiting in the church square to hear what sort of devilry was in the air.

"Sheeer nonsense!" said Don Camillo. "If the old woman weren't in such a bad way, it would be laughable."

382

As a matter of fact, she had told a tale that made very little sense.

"Father! I saw him!"

"Saw whom?"

"The headless man, the one buried under the black stone. I came face to face with him, all of a sudden."

"Face to face? But if he didn't have any head? . . ."

"He didn't have any head, that's just it. He was riding slowly along on a bicycle . . ."

Here Don Camillo couldn't help smiling.

"That's a good one! How could he ride a bicycle if he died in 1752, before bicycles were invented?"

"I don't know," she stuttered. "He must have learned how in the meantime. But I know it was him for sure, the man without a head."

Don Camillo's retelling of this account proved to be highly amusing and the notion of the headless man's having learned to ride a bicycle after his death was repeated from one house to another. For a couple of weeks, nothing out of the way happened, and then suddenly the man without a head reappeared. Giacomone, the boatman, met him shortly after dusk, on the path leading through the acacia grove. This time he was not on a bicycle, but on foot, a means of locomotion much more suitable to an eighteenth-century ghost. Giacomone himself told the story to Don Camillo.

"You've been drinking too much, Giacomone," was the priest's comment.

"I've sworn off for the last three years," Giacomone replied. "And I'm not the sort to be easily scared. I'm just telling you what I saw with my own eyes: a man minus a head."

"Don't you think he might have been a man with his jacket pulled up over his head in order to protect himself from the rain?"

"I saw the stump of his neck, I tell you."

"You didn't really see any such thing; you just fancy you did. Go back tomorrow to the exact place where you thought you saw him and you'll find the branch or bush that gave you the illusion."

The next day Giacomone did go back, and some twenty other villagers with him. They located the exact spot of the encounter, but they saw no feature of the landscape which might have seemed to be a man without a head. But the headless man appeared a week later to a young man, and at this point people stopped wondering whether or not the apparitions were genuine. They asked, rather: "Why is the headless man among us? What is he after?" And they did not have to look far for an answer. The headless man was looking for his head. He wanted it to lie with the rest of his body, in consecrated ground. Only Don Camillo refused to offer any guess as to the motive which caused the headless man to wander about the river roads and embankment. "I don't want to hear such foolishness," he said to anyone who questioned him. But one day he was deeply disturbed and confided his trouble to the Christ above the altar.

"Lord, since I've had this parish, I've never seen so many people come to church. Except for Peppone and his henchmen, the whole village has turned up, old and young, infirm and healthy."

"Well, aren't you glad, Don Camillo?"

"No, because they're driven only by fear. And I don't mean the fear of God, either. And it bothers me to see them in distress. I wish the nightmare could have an end."

Christ sighed.

"Don Camillo, aren't you one of these fear-stricken people yourself?"

Don Camillo threw out his arms in protest.

"Don Camillo doesn't know what fear is!" he said proudly.

"That's very important, Don Camillo. Your fearlessness is sufficient to liberate the others from their fear."

Don Camillo felt better, but the apparitions of the headless man continued, and they were further complicated by the intervention of Peppone, who came up to him one day in the square and said in a voice loud enough to be heard on the other side of the river:

"Father, I hear strange talk of a man without a head. Do you know anything about him?"

"Not I," said Don Camillo, feigning astonishment. "What's it all about?"

"It seems that a man without a head has been seen at night around the village."

"A man without a head? It must be someone looking for the People's Palace in order to sign up with your party."

Peppone did not bat an eyelash.

"Perhaps it's a ghost cooked up in the rectory and sent out to scare people into hiding behind the skirts of the priest."

384

"No ghosts are cooked up in the rectory, either with or without a head," retorted Don Camillo.

"Oh, do you import them from America?"

"Why should we import them, when your party manufactures the best headless ghosts to be found?"

Peppone gave a mocking laugh.

"It's a known fact that the ghost is of your fabrication."

"It's fabricated by diseased minds. It's true that I told the story of the headless man, but that's history. Anyone can see the document for himself."

Don Camillo led the way to the rectory, with Peppone, Smilzo, Brusco, Bigio and the other Red big shots following after. The book was still on the priest's desk, and now he pointed it out to Peppone.

"Look up November 8, 1752, and read what you can find there."

Peppone leafed through the diary until he came to the passage in question. He read it twice through and then handed the book to the others.

"If you have any doubts as to the authenticity of the document, you're free to submit it to any expert you please for study. My only fault is not to have foreseen that a two-hundred-year-old story would work so dangerously upon people's imaginations."

Bigio nodded.

"So there's some truth to the story of the headless man, after all," he mumbled.

"The truth is just what's set down in that diary," said Don Camillo. "All the rest is reckless imagination."

Peppone and his henchmen went thoughtfully away. That same evening two more villagers ran into the headless man, and the next day a delegation of mothers came to Don Camillo.

"Father, you must do something," they told him. "You must bless the grave marked by the black stone or say a Mass for the repose of the occupant's tormented soul."

"There's no tormented soul," said Don Camillo firmly. "There are only your benighted imaginings, and I don't want to bolster them by appearing to take them seriously."

"We'll go to the Bishop!" the women shouted.

"Go where you please. But no one can compel me to believe in ghosts!"

The nightmare became more and more of a menace.

Dozens of people had seen the headless man and even the most hard-headed of the villagers were tainted with the contagion of fear. Don Camillo finally resolved to do something about it. Late one night, after everyone had gone to bed he knocked at Peppone's door.

"I've been called to the bedside of a dying man. It's too far for me to go by bicycle. Will you take me in your car?"

It was pouring rain, and this request seemed logical enough. Peppone took out the car which served by day as a public bus.

"Just drive me by the rectory first," said Don Camillo.

Once they were there he got out and insisted that Peppone come inside.

"I've got to talk with you," he explained once they were in his study.

"And was it necessary to put up such a show?"

"Yes, and this isn't the end of it, either. The whole village is going mad and those of us with our wits still about us must do something to dissipate this terror. What I am about to propose isn't honest, but I assume full responsibility for it before God and man. We must pretend to have found a skull. We'll decide together on the most appropriate place, and I'll bury it there, together with half of an eighteenth century coin. The other half, of course, will go under the black stone. Then you, as mayor, will order some digging in the place where we have left the skull. Is that clear?"

"It seems rather gruesome to me," Peppone stammered, with perspiration breaking out on his forehead.

"It's more terrible to see the growth of a collective frenzy among our people. We must drive out one fear with another. Now, let's get down to details."

It was two o'clock in the morning when Peppone went out to his car. Almost immediately he began cursing.

"What's the matter?" called Don Camillo from the door.

"The battery must be run down; it won't start."

"Leave it here and come back tomorrow morning," said Don Camillo. "I'll walk home with you. Getting wet doesn't bother me."

They had walked some distance along the road skirting the village when all of a sudden Peppone halted and gripped Don Camillo's arm. There walking ahead of them was the headless man. A flash of lightning allowed them to make him out quite clearly. He walked slowly on, and Peppone and

Don Camillo followed. At a certain point he took a narrow road leading toward the river, and stopped under an old oak tree. Don Camillo and Peppone stopped too, and once more they saw his figure in a flash of lightning. A third flash followed, and almost simultaneously a blast of thunder. The lightning had struck the hollow oak and levelled it to the ground. And the headless man had disappeared.

Don Camillo found himself curled up in bed without the slightest idea of how he had got there. They awakened him early the next morning and dragged him outside. Half the village was gathered around the fallen oak and amid the uptorn roots there shone a white skull. No one had any doubt whatsoever. The skull belonged to the man without a head, and the way it had appeared proved it. That same morning they buried it under the black stone, and everyone knew for certain that the nightmare was over. Don Camillo went home in a daze and stopped to kneel before the altar.

"Lord," he stammered, "thank you for having punished my presumption. Now I know what it is to be afraid."

"Have you taken up a belief in headless ghosts, Don Camillo?"

"No," the priest replied. "But for a brief moment last night, my mind was invaded by the collective fear."

"That's practically a scientific explanation," Christ murmured.

"It's just a way of covering up my shame," Don Camillo said humbly.

Anyhow, the headless man acquired a head. Was it rightly his, or no? The main thing is that it pacified him and he no longer inflamed the popular imagination. And the great rolling river quietly carried one more story, like a dead leaf, down to the sea.

THE STRANGER

THE DILAPIDATED little car drove slowly around the village square, skirting the arcades, and came to a stop in front of the draper's. A thin, almost distinguished looking man about forty-five years old, got out. His left arm seemed to be glued to his side, all the way down to the elbow, and this detail contributed to the definite picture his appearance left in the mind of an onlooker. He took a big leather case out of the car and strode decisively into the draper's shop. The draper didn't need to look at the calling-card held out by the visitor to know what he was after.

"I'm overstocked," he explained. "Business has been slow for some time, and the floods gave it a knockout blow."

The stranger opened his case and showed his samples. The material was very fine, and the draper couldn't help eyeing it with interest.

"I can't buy a thing just now," he said finally. "Try coming back in the spring. I can't make any promises, but I hope we can do some business together."

The salesman thanked him politely, asked if he might jot down the name and address, put his samples back in the case and returned to the car, which sputtered some twenty yards down the street and then stopped, obviously because there was something drastically wrong with the engine. Luckily for the stranger, Peppone's workshop was only fifty yards farther on, and he was able to cover this distance fairly fast in spite of the fact that he had to get out and push the car. When Peppone heard the blast of a horn, he came promptly to the door.

"Hello there," said the stranger. "I'm having a little trouble. Can you see what it's all about?"

Peppone had shuddered when he heard the stranger's voice, and now he said rudely:

"Not now. I'm too busy."

"Well, I can't get it started, so I'll just leave it here. Have a look at it as soon as you can, will you?" And he walked away, while Peppone stared after him from the door.

"As soon as I can, eh? No, as soon as I feel like it!"

He went back to his lathe in the workshop, but try as he would to put the matter behind him, he couldn't get the stranger off his mind. No matter how often he told himself that the similarity was a matter of pure coincidence, the more he was persuaded that it wasn't coincidence at all. Finally he interrupted his work, threw open the wide glass-paned door of the workshop and pushed in the car. Shutting the door behind him, he searched the car's dashboard compartment for its registration papers. He took a quick look at them and quickly put them back where he had found them. No, it wasn't a coincidence at all. He had a wild impulse to kick the car to pieces, but on second thought he decided to repair it. The roar that burst from the engine when he pulled out the self-starter caused him to chortle with joy.

"I'd like to see his face when he finds out what a mess it's in!" he said to himself. He lifted off the bonnet and started to work. When he had taken out the cylinder block, he called his boy and sent him to find Smilzo. A few minutes later he was giving Smilzo some very definite instructions.

"I'm your man, Chief," said Smilzo. "I'll stand out there under the arcade and as soon as I see the fellow coming, I'll run to call the police. Then, when a policeman arrives, I'll follow."

Ten minutes later the stranger returned and immediately scrutinized the engine of the car.

"I thought so," he said after a while.

"It's a serious business," Peppone explained, enumerating all the minor bits of business connected with it. But he was interrupted by the arrival of the village policeman, in full uniform.

"Good morning, Mr. Mayor," said the policeman, lifting his fingers to his cap in a salute. "There's a paper here which you must sign."

Peppone looked at him with annoyance.

"Tell the clerk that this isn't my time for signing papers. I'll sign it when I come to the Town Hall this afternoon."

The policeman saluted again and about-turned. Peppone continued to list the deficiencies he had found in the engine until for the second time he was interrupted. Smilzo drew himself to attention before him, raising his left arm and a clenched fist.

"Chief," he said, "the proofs of our poster are here. We've got to decide whether the speech will be at nine o'clock or ten."

"Ten," Peppone answered decisively.

"Very good, Chief," said Smilzo, raising his fist again and swinging about on his heels.

This time Peppone managed to finish his description of the engine's woes. And at the end the stranger said:

"Now tell me whether you can make the repairs, and if so how long you will take and what you will charge me."

Peppone shrugged his shoulders.

"If we telephone to the bus station in the city, we may be able to get the necessary parts out by the evening bus. The work will take two and a half days and the cost will be, in round figures, between twenty and twenty-five thousand liras."

The stranger did not blench.

"I'll put in a telephone call to Milan and an hour from now I can give you an answer."

Peppone went back to his lathe.

"Nuts to you!" he whispered to himself as the door closed behind the stranger.

Early in 1943, when Peppone had received his call-up papers, he went to the nearest recruiting station to say:

"I'm forty-four years old and I went all through the last war. Why do you have to pick on me?"

"If you hadn't been called up and were left at home, what would you do?"

"I'd keep up my usual trade, which is that of a mechanic."

"Then just pretend you're still at home. It's because you're a mechanic that the army needs you."

Peppone was sent to some old barracks, which had been turned into a repair depot for army vehicles, and there, in the uniform of a corporal, he went on with his old trade. For a month this job was quite a soft one, because in spite of the grey-green uniform and insignia, Peppone and his fellows enjoyed considerable liberty. Until one day a cursed captain came into the picture, and then their troubles began.

The cursed captain had been on active service all over the map. On his chest he wore a complete assortment of decorations and in his buttonhole a German ribbon. During the retreat from Russia a shell fragment had put his left arm out of commission, and because he didn't want to be invalided home, they had sent him to create some order in the depot where Corporal Giuseppe Bottazzi was working. At first the boys thought that within a week they could make mincemeat of the captain with the withered arm. But instead, after a week had gone by, they found that their soft job had turned into a very tough one, for the captain was a martinet who had army regulations on the brain.

Corporal Peppone, the top mechanic, simply couldn't believe it when he was confined to the guardhouse for ten consecutive days. One morning, in the courtyard, when the captain with the withered arm passed by, he presented arms with a shaft of cement which the strength of three ordinary men would not have sufficed to lift off the ground. But the captain was not impressed. He looked at Peppone and said coldly:

"An ordinary crane, without even the rank of corporal, can lift heavier weights than that with less waste of energy. Perhaps that's because the crane is more intelligent than you are. Ten more days of confinement will give you time to think it over."

Two days later Peppone's wife and child came to the nearby town for a visit, but Peppone wasn't allowed to see them. When the captain looked in at his cell he found him a raging tiger.

"Take it easy, Corporal," he said, "or you may get into really hot water."

"I want to see my wife and son!" howled Peppone.

"Thousands of better men than you would like to see their mothers and wives and children, but they've given their lives for their country. You're a very poor soldier and you're only getting what you deserve."

Peppone could have knocked the captain down with a single blow, but all he did was grit his teeth and protest:

"I went all through the last war and brought home a silver medal!"

391

"The fact that you were of age when the last war came around isn't any particular virtue. And it isn't enough to win a medal; you've got to live up to it."

Every last man at the depot had it in for the captain with the withered arm. He stood over them from reveille to taps, and because he knew a thing or two about motors, he wouldn't let them get away with any work that wasn't absolutely first class.

On the evening of July 26, 1943, Mussolini suffered his well-known eclipse from the political scene. The next morning the captain was in the sleeping quarters when the men got up. Before they could go to breakfast he addressed them as follows:

"There's to be no change here. The same repair jobs are waiting for us, and it's still our duty to carry them out as best we can."

During the heavy air-raids of that August, the captain arrived at the men's quarters along with the first signal of alarm and stayed until the all-clear had sounded. On September 8, the Germans' liberation of Mussolini complicated the political situation further. There were panic and disorganization everywhere. The captain gave each of his men a gun and a round of ammunition and said simply:

"You'll sleep fully dressed, in order to be prepared for any emergency."

He slept on a table in the quartermaster's office and the next morning, after inspecting his men, he told them:

"The colonel has assigned us to the defence of the west side of the barracks and the vehicle entrance. Our orders are to let nobody in."

The west side of the barracks, including the repair depot, was located in the former stables, adjacent to the open fields, and when Peppone and the others heard the word "defence," they thought of the single round of ammunition each one of them had upon him, and stared nervously at one another. At ten o'clock, the place was surrounded by German tanks and a German officer came to ask the colonel to surrender. Upon the colonel's refusal, the heavy *Panzer* in front of the main gate shattered it with a single shot and rolled in. Meanwhile, the *Panzer* at the vehicle entrance didn't even bother to fire. It just bumped the rusty gate, and with the first bit of pressure put upon the hinges, the whole thing collapsed, as if it had been attached to the walls with thread.

Some of the mechanics were drawn up along the wall, while Peppone and four others were stationed in the sentry-box which guarded the gate. Now, where the gate had been, there stood the cursed captain with the withered arm, his legs spread far apart and a pistol in his hand, pointing at the *Panzer*. It was a ridiculous thing, if you like, but the captain wore a German ribbon in his buttonhole and this brought the German tank to a stop. These professional military types have a special way of looking at things and you can't take it away from them. Out of the tank turret popped a German officer, who proceeded to give a salute. The captain put his pistol into its holster and answered in kind. The German jumped down from the *Panzer*, drew himself up with puppet-like stiffness in front of the Italian and saluted him again, receiving the same salute in return.

"I'm sorry to say, I must ask you to surrender," said the German type in hesitant Italian.

The Italian type took the decoration out of his buttonhole and handed it to the German. Then he stepped out of the way. The German made a slight bow, climbed back into the tank, stood up to his waist in the turret and shouted an order, which caused the vehicle to move forward. As he passed before the Italian, the German raised his hand to his cap in a salute, which the Italian duly returned. After that, the Italian calmly lit a cigarette and when two German soldiers approached, he preceded them to the centre of the court-yard, where the colonel, along with the other officers and men who had been made prisoners, had been standing waiting.

The mechanics made for the open fields. Peppone was the last of them to run for freedom, because he wanted to see the business of those two military types through to the end. Two hours later he was in civilian clothes, and the next day, from the attic in which he was hiding, he saw a little group of Italian soldiers marched off under German tommy-guns to the train that was to take them to a prison camp far away. At the end of the group were the officers, and among them the cursed captain with the withered arm.

"I hope you don't come back until I call for you in person," Peppone mumbled to himself.

But he did not forget the captain. The final insult still rankled in his mind. When the *Panzer* was still outside the gate and the captain was on his way to meet it, he had called out to Peppone, who was trembling in the sentry box with his four companions:

"Now we'll see if Corporal Bottazzi is a real weight lifter!"

Peppone had sworn that one day he would make the captain with the withered arm eat these words, and now by some miracle he had the fellow at his mercy. It gave him no little satisfaction to see that cocky "active service" officer reduced to the status of travelling salesman.

The stranger didn't go to make a telephone call. He went to sit down in the church, where he could quietly count his resources. Turning his pockets inside out and squeezing the last penny from them, he figured that he had twenty-two thousand three hundred liras. And he would have to spend two or three days in the village.

"If it comes to the worst, I can always pawn my watch," he concluded, and he went back to Peppone's workshop.

"All right, you can go ahead with the work," he said. "And when you've finished, send word to me at the tavern, where I expect to rent a room. Try to get it done as fast as you can."

Without looking up Peppone muttered:

"*As fast as I can*, eh? We're not in the army now, good-looking! Here I work as I please."

That evening, before he laid off, he cast a scornful glance at the dilapidated car.

"His good times are over, all right!" he sneered.

At the tavern he saw the stranger sitting in a corner over a plate of bread and sausage, with a bottle of water in front of him.

"If all your customers are so lavish, you'll soon be a rich man!" he whispered to the proprietor.

The proprietor grimaced.

"They're just as proud as they've poor," he grumbled.

Peppone went home early. Sleepy as he was, he went into the workshop first. The bus had brought the parts necessary for the repair of the car. Peppone looked at the package and then swung it against his bench.

"*As fast as you can*, eh?" he exclaimed angrily, "Half starving, and he thinks he can still give out orders in the old way! I'll take three or four days, or a whole week, if I want to! And if that doesn't suit you, push your rattle-trap straight to hell. If you start kicking, I'll give you a couple of punches to go with it!" And as he passed in front of the midget car, he spat into the engine. "There's for you and your driver, you little fool!" he exclaimed.

After he had gone to bed he thought with irritation of the stranger, sitting there in the tavern.

"Stony broke, and yet he eats his salami with a fork!" he said disgustedly.

"Who's that?" asked his wife, waking up with a start.

"A pretty rascal, I can tell you! If he has the nerve to open his mouth, I'll murder him!"

"Don't get yourself in trouble, Peppone," murmured his wife, going back to sleep.

His anger at the rascal with the withered arm so upset Peppone's stomach that he got up after half an hour and went down to the kitchen for some bicarbonate of soda. He fancied he heard a noise from the workshop and took a look inside. Everything was in good order, and the dilapidated midget car was waiting peacefully, with its guts exposed to the air.

"*As fast as you can,* eh?" he exclaimed ironically. "Go and give orders in your own house, jackass! The days of the puppets in uniform are over, you beastly reactionary warmonger!"

A moment later he turned back from the door.

"I want to look at those parts that came down by bus," he said to himself. "Here's hoping there are a few mistakes, such as to cause further delay. And you'll have to grin and bear it, that is unless you want to push your car away."

The parts seemed to be quite satisfactory. In order to be quite sure, Peppone took the worn parts out of the engine and compared them. One piece had to be fitted more closely, and he started to adjust it.

At six o'clock in the morning, Peppone was still working frantically, sweating and swearing all the while.

"I want to get this thing out of the way," he shouted between clenched teeth. "Otherwise I'll find myself in trouble."

At noon Peppone got into the car, slammed the door and tested the engine.

"It moves, and that ought to be enough to suit you," he grumbled. "If once you're out on the highway it breaks down, that's just too bad."

The important thing was to be sure it really would reach the highway. With this end in view, it was natural enough for Peppone to regulate the engine again, change the oil, test

395

the clutch, brakes, points, carburettor and tyres, tighten some screws on the chassis, fill the battery with distilled water, grease all the points that needed greasing and finally take a hose and wash the body. There is a limit to everything, and logically enough Peppone did not feel like doing any more. So Peppone's wife was the one to brush the upholstery, and not knowing anything about the rascal of an owner she did the job with impartiality and care.

When everything was done, Peppone sent his boy to tell the proprietor of the tavern to pass on the word that the car was ready. Meanwhile Peppone went upstairs. He wanted to impress the stranger with his physical appearance as well as his accomplishment, and so he washed, shaved and put on a clean shirt.

"Now is the time for the real fun!" he said, inwardly rejoicing. From the living-room he took a big sheet of paper with the heading: *Giuseppe Bottazzi. Repairs. Welding, Brakes. Ignition. Grease and oil."* He had always been proud of this paper, and now if ever was the time to use it. "*Bill no ...*" And he proceeded to add the date and the debtor. He knew the stranger's first and last name perfectly well, but it seemed to him more impressive to leave them out. Let him appear to be someone totally unknown. Then he began to itemize the charges.

New Parts (detailed)	.	.	.	11,000 liras
3 quarts of oil	.	.	.	1,200
Greasing and washing	.	.	.	800
Telephone call and bus delivery		.	.	500
Total expenses	.	.	.	13,500
Labour	.	.	.	7,000
Overtime	.	.	.	4,500
Grand total	.	.	.	25,000

Twenty-five thousand liras, and he could cough up every last one of them, if he wanted his car back. "*As fast as you can*, eh?" But it costs more to get something in a hurry. It used to be different, but that was in the army!

Peppone came downstairs upon the stranger's arrival.

"Your car's ready," he said coldly.

"All fixed?"

"All fixed."

"And how much do I owe you?"

Peppone was inwardly jeering. This was the big moment. He took the bill out of his pocket, looked at it and then put it back.

"Everything included, parts and labour, 13,100 liras."

The stranger took three five-thousand lira notes from his wallet.

"Keep the difference," he said, getting into the car.

At the door he leaned out to ask:

"Do I make a left turn for the highway?"

"Yessir!" said Peppone, clicking his heels.

"Good-bye, Sergeant Bottazzi," said the stranger.

A quarter of a mile along the road, the stranger wondered why the devil he had dubbed the fellow a sergeant when he knew perfectly well that he was only the most pestiferous of corporals? Then he listened to the hum of the engine, which was acting as if it had only three instead of thirty thousand miles behind it.

Peppone stood at the door to the workshop, looking after the car.

"Devil take you and whoever brought you this way!" he exclaimed angrily as he went back inside. But he felt as puffed up as if he really were a sergeant.

THE GOLD RUSH

THE BOMBSHELL exploded around noon on Monday, when the newspapers arrived from the city. Someone from the village had won ten million liras in the National Lottery. The papers gave the names as Pepito Sbezzeguti, but there was no one in the village by either of these names. The local ticket-seller was besieged by questioners, but he could only throw out his arms discouragingly and say:

"Saturday was a market day and I sold tickets to any number of strangers. Probably one of them bought it. It's bound to come out, sooner or later."

But nothing came out at all, and curiosity remained at a high pitch, because people were convinced that Pepito Sbezzeguti was a false name. Sbezzeguti alone was plausible enough. Among the country people who came to the market there might be a Sbezzeguti. But a Pepito was out of the question. No exotic Pepito could possibly have come to a village market, where the trading was in corn, wheat, hay, livestock and cheese.

"I say it's an assumed name," said the keeper of the Molinetto tavern. "And if somebody goes under an assumed name, it means he's not a stranger, but a local man who wants to remain under cover."

This was a debatable point, but it was received as a piece of perfect logic, and people transferred their attention from the idea of a stranger to that of someone right among them. They conducted the search as ferociously as if they were looking for a criminal rather than a lottery winner. Even Don Camillo, with less ferocity, but almost equal curiousity, took an interest in the search. And because he had an idea that Christ didn't altogether approve his bloodhound activities, he went to justify himself before the altar.

"Lord, I'm not merely curious. I have a duty to perform. Anyone who has received such a favour from Divine Providence and not told his neighbours about it, deserves to be branded as an ingrate."

"Don Camillo," Christ replied, "even if Divine Providence takes an interest in lotteries (a point which is not necessarily to be granted), I don't see that it needs to beg for publicity. The fact in itself is all that matters, and you know its most important feature. Someone has won the jackpot, but why should you care to discover his identity? People who are less favoured by fortune require your care."

But Don Camillo had the lottery prize on the brain and could find no rest until the mystery was solved. Finally a light shone upon his darkness. When the solution dawned upon him he was tempted to tug at the rope and ring the church bell. He managed to overcome this impulse, but he did go so far as to put on his cape and stroll about the village. When he came to Peppone's workshop he couldn't resist sticking in his head and wishing good-day to the mayor.

"Comrade Peppone, how do you do!"

Peppone looked up from his hammering and shot the priest a nervous glance.

"What's on your mind, Father?"

"Nothing. It just occurs to me that Pepito is a diminutive of Peppone. And I have an idea that by unscrambling all the letters of Pepito Sbezzeguti, the result would be something strangely like Giuseppe Bottazi."

Peppone went right on hammering.

"Go and give that to the Sunday puzzle page," he answered. "This is no place for anagrams; it's an honest man's workshop."

Don Camillo shook his head.

"I'm truly sorry that you're not the Pepito with ten million in his pocket."

"I'm just as sorry as you are," said Peppone. "If I had them, I'd give you a couple just to persuade you to go home."

"Don't worry, Peppone, I'm happy to do you a favour free," said Don Camillo as he went his way.

Two hours later the whole village knew the meaning of an anagram, and in every house Pepito Sbezzeguti was dissected to see if he would yield up Giuseppe Bottazzi. That evening the Reds' general staff held a meeting at the People's Palace.

"Chief," said Smilzo, who was the first to speak, "the reactionaries have gone back to their old propagandistic device of spreading malicious slander. The whole village is up in arms over the suspicion that you're the winner of the ten million liras. We must make a quick comeback and nail the mud-slingers to the wall."

Peppone threw out his arms.

"To accuse a man of having won ten million liras isn't slander. It's slander to accuse a man of dishonesty. But there's nothing dishonest about winning a lottery prize."

"Chief," Smilzo insisted, "even the accusation of having done a good deed can constitute political slander. Slander is any accusation harmful to the Party."

"People are laughing behind our backs," put in Brusco. "We've got to stop them."

"We must post a printed statement for everybody to see," suggested Bigio, "a statement that makes the whole thing perfectly clear."

Peppone shrugged his shoulders.

"All right. We'll do something about it tomorrow."

Smilzo took a sheet of paper out of his pocket.

"Chief, in order to save you trouble, we've drawn up a statement for you. If you approve, we'll print it tonight and paste it up in the morning."

And he proceeded to read aloud:

"The undersigned, Giuseppe Bottazzi, hereby declares that he has no connection with Pepito Sbezzeguti, winner of ten million liras at the Lottery. It's useless for the reactionaries to slanderously link my name with that of the new millionaire.
"GIUSEPPE BOTTAZZI."

Peppone shook his head.

"Until I see the accusation in print, I see no need for making a printed reply."

But Smilzo didn't agree.

"Chief, it seems to me foolish to wait for someone to take a potshot at you before shooting in reply. The rule is to beat your enemy to the draw."

"The rule is to administer a swift kick to anyone who interferes in my personal affairs," said Peppone. "I don't need any defenders, thank you just the same. I'm quite capable of looking after myself."

Smilzo shrugged his shoulders.

"If that's the way you take it, there's nothing anyone can say."

"That *is* the way I take it!" shouted Peppone, pounding the desk with his fist. "Every man for himself and the Party for all of us together!"

His henchmen went away without being convinced by anything he had said.

"This supine acceptance of the accusation seems very feeble to me," said Smilzo on the way home. "And then there's the complication of the anagram, too."

"Let's hope it turns out for the best," sighed Bigio.

After it had come out in gossip, the accusation finally did appear in print as well. The farm paper carried an italicized item which read: *Scratch a Peppone, and find a Pepito,* and this made everyone rock with laughter. As a result, Peppone's general staff held an emergency meeting and insisted that something must be done.

"Very well," said Peppone, "print the statement and plaster it up on the walls."

Smilzo made a beeline for the printer's and an hour later Don Camillo's friend, Barchini, brought a sheet of proof to the rectory.

"This is a black eye for the paper," Don Camillo said glumly. "If Peppone had won the millions, he wouldn't dare print so categorical a denial, unless he cashed them on the sly."

"He hasn't left the village for a single second," Barchini assured him. "Everyone has his eyes peeled."

It was late by this time and Don Camillo went to bed. But at three o'clock in the morning he was awakened, and the intruder was Peppone. He came in from the garden behind the house, and paused in the hall to look back through the half-closed door.

"I hope no one saw me," he said. "I feel as if I were under watch the whole time."

"Are you stark crazy?" Don Camillo asked him.

"No, but I may be soon."

He sat down and wiped the perspiration off his forehead.

"Am I talking to the priest or to the town crier?" he inquired.

"That depends on what you have to say."

"I came to talk to the priest."

"Then the priest is listening," said Don Camillo gravely.

Peppone twisted his hat in his hands for a while and then came out with it.

"Father, I told a big lie. I *am* Pepito Sbezzeguti."

That bombshell hit Don Camillo so hard that he could hardly catch his breath.

"You won those ten million liras!" he exclaimed, after he had come to. "Why in the world didn't you say so?"

"I'm not saying it even now for public consumption," said Peppone. "I came to tell the priest, and all the priest should care about is the fact that I was guilty of a lie."

But Don Camillo couldn't resist this opportunity to preach to Peppone in no uncertain terms.

"Shame on you! So one of the comrades wins ten million liras! Why don't you leave those dirty deals to the bourgeois reactionaries? A good Communist should earn money by the sweat of his brow!"

"I didn't come here to joke, Father. Surely it's no crime to buy a lottery ticket."

"I'm not joking, and I never said it was a crime. I simply said that a good Communist wouldn't do it."

"Ridiculous! They all do."

"To bad. And especially on your part, because you're a leader, with the guidance of the proletariat in your hands. Lotteries are one of the capitalists' most subtle weapons against the people, and one which costs them nothing. On the contrary it makes money for them. A good Communist ought to be dead set against lotteries, in any form whatsoever."

Peppone stared at him in amazement.

"Father, have you water on the brain?"

"No, but you have," said Don Camillo. "What is a lottery and how does it work? Imagine a thousand poor devils sentenced by a despot to hard labour in a prison camp, with only a miserable crust of bread for their daily pay. And what do they do to combat their hunger? Each one of them gives up a fifth of one day's ration to the despot, along with a piece of paper containing his own name. The despot puts all these papers into a hat and every Sunday draws one out. The bearer of the lucky name receives half the total amount of bread contributed by his companions and the despot keeps the other half for his trouble. So that nine hundred and ninety-nine poor devils have hopefully deprived themselves of a fifth of their daily bread for his enrichment. After all, the despot is the only one to steadily gain thereby. It's the same old story of capitalist exploitation."

Peppone shrugged his shoulders impatiently, but Don Camillo continued:

"Don't chafe at the bit, Comrade! Anything that makes the working man believe there is any improvement of his lot outside the proleterian revolution operates against him and in favour of his enemies. In patronizing the lottery, you are betraying the cause of the people."

Here Peppone lost all patience.

"I'm not betraying anybody," he protested. "I know what I'm doing."

"I don't doubt that, Comrade Peppone. Since your aim is to win the people's cause and no one can hope that the capitalists are going to finance it, then it's logical to make money to finance it yourself. In other words, if you are a good Communist, then you play the lottery in a Communist spirit, in order to make money with which to carry on the class struggle. Of course, as a good Communist, you'll put those ten million liras in the Party coffers."

Peppone waved his arms.

"Look here, Father," he said, "do we have to turn everything into politics?"

"Comrade! What about the revolution?"

Peppone stamped angrily on the floor.

"I understand, Comrade," Don Camillo said with a smile. "You're right. Better ten million liras in your own pocket today than the revolution tomorrow!"

Don Camillo poked the fire for a minute or two and then turned again to Peppone.

"Is that all you came to tell me? That you had won the ten millions?"

Peppone was perspiring heavily.

"How can I cash them without letting anyone know?"

"Go straight to Rome."

"I can't. They're watching me too closely. And then my denial is coming out tomorrow."

"Send a trusted emissary."

403

"I can't trust a soul."

"Well, what can I say?" said Don Camillo, shaking his head.

"Then you go to collect the money for me."

Peppone got up and went away, leaving an envelope in front of Don Camillo. The priest went off the next morning and was gone for three days. He arrived late at night and on his way to the rectory stopped in the church at the main altar. With him he had a briefcase which he laid open on the altar rail.

"Lord," he said grimly, "here are ten packages, each one containing a hundred ten-thousand lira notes, in other words Peppone's ten millions. I'd only like to say that he is totally undeserving of any such prize."

"Tell that to the Lottery!" Christ advised him.

Don Camillo took the briefcase and went to the second floor of the rectory, where he switched the light on and off three times in succession, as he had previously agreed with Peppone.

The latter was on the lookout, and signalled back with the light in his own bedroom, twice in succession. Two hours later he sneaked over to the rectory, with his coat collar up to the eyes. He came in through the garden and slipped the chain off the back door.

"Well?" he said to Don Camillo, who was waiting in his study.

Don Camillo pointed to the briefcase in reply. Peppone opened it with trembling hands and a burst of perspiration.

"Ten millions?" he asked in a whisper.

"Ten millions. Count them for yourself."

"No, no!" protested Peppone, staring at the money with fascination.

"Ten millions make a pretty pile, at least for the time being," said Don Camillo with a sigh. "But what will they be worth tomorrow? Just a little bad news, and their value is deflated, leaving nothing put a heap of worthless paper."

"They'd better be invested without delay," said Peppone anxiously. "Ten millions are enough to buy a sizable farm. Land always keeps its value."

"Land belongs to the people, Malenkov tells us. If Malenkov comes, he'll take your land away."

"Malenkov? Why should he come here? He's no imperialist."

404

"When I say Malenkov, I mean Communism. Communism is going to win, Comrade. The world's moving to the Left ..."

Peppone was still staring at the money.

"Gold," he said, "that's the thing to buy. Gold can be hidden in the ground."

"And when it's hidden in the ground, what good will it do you? If Communism comes, everything will be rationed by the State and you won't be able to buy anything with your gold."

"Then I'd better send it abroad."

"Aha! Just like a capitalist, eh? You'd have to send it to America, because Europe is going Communist for sure. And when America is completely isolated, it will have to surrender."

"America's strong," said Peppone. "Communism will never get there."

"You can never tell, the future is in Malenkov's hands, Comrade."

Peppone sighed and sat down.

"My head's whirling," he said. "Ten millions!"

"Well, gather it up and take it home. But send back the briefcase; that belongs to me."

"No," said Peppone. "Just keep it all here, will you? We'll talk about it tomorrow. I can't think straight just now."

Peppone made his way home, and Don Camillo picked up the briefcase and went to bed. He was dead tired, but he didn't sleep for long because at two o'clock he was awakened. Peppone and his wife were standing, all bundled up, downstairs.

"Father, try to understand," said Peppone. "My wife wants to know—wants to know what ten million liras look like. . ."

Don Camillo fetched the briefcase and opened it upon the table. Peppone's wife paled when she saw the money. Don Camillo waited patiently for the spectacle to be over. Then he closed the briefcase and escorted the two of them to the door.

"Try to go to sleep," he said in farewell.

He went back to bed, but at three o'clock Peppone roused him again.

"Isn't the pilgrimage over?" the priest asked.

"Father, I came to take the money."

"At this hour? Not on your life. I've just stowed it away in the attic and I have no intention of bringing it down so soon.

Come back tomorrow. I'm cold and sleepy. . . . Don't you trust me?"

"It's not a question of trust. Imagine . . . just for instance . . . that you were to suffer an accident. . . . How would I prove the money was mine?"

"Don't worry about that. The briefcase is locked and has your name on it. I've thought of everything."

"Of course . . . but it would be better to have the money in my own house."

There was something in his tone of voice that Don Camillo didn't like. And so he changed his tone to match it.

"What money do you mean?" he asked.

"My money! The money you got for me from Rome."

"You must be mad, Peppone, I never got any money of yours."

"The receipt was mine," panted Peppone. "Pepito Sbezzeguti, that's me."

"But it's plastered up all over the walls that you aren't Pepito Sbezzeguti at all. That's your own statement."

"But I am! Pepito Sbezzeguti is an anagram of Giuseppe Bottazzi."

"Not a bit of it. Pepito Sbezzeguti is an anagram of Giuseppe Bott*ezzi*. And your name is Bott*azzi*. I have an uncle called Giuseppe Bott*ezzi* and I bought the lottery ticket for him."

With a trembling hand Peppone wrote Pepito Sbezzeguti in the margin of a newspaper lying on the table. Then he wrote his own name and checked the letters.

"Damnation!" he shouted. "I put an *e* instead of an *a*. But the money's mine! *I* gave you the receipt!"

Don Camillo started upstairs to bed and Peppone followed him, calling for his money.

'Don't take it so hard, Comrade," said Don Camillo, climbing quietly into bed. "I shan't spend your money. I'll use it for your cause, for the cause of the People. In other words, I'll give it to the poor."

"Devil take the poor!" shouted Peppone.

"You reactionary swine!" exclaimed Don Camillo, settling down between the sheets. "Go away and let me sleep!"

"Give me my money or I'll kill you like a dog!"

"Take the filthy stuff and go away!" Don Camillo mumbled without even turning around.

The briefcase was on the chest of drawers. Peppone picked

it up, hid it under his coat and hurried home. Don Camillo sighed when he heard the door slam.

"Lord," he said grimly, "why did you let him win? He's ruined for life! And the poor fellow didn't deserve such punishment."

"First you told me the money was an undeserved prize and now you say it's an undeserved punishment. I'm always rubbing you the wrong way, Don Camillo."

"Lord, I'm not really talking to you; I'm talking to the Lottery!" And at last Don Camillo fell asleep.

THE WHISTLE

As usual, whenever he went shooting, Don Camillo started out from the orchard, and this time, in the farther field, behind the church, he saw a boy sitting on the stump of a tree and apparently waiting for him.

"Can I go over with you?" the boy asked, as he got up and started to walk over.

Don Camillo looked hard and saw at a glance who the boy was.

"Go along with you," he answered brusquely. "You don't think I want one of you little devils for company, do you?"

The boy stood stock-still and watched the priest and his dog Thunder go on their way. Pino dei Bassi was not even thirteen years old, but he had already been enlisted by the Reds. They had signed him up in their youth organization and sent him out to distribute propaganda leaflets or to dirty the walls with diatribes against this, that and the other. He was the most active of the lot, because while the other boys had chores to do at home, he hung about the streets all day long. His mother, the widow of Cino dei Bassi, carried on her husband's trade. Every morning she hitched the horse to the wagon and went around the countryside selling pots and pans and cotton goods of every description. The boy had weak lungs and could not help her, so he was left in charge of his grandmother, who had a mere glimpse of him at noon, when he came home for something to eat. One day Don Camillo stopped the widow and told her she'd better keep an eye on the boy or else the company he was keeping would get him into trouble. But she answered tartly:

"If he goes with them, it's because it's more fun than going to church."

Don Camillo saw that there wasn't any use insisting. And he knew it was useless to preach at a good woman who wore herself out with hard work every day in order to keep body and soul together. Every time he saw the horse and wagon go by he thought of Cino dei Bassi, one of his very best friends, whom he had seen die before his eyes. And he thought of Cino again whenever he went shooting. If Cino had known Thunder, he would have been wild about him. Cino had shooting in his blood and was one of the best shots in the countryside. He had an unerring nose for game and an unerring eye for shooting, and his expeditions carried him to places no one had visited before. Whenever Cino went to a duck shoot or target competition, half the village tagged along behind, as if he were a one-man football team. He was Don Camillo's boon companion, and it was while they were out shooting together that Cino had stumbled into a ditch and by some mischance fallen on the trigger of his shotgun. He had sent a volley into his own chest and died in Don Camillo's arms.

This kind of death seemed to be written into the fate of the Bassi family. Cino's grandfather, who was a mighty nimrod in his time, had accidentally killed himself with a gun, and Cino's father had been shot in the course of a shoot. Then death came to Cino the same way. And he had left his gun to Don Camillo.

"You keep it," were his dying words, "and put it to good use."

Now the sight of Cino's son sharpened Don Camillo's memory of his old friend, and when the boy asked if he could come along, he wished violently that he could knock some sense into his head and wipe out the disgrace he was bringing upon his father's good name.

"Thunder," he said, relieving himself of his feelings to his dog, "the next time we meet the little rascal, we'll practically shave the hair off him. It's plain as day that they're training him to make trouble and sent him to pester me."

Thunder did not swerve from the path, but growled lightly in reply.

Four or five days later, Don Camillo found Pino waiting for him in the same place.

"I've quit," said the boy. "Can I go with you this time?"

"Quit? What do you mean?" asked Don Camillo.

"I'm not with them any longer. I resigned."

Don Camillo looked him over with a feeling of perplexity. The boy had a welt under his left eye and a slightly battered air.

"What did you do?" he asked.

"They beat me up. But I'm not with them any longer. Today, will you take me?"

"Why do you want to go?"

"I'd like to see some shooting."

Don Camillo walked on and the boy trailed him as silently as a shadow. He did not get in the way and his footsteps made no echo upon the ground. His pockets were stuffed with bread and he did not ask for a thing during all the hours they were walking. Don Camillo did a good bit of shooting, and although he made no sensational hits he gave a very creditable performance and Thunder wasn't vexed with him too often. For when it came to his profession, Thunder was a strict taskmaster. He operated by the book and when Don Camillo made a whopping error he growled at him. On one occasion, early in their acquaintance, when the priest missed a hare almost the size of a calf, Thunder stood in front of him and bared his teeth.

Now Don Camillo had made a better-than-average record. He was ready to call it a day and go home, when suddenly Thunder showed signs of excitement.

"Can I have a shot?" whispered Pino, pointing to the shotgun.

"Of course not. You don't even know how to hold a gun to your shoulder."

Thunder took a few cautious steps forward and then froze into a pointing position.

"Give it here!" said the boy.

Don Camillo put the gun into his hands, but it was too late. A bird rose up out of the field, and only the kind of sportsman that likes to hear the sound of his own weapon would have taken a shot at it. That is, only a perfect fool, or else a marksman of the calibre of the late Cino dei Bassi. The boy raised the gun to his shoulder and fired. And the bird fell like a stone, because this was Cino's son, wielding his father's gun.

Don Camillo broke out into perspiration and there was a tight feeling about his heart as he remembered that this gun was responsible for the death of Cino. Impulsively he snatched it. Meanwhile Thunder had streaked away and come back to deposit a quail at the boy's feet. The boy leaned over to pat his head, and a second later the dog raced off to the far end of the field to show off the power of his lungs and legs together. There he stopped and waited. At this point the boy gave out a whistle that Don Camillo hadn't heard since the days when Cino was his hunting companion, and the dog responded instantly. A shiver ran down Don Camillo's spine. Meanwhile the boy handed the quail over to him.

"You shot it, so it's yours," said the priest roughly.

"Mother doesn't want me to shoot," the boy mumbled, and two minutes later he had gone away.

Don Camillo stuffed the quail into his bag and walked homeward, with Thunder frolicking before him. All of a sudden the dog stopped in his tracks, bringing Don Camillo to a halt just behind. In the distance sounded Cino's special whistle, and Thunder was off like a shot in reply.

"Thunder!" Don Camillo shouted, causing the dog to pause and look around. "Thunder, come here!"

But the whistle sounded again, and after a brief whinny of explanation, Thunder ran on, leaving Don Camillo in the middle of the narrow road. The priest did not continue straight on his way. Instead of crossing the ditch, he walked along it for at least a quarter of a mile. The evening mist was descending, filling up the rents left in the sky by the dried branches of the bare trees. Beside the ditch, at a spot marked by a wooden cross, Cino had fallen, releasing the trigger of his gun. Don Camillo bowed his head, took the quail out of the bag and laid it at the foot of the cross.

"I see you're still in good form, Cino," he whispered, "but please don't do it again."

Don Camillo had no more taste for shooting. The episode of Pino had given him such a chill that merely to look at the shot-gun hanging on the wall sent a tingle down his spine. And Thunder kept him company. The dog had received a major whacking and his demeanour was so humble that it seemed as if he must have understood every word, from the first to the last, of the little speech that had gone with it. If his master went out on the church square for a breath of air, he followed, but with his tail hanging. Then one afternoon, while the dog lay on the ground looking up at Don Camillo, who was pacing up and down with the usual cigar butt between his lips, the famous whistle sounded again. Don Camillo stopped and looked down at Thunder. Thunder did not budge. The whistle sounded again, and this time, although Thunder did not move, he traitorously wagged his tail and kept on wagging it until Don Camillo shouted at him. The confounded whistle sounded for a third time, and just as Don Camillo was about to grab his collar and pull him indoors, Thunder slipped away, jumped over the hedge and disappeared.

When he came to the field behind the church Thunder stopped to wait for further orders. Sure enough, he heard another whistle, which led him farther. The boy was waiting for him behind an elm, and they walked on together in the direction of an old mill which for the last fifty years had been nothing but a pile of stones beside a dried-up canal. When a dike had been thrown up to prevent floods, the course of the river had been changed, and the mill served no longer.

Now the boy climbed among the ruins, with Thunder at his heels. When they came to a half-collapsed arcade, he took away a few stones, revealing a long, narrow box behind them. Out of this he took an object wrapped in oily rags. Thunder looked on with a puzzled air, but in a minute he saw what it was all about. Enveloped in the rags was an old musket, as highly polished as if it had just come from the maker.

"I found it in the attic," the boy explained "It belonged to my great-grandfather, who was a keen shot in his day. It takes a while to load it, but it shoots perfectly well." With which, he proceeded to load it. Then he put the powder-horn in his pocket, hid the musket under his coat and led the dog away.

Thunder had very little confidence in this strange contraption. And when he heard a bird stir in the grass, he pointed without any particular enthusiasm. But when he saw the bird drop to the ground he put his heart into his work, because he knew that it was worth while. This boy shot as Thunder had never seen anyone shoot before, and when they came to tuck the musket away in its hiding-place at the old mill the boy's pockets were bulging with quail.

"I can't take them home, because if my mother and grand-mother were to find out that I had been shooting, they would raise the roof," Pino explained. "I give my catch to a fellow from Castelletto who deals in poultry, and he lets me have powder, tow, buckshot and cartridges in exchange."

Thunder's reaction to the announcement of this trade was not expressed very clearly. But then boy and dog alike were true artists. They didn't shoot for the sake of garnishing spits or frying pans, or just because they had a barbaric taste for bloodshed.

From this time on Thunder led a double life. He stayed quietly at home for days on end, but whenever he heard Pino's whistle he threw off all restraint and made for the field behind the church. Eventually Don Camillo took offence and put Thunder out of the front door.

"You're not to set foot in my house until you've given up this shameful behaviour," he said aiming a swift kick to underline his meaning.

And Thunder rejoiced, because his newly won independence favoured the enterprise on which he had set his heart.

Pino got it into his head that he must bring down a pheasant.

"I'm tired of these small pickings," he explained to the dog. "Now I want to do some real shooting. We've got to find a pheasant. To have bagged a pheasant is the badge of a true shot."

Thunder did the best he could, but even a blue-ribbon shooting dog can't find a pheasant where none is to be found. And yet there were some pheasants not too far away. They had only to go to the game preserve and worm their way through the wire fence. There thousands of pheasants awaited them.

But three wardens reigned over the preserve, and they were no joking matter.

However, the prospect of bringing down a pheasant was overwhelmingly attractive. And so one day Pino and Thunder found themselves up against the fence. They had chosen just the right sort of weather, for there was a mist in the air just thick enough to afford vision combined with invisibility and to muffle the sound of gunshot. Pino had a pair of pincers and he lay down on the ground to loosen just enough of the wire to allow himself and the dog to squeeze under. They stalked silently through the tall grass, and before they had gone very far Pino found a pheasant to shoot at. The bird came down like a ton of bricks, but once it hit the ground it recovered sufficient strength to make a last flight which ended in a thicket. Thunder was just about to go for it when the boy called him back. Someone was running after them and calling upon them to halt or else. Pino ran like a demon, holding his head low, and Thunder followed after. The thickness of the mist and the general excitement caused the boy to strike the fence at a point slightly to the right of where he had made the hole. He realized this too late and lost time finding the right place. Just as he was bending down to slip through he was felled by the warden's gun.

He sank noiselessly to the ground and in spite of his ebbing strength tried to squeeze himself under. Just then the warden overtook him. Thunder stood in front of the boy, barking and baring his teeth. The man stopped short and when he saw the boy's bloodstained body on the ground he turned pale and did not know what to do. Pino was still trying to propel himself with his hands across the ground and Thunder, without taking his eyes off the warden, took the lapel of his jacket between his teeth and pulled him along. The warden stood there in a daze until at last he ran away. Pino had reached the other side of the fence, but he lay still and was apparently no longer breathing.

Thunder ran up and down, howling like one of the damned, but no one came by and finally he ran straight as an arrow to the village. Don Camillo was in the process of baptizing a baby when the dog rushed into the church, caught hold of his cassock and dragged him to the door. There Thunder let go, ran ahead, paused to bark came back to take the priest's cassock between his teeth again, pull him forward and then dash on ahead to show the way. Now Don Camillo followed of his own free will, wearing his vestments and with his book in hand. And as he ran along the road, people from the village came after him.

Don Camillo brought the boy back in his arms, accompanied by a silent procession. He laid him down on his bed, while the old grandmother stared at him and murmured:

"There's fate for you! All of them died the same way."

The doctor said there was nothing to do but let him die in peace, and the onlookers lined up against the wall like so many statues. Thunder had disappeared, but he came back all of a sudden and took up his place in the middle of the room. In his mouth was the pheasant, which he had fetched from the thicket where it had fallen inside the preserve. He went over to the bed and put up his front legs and laid it on the boy's right hand which lay motionless on the bed-cover. Pino opened his eyes, saw the bird, moved his fingers to stroke it and died with a smile on his face.

Thunder made no fuss but remained lying on the floor. When they came the next day to put Pino into his coffin they had to call upon Don Camillo to take the dog away, because he would not let anyone come near. Don Camillo put the body into the coffin himself and Thunder realized that if his master did it then it must be done. The whole village came to the funeral, and Don Camillo walked before the coffin, saying the office of the dead. At a certain moment his eyes fell upon the ground, and there was Thunder with the pheasant between his teeth. When they threw the first hand-fuls of earth over the coffin, Thunder let the pheasant drop among them. Everyone was scared by the dog's uncanny behaviour and left the cemetery in a hurry. Don Camillo was the last to go, and Thunder followed him, with his head hanging low. Once they were outside he disappeared.

The three wardens of the game preserve were grilled for forty-eight hours by the carabinieri, but every one of them made the same reply: "I know nothing about it. There was a heavy mist, and I saw and heard nothing in the course of my rounds. Some other poacher must have shot him." Finally they were all dismissed for lack of proof.

Thunder lay all day in the rectory, but when night came he ran away and did not come back until dawn. For twenty nights in succession he did the same thing, and for twenty nights a dog howled under the window of one of the three wardens. He howled uninterruptedly and yet no one could find the place where he was hiding. On the twenty-first morn-ing the warden gave himself up to the sergeant of the carabinieri.

"You may as well lock me up," he said. "I didn't mean to kill him, but the shot was mine. Do what you like with me, because I can't stand that confounded dog's howling."

After this everything returned to normal, and Don Camillo resumed his shooting. But every now and then, in the middle of some remote, deserted meadow, Thunder came to a sudden stop. And in the silence there rang out the whistle that was peculiar to Cino dei Bassi.

THE EXCOMMUNICATED MADONNA

ONE MORNING a young man rode up on a bicycle to the square in front of the church and began to look inquiringly around him. Having apparently found what he wanted, he leaned his bicycle up against a pillar of the arcade and unpacked the bundle on the carrier behind the saddle. He took out a folding stool, an easel, a paint box and a palette, and a few minutes later he was hard at work. Fortunately the village children were all at school and he had a good half hour of peace and quiet. But gradually people crowded around and a hundred pairs of curious eyes followed his every brush-stroke. Just then Don Camillo came along, walking as casually as if he just happened to be passing that way. Someone asked him what he thought of the painting.

"It's too early to say," the priest answered.

"I don't see why he chose the arcade for a subject," said a member of the would-be intelligentsia. "There are far more picturesque scenes along the river."

The painter heard this remark and said without turning around:

"Picturesque scenes are for penny postcards. I came here to paint just because it isn't picturesque."

This statement left the villagers puzzled, and they continued to stare somewhat mistrustfully at the artist's work for the rest of the morning. At noon they went away and he was able to put in two solid hours without interruption

416

When the villagers returned they were so agreeably surprised that they ran to the rectory.

"Father, you must come and see. His picture's a beauty."

The painter was, indeed, a talented fellow, and Peppone, who happened to be among the onlookers, summed it up aptly by saying:

"There's art for you. I've been looking at that arcade for for almost fifty years and I never realized that it was so beautiful!"

The painter was tired and packed his painting things away.

"Have you finished?" someone asked.

"No, I'll finish tomorrow. The light's changed and I can't get the same effects at this hour."

"If you'd like to leave your things at the rectory, there's plenty of room and I can answer for their safety," said Don Camillo, who saw that the young man didn't know what to do with his wet canvas.

"I knew the clergy would try to take him over," said Peppone disgustedly, as the artist gratefully accepted Don Camillo's offer.

After the young man had put his things in the hall closet he asked Don Camillo to recommend some simple lodgings.

"You can stay here," said Don Camillo. "I'm happy to have an artist under my roof."

A fire was lit in the rectory and supper was on the table. The young man was cold and hungry, but after he had eaten the colour came back into his cheeks.

"I don't know how to thank you," he said.

"You mustn't even try," said Don Camillo. "Will you be staying in these parts for long?"

"Tomorrow afternoon I must go back to the city."

"Has your enthusiasm for the river country suddenly left you?"

"No, it's a question of money," sighed the young man.

"Have you work waiting for you?" the priest asked him.

"Oh, I just scrape along from one day to the next," the artist told him.

"Well, I have no money," said Don Camillo, "but I can give you board and lodging for a month if you do some work in the church for me. Think it over."

"That's quickly done," said the young man. "It's a bargain. That is, if you let me have some time to paint for myself."

"Of course," said Don Camillo. "I need you for only a couple of hours a day. There's not so much to be done."

The church had undergone some repairs a month before and where the workmen had replaced some fallen plaster there was a gap in the decoration.

"Is that all?" asked the painter. "I can do that in a single day. You're offering me too much in return and it would be dishonest to accept it. You'll have to find something more for me to do."

"There is something more," said Don Camillo, "but it's such a big job, I haven't the courage to mention it."

"Let's hear."

Don Camillo went over to the rail of a side-chapel and threw on the light. A great spot filled the space above the altar.

"There was a leak," Don Camillo explained. "We caught on it too late, and even though we mended the roof, the seepage had loosened the plaster. And so the painting of the Madonna was completely destroyed. The first thing to do, of course, is to replace the plaster. But I'm much more concerned over the repainting of the Madonna."

"You can leave that to me," said the artist. "Go ahead and get the plaster put in order, and meanwhile I'll make a sketch and have it ready to transfer to the wall when the mason gives me the word. I've had some experience in frescoes already. But I'll have to insist upon some privacy. You can see the job when it's done, but I can't bear to work with people staring at me."

Don Camillo was so pleased that he didn't have breath enough even to answer: "Yes, sir!"

The young man had a genuine passion for painting, and the agreeable surroundings plus three square meals a day fired him to tremendous enthusiasm. When he had finished his widely admired picture of the arcade on the church square, he set off to explore the surrounding country and to find a model for the Madonna. He didn't want to paint a conventional figure, but to spiritualize a genuine face, which he hoped to discover in the vicinity of the village. During the first week he patched up the decorations in the main body of the church and restored an oil painting over the choir stalls. But he was restless and dissatisfied because he had not yet found his model. By the end of the second week

418

the replastered chapel wall was ready for him to work on, but he was unable to begin. He had looked at hundreds of women in and around the village without finding a single face that interested him. Don Camillo became aware that something was wrong. The young man seemed listless and often came back in the evening without a single sketch in his notebook.

"Don't you care for this country any longer?" he asked. "There are all sorts of beauty you haven't yet discovered."

"Only one kind of beauty interests me just now," the artist complained. "And that I can't seem to find."

The next day the young man mounted his bicycle, making this resolution: "If I don't find what I'm after today, then I'm going home." He rode at random, stopping in farmyards to ask for a glass of water or some other trifle and looking into the face of every woman he saw along the way. But he was only confirmed in his disappointment. At noon he found himself in the settlement of La Rocca, a small place not far from the village, and rather than communicate his chagrin to Don Camillo he stopped for a bite to eat at the Pheasant Tavern. The big, low-ceilinged room with prints of characters from Verdi's *Othello* on the walls was completely deserted. An old woman appeared and he asked her for bread, sausage and a bottle of wine. A few moments later, when a hand deposited this simple fare on the dark table before him he raised his eyes and was startled almost out of his skin. Here was the inspiration for which he had been searching. The inspiration was about twenty-five years old and carried herself with the nonchalance of eighteen. But what captured the artist's fancy was the girl's face, and he stared at it, hardly daring to believe it was true.

"What's the matter?" the girl asked. "Have I done something to annoy you?"

"Please forgive me . . ." he stammered.

She went away but returned a little later to sit down over some sewing at the door. At once the young man took a pad and pencil and began to sketch her. She felt his eyes upon her and broke in upon his work with a question:

"May I ask what you're doing?"

"If you don't mind, I'm drawing you."

"What for?"

"Because I'm a painter and take an interest in everything beautiful."

She gave him a pitying smile, shrugged her shoulders and went on with her work. After an hour she got up and went to look over the young man's shoulder.

"Do I really look like that?" she asked him, laughing.

"This is just a preliminary sketch. If you'll allow me, I'll come back to finish tomorrow. Meanwhile, how much do I owe you for lunch?"

"You can pay when you come back."

As soon as the artist got back to the rectory he shut himself up in his room to work. The next day he worked until noon, when he went out, locking the door behind him.

"I've got it, Father!" he exclaimed as he rode away.

When he reached the Pheasant he found things just as they had been the day before: bread, sausage, wine and his inspiration sitting at the door. This time, after he had worked for a couple of hours, the girl showed more satisfaction with what he had accomplished.

"It will be better yet if I can come back tomorrow," he sighed.

He came back for the two next afternoons and then no more, for he had reached another stage of his work. For three whole days he remained in his room and then, in agreement with the mason, started in on the chapel. No one could see what he was doing, because a board partition had been thrown up to protect him from the public view and he alone had the key to the door leading through it. Don Camillo was consumed with curiosity, but he contained himself and did no more than ask every evening:

"How's it going?"

"You'll soon see," said the young man excitedly.

Finally the great day came. The young man put a cloth over the fresco and tore down the boarding. Don Camillo rushed to the rail and waited, with his heart pounding. Then the young man took a pole and lifted the cloth off his "Madonna of the River." It was a most impressive painting, and Don Camillo stared at it with his mouth hanging open. Then all of a sudden something caught at his heart and perspiration broke out on his forehead.

"Celestina!" he shouted.

"Who's Celestina?" the young man asked.

"The daughter of the tavern-keeper at La Rocca."

"Yes," said the young man calmly. "She's a girl I found at the Pheasant Tavern."

Don Camillo took hold of a ladder, carried it over to the far end of the chapel, climbed up and draped the cloth over the fresco. The young man couldn't imagine what was wrong.

"Father, are you out of your head?" he asked him, but Don Camillo only ran back to the rectory, with the young man at his heels.

"Sacrilege!" he panted, once he had reached his own study. "Celestina from the Pheasant Tavern! You mean you don't know about Celestina? She's the most ardent Communist anywhere around and to present her face as that of the Madonna is like painting Jesus Christ in the likeness of Stalin."

"Father," said the artist, recovering some of his calm. "I was inspired not by her political beliefs but by her beauty. She has a lovely face, and that was given her by God, not by the Party."

"But the black soul behind it came straight from the Devil!" shouted Don Camillo. "You don't appreciate the gravity of the sacrilege you've committed. If I didn't realize that you were completely innocent about it, I'd send you packing."

"I have nothing on my conscience," said the artist. "I gave the Madonna the most beautiful face I could find."

"But the portrait doesn't reflect your good intentions, it represents a damned soul! Can't you see the sacrilege involved? The only fitting title to the fresco is 'The Excommunicated Madonna!'"

The young man was in terrible distress.

"I put everything I had in me into bringing out the spiritual qualities of that face. . . ."

"How do you expect to spiritualize the face of such a wanton creature? Why, when she opens her mouth, teamsters blush at the words that come out of it! No one can wish a face like that upon the Madonna."

The artist went to throw himself on his bed and did not come down to supper. About ten o'clock Don Camillo went up to see him.

"Well, are you awake now to the sacrilege you have committed? I hope that a second look at your sketches has revealed to you the essential vulgarity of that face. You're a young man and she's a provocative girl. She spoke to your senses, and your artistic discrimination went by the board."

"Father, you're misjudging and insulting me."

421

"Just let's look at your sketches together!"

"I've torn them all up."

"Then let's have another look at the chapel."

They went down to the empty church and Don Camillo took the pole to pull down the cloth covering the fresco.

"Look at it calmly and tell me if I'm not right."

The artist turned two powerful lights on the painting and shook his head.

"I'm sorry, Father," he said, "but there's nothing wanton or vulgar in that face."

Don Camillo stared at it again, scowling. The expression of the Madonna of the River was calm and serene and her eyes were pure and clear.

"Incredible!" exclaimed the priest angrily. "I don't know how you managed to get anything spiritual out of that creature."

"Then you admit that my picture has a spiritual and not a vulgar quality about it!"

"Yes, but Celestina hasn't. And anyone looking at it can't help saying: 'There's Celestina playing the part of the Madonna.'"

"Well, don't take it so tragically, Father. To-morrow I can destroy it and start all over."

"We'll decide that to-morrow," said Don Camillo. "As a painting it's stupendous, and it's a crime to wipe it off the wall. . . ."

Indeed, this Madonna of the River was one of the most stunning things Don Camillo had ever seen. But how could he tolerate Celestina in the guise of Our Lady? The next day he called five or six of his most trusted parishioners together, unveiled the fresco before them and asked for their honest opinion. Without exception they exclaimed:

"Marvellous!" and then a second later: "But that's Celestina from the Pheasant Tavern!"

Don Camillo told them of the painter's misadventure and concluded:

"There's only one thing to do: wipe the whole thing out!"

"Too bad, because it's a masterpiece. Of course, it wouldn't do for our Madonna to have an excommunicated Communist's face. . . ."

Don Camillo begged the members of this little group not to say a word, and as a result the story spread like wildfire.

People began to pour into the church, but the fresco was draped with a cloth and the entrance to the chapel barred. The news travelled outside the village and that evening, when Don Camillo was closing up the church he detected in the shadows the malicious face of Celestina in person.

"What do you want?" he asked gruffly.

"I want to see that idiot of a painter," she told him, and just then the idiot came upon the scene.

"Aside from the fact that you ate four meals at the Tavern without paying for them," Celestina said to him threateningly, "I'd like to know who gave you permission to misuse my face!"

The young man looked at her in amazement: here indeed was the face of which Don Camillo had spoken. He wondered how in the world he had seen anything spiritual in it. He started to make a hesitant reply, but she overrode him:

"You fool!" she exclaimed.

"Let's have less noise, my girl," Don Camillo interrupted. "We're in church, not in your father's tavern."

"You have no right to exploit my face and pin it on to a Madonna," the girl insisted.

"No one's exploited you," said Don Camillo. "What are you driving at, anyhow?"

"People have seen a Madonna with my face!" Celestina shouted. "Deny it if you can!"

"Impossible!" said Don Camillo. "But since it's true that some people see a slight resemblance, the fresco is going to be scraped away and done over."

"I want to see it!" Celestina shouted. "And I want to be present when you take my face out of it!"

Don Camillo looked at her ugly expression and thought of the gentle countenance of the Madonna of the River.

"It isn't your face," he said. "Come and see for yourself."

The girl walked quickly to the chapel and came to a halt in front of the rail. Don Camillo took the pole and removed the cloth cover. Then he looked at Celestina. As she stood motionless, staring up at the picture, something extraordinary happened. Her face relaxed while her eyes lost their malice and became gentler and more serene. The vulgarity disappeared, and gradually she seemed to take on the expression of the painting. The artist gripped Don Camillo's arm.

"That's how I saw her!" he exclaimed.

Don Camillo motioned to him to be silent. A few moments later Celestina said in a low voice:

"How beautiful!" She could not take her eyes off the picture, and finally she turned to say to Don Camillo: "Please don't destroy it! Or at least, not too soon." And to his surprise she knelt down in front of the Madonna of the River and made the sign of the cross.

When Don Camillo was left alone in the church, he covered the fresco and then went to talk to the Crucified Christ over the main altar.

"Lord, what's going on?" he asked anxiously.

"Painting's not my business," answered Christ with a smile.

The next morning the young artist rode off on his bicycle to La Rocca. The tavern was empty, as usual, and Celestina sat, leaning over her sewing, at the door.

"I came to pay what I owe you," said the young man.

She raised her head, and he felt better because she had the gentle and serene expression of the painting on her face.

"You're a real artist!" she sighed. "That Madonna is a beauty. It would be a shame to take her away."

"I quite agree. I put my heart and soul into her, but people say an excommunicated Madonna won't do."

"I'm not excommunicated any longer," said Celestina with a smile. "I fixed that up this morning." And she proceeded to explain what steps she had taken.

Then she took advantage of the young man's surprise to ask whether it was his wife that kept his clothes so well mended and in such good order. He said that it wasn't, because he lived all alone and had no one to look after him. She observed with a sigh, that after a certain age, living alone was a tedious affair, even when a girl had any number of suitors. The time came when the thing to do was to settle down and have a family. He agreed on this point, but said that he had barely enough money to support himself. That, said Celestina, was because he lived in the city, where things were twice as expensive. If he were to move to the country, life would be much simpler, especially if he found a girl with a little house of her own and a parcel of land that only needed further development. He started to say something else, but just then the clock rang out noon. The hours have a way of flying when one engages in a conversation of this kind. Celestina went to fetch the usual bread, sausage and wine, and when he had finished eating he asked her:

"How much do I owe you?"

"You can pay to-morrow," she answered.

The Madonna of the River remained concealed for about a month longer. But on the day when the artist and Celestina were married, with all possible splendour, including organ music, Don Camillo drew the curtain and threw on the lights in the chapel. He was slightly worried about what people might say about the Madonna's resemblance to Celestina. But their only comment was:

"Celestina must wish she were equally beautiful! But she doesn't really look like Her at all!"

THE PROCESSION

DON CAMILLO waited patiently for things to come to a head, and although he waited a long time, it was not in vain. One morning the man he was expecting turned up at the rectory.

"Is there any change in the programme, Father," he asked, "or is it just the same as other years?"

"Just the same," said Don Camillo, "except for one detail: no music in the procession."

This "one detail" made Tofini, leader of the local band, suffer considerable distress.

"No music?" he stammered. "Why not?"

"Orders from higher up," said Don Camillo, throwing out his arms helplessly.

Still Tofini couldn't believe it.

"Do you mean there's to be no more band-playing in any parades?"

"No," said Don Camillo, with icy calm. "It means that there's no more room in *my* procession for *your* band."

Tofini's collection of brasses was known as the "Verdi Band," but it was no great shakes from a musical point of view. However, it was no worse than other bands in that part of the country and no one had ever dreamed of looking elsewhere for the musical accompaniment to a religious or patriotic display.

"If we suited you in previous years and now you don't want us any more, what's the matter?" asked the dismayed Tofini. "Have we lost our art?"

426

"That's something you never had. But you know the reason perfectly well."

"Father, I don't know a thing!"

"Then ask around until you find out who played the *International* in the village square two months ago?"

"We did," answered Tofini, "but I don't see anything wrong in that."

"I do, though."

"But you know us, Father. You know we don't go in for politics. We play for anyone that hires us. Two months ago the mayor asked us to play in the square and we put on a programme of marches and operatic airs. Then people called for the *International*, the mayor said to play it, and we obliged."

"And if you'd been asked for the Fascist anthem, *Giovinezza*, or the *Royal March*, would you have played them too?"

"No. They're forbidden by law. But the *International* isn't forbidden."

"It's forbidden by the church," said Don Camillo. "If you respect the laws of the State and not those of the Church, you may be a good citizen, but you're a very bad Christian. As a good citizen, you can go on playing in the square. But as a bad Christian, you can't play in a Church procession."

"Father, that's no way to reason. Everyone has his own way of making a living. And if everyone that works for the Communists were a bad Christian, where would we be now? Printers couldn't put out Communist papers, chemists couldn't sell medicine to Party members. . . . When a man pursues his regular trade, politics and religion don't come into it. A doctor takes care of anyone that's sick, regardless of his party. And when we make music for money, we're simply dealing in the only commodity we have to sell. The *Overture to William Tell* and the *International* are all the same to us. The notes may be in different order, but they're still the same old A B C."

"Quite so," said Don Camillo, warming up to the debate. "One piece is as good as another, within the law. So if I'd come to the square on that occasion and asked for the anthem of the Christian Democrat Party, you'd have played that too?"

"Certainly, if I wanted a beating," said Tofini with a shrug of his shoulders.

"It's not forbidden by law," said Don Camillo, "so why wouldn't you have played it?"

"If the Reds pay me, I can't very well play their opponents' song."

"When you say that, you're talking politics, after all. You appreciate the propaganda value of the *International* and you're a bad Christian to play it."

"Theory's one thing and practice is another," said Tofini. "A man's got to live."

"What matters more is that he's got to die. And our accounts with God are more important than those with any shopkeeper."

"God can wait," laughed Tofini, "the shopkeeper won't give me anything to eat until I pay."

Don Camillo threw out his arms.

"Are you reasoning like a good Christian?" he asked.

"No; like a poor devil that has to live as best he can."

"Very well, but there are other poor devils who manage to be very good Christians just the same. So why should I give you the preference? From now on the bands from Torricella, Gaggiolo and Rocchetta will play at funerals and all other religious processions. They're just as much out of tune, but at least they have more sense."

Tofini was so perturbed that he went to Peppone and a few hours later Peppone went to Don Camillo.

"Are fellows to be thrown out of work just because they played the anthem of a legally constituted party?" he shouted.

"Orders from higher up, Mr. Mayor," said Don Camillo regretfully. "Like you, I have to do what my superiors say."

"Even if their orders are stupid?"

"That's never been the case, where my superiors are concerned," said Don Camillo, calmly.

"Don't try to be funny," said Peppone. clenching his fists. "It hurts my conscience to see this man harmed through a fault of mine."

"There's no fault of yours. You didn't play the *International*. Tofini's band did, and that's why I must look for another."

"All right, then. You'll see," said Peppone, as he took his leave.

Don Camillo waited until the last minute to engage another band. And when he got around to it, he found that all three nearby bands had previous commitments. He searched farther afield, only to meet everywhere the same answer. Don Camillo smelled a rat, and sure enough he finally came upon a band leader willing to tell him the truth.

"Father, we're willing to play but not to take a beating."

"Did someone threaten you?"

"No, but we were given some friendly advice."

Don Camillo went home feeling considerably depressed. The procession of the Madonna was scheduled for the next evening and no band was to be found. He spent a night haunted by musical nightmares and woke up feeling even worse than when he had gone to bed. Around ten o'clock Tofini dropped by.

"I heard you were looking for me, Father," he said.

"You're wrong, Tofini. You were looking for me, but I wasn't in."

"Very well," said Tofini. "At your service, in case of need."

"You may serve the mayor," said Don Camillo, "but you won't serve me."

After noon the village was in a ferment. That was always the way during the hours preceding the night-time procession of the Madonna. Every window was decorated with paper lanterns, luminous stars, candles and tapers, and out of every windowsill hung a rug, a piece of crimson damask, a garland of paper flowers, a bedspread, a linen sheet or a strip of lace or embroidery. The poorest houses were often the most artistically decorated, because ingeniousness took the place of money.

The village was in a ferment, then, during the afternoon, but towards evening, when the decoration was done, it grew calm. This year, however, the calm was only skin-deep, for everyone was curious. Would Don Camillo call upon Tofini or would he give up the idea of a band? And what about the People's Palace? The year before, the People's Palace was the only building which displayed no light. But at the last minute, just as the procession was getting under way, a red, white and green star appeared at a second-story window, only to disappear after the marchers had gone by. No one ever knew quite how that came about but everyone was speculating upon what would happen this year. Either there would be a star or there wouldn't. Or else the star would be all red, instead of a patriotic red, white and green. Don Camillo threatened a fourth hypothesis:

"If they show a red star with a portrait of Malenkov in the centre, and they make me furious over the absence of music, I'll hold up the procession. . . ."

But his hypothesis did not go any further. He knew that if the Reds deliberately provoked him, he would come to a halt. But he didn't know what he would do next. And this unknown worried him intensely.

Night fell, and when the bells rang, every window was illuminated, that is, all except those of the People's Palace. The procession began to move, and the voices of women and children sang out the hymn *Behold this Thy people*. But the song was a melancholy one without the reinforcement of Tofini's band. Everyone felt uneasy, and as they approached the People's Palace, the uneasiness grew. It looked as if, this time, there would be nothing but grim darkness. The head of the procession was within twenty-five feet of the People's Palace when Don Camillo began to pray:

"Lord, let there be a star, no matter what the colour! That dark, hermetically closed building gives me the impression of a world deprived of Your Divine Grace. Let some light be lit behind those dark windows in order to demonstrate Your presence. To tell the truth, Lord, I am afraid. . . ."

Now the head of the procession was passing right in front of the People's Palace, and still there was no sign of life or light. All hope was gone, and the procession wound slowly on. The picture of the Madonna was about to pass by, but it was too late now to hope for a miracle. And no miracle happened. What happened was that all the windows were suddenly thrown open, flooding the street with light. A volley of fireworks went off in the sports field, and in the courtyard Tofini's band, flanked by the bands from Torricella, Gaggiolo and Rocchetta, burst into *Behold this Thy people*.

An atomic bomb could not have made any more of an impression. With their eyes glued to the fireworks and their ears deafened by the din of the music, the marchers were completely at a loss. Don Camillo was the first to recover his aplomb. When he realized that the procession had come to a stop and the Madonna was stalled in front of the People's Palace, he shouted:

"Forward!"

The procession went on, and a thousand voices rose as a single voice, because they had four rival bands to sustain them.

"Lord," said Don Camillo, raising his eyes to heaven, "they did it all just to spite me!"

"But if in spiting you they've honoured the Holy Mother of God, why should you worry?"

"They don't mean to honour anyone, Lord. It's all a trick played upon poor, innocent people."

"They can't trick me, Don Camillo."

"I see, Lord. I was wrong, then, not to take the band that had played the *International* in the public square."

"No, you weren't wrong, Don Camillo. The proof is that four bands, instead of one, have gathered to give thanks to the Mother of God."

"Lord, this is just a deceitful game," Don Camillo insisted. "It's all because Russia's putting out peace feelers!"

"No, Don Camillo; I say it's all because Peppone isn't Russia."

Deep down in his heart, Don Camillo thought so too, and was thankful for geography.

HOLIDAY JOYS

IN RETALIATION for excommunication, the Reds decided to abolish Christmas.

And so on Christmas Eve Peppone came out of the People's Palace without so much as a glance at Bigio, who was waiting for him at the door, and hurried home, avoiding the main square in order not to run into the crowd returning from the Midnight Mass. Smilzo trailed after him in disciplined style, but got no reward for his pains, because Peppone slammed the door of his own house behind him without so much as a good-night. He was dead tired and lost no time in falling into bed.

"Is that you?" asked his wife.

"Yes," mumbled Peppone. "Who do you expect it to be?"

"There's no telling," she retorted. "With the new principles you've just announced, it might just as well be some other official of your Party."

"Don't be silly," said Peppone. "I'm not in a joking mood."

"Neither am I, after this very uninspiring Christmas Eve. You wouldn't even look at the letter your son had left under your plate. And when he stood up on a chair to recite the Christmas poem he learned in school you ran away. What have children to do with politics, anyhow?"

"Let me sleep, will you?" shouted Peppone, rolling over and over.

She stopped talking, but it took Peppone a long time to fall asleep. Even after he finally dozed off, he found no peace, 'for nightmares assailed him, the kind of nightmares that go with indigestion or worry. He woke up while it was still dark, jumped out of bed and got dressed without putting on the light.

He went down to the kitchen to heat some milk and found the table set just the way it was the evening before. The soup bowl was still there and he lifted it up to look for the little boy's letter, but it was gone. He looked at the spotted tablecloth and the scraps of food upon it, remembering how his wife once decorated the table on past Christmas Eves. This led him to think of other Christmases, when he was a boy, and of his father and mother.

Suddenly he had a vivid memory of Christmas 1944, which he had spent in the mountains, crouching in a cave in danger of being machine-gunned from one moment to the next. That was a terrible Christmas, indeed, and yet it wasn't so bad as this one because he had thought all day of the good things that went with a peacetime celebration, and the mere thought had warmed the cockles of his heart.

Now there was no danger, and everything was going smoothly. His wife and children were there right in the next room, and he had only to open the door in order to hear their quiet breathing. But his heart was icy cold at the thought that the festive table would be just as melancholy on Christmas Day as it had been the evening before.

"And yet that's all there is to Christmas," he said to himself. "It's just a matter of shiny glasses, snow-white napkins, roast capons and rich desserts."

Then he thought again of Lungo's little boy, who had built a clandestine Manger in the attic of the People's Palace. And of the letter and poem of his own little boy, which had no connection with all the foodstuffs he had insisted were only the true symbols of the season.

It was starting to grow light as Peppone walked in his long black cape from his own house to the People's Palace. Lungo was already up and busy sweeping the assembly room. Peppone was amazed to find him at the door.

"Are you at work this early?"

"It's seven o'clock," Lungo explained. "On ordinary days, I start at eight, but today isn't ordinary.

Peppone went to his desk and started looking over the mail. There were only a dozen routine letters, and within a few minutes his job was done.

433

"Nothing important, Chief?" asked Lungo, sticking his head around the door.

"Nothing at all," said Peppone. "You can take care of them yourself."

Lungo picked up the letters and went away, but he came back soon after with a sheet of paper in his hands.

"This is important, Chief," he said. "It must have escaped your notice."

Peppone took the letter, looked at it and handed it back.

"Oh, I saw that," he said; "there's nothing unusual about it."

"But it's a matter of Party membership and you really ought to make an immediate reply."

"Some other day," mumbled Peppone. "This is Christmas."

Lungo gave him a stare which Peppone didn't like. He got up and stood squarely in front of his subordinate.

"I said it's Christmas, did you understand?"

"No, I didn't," said Lungo, shaking his head.

"Then I'll explain," said Peppone, giving him a monumental slap in the face.

Lungo made the mistake of continuing to play dumb, and because he was a strapping fellow, even bigger than Peppone, he gave him back a dose of the same medicine. With which Peppone charged like an armoured division, knocked him on the floor and proceeded to change the complexion of his hindquarters with a series of swift kicks. When he had done a thorough job, he grabbed Lungo by the lapels and asked him:

"Did you understand what I was saying?"

"I get it; to day's Christmas," said Lungo darkly.

Peppone stared at the little Manger Lungo's son had built.

"What does it matter if some people choose to believe that a carpenter's son, born two thousand years ago, went out to preach the equality of all men and to defend the poor against the rich, only to be crucified by the age-old enemies of justice and liberty?"

"That doesn't matter at all," said Lungo, shaking his big head. "The trouble is that some people insist he was the son of God. That's the ugly part of it."

"Ugly?" exclaimed Peppone. "I think it's beautiful, if you want to know. The fact that God chose a carpenter and not a rich man for a father shows that He is deeply democratic."

Lungo sighed. "Too bad the priests are mixed up in it," he said. "Otherwise we could take it over."

"Exactly! Now you've hit the real point. We must keep our heads and not mix up things that have no real connection. God is one thing and priests are another. And the danger comes not from God but from the priests. They're what we must seek to eliminate. It's the same thing with rich people's money. We must eliminate them and distribute their money among the poor."

Lungo's political education had not gone so far, and once more he shook his head uncomprehendingly.

"That isn't the essential question. The fact is that God doesn't exist; he's merely a priests' invention. The only things that really exist are those that we can see and touch for ourselves. All the rest is sheer fancy."

Peppone didn't seem to put much stock in Lungo's cerebrations, for he answered:

"If a man's born blind, how is he to know that red, green and the other colours exist, since he can't see them? Suppose all of us were to be born blind; then within a hundred years all belief in the existence of colour would be lost. And yet you and I can vouch for it. Isn't it possible that God exists and we are blind men who on the basis of reason or experience alone can't understand His existence?"

Lungo was completely baffled.

"Never mind," said Peppone abruptly. "This isn't a problem that requires immediate solution. Forget about it."

Peppone was on his way home when he ran into Don Camillo.

"What can I do for Your Grey Eminence?" he asked gloomily.

"I wanted to offer you my best wishes for Christmas and the New Year," said Don Camillo blandly.

"You forget that we Reds have been excommunicated," said Peppone. "That makes your good wishes somewhat illogical."

"No more illogical than the care which a doctor gives a sick man. He may quarantine him in order to protect others from his contagious disease, but he continues to look after him. We abhor not the sinner but his sin."

"That's a good one!" said Peppone. "You talk of love, but you'd kill us off without hesitation."

435

"No, we'd be very poor doctors of men's souls if we killed them in order to obtain a cure. Our love is directed at their healing."

"And what about the violent cure you spoke of at the political rally the other day?"

"That had nothing to do with you and your friends," Don Camillo answered calmly. "Take typhus, for instance. There are three elements involved. The typhus itself, the lice that carry it and the suffering patient. In order to overcome the disease we must care for the patient and kill the lice. It would be idiotic to care for the lice and insane to imagine that they could be transformed into something other than a vehicle of contagion. And in this case, Peppone, you are a sick man, not the louse."

"I'm perfectly well, thank you, Father. You're the sick one, sick in the head."

"Anyhow, my Christmas wishes come not from the head but from the heart; you can accept them without reservation."

"No," said Peppone, "head, heart or liver, it's all the same. That's like saying: 'Here's a nice little bullet for you; it's a gift not from the percussion cap but from the barrel.' "

Don Camillo threw out his arms in discouragement.

"God will take pity on you," he murmured.

"That may be, but I doubt that He'll take pity on you. Come the revolution, He won't prevent your hanging from that pole. Do you see it?"

Of course Don Camillo saw the flagpole. The People's Palace was on the right ride of the square and from his study window he couldn't help seeing the pole sticking insolently up into the free air, with a shiny metal hammer and sickle at its summit. This was quite enough to ruin the view.

"Don't you think I may be a bit too heavy for your pole?" he asked Peppone. "Hadn't you better import some gallows from Prague? Or are those reserved for Party comrades?"

Peppone turned his back and went away. When he reached his own house he called his wife outside.

"I'll be back about one o'clock," he told her. "Try to fix everything in the usual Christmas way."

"That's already attended to," she mumbled. "You'd better be back by noon."

Shortly after noon, when he came into the big kitchen, Peppone rediscovered the atmosphere of Christmases gone by and felt as if he were emerging from a nightmare. The little boy's Christmas letter was under his plate and seemed to him unusually well written. He was ready and eager to hear the Christmas poem, but this did not seem to be forthcoming. He imagined it would come at the end of the meal and went on eating. Even when they had finished dinner, however, the child showed no intention of standing up in his chair to recite, in the customary manner. Peppone looked questioningly at his wife, but she only shrugged her shoulders in reply. She whispered something in the little boy's ear and then reported to her husband:

"Nothing doing. He won't say it."

Peppone had a secret weapon: a box of chocolates which he extracted from his pocket with the announcement:

"If someone recites a poem, this is his reward!"

The child looked anxiously at the chocolates but continued to shake his head. His mother parleyed with him again but brought back the same negative reply. At this point Peppone lost patience.

"If you won't recite the poem, it means you don't know it!" he said angrily.

"I know it, all right," the child answered, "but it can't be recited now."

"Why not?" Peppone shouted.

"Because it's too late. The Baby Jesus is born now, and the poem is about the time just before."

Peppone called for the notebook and found that, sure enough, the poem was all in the future tense. At midnight the stall at Bethlehem would be lit up, the Infant would be born and the shepherds would come to greet Him.

"But a poem's not like an advertisement in the paper," said Peppone. "Even if it's a day old it's just as good as it was to start with."

"No," the child insisted, "if Baby Jesus was born last night, we can't talk about him as going to be born to-morrow."

His mother urged him again, but he would not give in.

In the afternoon Peppone took the little boy for a walk and when they were far from home he made one more attempt to bring him around.

"Now that we're all alone, can't you recite the poem?"

"No."

"No one will hear you."

"But Baby Jesus will know."

This sentence was a poem itself, and Peppone appreciated it.

The allotted number of days went by and then New Year's Eve arrived in the village. In the little world as everywhere else it was the custom to welcome the New Year with lots of noise. The irrepressible high spirits of the villagers found this an excellent excuse of letting go with every available firearm at midnight. So the New Year was started off right and the dying year killed for good and all. Don Camillo had a hundred good reasons for disliking this custom, but this year he felt a perverse desire to kill the old year and have done with it. A few minutes before midnight he opened his study window and stood there, gun in hand, waiting for the bell in the church tower to ring. The lights were out but there was a fire in the fireplace and when Thunder, his dog, caught the gleam of the gun in Don Camillo's hand he was highly excited.

"Quiet there," Don Camillo explained. "This isn't my shooting gun. It's the old firing-piece I keep in the attic. It's a matter of shooting the old year out, and a shotgun won't answer the purpose."

The square was empty and the lamp in front of the People's Palace lit up the flagpole.

"It's almost as conspicuous by night as it is by day," muttered Don Camillo. "Seems as if they put it there just to annoy me."

The first of the twelve peals of midnight sounded, and at once the shooting began. Don Camillo leaned on the window-sill calmly and fired a single shot. Just one, because the gesture was a symbolic one and this was quite sufficient to give it meaning. It was very cold. Don Camillo carefully shut the window, leaned the gun against a chest and stirred the fire. All of a sudden he realized that Thunder wasn't there. Obviously he was so excited over the shooting that he had run out to join the fun. The priest was not particularly worried. The dog would slip back in just as easily as he had slipped out a few minutes before. Soon after this the door creaked and he looked up expectantly. The cause was not Thunder but Peppone.

"Excuse me," he said, "but the door was ajar and I came to pay you a call."

"Thank you, my son. It's always pleasant to be remembered."

"Father," said Peppone, sitting down beside him. "There's no doubt about it truth is stranger than fiction."

"Has something unfortunate happened?" asked Don Camillo.

"No, just a curious coincidence. Someone shooting into the air hit our flagpole just at the top, where the metal emblem is joined on to the wood. Don't you find that extraordinary?"

"Extraordinary indeed," Don Camillo agreed, throwing out his arms.

"And that's not all," Peppone continued. "In its fall the emblem very nearly hit Lungo on the head. He thought someone had thrown something at him on purpose and gave the alarm. We all went out to look, and although there was nothing on the ground we noticed when we looked up that the emblem was missing from the flagpole and that, as I told you, it had been clipped off very neatly. Now who do you think can have taken it away as a trophy from the deserted square?"

"To be quite frank," said Don Camillo, "I can't imagine who would be interested in a piece of junk of that kind."

Meanwhile Thunder had come back in and sat motionless between the two men. The hammer-and-sickle emblem was between his teeth and at a certain point he dropped it on to the floor. Don Camillo picked it up and turned it around in his hand.

"A poor quality of metal," he said. "From a distance it didn't look so frail. Take it home if it interests you."

Peppone looked at the emblem which Don Camillo was holding out to him and then looked into the fire. Since no hand was extended to take it, the priest threw it into the flames. Peppone gritted his teeth but said nothing. The emblem grew red hot, its joints melted and the various parts curled up like so many snakes.

"If Hell weren't just an invention of us priests . . ." Don Camillo murmured.

"It's the other way around," muttered Peppone. "Priests are an invention of Hell!"

While the priest poked at the fire Peppone went to look out the window. Through the glass he could see the decapitated flagpole.

"How many shots did it take you?" he asked without turning around.

"One."

"American model with telescope attachment?"

"No, a regular old ninety-one."

Peppone came to sit down again by the fire.

"That's still a good gun," he mumbled.

"Guns are ugly things at best," murmured Don Camillo.

"Happy New Year!" muttered Peppone as he went out the door.

"Thanks, and the same to you," Don Camillo answered.

"I was speaking to Thunder," said Peppone roughly.

And Thunder, who was stretched out in front of the fire, responded to the mention of his name by wagging his tail.

A LESSON IN TACTICS

A MASSIVE piece of machinery distinctly resembling a car, with a "U.S.A." licence plate at the rear, drew up in front of the rectory, and a thin man, no longer young, but of erect and energetic bearing, got out and walked over to the door.

"Are you the parish priest?" he asked Don Camillo, who was sitting on a bench just outside, smoking his cigar.

"At your service," said Don Camillo.

"I must talk to you," said the stranger excitedly, stalking into the hall for all the world like a conqueror. Don Camillo was momentarily taken aback, but when he saw that the stranger had reached a dead end and was about to descend into the cellar he moved to restrain him.

"This way!" he interjected.

"Everything's changed!" said the stranger. "I don't get it."

"Have you been here before, when things were differently arranged?" Don Camillo asked, leading him into the parlour, near the front door.

"No, I've never set foot in this house," said the stranger, who was still in a state of agitation. "But I still don't get it! Sermons won't cure the situation, Father. Nothing but a beating-up will teach those Reds a lesson."

Don Camillo maintained an attitude of cautious reserve. The fellow might be an escaped lunatic, for all he knew. But when a lunatic travels in a car with a "U.S.A." licence and a liveried chauffeur, it is best to handle him with kid gloves. Meanwhile the stranger wiped his perspiring forehead and

441

caught his breath. The priest scrutinized the somewhat hard lines of his face and tried to connect them with something in his memory, but to no avail.

"May I offer you some sort of refreshment?" he asked.

The stranger accepted a glass of water, and after he had gulped this down, apparently he felt a little calmer.

"You have no reason to know me," he said. "I come from Casalino."

The priest scrutinized him again, this time mistrustfully. Now Don Camillo was a civilized man and one ready to acknowledge his own mistakes; he had plenty of common sense and a heart as big as a house. Nevertheless he divided mankind into three categories: good people who must be encouraged to stay good; sinners who must be persuaded to abandon their sin and, last of all, people from Casalino, a village which from time immemorial had feuded with his.

In ancient times the struggle between the two villages had been violent and men had lost their lives in it. For some years past it had degenerated into a cold war, but the substance of it was still the same. Politicians from Casalino had wormed their way into the provincial administrations and the national government, particularly the departments of public works and engineering. As a result, whenever there was any plan to do something for Don Camillo's village, these politicians blocked it or turned it to their own advantage.

So it was that although Don Camillo worked hard to keep good people good and to persuade sinners to abandon their sin, he left Casalino in God's care. When things got especially tense he would say to Christ, "Lord, if You created these people, there must be some reason for it. We must accept them like death and taxes, with Christian resignation. May Your infinite wisdom rule over them and Your infinite kindness deliver us from their presence!"

"Yes, I'm from Casalino," the stranger repeated. "And if I have humiliated myself to the point of coming here, you can imagine that I must be very angry."

This was easy enough to understand, but Don Camillo could not see the connection with the big American car.

"I was born in Casalino," the stranger explained, "and my name is Del Cantone. Until 1908, when I was twenty-five years old, I lived on a farm with my father and mother. We worked like dogs, because we had no peasants to help us. Then all of a sudden, those damned souls . . ."

He turned red in the face again and perspired profusely.

"What damned souls do you mean?" asked Don Camillo.

"If you, a priest, don't know that the Reds are damned souls, then you must be blind as a bat!" the stranger shouted.

"Excuse me," said Don Camillo, "but aren't you speaking of events of some forty years ago?"

"The Reds have been damned souls from the beginning, ever since Garibaldi invented that infernal red shirt. . . ."

"I don't see much connection with Garibaldi," demurred Don Camillo.

"You don't? Wasn't the doctor who introduced socialism to this part of the world a follower of Garibaldi?" the stranger retorted. "Didn't he put all sorts of ideas into people's heads and start subversive organizations?"

Don Camillo urged him to tell the rest of his own story.

"Well, in 1908 those damned souls made a big splash, with a farm-workers' strike and nonsense of that kind. They came to our place and insulted my father, and I took a shotgun and shot a couple of them down. No one was killed, but I had to run away to America. There I worked like a dog, too, but it took me a number of years to make any money. Meanwhile my father and mother died, in extreme poverty. All because of those damned souls. . . ."

Don Camillo gently remarked that after all the shotgun was to blame. But the other paid no attention.

"When I heard about how Mussolini was taking care of the Red menace, I thought of coming back to settle my private account with them. But by that time, I was thoroughly tied up with a growing business. I did send someone to raise a gravestone to my parents in the cemetery. After that, more time went by, and now I'm in my seventies. . . . Anyhow, here I am, after four decades of absence. And I haven't much time. I came back to do something to commemorate my father and mother. A gravestone is something as lifeless as those that lie beneath it. What I wanted to do was to give their name to some charitable institution, a fine, modern building with plenty of grounds around it. And my idea was to have the building divided in two parts: one a children's home and the other a home for old people. Old people and children could share the grounds and come to know one another. The end of life would be drawn close to the beginning. Don't you think it's a good idea?"

"Very good," said Don Camillo. "But the building and grounds aren't all that's necessary——"

"I didn't come all the way from America to learn anything so elementary. You don't think I imagine that an institution can live on air, do you? I meant to endow it with a thousand-acre self-supporting farm. In fact, for the whole project I have put aside a million dollars. I haven't much longer to live and there are no children to inherit from me. Taxes and lawyers' fees will eat up most of what I leave behind. And so I transferred the million dollars to this, my native land. But now I've decided to take them back to America."

Don Camillo forgot that the loss of this sum would be a loss to Casalino. In fact, with the notion of a million dollars ear-marked for charity coursing through his mind he was willing to take the inhabitants of Casalino out of the category of untouchables and consider them in the same light as the rest of mankind.

"Impossible!" he exclaimed. "God inspired you with a truly noble idea. You mustn't go back on His inspiration."

"I'm taking the money home, I tell you," the stranger shouted. "Casalino shan't have a penny of it. I went there straight from Genoa, and what did I find? Red flags all over the village and on every haystack around! Red flags, posters bearing the hammer and sickle and threatening death to this one and that. There was a rally in the public square and the loudspeakers brought me every word of it. 'Now let us hear from our comrade the Mayor,' they were saying. And when they saw my licence plate, they shouted at me: 'Go back to Eisenhower! Go back to America!' One of them even damaged the top of my car. You can see for yourself if you don't believe me."

Don Camillo looked out of the window and saw that this was indeed true.

"Well, I'm going back, never fear," concluded the stranger, "and taking my money with me. I'll give it to the Society for the Prevention of Cruelty to Animals, rather than to the damned souls of Casalino!"

"But not all of them are Reds," protested Don Camillo.

"They're all swine, though. The Reds because they're Reds, and the others because they're too weak to kick them out. Yes, I'm going back to America."

Don Camillo thought it was pointless to argue. But he wondered why the old man had come to him with this story.

"I understand your disappointment," he said. "And I'm ready to do anything I can to help you."

"Of course . . . I had forgotten the most important thing of all," said the stranger. "I came to you for a very good reason. I've money to burn and expenses don't matter. I'm willing to make this my legal residence or do whatever else is necessary, to organize a secret raid and enlist the devil himself to carry it out. But my parents can't be at rest in the cemetery of Casalino, and I want to bring their bodies here. I'll erect a new gravestone in your cemetery, a monument of colossal proportions. All I ask is that you take care of the whole thing, I'm content to pay."

And he deposited a pile of banknotes upon the table.

"Here's for your preliminary expenses," he added.

"Very well," said Don Camillo. "I'll do whatever's possible."

"You may be called upon to do the impossible," said the stranger.

Now that he had got all this off his chest, he seemed to be in a more reasonable frame of mind. He consented to drink a glass of sparkling Lambrusco wine, which brought back memories of his youth and restored his serenity.

"How are things here, with you Father?" he asked. "Terrible, I suppose. I have an idea that the whole area is pretty much like Casalino."

"No," answered Don Camillo. "Things are quite different here. There are Reds, of course, but they aren't on top of the heap."

"Isn't your local government in Red hands?"

"No," Don Camillo said shamelessly. "They're on the village council, but not in the majority."

"Wonderful!" exclaimed his visitor. "How do you do it? You can't tell me that sermons have turned the tide."

"There you're wrong," said Don Camillo. "My sermons aren't without effect. The rest is a matter of tactics."

"What do you mean?"

"Well, it's hard to put into words, so I'll give you a concrete example." And out of a drawer he took a pack of cards. "Say each one of these cards is a Communist. Even a tiny child can tear them up one by one, whereas if they're all together it's almost impossible."

"I see," said the stranger. "Your tactics are to divide your enemies and overcome them one by one."

"No," said Don Camillo; "that's not it at all. My tactics are to let the enemy get into a solid block in order to size up their strength correctly. Then when they're all together, I go into action."

So saying, he tore the pack of cards in two in his big, bare hands.

"Hooray!" the old man shouted enthusiastically. "That's terrific! Will you give me that pack of cards with your autograph on one of them? The only trouble with such tactics is that they require unusually strong hands!"

"Strong hands aren't lacking," said Don Camillo calmly. "We can handle a pack easily enough. But what shall we do when there are sixty or more? We're still on top, but they're working day and night to put us down. And they have powerful weapons."

"Weapons? And you haven't any? I'll send you plenty of those!"

"That's not the sort of weapons I mean. The Reds' chief weapon is other people's selfishness. People who are well off think only of holding on to their possessions; they show no concern for their neighbours. The richest people are often the more stingy; they fail to see that by clinging to their individual piles the whole lot of them will lose everything. But don't let's worry over that, Signor Del Cantone. Have another glass of wine."

"There's the Old World for you!" sighed the stranger, turning down the offer of a second drink. "I want to speak with the mayor right away. I see a way of killing three birds with one stone. I'll raise an enduring monument to my father and mother, save Western civilization and madden those damned souls of Casalino by making this village the seat of my institution."

Don Camillo saw stars. Then he hastily pulled himself together.

"The mayor's not here today. But I'll have him on deck here at the rectory tomorrow morning."

"Good. I'll be here. Remember I have very little time, and be ready to present your choice of a location. I have the building plans in my pocket. And my agent has rounded up several big farms for raising all the produce the institution can consume."

"No," said Peppone, "I won't take part in any such

446

dirty comedy. I am what I am and I'm proud of it."

"There's nothing dirty about it," said Don Camillo. "All you have to do is pretend to be a decent sort of person."

"And there's no use your trying to be funny, either. I'm no puppet! I'll turn up at the rectory tomorrow morning, if you like, but with my red kerchief around my neck and three Party membership pins."

"Then you may as well save yourself the trouble. I'll tell him to hang on to his million, because the mayor has no use for it. Our mayor intends to build a children's and old people's home with the funds they send him from Russia. In fact, I'll have the whole story put into print so that everyone can know."

"That's blackmail!" said Peppone angrily.

"I'm only asking you to be quiet and let me do the talking. Politics shouldn't come into it. Here's a chance to do something for the poor, and we must make the best of it."

"But it's a fraud!" said Peppone. "Among other things, I have no intention of tricking that poor old man."

"All right," said Don Camillo, throwing out his arms. "Instead of tricking a millionaire, let's trick the poor! To think that you claim to be fighting for a fairer distribution of rich people's money! Come, come! Is there any trickery in persuading a madman that you're not a Communist, in order to obtain funds for the needy? I see nothing wrong. Anyhow, I leave it up to the Last Judgment, and if I am found guilty I shall pay. Meanwhile our old people and children will have shelter and a crust of bread. This madman wants to build something to commemorate his parents. Why shouldn't we help him?"

"No! I say it's dishonest and I won't have any part of it!"

"Very well," said Don Camillo. "You're sacrificing a cool million to Party pride. Perhaps tomorrow, when you're polishing up the weapons you've stowed away for the Revolution, a bomb will explode in your hands, leaving your son an orphan."

"I hope you explode first," retorted Peppone. "And my son will never beg for your reactionary charity!"

"That's true. He'll have your pension from Malenkov. But what if you live long enough to achieve second childhood and there's no old people's home to take you in?"

"By that time Malenkov will have fixed things so that every old person has a home of his own."

447

"What if Malenkov disappoints you?"

"I'm not worried about that. Meanwhile, I'll have nothing to do with this plan."

"All right, Peppone. I have to admit that you're right. I was so carried away by the idea of doing something for the poor that I lost my head completely, and it took a hardened unbeliever like yourself to remind me of God's law against lying. It's never permissible to sacrifice principle to profit. Come along tomorrow morning, and we'll tell that madman the truth. I have sinned and it's up to me to atone."

Don Camillo did not have the courage to speak to the Crucified Christ over the altar that evening. He slept uncomfortably and waited for the next morning to restore his peace of mind. Sure enough, the big American car pulled up in front of the rectory and the stranger walked in. Peppone, who was waiting outside with Brusco, Smilzo and Bigio, followed after.

"Here are the mayor and three members of the village council," said Don Camillo.

"Good!" said the old man, shaking hands all round. "I suppose that Don Camillo has already told you my story. . . ."

"Yes," said Peppone.

"Splendid. I presume you belong to the clerical party."

"No," said Peppone.

"We're independents," put in Smilzo.

"So much the better!" said the old man. "I don't hold particularly with the priests. If you're free and independent, then of course you're against the Reds. Castor oil and a beating, those are the only treatments for them. Don't you agree?"

His slightly wild eyes were fastened upon Peppone.

"Yessir," Peppone answered.

"Yessir," echoed Bigio, Brusco and Smilzo.

"These cursed Reds . . ." the old man continued, but Don Camillo broke in.

"No more!" he said firmly. "This comedy has gone far enough."

"Comedy? What comedy do you mean?" the old man asked in amazement.

"You were so excited when I saw you yesterday, that in order to calm you down I said some things that are not exactly true," explained Don Camillo. "Things are just the same here as they are at Casalino. The mayor and most of the members of the Village Council are Reds."

"Did you want to make a fool of me?" the stranger asked with a grim laugh.

"No," answered Peppone calmly. "We simply wanted to help the poor. For their sake we were willing to stoop to almost anything."

"And what about those famous tactics of yours?" the stranger said ironically to Don Camillo.

"They're still valid," the priest answered determinedly.

"Then why don't you explain them to the mayor?" the old man asked vindictively.

Don Camillo gritted his teeth and took a pack of cards from a desk drawer.

"Look," he said. "Even a tiny child can tear them up one by one, whereas if they're all together it's almost impossible . . ."

"Just a minute," said Peppone. And taking the pack out of Don Camillo's hands he tore it in two with his own.

"Amazing!" exclaimed the old man. "Record-breaking!" And he insisted that Peppone give him a split card with an autograph upon it.

"I'll display them both in the window of my shop in America," he said, putting the whole pack in his pocket. "On one side the priest's and on the other the mayor's. And in between their story. The fact that both of you can split a pack of cards is important," he added. "Likewise the fact that you can league together for the good of the village against an outsider. I still have the same low opinion of you cursed Reds. But I don't care if they burst with envy at Casalino; this is the place where I want to build my institution. Draw up a charter for it tomorrow and choose a board of directors with no politicians among them. All decisions made by this board must be approved by two presidents, who have a life-long term and the power to choose their successors. The first two men to hold this office shall be Don Camillo and (if I have the name right) Giuseppe Bottazzi. Before we American businessmen embark upon any enterprise we obtain a thorough report on the people and places with which we expect to be concerned. Yesterday, when your priest told me that the local government was not predominantly Communist in character, I had a good laugh. Today I didn't find it quite so funny. But I have learned something I didn't know before and I shall go home happy. Push this thing through fast, because I want to settle it tomorrow. I'm buying the farm today."

Don Camillo went to kneel before the Crucified Christ over the main altar.

"I'm not especially pleased with you, Don Camillo," Christ said. "The old man and Peppone and his friends behaved themselves more creditably than you did."

"But if I hadn't stirred up the situation a bit, nothing would have come out of it," protested Don Camillo weakly.

"That doesn't matter. Even if some good comes out of your evil-doing, you're responsible to God for what you did. Unless you understand this, you've misunderstood God's word completely."

"God will forgive me," murmured Don Camillo, lowering his head.

"No, Don Camillo, because when you think of all the good which your sin has done for the poor you won't ever honestly repent."

Don Camillo threw out his arms and felt very sad, because he knew that Christ was quite right.

PEPPONE HAS A DIPLOMATIC ILLNESS

"THIS IS an outrageous hour," grumbled Don Camillo when Peppone's wife came to the rectory.

"I thought priests and doctors were available twenty-four hours a day," she answered.

"All right, all right, but say what you have to say without sitting down. That way you won't stay too long. What is it you want?"

"It's about the new house. I want you to bless it."

Don Camillo clenched his fists.

"You've come to the wrong counter," he said sternly. "Good-night."

The woman shrugged her shoulders.

"You must forgive him, Father. He had something on his mind."

Don Camillo shook his head. The matter was too serious to be forgotten, even after six months had gone by. Peppone had had an irresistible impulse to make a change; he had sold his shabby, run-down workshop, borrowed money until he was in debt up to his ears and built himself a new house just outside the village, on the main road running parallel to the river. The workshop was as well equipped for making repairs as that of any big city garage, and there were living quarters on the second floor. He had acquired the franchise for a well-known brand of petrol, and this promised to bring him many customers from the heavy traffic on the highway.

Of course Don Camillo couldn't resist his curiosity, and one fine morning he went to see. Peppone was deep in a disembowelled engine and decidedly not in talkative mood.

"Fine place you've got here," said Don Camillo, looking around.

"Yes it is, isn't it."

"A big courtyard, a flat on the second floor, a petrol pump and everything," Don Camillo continued. "There's only one thing missing."

"What's that?"

"Once upon a time, when a man moved into a new house he called upon the priest to bless it. . . ."

Peppone drew himself up, wiping the sweat off his forehead.

"Here's the holy water of our day and age," he said aggressively, "consecrated by good hard work instead of by one of your priestlings."

Don Camillo went away without saying a word. There was something alarming in Peppone's words, something he had never heard before. Now this request from Peppone's wife carried him back to the feeling of disgust he had suffered six months before.

"No," he told her.

"You've simply got to come," she said, no whit discouraged. "My husband's not the only one in the house. There's myself, and my children. It's not our fault if Peppone was rude to you. If Christ were to . . ."

"Christ doesn't come into it at all," interrupted Don Camillo.

"He does, though," she insisted.

And so, after pacing for several minutes around the room, Don Camillo answered:

"All right, then. I'll come tomorrow."

"No, not tomorrow," she said, shaking her head. "You must come right now, while Peppone's out. I don't want him to know, or the neighbours to see and report to him, either."

This was too much for Don Camillo.

"So I'm to be an underground priest, am I? Perhaps in order to bless a house I should disguise myself as a plumber. As if it were something shameful that had to be hidden! You're more of a heathen than your wretched husband!"

"Just try to understand, Don Camillo. People would say that we were having the house blessed because we're in trouble."

"Because you're in trouble, eh? And actually you want it blessed for some totally different reason. Out with it, woman!"

"Because we *are* in trouble, to tell the truth," she explained. "We've had bad luck ever since we moved into the new house."

"So because you don't know where to turn, you thought you might try God, is that it?"

"Well, why shouldn't I? When things go well, we can look out for ourselves, without bothering God Almighty."

Don Camillo took a stick out of the pile beside the fireplace. "If you aren't at least as far away as the square in the next two seconds, I'll break this over your head!" he told her.

She went away without a word, but a second later she stuck her head through the door.

"I'm not afraid of your stick," she shot at him. "I'm afraid of your unkindness and bad temper."

Don Camillo threw the stick on to the fire and watched it go up in flames. Then brusquely he threw his overcoat over his shoulders and went out. He walked through the darkness until he came to Peppone's house and there he knocked on the door.

"I knew you'd come," said the wife of Peppone.

Don Camillo took the breviary out of his pocket, but before he could open it, Peppone came like a whirlwind into the hall.

"What are you doing here at this hour?"

Don Camillo hesitated, and Peppone's wife spoke up: "I asked him to come and bless the house."

Peppone looked at her darkly. "I'll settle accounts with you later. As for you, Don Camillo, you can go at once. I don't need you or your God either."

This time Peppone's voice was hardly recognizable. To tell the truth, Peppone was not the man he had been before. He had bitten off more than he could chew, and in throwing himself into this new venture he had borrowed on everything he had and some things he hadn't. Now he was in really hot water and didn't see how he was ever going to get out of it. That evening, for the first time in his life, he had surrendered and asked for help.

After Don Camillo had left, Peppone exploded. "So you'd betray me too, would you?"

"I wouldn't betray you. There's a curse on this house and I wanted to break it. I didn't do anything wrong."

Peppone went into the large kitchen and sat down at the table.

"Bless the house, indeed!" he shouted. "He didn't come to bless the house; he came to spy on us, don't you understand? To see how things are going and dig up some proof of our desperate situation. If he'd got into the workshop, he'd have noticed that my new lathe is gone . . ."

"Tell me, what happened?" his wife broke in.

"Well, the lathe's taken care of, and no one saw me carrying it away."

"Someone will notice tomorrow," his wife sighed. "The first man to come in will see that it's not there."

"No one will see a thing," Peppone reassured her. "With the money I got for the lathe, I paid off our two most pressing creditors, and tomorrow I won't open the shop for business. I've taken care of that too."

His wife looked at him questioningly.

"I called the village council together and told them that I was ill and needed a long rest. I'm going to shut myself up in the house and not let anyone see me."

"That won't do any good," she answered. "Notes will fall due, no matter how tightly you shut yourself up."

"The notes will fall due in another month. Meanwhile, the lathe is gone, and that's a fact we must cover up. There are all too many people who'd be happy to know that I'm in trouble."

Then Peppone asked his wife for a big sheet of paper and printed on it in big letters:

WORKSHOP TEMPORARILY CLOSED
DUE TO ILLNESS OF OWNER

"Go and stick that on the door," he ordered.

His wife took a bottle of glue and started out, but Peppone stopped her.

"That won't do," he said sadly. "*Owner* is far too bourgeois a word."

He sought in vain for some less reactionary term and finally had to content himself with a vague:

CLOSED, DUE TO ILLNESS

As a matter of fact, the whole business was sick, and not just Peppone.

Peppone did not stick his nose outside, and his wife explained to everyone that he was in a state of exhaustion and mustn't be disturbed until he got better. Ten days went by in this way, but on the eleventh day there was bad news. In the local column of the farm paper there was an item that ran:

LOCAL CITIZEN IN THE LIMELIGHT
We are happy to say that the popularity of our mayor, Giuseppe Bottazzi is always on the increase. Today's list of call-in promissory notes carries three mentions of his name. Congratulations on the well-deserved publicity.

Peppone ran a genuine temperature and went to bed, asking his wife to leave him completely alone.

"I don't want to see any letters or newspapers. Just let me sleep."

But three days later she came sobbing into the room and woke him up.

"I've got to tell you something," she said. "They've seized all the new tools in your workshop."

Peppone buried his head in the pillow, but he heard what she was saying. He sweated all the fever he could out of himself and then suddenly decided to jump out of bed.

"There's only one thing to do," he exclaimed. "I'll have to go away."

"Just forget about the whole thing," his wife begged him, in an attempt to bring him back to reason. "Let them seize and sell whatever they like. There's a curse on the whole business. We still have the old house and the old workshop. Let's start all over again."

"No!" Peppone shouted wildly. "I can't go back to the old place. That would be too humiliating. I must go away, that's all. You can say that I've gone to the mountains on account of my health, and meanwhile I'll try to think up a solution. I can't concentrate in these surroundings, and there's no one to advise me. I'm not breaking off for good; I'll leave everything as it is. If things continue to go badly, they'll blame it on my poor health. But I can't bear to take a step backward and give satisfaction to my enemies."

"Whatever you say," his wife conceded.

"I still have my lorry," said Peppone. "That's something.

455

I don't know where I'll go, but you'll be hearing from me. Don't breathe a word to a soul, even if they kill you."

At two o'clock in the morning, Peppone started up the lorry and drove away. No one actually saw him, but he was the subject, even at this late hour, of many conversations.

"His creditors have jumped on him just because he's sick," some people were saying.

"That illness of his is just an excuse to cover up his crimes," said others.

"He's a coward."

"Serves him right!"

"The main thing is for him to get well and come back to his job as mayor."

"If he has any decency, he ought to resign."

Peppone's name was on hundreds of mouths, and all the while he was hurrying away in his old lorry, pursued by the "complex of bourgeois respectability," whose influence is felt in every class, including the proletariat.

The days went by and after the news of the seizure came an announcement of a public auction of Peppone's new tools and machinery.

"Lord," said Don Camillo, pointing to the newspaper, "here's proof that God does exist!"

"You're telling Me!" Christ answered.

Don Camillo lowered his head. "Forgive my stupidity," he murmured.

"The stupid things you say are entirely forgivable. I know how that tongue of yours is always getting you in trouble. But what worries Me is your way of thinking. God doesn't care about seizures and auctions. Peppone's bad luck has nothing to do with his demerits, any more than a rascal's rapid rise to riches has anything righteous about it."

"Lord, he has blasphemed Your Name, and ought to be punished. All the decent people of the village are sure that it's because he refused to have the house blessed that he ran into difficulty."

Christ sighed. "And what would these decent people say if Peppone had prospered? That it was because he turned down the blessing?"

Don Camillo threw out his arms impatiently.

"Lord, I'm only telling you what I hear. People——"

" 'People?' What does that mean? 'People' as a whole are never going to get into Heaven. God judges 'people' individu-

456

ally and not in the mass. There are no 'group' sins, but only personal ones, and there is no collective soul. Every man's birth and death is a personal affair, and God gives each one of us separate consideration. It's all wrong for a man to let his personal conscience be swallowed up by collective responsibility."

Don Camillo lowered his head. "But, Lord, public opinion has some value. . . ."

"I know that, Don Camillo. Public opinion nailed Me to the Cross."

On the day of the public auction, a flock of vultures arrived from the city. They were so efficiently organized that for a mere pittance they divided up and carried away the worldly goods of Peppone. Don Camillo was somewhat depressed when he came back from the sale.

"What are people saying, Don Camillo?" Christ asked him. "Are they happy?"

"No," Don Camillo answered; "they say it's too bad that a man should be ruined because he's ill and far away and can't defend himself."

"Be honest with me, Don Camillo, and tell me what people are actually saying."

Don Camillo threw out his arms. "They're saying that if God really existed, such things wouldn't happen."

Christ smiled.

"From the 'Hosannas!' of the acclaiming crowd to the same crowd's cry of: 'Crucify him!' there isn't so very far to go. Do you see that, now, Don Camillo?"

That same evening there was a stormy meeting of the village council. Spiletti, the only councillor belonging to the Opposition, raised the subject of the mayor.

"For two months we've had no news of him. He's lost all interest in the village and even in his own private affairs. Where is he, and what's he doing? On behalf of a large number of my fellow-citizens, I demand a definite answer."

Brusco, who was serving as deputy mayor, got up to reply.

"I shall give you a detailed answer tomorrow."

"I'm not inquiring into any top secret, am I?" objected Spiletti. "I demand an answer right away. Where is the mayor?"

Brusco shrugged his shoulders.

"We don't know," he admitted.

There was a grumbling protest from all those present. The thing was simply incredible.

"Nobody knows the whereabouts of the mayor!" Spiletti shouted. "Then let's put an ad in the paper: *Reward to anyone who can find one Red mayor, two months missing.*"

"It's not so funny as all that," said Brusco. "Not even his wife knows where he is."

Just then a voice boomed out from the back of the room. "I know," said Don Camillo.

Everyone was silent, until Brusco spoke out: "If you know, tell us."

"No," said Don Camillo. "But I can bring him here tomorrow morning."

In a gloomy section of the suburbs of Milan, Peppone was shovelling scrap iron and plaster from a recently demolished building into his lorry. When the noon whistle sounded, he threw down his shovel, took out a sandwich and a copy of the Communist paper, *Unity*, out of the pocket of his jacket and went to sit down with his back against a fence, alongside his fellow-workers.

"Mr. Mayor!"

The shrill voice of Spiletti brought him to his feet with a single-bound.

"There aren't any mayors around here," he answered.

"And the trouble is we have no mayor in our village, either," said Spiletti. "Can you tell me where to find one?"

"That's none of my business," said Peppone, sitting down on the ground.

"You look to me as if you'd recovered your health," Spiletti insisted. "You must be well enough to send us a postcard."

"You don't catch me sending a postcard to you, you tool of the clergy! How happy I am not to have you on my mind!"

"That's no way for a mayor to talk!" Spiletti protested.

"I'm speaking as a free man."

"Well said!" said the other workers, who had left their lunch to gather around Peppone.

"If you want to be free, then resign from your position!" Spiletti shouted.

"Just to please you, eh?" grumbled the workers. "Hold on to it, Comrade!"

"Well, if you're not resigning, we'd like at least to know your intentions."

Peppone shrugged his shoulders.

"If you'd rather have fun in Milan than do the job to which you've been appointed, then you've simply got to give up the job."

"We'll take *your* job away, that's what," threatened the workers. But Peppone turned around.

"Easy, boys," he said authoritatively. "This is a democratic country, and threats don't go."

Meanwhile Brusco, Bigio and the rest of Peppone's henchmen had appeared upon the scene and sat silently down around him.

"Chief," said Brusco sadly, "why did you desert us?"

"I'm not deserting anybody."

"What are we to do about the new road? Here's a letter from the Ministry of Public Works."

And Brusco held out a sheet of paper, which Peppone proceeded to read.

"As long as there's a certain crowd in the government, we'll never get anywhere," he observed.

"Never mind about the national administration!" Spiletti shouted. "It's up to you to make a concrete proposal."

"We made one, long ago," Bigio put in.

"That was just propaganda!" Spiletti shouted. "There was nothing concrete about it."

Smilzo had a word to put in at this point, and so did Peppone. Soon they were in the middle of a heated discussion. Amid the refuse from a demolished building in Milan, they held one of the most unusual village council meetings ever to be seen. When five o'clock came and they were still debating, the night watchman said he must close the gate and send them away. The whole council, including the Opposition, transferred the debate to Peppone's lorry.

"Let's go and find a quieter place," said Peppone, starting up the motor.

There was no telling how it happened, perhaps because none of them knew the layout of the city too well, but soon the lorry was rolling down the highway. Peppone bent with clenched teeth and tense muscles over the wheel. There was something on his mind, which for a long time he had been unable to say. All at once he threw on the brakes. One of those cursed hitch-hikers was standing practically in front of the truck and signalling that he wanted a lift in the same direction. He had a cake and a toy balloon in one hand and a priest's hat on his head. Smilzo got down from the seat beside Peppone and went to sit in the back of the truck, along with the rest of the village council. Don Camillo climbed up to take his place, and Peppone started off with a jolt like that of a tank.

"Do certain people always have to be hanging around?" he grumbled.

The lorry was travelling like a racing car, and the roar coming out of the engine was like the orchestra of Toscanini. All of a sudden, over the crest of the river embankment, they saw the church tower.

"Ah!" Peppone exclaimed ruefully.

" 'Ah' doesn't make the first two letters of 'happy,' " observed Don Camillo.

"Yes, it does, even if the letters aren't in the right order," said a voice that only Don Camillo could hear.

A BALL BOUNCES BACK

WHEN WOMEN go in for politics they're worse than the most rabid of the men. The men throw their weight around for the sake of "the cause," whereas the women direct all their wiles toward the discomfiture of the enemy. The same difference as there is between defending one's country and going to war in order to kill as many people as possible on the other side.

Jo del Magro was up to her ears in politics, and because of her fiery temperament she did not only her share but that of her husband as well. He died, poor fellow, leaving her with a three-year-old son, but her grief for his loss must have been to some degree compensated by the fact that she ignored the priest and carried him to the grave to the muted notes of the Red anthem.

Jo was good-looking enough, in her way, and could perfectly well have found a second husband to look after her. But she clung obstinately to her hard lot, feeding upon it the embitterment which held the place of faith in her heart. She supported herself by heavy farm work—sowing, reaping, threshing and wine-pressing—in the summer, and in the winter by making reed baskets which she peddled about the country. She worked fiercely, as if weariness were an end in itself and her only satisfaction. And even the boldest men took care not to bother her, because she was not only strong-armed, but had a vocabulary coarse enough to put theirs to shame.

The little boy grew like a weed. When he wasn't left alone

461

in their isolated shack but was allowed to trail after his mother, she set him down in the farmyard where she was working and told him to shut up and "keep out of her hair." When he was five years old he could throw stones as well as a boy of ten and destroy a laden fruit-tree in less than half an hour. He nosed about like a hunting-dog among the chicken coops, leaving a mess of broken eggs behind him; he strewed bits of glass on the roads and perpetrated other tricks of the same kind. His only distinction lay in the fact that he was a lone wolf and preferred to operate on his own rather than to run with the pack. When two gangs of boys were engaged in battle he hid behind a bush or tree and threw stones indiscriminately at both factions. He was anti-social by nature and had an extraordinary ability to disappear from the scene of his misdemeanours. The evening of the grape-gathering festival he let the air out of the tyres of some fifty bicycles and threw the valve caps away. No one could lay hands on him, but everyone was saying:

"It must be that confounded little Magrino!"

A few days later some well-meaning ladies went to call on his mother and tactfully intimated that instead of letting him run wild she should turn him over, during her working hours, to the day nursery. Jo grew red in the face and shouted that rather than give her son over to a priestly institution she'd leave him with certain women whose reputation they knew all too well.

"Tell Don Gumshoe Camillo to look after his own business!" she said, adding a volley of oaths which caused the well-meaning ladies to pull up their skirts and run. Their leader reported the upshot of their visit to Don Camillo, concluding:

"Father, I can't repeat the name that unfortunate creature fastened upon you!"

"I know it already," he answered gloomily.

The weather was fine and the children of Don Camillo's day nursery were out on the playing field most of the afternoon. The swings and see-saws had been restored to good order and even the grumpiest children were all smiles. Don Camillo lay in a deck chair, smoking his cigar and enjoying the warm sun, when he had a sudden feeling that something was wrong.

The playing field bordered, on the river side, on a field of alfalfa, from which it was separated by a galvanized wire fence. Now Don Camillo was struck by an unaccustomed ripple in the alfalfa, and his sportsman's instinct told him that it was neither a dog nor a chicken. He did not move, but half closed his eyes in order to observe without being detected. Slowly something rose out of the grass and Don Camillo felt Magrino's eyes converging upon him. He held his breath while Magrino, feeling sure that he was not watched, transferred his gaze to another objective. He was following the children's game and such was his curiosity that at one point he forgot himself and raised his whole head above the alfalfa. No one noticed, and of this Don Camillo was glad. All of a sudden his head disappeared. A big ball, with which some of the bigger boys were playing, had been kicked over the fence and they called out to ask Don Camillo if they could go and get it. The priest pretended to wake up with a start.

"Is the ball out of bounds again?" he shouted. "I've told you to be more careful. That grass can't be trodden down. No more ball-playing today. You can go and get the ball to-morrow, and meanwhile let me sleep!"

The boys grumbled a bit; then they found another ball and played with that, while Don Camillo pretended to be sleeping. Actually, he was more alert than ever. Ten minutes later the alfalfa stirred again, but this time the line of rippling moved farther and farther away. Magrino was leaving, but he was following an odd course, which for the moment led him to the centre of the alfalfa field.

"He must be cutting across diagonally," thought Don Camillo, "in order to emerge along the hedge parallel to the canal."

Instead, Magrino stopped short and made an abrupt turn to the left. Obviously he had found the ball, picked it up and now was carrying it away.

"Rascal!" muttered Don Camillo. "You've pulled off the trick handsomely. But when you reach the row of trees at the end of the alfalfa you'll have to show yourself!"

But Magrino knew better. When he was out of the tall grass he slid on his stomach until he came to a ditch which ran at right angles to the trees and afforded him perfect cover.

"Lord," Don Camillo murmured, "how can a five-year-old boy have learned to be so tricky?"

"Don Camillo," the Lord answered, "how do fish learn to swim? By instinct, of course."

"Instinct?" Don Camillo exclaimed gloomily. "Are men instinctively evil?"

Don Camillo bought the boys another ball and made no mention of the escapade of Magrino. He hoped that the stolen ball would act like bait and bring Magrino back later. Every day he scanned the field of alfalfa, but there was no ripple. Then someone told him that Magrino was ill and confined to the house. As a matter of fact, Magrino had come down with a fever the night after he had taken the ball. The ditch was full of water, and in crawling through it he was chilled to the bone. Then, before going into the shack he had buried the ball in a hole. His mother came home late, and found him shivering all over. At first it seemed like nothing at all, at least nothing that couldn't be cured with a few pills and a hot-water bottle. Then things took a turn for the worse and one evening he became half delirious. He muttered something over and over, and finally Jo understood him to mention a big rubber ball.

"Don't worry," she said. "Hurry up and get well, and I'll buy a ball for you."

Magrino quieted down, but the next night, when his fever rose again, he resumed his insistence upon the ball.

"Take it easy!" said Jo. "I told you I'd get it as soon as you're well."

"No ... no ... "

"Do you want me to get one right away?"

"No ... no ... The ball ..."

Evidently he couldn't take his mind off it. But the doctor said there was no use looking for a meaning in the ravings of a delirious child. And so, on the third night, Jo simply answered:

"All right. ... Whatever you say. ..."

He raved until one o'clock when the fever went down sufficiently for him to sleep. Then, at last, the exhausted Jo was able to go to bed.

The next morning at five o'clock Don Camillo stood shaving in front of the mirror hanging from the sash bolt of his window. It was a clear, cool day, and he took his time, looking out over the fields to the row of poplars along the river bank and beyond them the gleaming river. Directly below him lay the playing field, empty and silent at this hour, but soon to

464

be overrun by the day nursery. He smiled to himself at the thought of all the freshly washed little faces.

As his glance fell upon the field of alfalfa and the wire fence, he murmured to himself: "The little rascal! . . ." Then he started as a moving white object caught his attention. Only when it was within a few yards of the fence did he recognize it. It was little Magrino, bundled up in a long white night-shirt, which his father had formerly worn by day, weaving in and out of the tall grass, like a drunkard or a sleepwalker. He stumbled and fell, but stood up again and went on, clutching all the while a big rubber ball. When he reached the fence he threw it up in the air, but the fence was too high and it fell back on the same side. He threw it again and it hit the wire. Don Camillo's forehead was covered with perspiration.

"Lord," he prayed, "give him the strength to throw it over!"

Magrino was tired out and the tiny arms sticking out of the shirtsleeves seemed to have lost all their former skill. He staggered in order to remain erect and paused for several minutes before making another try. Don Camillo shut his eyes, and when he opened them the ball was in the playing field, while Magrino lay motionless among the afalfa. The priest went like an avalanche down the stairs. When he picked up the little boy the lightness of his burden struck terror into his heart. Magrino's eyes flickered open, and finding himself in the enemy's grasp he whispered:

"Don Gumshoe . . . the ball's inside. . . ."

"Good fellow!" said Don Camillo.

The bell-ringer, who went to tell Jo, found her beside herself over the disappearance of her son. When she saw him lying on a couch before the fire in Don Camillo's study her amazement knew no bounds.

"I found him in a dead faint among the alfalfa, just twenty minutes ago," Don Camillo told her.

"And what in the world was he doing there? My head is completely woozy."

"Always has been, hasn't it?" asked Don Camillo.

The doctor told Jo not to dream of taking the boy away but gave him an injection and left precise instructions for his care. Meanwhile Don Camillo was in the sacristy, preparing for Mass.

"Lord," he said to the Crucified Christ as he stood before

the altar, "how did it all happen? After the upbringing that boy's had, how could he know the difference between good and evil?"

"Don Camillo," said Christ, "how do fish learn to swim? By instinct. And conscience is instinctive in the same way; it's not something that can be transmitted from one person to another. It's not like taking a light into a dark room. The light is burning all the time, covered by a thick veil. When you take the veil away, the room is lit."

"Very well, Lord, but who unveiled the light in that boy's soul?"

"Don Camillo, when the darkness of death is impending, everyone instinctively searches within himself for a ray of light. And now, don't you bother your head about how it came about; just rejoice in it and thank God."

Magrino stayed for a fortnight in the rectory and Jo came morning and evening to see him; that is, she knocked at the window and when Don Camillo opened it, she said:

"I've come to see the prisoner."

Don Camillo made no reply but let the two of them talk together. After a fortnight had gone by he came home one day to find Magrino letting the air out of his bicycle tyres. He gathered together the boy's few clothes and took him to the door saying:

"You're cured. Go along home!"

That evening Jo came boldly to the door.

"How much do I owe you?" she asked.

"Nothing. The most that you can do for me is to stay out of my sight for ever, *per omnia saecula saeculorum.*"

"Amen," mumbled Jo.

But out of sheer spite she appeared at eleven o'clock Mass the following Sunday, sitting in the front pew, with Magrino beside her. Don Camillo shot her a terrifying glance, but from the bold way in which she stared back at him he knew perfectly well that she was saying to herself:

"Don Gumshoe, don't make those ferocious eyes at me. I'm not the least bit afraid!"

THE CARD SHARPERS

SMILZO HAD the post office job of taking around special delivery letters, and now he braked his bicycle in breakneck Mao Tse-tung style right in front of the sunny bench where Don Camillo was quietly reading his paper.

The method of stopping a bicycle by sliding off the saddle towards the rear and at the same time jerking up the handlebars in such a way as to lift the front wheel off the ground and produce the effect of a bucking broncho had been known until recent years as "Texas Cowboy" style. Now, for obvious political reasons, this reactionary Western name had given way to an appellation from the proletarian and revolutionary East.

Don Camillo raised his eyes and viewed Smilzo's cyclonic arrival distrustfully.

"Does a certain Jesus Christ live here?" Smilzo asked, pulling a letter out of the bag hanging over his shoulder.

"Someone lives here that may give you a swift kick," Don Camillo answered tersely.

"Due respect must be paid to all officials engaged in the public service," said Smilzo. "The address on this Special Delivery letter is: *Jesus Christ, Parish House*. If no such person resides here, then I write: *Unknown at the above address*, and that's all there is to it."

Don Camillo took hold of the letter and, sure enough, the address was just what Smilzo had represented it to be.

"I'll take it," he said. "It will give me grounds for a complaint to the postal authorities. They have no right to encourage such a piece of sacrilegious imbecility."

"The postal authorities are only doing their duty," said Smilzo. "The parish house exists, and they don't have to know who's inside. A man can have anyone in his house he wants to. And the name doesn't matter; it may be an alias for all we care."

Don Camillo bent over with studied indifference and the intention of taking off his shoe to serve as a missile, but Smilzo rode off like a flash, before he could reach it.

The joker who had written the sacrilegious address had added the word *Personal,* and underlined it, and Don Camillo went to give vent to his indignation before the Crucified Christ over the altar.

"Lord," he exclaimed, "won't You tell me who pulled off this disgraceful trick? Won't You enable me to go and wring his neck and force him to eat the letter?"

"Don Camillo," Christ answered with a smile, "we must respect the privacy of the mails. We can't go against the principles of the Constitution."

"Then, Lord, are we to allow these fellows to blaspheme You with the written word as well as the spoken one?"

"How do you know that the author of the letter is a blasphemer?" Christ asked. "Mightn't he be a simple-minded man or a mad one? You'd better read it before you condemn him."

Don Camillo threw out his arms in resignation, tore open the envelope and took out a sheet of paper with words printed in capital letters upon it, which he read slowly to himself.

"Well, Don Camillo? Is it as dreadful as you imagined?"

"No, Lord; it's the work of a madman, who deserves only compassion."

Don Camillo stuffed the letter into his pocket and started to go away, but Christ called him back.

"What does this madman ask of Me, Don Camillo?"

"Nothing in particular. His letter's a mass of chaotic sentences, with no order or meaning."

"All well and good, but you mustn't pass such a quick judgment upon the expression of a troubled mind. Madness has a logic all its own, and the understanding of this leads to a discovery of the cause of the trouble."

"Oh, the trouble is a vague sort of affair," said Don Camillo hurriedly. "It's impossible to understand it."

468

"Read it to Me, Don Camillo."

Don Camillo shrugged his shoulders in resignation, drew the letter out of his pocket and read it aloud.

"Lord, I beg you to illuminate the mind of a certain priest and convey to him that he is carrying his political activity too far. In fact, if he carries it much farther, he may find his hind quarters in contact with a hickory stick. To exercise the priesthood by vocation is one thing, and by provocation is another. Signed—A friend of democracy."

"What priest do you suppose he means?" Christ asked at the end of the letter.

"I haven't the slightest idea," said Don Camillo.

"Do you know any priest who carries his political activity too far?"

"Lord, I get around so very little. . . . All the priests in this part of the country are quiet, well-balanced fellows. . . ."

"What about yourself, Don Camillo?"

"Lord, we were speaking of priests in this part of the country. If the letter had referred to me, it would have said 'the local priest,' or 'the priest of this parish,' instead of 'a certain priest.' As You so rightly remarked, madness has a logic all its own, and I am trying to reason along the lines of this logic."

"Don Camillo," Christ sighed, "why are you trying to keep the truth from Me? Why don't you admit that you are the priest in question?"

"Lord, do You pin Your faith on poison-pen letters and anonymous accusations?"

"No, Don Camillo, but I'd pin My faith on any accusation you care to make against yourself."

"Lord, the election is very near, and we're waging an important battle. I must be loyal to the parish priest. I can tell him to be careful, but I can't bring any accusation against him."

"You mean you'll advise him to keep his hind quarters out of contact with a stick, is that it?"

"No, Lord, I'm concerned not with my body but with my soul."

With which Don Camillo went to meditate in his study, and as a result the next day Smilzo brought a Special Delivery letter to Peppone.

"What are we to do with this, Chief?" he asked.

Peppone saw that the address on the envelope was: *Mr. Malenkov, People's Palace*. Undaunted, he took out the letter and read the printed text:

> *"Mr. Malenkov, please inform your follower known as 'a friend of democracy' that his interesting letter will be photographed for reproduction in the local reactionary press. Gratefully yours, A Certain Priest."*

Peppone turned purple with anger, but Smilzo calmed him down.

"Chief, you'll just have to take it and let the whole thing blow over. He's manoeuvred himself into a favourable position."

"He's got himself out of range of a hickory stick," roared Peppone, bringing his massive fist down on the deck. "But if I beat him up with a branch of elm or acacia, then no one will suspect me."

"Naturally, Chief. There are dozens of ways you can get the better of him, without giving yourself away by the use of hickory. All nature is on the People's side!"

The publication of the letter aroused considerable talk and everyone accused the Reds of its authorship. In self-defence Peppone decided to relax the general tension by organizing a "Poker Tournament for the Peace Crusade." In this part of the world, which is cut off by the winter fog from the rest of humanity, poker is not so much a game as it is a vital necessity and a tournament of this kind, even if it was organized under the shadow of the wings of Stalin's Peace Dove, was bound to be a success.

Tournament headquarters was set up at the Molinetto tavern, which was filled every evening with people of every class and condition. The match grew more and more exciting as poor players were eliminated and undisputed experts held the field. At last it came to a final showdown, which brought two champions face to face. Don Camillo informed Christ of the latest developments.

"Lord, this evening brings the last round. Everyone's excited, because, as always happens in these parts, politics has entered the situation. I shouldn't be surprised if fists were to fly before the evening's over."

"How does that happen, Don Camillo?"

"Lord, politics has a way of changing the aspect of everything it touches, and so the last round of the tournament has turned into a duel between the People's champion and the champion of Reaction. The finalists are Farmer Filotti and Peppone. If Filotti wins, then it is a victory for Reaction, and if, instead, Peppone manages to beat him, then the proletariat will rejoice."

"This is all very silly," said Christ. "What interests are tied up in this game?"

"It's just a matter of prestige. Foolish, if you like, but in politics it makes a big difference. Anyhow, we're certain to be defeated. I say 'we' because the Reds are our natural enemies. But it had to end this way. Peppone isn't coming up against our best player. Filotti may be good, but he's not our top man. And Peppone's such a schemer that he's not above pulling off some funny business with the cards. Now, it may be blasphemous to speak of 'Justice' in something so frivolous as a game of poker. But, if I may be allowed to say so, it's unjust that victory should go to someone who doesn't deserve it. . . ."

"Don't take it too hard, Don Camillo," Christ interrupted. "You said yourself that it's a frivolous matter. As a matter of fact, all such games are bad for a man, even if they are playing for nothing more than fun. Card-playing is a vice, just like everything else that serves merely to kill time."

"Of course," said Don Camillo, with a blow. "But if it's legitimate to draw up a scale of values among all these vicious games, I should say that poker was the least harmful of the lot, because it's based on reason and provides mental gymnastics as well as wholesome reaction."

"Don Camillo, you talk like a real fan."

"No, just like someone that knows the game. Like a very mediocre player, but one that could beat three Peppones to a frazzle. . . . But of course it's unthinkable for a priest to mingle with card-players in a tavern, even if he is motivated by a noble desire to prevent a leader of godlessness from carrying off an undeserved victory."

"Quite right," Christ answered. "A priest must never set foot in a tavern simply in order to take part in some petty game. Priests serve the King of Heaven, not the kings of clubs and diamonds."

It was late by now, and Don Camillo started off to bed. Meanwhile the crowded Molinetto tavern was the scene of the final battle. Peppone was in good form; indeed, he seemed to have a calculating machine in place of his brain. The last game won him deafening applause. Filotti threw his cards down on the table and called for a glass of white wine.

"Let's have a drink on it," he said. "There's nothing else I can do."

Peppone was the winner and the Reds were so wild with joy that they began to shout for a speech. Amid general silence Peppone took the floor.

"Comrades! In the battle of sport as well as the battle of labour, the working man must win. This victorious tournament, played under the auspices of . . ."

But at this point he stopped short, because someone was knocking at the window which gave on to the street. Smilzo prudently opened it, and there behind the grating was the face of Don Camillo. There was a dramatic silence.

"What do you want?" Peppone asked threateningly.

"I want to play," answered Don Camillo.

"To play? Play with whom?"

"Anyone that's not afraid to play with me."

Peppone shot him a pitying glance.

"I'm not afraid of anybody. But the tournament is over. If you wanted to play, you should have signed up for it."

"I did sign up," Don Camillo explained. "If you look at the list, you'll find a registration under the name of *Il Calmo*, or 'The Calm Man.'"

"That doesn't mean anything," retorted Peppone. "Anyone can come along and claim to have signed up under that name."

"No, because *Il Calmo* is an anagram for 'Camillo.'"

"This isn't an anagram contest or a Latin lesson; it's a serious card game."

Don Camillo explained the nature of an anagram, and after Peppone had counted the letters he had to admit that Camillo and *Il Calmo* came to the same thing.

"Of course if His Honour the Mayor is afraid of coming a cropper, then I'll go away."

"Come on in," shouted Peppone.

"I can't do that," said Don Camillo; "it wouldn't be proper. I'll stay here and we'll play on the windowsill."

"That may be a good idea," said Peppone. "You'll feel safer that way."

Don Camillo grasped two bars of the grating in his hands and twisted them back.

"That makes it more convenient," he explained, "but if the fresh air bothers you, you can fix it the way it was before."

"It does bother me," said Peppone, grasping the bars and pulling them back into their original position.

The crowd had never seen a more formidable sight. People held their breath the way they do at the circus when two tightrope walkers advance to the roll of drums. Peppone took a pack of cards and laid it on the windowsill; Don Camillo picked it up and shook his head.

"These are too thin and frail for a temperament like mine," he objected. And taking the pack in his big hands, he tore it in two. Peppone paled, and Smilzo came up with another pack of cards.

"Will this do?" asked Peppone.

"No," said Don Camillo.

"I don't like it myself," said Peppone, picking up the pack and mangling it in the same way.

Someone offered them a third pack.

"It has to be brand new and in its original wrapping," Don Camillo insisted. "Trust is all very well, but mistrust is better."

Smilzo brought out a pack of cards still wrapped and sealed in cellophane paper, which Peppone examined carefully and then handed to Don Camillo.

"I'm satisfied," he said. "What about you?"

"It's all right with me," said Don Camillo, turning the cards over in his hands and giving them back to Peppone. "Go ahead and shuffle, but keep your hands out of mischief."

Peppone gritted his teeth, shuffled the cards and laid them on the windowsill.

"The tournament's over, and I won it," he said. "The Cup goes to the Party, and no one can take it away. But in order to make this a good game and lend it some social significance, I'll put up my shotgun as stakes. What about you?"

A murmur went through the room. Peppone's gun was the finest for miles around and everyone knew how he prized it. He would have cut off a leg rather than give up that precious gun. Everyone waited for Don Camillo to make a fitting reply. And it did not disappoint them.

"I'll put up my dog!" he said boldly. And everyone knew that the dog was the apple of Don Camillo's eye.

The game that followed was of an epic character. If Homer's heroes had played poker they would have played it in just the same way. The two men fought with all their wits until the bitter end, and Don Camillo won. No one dared applaud him. Finally Don Camillo tipped his hat.

"Thanks for the good game, and good-night. Gambling debts are due within twenty-four hours."

Don Camillo went straight to the rectory, without passing through the church, but Christ's voice overtook him.

"At this late hour, Don Camillo!"

"I went to look in at the last round of the tournament. But I didn't set foot in the tavern; I stayed just outside the window. And just as I thought, Peppone was the winner."

"Did that cause any trouble?"

"No, everything went smoothly, and there was general agreement that the best man won."

"Don Camillo, this game of poker interests me. I gather from what you say, that it must be played with a pack of brand-new cards, in their original wrapping."

"That's a wise precaution, especially if you're playing with nimble-fingered fellows who may connive with the tavern-keeper to use marked cards."

"I see. So a pack of new cards is brought out; the first player examines it and passes it to the second, who then slips it into his pocket and puts in its place another identical pack, inconspicuously marked with his thumb-nail and rewrapped in the original paper. Isn't that the system?"

"Oh, I wouldn't put it that way," said Don Camillo.

"Then what have you got in your pocket?"

"I can't imagine how in the world it got there," stammered Don Camillo, pulling out a pack of new cards and laying it on the table.

"Peppone gave it to you and you slipped his pack into your pocket and gave him back another pack which you had brought with you."

"Obviously there was a mix-up of some kind," said Don Camillo.

"Yes, you mixed up right and wrong, and added to the immorality of a gambling game. But you're the real loser, Don Camillo."

Don Camillo was wiping the perspiration off his forehead

474

when Peppone came into the room. He took his famous shotgun out from under his coat and handed it over.

"Gambling debts are paid promptly," he said, "but if you're an honest man, you'll give me a chance for revenge."

Then he noticed the pack of cards on the table.

"This is luck," he added. "Here's a brand-new pack, which guarantees a fair game. Open it and shuffle the cards."

They sat down at the table and Don Camillo opened the pack and shuffled. The game was just as Homeric in character as the one that had gone before, but this time Peppone won.

"Shall we play a third game to break the tie?" he suggested.

Don Camillo did not answer, because he was fingering the cards.

"Aha!" he said all of a sudden. "So you mark the ace like this, do you?"

Peppone did not blench. He pulled another pack of cards out of his pocket and searched for the seven.

"And your mark is these two fine lines, isn't it?" he countered.

Don Camillo picked up Peppone's pack and threw it on to the fire. And Peppone did the same thing with Don Camillo's.

"Well, we're even," said Peppone as he got up to leave.

"No," said Don Camillo; "I'm the loser."

And he said it so sorrowfully that Peppone was touched.

"Father, don't take it too hard. In a game of poker the prospect of winning addles a man's brain and he can't help himself. I'll lend you my gun to go hunting, and you can lend me your dog in return. How about it?"

After Peppone had gone, Don Camillo stared into the fire.

"Don Camillo, I said that you were in the service of the King of Heaven, not of the kings of clubs and diamonds. You ought to be ashamed!"

Don Camillo threw out his arms, raised his eyes to heaven and exclaimed:

"Lord, I know I'm in the wrong. But you heard what he said about the game and how it addles a man's brain."

Then something caught Don Camillo's eye. It was Peppone's pack and the flames of the fire were just beginning to curl round it. In a moment it would be too late to find out how an expert like Peppone marked the kings and queens.

Christ sighed.

"Don Camillo, who's going to save you from burning in Hell?"

Don Camillo did not answer, but he sat quite still and did not go up to bed until the glowing coals had turned to ashes.

HUNGER STRIKE

SMILZO'S MOTHER had paralysed legs, but she also had a head on her shoulders, and even though she had been confined to a chair for five or six years, she knew exactly what was going on. When she was present Smilzo and his wife didn't dare talk politics, but she had a keen ear and heard much of what they didn't even say. They thought they had everything under control but a few days after their son was born the old woman came out and said:

"It's time to baptize him."

Smilzo was taken by surprise and stood there gaping, but his wife jumped into the breach.

"There's no hurry," she said. "Let's wait at least until this cold spell is over."

The old woman said nothing, but two days later she attacked again.

"Well, is he going to be baptized or isn't he?"

With the passage of time she became more and more insistent, and finally Smilzo screwed up his courage to say: "Don't let's hear any more talk about this business of baptism. Times have changed in a great many ways that you don't know."

The old woman shook her head. "From the day when Jesus Christ started this business of baptism, times have changed over and over and any number of things have happened, but newborn babies have always been baptized."

Smilzo muttered something about political parties and

477

excommunications but the old woman knew what she was talking about and stuck to it.

"Newborn babies aren't party members. And so they've got to be baptized."

Smilzo repeated that she didn't understand, but she went on shaking her head.

"I understand perfectly well. Your father was worse than you are when it comes to political notions, but you were baptized shortly after you were born."

"Things were different in those days," Smilzo's wife exclaimed.

"And wives were different too!" retorted the old woman.

"Wives were different? What do you mean? What have you got against me?"

"The fact that you're a silly girl?"

"All right, then," the wife shouted. "I won't have my baby baptized for certain. If when he's older he feels like being baptized, then he can do something about it."

The old woman looked at her son, but he failed to agree with her.

"It's putting something over on children to baptize them when they don't know what it's all about," he mumbled.

"Very well," said the old woman. "From now on, I'm not eating. I shan't eat until the baby's been baptized.

"You'll starve for years, then," said her daughter-in-law with a mocking laugh.

Smilzo said nothing, but brought his fist down on the table and went out of the house.

The next day the old woman did not drink her usual cup of milk for breakfast and at noon she sat quietly in her chair, watching the others eat their lunch. It was the same thing at supper, and finally Smilzo lost his patience.

"You've behaved quite long enough like a spoiled child," he said. "Go ahead and eat, instead of trying to upset me."

"She'll eat when she's hungry," his wife reassured him. But another day went by in the same way, and the daughter-in-law began to be worried.

"We must call the doctor," she said, "tell him what's happened and have her taken away. Otherwise, if she dies of starvation, we'll be blamed for it. Can't you see her little game? She wants to ruin our reputation."

At this point the old woman spoke up.

"Give me pen and paper and I'll write down that I'm

dying of my own free will. I'm not trying to ruin your reputation; I simply want to save my grandson's soul."

Smilzo's wife had an attack of nerves and began sobbing: "She hates me! I won't have any milk for the baby if she goes on this way."

"What of it?" said the old woman. "Snake's milk won't do him any good."

Smilzo ran out of the house in despair. But he could just as well have stayed at home, because the old woman did not open her mouth to speak again. The third day she chose to stay in bed.

"I'd rather die in this position," she explained. "Please call the priest."

"No!" shouted her daughter-in-law. "No!"

"It doesn't really matter," said the old woman. "God will listen to me just the same."

"You'll die with a curse upon you!" shouted her daughter-in-law. "It's a clear-cut case of suicide, because you won't eat."

"No, you've prevented me from eating by refusing to have the baby baptized."

She closed her eyes and sank back on the pillows, while her daughter-in-law withdrew uneasily. Smilzo had been listening just outside the door.

"Something must be done in a hurry," he said.

"Are you going to give in to the priests?" his wife panted. "They've thrown you out of the Church and you ask them to baptize your son? That doesn't go very well with the beliefs you profess in public."

"Take it easy!" said Smilzo. "We've got to find a way to kill two birds with one stone. I'm going to see Peppone."

Peppone was in his workshop when Smilzo burst in upon him.

"Chief, you've got to help me. I'm in hot water." He proceeded to tell his thorny story and concluded: "Chief, I don't want to betray my political principles, but I can't let my mother die. Suppose I get a fancy, lace-trimmed baptismal dress; you put on your best clothes and come for us in your car. We'll have the baby all rigged out in white and show him to his grandmother, with you in a godfather's robe. We'll drive to the People's Palace, sneak in through the courtyard, drink a bottle of wine and then go back and say to my mother: 'Here he is, fresh from the font, just as you

479

wanted!' Then she'll start eating again and my conscience will be clear."

"I see," said Peppone. "But what if she ever finds out?"

"She won't," said Smilzo curtly. "And the main thing just now is to get her to eat."

Peppone shrugged but agreed to co-operate and while Smilzo went to buy a robe he put on his best clothes. Half an hour later they were at Smilzo's house. The house was in a lonely spot and there was a heavy fog in the air, both of them favourable circumstances. Smilzo's wife ran to wake up the old woman.

"If you really don't want to ruin our reputation, then get up for a minute. The baby's godfather is here."

"His godfather?" exclaimed the old woman, opening her eyes wide.

"Yes, the mayor himself, who's honoured us by consenting to present him for baptism."

Voices rang out downstairs, and the old woman pulled herself into an upright position and threw a shawl around her shoulders.

"Where's the baby?" she asked.

"They're dressing him now."

"Is he fitted out properly?"

"You'll soon see."

There was a knock at the door, and Smilzo came in, carrying the baby wrapped in the most elaborate outfit that can be imagined. Behind this dazzling white vision was the massive figure of Peppone. But the old woman had eyes only for the baby.

"What a little beauty!" she sobbed, raising her gaunt hands as if before some miraculous apparition.

Even the mother was amazed to see her child in such festive array. She snatched him out of Smilzo's arms in order to smooth out the pleats and straighten the bows of the baptismal robe and put the cap at the proper angle on the tiny pink head.

"How are you?" Peppone asked the old woman.

At last she managed to take her eyes off the baby and look at Peppone.

"What an honour you are paying us, Mr. Mayor!" she exclaimed, grasping one of his big paws. "God bless you! I know it's thanks to you that my son came around to reason. But never mind about that; it's all over. . . ."

480

Peppone tried to free his hand, but she held it in an iron grasp.

"Don't say that!" he replied. "Your son doesn't need advice from anybody. He's a fine man. And the honour of being his child's godfather is all mine. . . . But tell me how you are feeling."

"Splendid, thank you," she answered. "I had a touch of flu, just like everyone else this winter, but I'm quite well now."

"Take good care of yourself!" Peppone admonished her in an authoritative tone. And after this he could find nothing else to say.

"We must hurry along," put in Smilzo. "The priest is waiting."

The old woman insisted on looking at the baby again and laid a finger on his forehead.

"He's smiling!" said Peppone. "Seems as if he knew you already."

The baby had clutched the old woman's hand and for a moment he would not let it go.

"He wants me to come along," she sighed, "but I'm in no condition to go. When I hear the church bells ring I'll be happy."

"You may not hear them at all," mumbled her daughter-in-law nervously. "There's a fog outside so thick you could cut it with a knife."

"I've a keen ear, and besides, I'll open the window," the old woman answered, smiling.

In the bar of the People's Palace, there was no one but Bigio, who was engaged in going over some accounts. He was startled to see Peppone and Smilzo come in, bearing the decked-out baby.

"Pull down the blinds," said Peppone, "and bring us a bottle of dry white wine."

Bigio brought the bottle of wine and three glasses.

"Aren't you having a drink too?" asked Smilzo.

"Well, there are three of us, aren't there? And I've brought three glasses."

"What about the fourth?" asked Smilzo, pointing with a laugh at the white bundle on the table.

"I don't get it," Bigio said.

"A proletarian baptism!" explained Smilzo, raising his glass. "To the health of a new comrade!"

Bigio and Peppone drained their glasses. Then, while Peppone told Bigio what it was all about, Smilzo dipped his finger into the wine and held it up to the baby's lips.

"Look how he sucks it!" he said proudly. "It's plain he'll grow up to be a very fine fellow!"

The others made no answer, and Smilzo drank down another glass of wine. For several minutes he was absorbed in his thoughts, but finally he said:

"The church bells! She wanted to hear them ringing!"

Just then the church bells actually rang, and the three men jumped as if in the presence of something supernatural.

"Oh yes," said Bigio. "To-day they were going to baptize the chemist's baby."

Smilzo gave a roar of joy.

"She wanted to hear the church bells, did she? Well, there they are! What luck!"

The bundle on the table began to wriggle and Peppone touched the baby's warm, rosy forehead with his enormous hand. The baby took hold of his middle finger and would not let it go. Peppone reflected that a short time before the baby had held his grandmother's old hands in the same way. Now the baby held fast again. Meanwhile Smilzo drank a third glass of wine.

"We can go home now," he said, slamming the empty glass down on the table.

Peppone and Bigio did not move.

"Ring down the curtain!" said Smilzo. "The play is over, and I'm a perfect swine."

Peppone and Bigio had never heard what the Party calls confession couched in such very honest and appropriate terms.

"Go to it, Bigio," said Peppone, "and make it snappy."

And Bigio was off like a shot.

"What's this?" asked Don Camillo, going over to the baptismal font.

"My son!" said Smilzo, straightening the ribbons which stuck out of the bundle on Peppone's arm.

"Poor boy!" sighed Don Camillo. "Couldn't he have chosen a better father?"

The baby was in good form by now and proceeded to grasp Don Camillo's middle finger. "Brat!" Don Camillo said severely. "Are you trying to take other people's belongings away from them so soon?"

Smilzo wanted to say something, but Don Camillo drowned out his voice.

"Silence! As you know, no convinced Communist can serve as a godfather. Are you a convinced Communist, Peppone?"

"No sir!" said Peppone.

"God only knows whether you are telling the truth, and He'll call you to account for it on Judgment Day."

After the ceremony was over and Peppone had gone out to the car, in which Bigio was waiting before the church, Smilzo went up to Don Camillo.

"How much do I owe you for your trouble?" he asked.

"Nothing. You too can settle your accounts with God Almighty."

Smilzo looked at him with mistrust.

"You won't get my next baby, though!" he said defiantly.

"The future is in God's hands, my son!" said Don Camillo, throwing out his arms. "But get out of here in a hurry, because the present might be in my feet!"

This was a theory just like any other. But Smilzo knew the size and strength of Don Camillo's feet and so he took it into due consideration.

PEPPONE GOES BACK TO SCHOOL

PEPPONE DECIDED to go all out against clerical interference in the primary schools, and an announcement to this effect came out in the bulletin nailed to the wall of the People's Palace. In it was the proposal that a supervisory committee be set up and empowered to visit the schools at any time to make sure that the teaching was in accord with democratic principles.

Of course, the next day, the bulletin of the Opposition printed a reply:

> "We don't for a moment criticize our Mayor for the fact that he never finished school. We believe that ideas are much more important than good grammar. But for purposes of the present discussion we must note that it seems singularly inappropriate for primary instruction to be in the hands of someone who never finished his own. Let the Mayor hand over this job to Smilzo, who stayed two years in first grade and three years in both second and third, thus acquiring considerably more experience in the field of education."

This piece caused considerable talk in the village, and Don Camillo made a copy of it which he took to read to the Christ over the altar.

"I am still of the same opinion," Christ told him. "This was written by a man just as stupid as the one who pencilled the word 'Donkey!' on the margin of some other declaration by Peppone."

"But, Lord," Don Camillo objected, "this is an entirely different matter. Isn't it stupid of a man with one leg to insist on entering a race?"

"Don Camillo, you're not playing fair! A man with only one leg can't acquire another in its place, but a man who doesn't know grammar can always learn it. If you know the person who wrote these words, tell him that they are very stupid."

"I'll try to explain," said Don Camillo, throwing out his arms, "but it's going to be uphill work, because he honestly believes he's in the right."

"He can't honestly believe that, when he's out of harmony with God's law. You know that perfectly well, because I've told you."

"Don Camillo is always in hot water," the priest sighed.

Peppone couldn't take the counter-attack lying down, and so he brought out another broadside:

"We can confidantly state that if our unknown adversary were to look after his priestly affairs instead of the affairs of other people, it would be a very good thing. There are two kinds of ignorance: the ignorance of those who for obvious reasons have not been able to continue their schooling and that of persons like the ignorant priest in question, who has studied a great deal but learned nothing. He reminds us of a shiny copper pot, with a hole in the bottom, looking down at a tarnished old pot, which is obviously much more serviceable for cooking."

This was only the beginning, and the rest was couched in much grosser terms. When Don Camillo went to kneel in front of the altar, Christ asked him if he had read Peppone's new innuendo.

"Yes, Lord."

"And have you resisted the temptation to reply?"

"Yes, Lord."

"Will you be able to keep up your resistance?"

Don Camillo threw out his arms.

"The future is in God's hands," he answered.

"But the draft of your reply is in your right-hand pocket, and so in this case the future is in the hands of Don Camillo."

Don Camillo took the sheet of paper out of his pocket and burned it in the flame of a candle.

"The election is just around the corner," he observed, "and

to my mind these are mistaken tactics, from a political point of view."

"That may be, Don Camillo. But don't worry about the election. I'm not for or against any ticket. I won my battle a long time ago."

When Peppone was beside himself with political passion, he proceeded with about as much delicacy as a Sherman tank, and so, naturally enough, this piece of prose which began with the famous "confid*a*ntly" was full of errors. People laughed immoderately at it, even without any instigation on the part of Don Camillo, and Peppone's pride was deeply injured. He tried throwing a few punches around and received a few from persons upon whom he had not inflicted any, but he was aware that this did not alter the situation and that his grammar was just as stumbling as ever. And so he dropped the fight for a supervisory committee and fastened his energies upon the fulfilment of a very ambitious dream. No one except his wife knew anything about it. Every evening, when he set off on his motorcycle, she gave an anxious sigh, and toward midnight, when he returned she immediately asked:

"How did you do?"

"It's hard going, but I'll make it."

This went on for three and a half months, until one night, upon his return from the mysterious trip, Peppone announced:

"This is it! I'm taking the plunge!"

"What if you don't succeed?"

"I must, that's all."

"Think how those wretched people will laugh if you fail. Couldn't you do it in the city, where nobody knows you and if you don't make the grade, it doesn't matter?"

"No, if I did it anywhere else, they'd say there was something tricky or dishonest about it. It's got to be done in the light of day, with everything legal. I'm putting in an application tomorrow."

"Well, be sure not to make any mistakes in the application!"

"You don't need to worry about that," Peppone reassured her. "I've got the application all ready. They typed it up for me in the city!"

"I, Giuseppe Bottazzi, etc., etc., respectfully ask permission of the Board of Education to take the eighth-grade examinations..."

The bomb burst with a noise almost atomic in intensity and Smilzo ran to Peppone's house with his eyes popping out of his head.

"Chief, people are saying that you want to take the eighth-grade examinations!"

"Well, what's so remarkable about it?"

"Chief, the eighth grade is tough!"

"Good! 'Live dangerously!' must be our motto."

"Chief, if you fail, you're a goner!"

"Verdi failed at the Conservatory, and then did pretty well."

In the face of such confidence, Smilzo could find nothing to say. With all the nonchalance of a gentleman flicking an ash off the end of his cigarette, Peppone added:

"If I haven't got an inferiority complex, why should you have one?"

This was the last straw. If Peppone knew the meaning of an inferiority complex, then he must be up to his ears in culture.

"Chief," Smilzo stammered, "have you been studying all these months? It must have cost you an awful lot of money?"

"Why? I took a cramming course at a night school in the city, for adults and children together. At the desk next to mine there was a twelve-year-old boy called Mario Bibelli, a little fellow that didn't come up to my shoulder. He'll pay me a visit here some Sunday."

"Amazing!" exclaimed Smilzo. "It sounds like an old-fashioned, romantic novel."

"Reality is the true romanticism of both yesterday and today," said Peppone didactically. "Both De Amicis and De Sica are neo-realists, even if the former did his writing a century ago."

Smilzo went away completely convinced of one thing: Peppone had turned into an intellectual.

"It wouldn't surprise me if he were to write for some literary magazine," he said to Brusco, Bigio and the rest of Peppone's henchmen. "This is going to be a bitter pill for some people to swallow."

It was a bitter pill for Don Camillo, who was burning up

487

with eagerness to talk to Peppone and size up his new education. Peppone seemed to be avoiding him, and this exasperated his curiosity all the further. Finally he did get hold of him, by means of a personal visit to the workshop. Peppone greeted him with gentlemanly indifference.

"What can I do for you?" he asked.

"I was just passing by," said Don Camillo, "and wanted to inquire about the health of our mayor."

"There's no mayor here. Here you have only Giuseppe Bottazzi, the blacksmith, descendant of the blacksmith of the same name who brought the family to this village several centuries ago and was beheaded because he stripped a priest of his ill-gotten gains. There's the nemesis of history for you!"

"The nemesis of history? How do you mean?" asked Don Camillo in utter astonishment.

"I mean that maybe this time there'll be a different ending and Giuseppe Bottazzi will not only strip the priest of his ill-gotten gains, but kill him!"

"Ill-gotten gains? But I have no more money than a jumping jack-rabbit!"

"I'm not speaking of money. You've captured the confidence of a great many ignorant people, and we shall take it away!"

The conversation was taking an unpleasant turn, but Don Camillo swallowed his pride for the sake of acquiring further information.

"What will be, will be," he said. "How about the examinations?"

"Trifles!" answered Peppone. "The important examination is the one I take every day with this hammer and anvil. And I pass it, time after time."

As Don Camillo was going away he saw Peppone's wife at the door.

"Did you come to rag him?" she said aggressively. "It's eating you up, isn't it, that you can't brand him as someone that never got through school?"

"No," said Don Camillo. "But it's still too early to say. We'll see what happens when he's put to the test."

Don Camillo went home in a gloomy state of mind.

"Lord," he said to the Christ over the altar, "that poor fellow is so swollen with pride that he deserves to fail every single subject."

488

"I don't know about that, Don Camillo. I'm not on the examination committee. That's for them to decide."

"God is everywhere," objected Don Camillo, "and He'll be in the schoolroom where that country bumpkin comes to make a fool of himself."

"Certainly, Don Camillo, God is everywhere. Right now He's here listening to the stupid things you are saying."

Don Camillo threw out his arms in discouragement.

"For some time now, I haven't been able to say the right thing!"

The matter of examining Mayor Peppone was a headache to the Board of Education. Things had to be conducted with such scrupulous care that no one could find an excuse for saying that either success or failure was due to the candidate's political office or party affiliation. A special commission was made up of the board's director and two teachers from another township, one a stiff, elderly woman and the other, a middle-aged man. Peppone was in a radiant mood, with no doubts at all as to his ability to get through. When he received notice that the examinations would be held the next day he burst out with:

"It's about time! I was beginning to be thoroughly bored."

He went to bed in a good humour and got up in one that was even better. Immediately he put on his best suit, filled his fountain-pen, tested it on a piece of paper and started to leave the house.

"I'll go with you as far as the school," his wife suggested.

"Don't let's be silly about it!" said Peppone.

"Your son insists on going," she told him.

"Don't make me look ridiculous; I'd seem like a schoolboy, and all those wretched people will be staring out their windows at me."

And so Peppone went off alone, but when he reached the school, his wife and son were already there, lurking behind a hedge, all red in the face from having run across the fields to beat him. As he started up the steps into the schoolhouse, they waved to him and he waved back at them with his hand hidden halfway down his back. The commission welcomed him with icy politeness.

"Sit down," said the director. "You will have written examinations in arithmetic and composition. Remember that the allotted time is four hours."

Then they set before him four sheets of officially stamped examination paper, two for a rough copy and two for the finished product.

"Shall we begin?" asked the director, after Peppone had sat down and taken out his pen.

"By all means," said Peppone.

"Then take this down: 'Problem: A cement basin of parallelepiped form has a base 40 by 60 centimetres in size and is fed by two taps. The first tap pours in 8 litres of water a minute and the second tap 5 litres of water every other minute. In thirty minutes the flow from the second tap alone fills two-fifths of the basin. How long will it take to fill the whole basin if both taps are open? How high is the basin?"

As Peppone diligently wrote down the problem, he noticed that his hand had begun to tremble. "I shouldn't have done so much hammering last night," he said to himself. "It has tired my hand." Meanwhile the director told him to shift to another sheet of paper and take down the composition theme set for him by the woman teacher.

"Theme: Narrate some event, either recent or long ago, which made a strong impression upon you."

Peppone took this down with some difficulty, for his hand continued to tremble. Then he ran a handkerchief over his perspiring forehead. He looked over the two sheets, and reread the arithmetic problem. A parallelepiped—what the devil was that? Two minutes earlier, he had known perfectly well, but now it had gone out of his head completely. The tap whose flow sufficed to fill two-thirds of the basin filled him with confusion. What could be meant by two-fifths of a parallelepiped? And what about the other tap, which poured in water continuously?

His head was empty, as he looked again at the theme for a composition. What was an event? What events had he witnessed, and how could he tell the story of any one of them? He thought back to his night school classes and tried to fish out of his memory some of all that he had heard there in the last three and a half months. But not a single word could he recapture. Then he thought of his wife and son waiting for him outside, and there was an ache in his heart.

The three examiners sat around a table at the far end of the room, as stiff as statues. Peppone wiped the perspiration off his brow. The clock in the church tower rang ten. How perfectly terrible! He looked out the window to make sure he had heard correctly. Yes, the hands were pointing to ten, and so were those of the clock in the schoolroom. He had barely written down the questions, and it was ten o'clock already. And those damned taps were still pouring water into that damned parallelepiped!

The old charwoman brought the news to the rectory.

"Father, I saw him with my own eyes. He's been staring for a whole hour and a half at the paper, and perspiring as if he had a high fever. Not a single word has he written!"

Don Camillo listened to her with satisfaction.

"That's what he gets for being so stuck-up," he exclaimed.

"He looked just like a schoolboy," the old gossip continued. "He came up the road alone, but he got his wife and son to walk along parallel to him, behind the hedge. They met him at the schoolhouse door and waved good-bye."

With that the charwoman went away, promising to come back later. She came at eleven o'clock, even more excited than before.

"Things are still exactly the same," she reported. "He's still perspiring, and still staring at the paper. In two more hours, time will be up. His wife and child are still hiding behind the hedge. She's chewed up half a handkerchief, she's so nervous. Father, I only wish you could see the state that big bully is in now!"

And Don Camillo thought he had every right to see the big bully brought so low.

The two strokes of half-past eleven rang out, and Peppone was thinking that he had only an hour and a half more. Just then the charwoman came to call the director. The director went out into the hall and met Don Camillo.

"Excuse me," said the priest, "but even if the mayor is playing schoolboy he can't neglect his municipal duties. There's a poor woman who may die if he doesn't sign the papers authorizing her immediate removal to a city hospital." And he held out a sheet of paper, adding: "Will you give it to him?"

"That's not regular," the director stammered.

"I know, but it would be still more irregular for a poor woman to die simply in order not to disturb an examination. I don't think this will upset your examinee."

The director shrugged his shoulders.

"Father," he said in a low voice, "it's positively nerve-wracking: all he's done is perspire!"

Don Camillo smiled.

"All these boys are the same way. Outside school they go in for a lot of big talk, but in class . . ."

The director took the sheet of paper and started to go back into the classroom. Then he changed his mind.

"Father, I'll send him out here and let you give it to him in person. I'll leave the door open."

Don Camillo glimpsed the sad state of Peppone and calmly waited for him. Meanwhile after Peppone had heard what the director had to say, he slowly got up and came out into the hall.

"Forgive me, Mr. Mayor," said Don Camillo, "but it's an urgent matter."

Peppone took the sheet of paper and read: "I, Angiolina Pateri, widow, without means of support, state as follows . . ."

"I've already told you that I can't do anything for her," he said, handing the paper back to Don Camillo. "I had this same statement in my hands two weeks ago."

"Two weeks ago, things were different," Don Camillo shot back at him. "Please read on. Here you have the notarized signature of the doctor."

Just then the director came out into the hall again.

"Mr. Mayor," he said, "since you're called upon to decide an important matter, this time won't be counted. The commission has noted the exact hour at which you left the room."

"Thank you," said Don Camillo. "I shouldn't want to have on my conscience the theft of time from a mathematics exercise or a literary masterpiece."

Peppone gritted his teeth and shot a bitter glance at Don Camillo.

"Come, Mr. Mayor, hurry!"

Peppone reopened the paper and scrutinized the declaration: "The undersigned certifies that Angiolina Pateri is in a desperate condition and must be sent away for a surgical intervention; *meanwhile, ten minutes from now, you ask for permission to go to the toilet.*"

He reread the last two lines, fearing that he had misunderstood them. Then he looked at Don Camillo and asked:

"Why?"

"If the doctor says so, then it's got to be done," answered Don Camillo. "Just sign here."

Peppone signed the paper and handed it back. When he returned to the classroom the commission took note of the

492

hour. Don Camillo thanked the director and then said to him in a whisper: "He may not seem to be so very bright, but you'll see. He's a slow starter."

"Very slow indeed, Father," said the director with a low laugh.

Ten minutes went by, and then suddenly Peppone raised the thumb and forefinger of his right hand.

"Go right ahead," said the director. "And smoke a cigarette while you're there, if you want to. We'll subtract the time."

Peppone walked unsteadily to the toilet, which was at the end of a long hall. A window looked out over some empty fields.

"Psss!"

Peppone nailed his face to the grating over the window. Just below there was a pile of dried grass and sticks, and this was the source of the whistle.

"Hurry up, you jackass! Light a cigar and pretend to take it easy. Quick, tell me the problem!"

Peppone told him the problem between one puff of smoke and another.

"Parallelepiped. . . . Basin . . . 40 by 60 centimetres . . ."

"What's 40 by 60 centimetres?" came the voice from outside.

"The base . . . two taps . . . one 8 litres a minute . . . other 5 litres every two minutes, but in 30 minutes fills two-fifths of the basin . . ."

"And what do they want to know?"

"How long it would take to fill the basin with both taps running. And the height of the parallelepiped."

"Jackass! That's child's play."

Don Camillo proceeded to explain it to him.

"Do you get it?" he said in conclusion.

"No, but now that you've given me a hint, I'll try to think it out."

"Beat it, then!"

Peppone jumped.

"How about the composition?"

"What's the theme?"

"An event which made a strong impression upon me."

"Well, you'll have to work that out yourself. What do I know of your affairs?"

"But I can't remember a single thing! What shall I tell?"

493

From the pile of grass came a suggestion, and Peppone took it back with him to the classroom. He thought hard over what Don Camillo had told him about the arithmetic problem, and having caught on to the general idea he was able to work it out on paper. He was still perspiring, but in a different way. And the trembling of his hand was not the same, either. The director's voice aroused him:

"It's one o'clock and allowing you ten minutes for each of the two interruptions, you've only twenty minutes left."

Peppone fell once more into a panic. Twenty minutes to make clean copies of both the problem and the composition! He looked around in search of help and his eye fell on the clock in the church tower.

"It isn't yet one o'clock," he exclaimed. "It's twenty minutes to."

The examiners remarked that the hands of the classroom clock pointed to one.

"But I came with the tower clock and it's only fair that I leave with it too."

"Very good," said the director, who wanted above all to have everything proceed smoothly.

Peppone copied first the problem and then the composition, and when the tower clock pointed to one-eighteen he handed in both papers. Don Camillo was watching with a spyglass from the bell tower, and when he saw Peppone coming down the steps he adjusted the mechanism of the clock.

"Now try to catch up on those twenty minutes I set you back!" he murmured.

Looking out again through his spyglass, he saw Peppone jump over the hedge and start home with his wife and son.

"Wretched creature!" the priest murmured. "I wonder if at the oral examinations tomorrow, you'll find another shady character to help you the way I did today!"

But the next day Peppone did very well without any help whatsoever and the old woman teacher felt impelled to say:

"Allow me to congratulate you not only on your thorough preparation but on your good manners and sensitivity as well."

Her fellow-examiner and the director both agreed, and Peppone went triumphantly home, not across the fields, this time, but down the street, with his head held high. Don Camillo sat in the church square, smoking his usual cigar butt, and Peppone marched decisively over to him.

"Did you get your diploma?" Don Camillo asked.

"Yes," said Peppone gloomily. "But you were your usual perfidious self to suggest 'The Day of my First Communion' as subject for a composition. I was down and out, and you took advantage of me."

"I can see that it puts you in real danger," admitted Don Camillo. "If Malenkov comes this way and this composition gets into his files, then you're done for! That's what you get for your pursuit of culture!"

As Don Camillo was passing in front of the main altar, Christ's voice stopped him.

"Where were you yesterday morning, Don Camillo?" Christ asked. "You were away from here for some time."

"Lord, please let it go by for the moment, will You? Later on we'll draw up accounts, and I'll pay up what I have to pay."

"You're shamefully lucky, Don Camillo," Christ said with a sigh. "Even when that time comes you'll find Someone to overlook what you owe Him and give you more credit."

"Forgive us our debts as we forgive our debtors," said Don Camillo, throwing out his arms. Then he remembered how Peppone's wife and child had waited for him behind the hedge.

"I did it for the sake of those two, Lord," he said.

"For the sake of those three," Christ corrected him.

"Oh well, one more or less doesn't matter," concluded Don Camillo.

A BABY CONQUERS

PEPPONE WOKE up at four o'clock that morning. He had gone to bed the night before with something on his mind, and hence there was no need of any alarm clock to arouse him. A little before midnight, when he was just about to retire, he had received news that the clerical group was holding a meeting at the house of Filotti. His informant, who was on watch in the vicinity, had overheard one of the big shots say in a loud voice as he came away from the meeting: "We'll have a good laugh tomorrow."

What could be going to happen? Peppone had no idea, and after cudgelling his brain in vain he had decided that the wisest thing was to go to bed and get up early the next morning in order to meet trouble wherever he found it.

Now, at a quarter past four, he left the house and made an inspection of the sleeping village. Apparently there was nothing new. The posters on the wall were the same as the day before, and so were the electoral pennants and banners. This was in a way reassuring, but in another it wasn't. If his rivals' latest trick was not connected with propaganda, what could it be? Perhaps it would come out in the newspaper, and in this case there was nothing to do but await the paper's arrival.

Peppone crossed the square in the direction of the People's Palace. His head hung low, heavy with thought, and when he raised it to fit the key into the lock he leaped back with surprise. On the step at the foot of the door was a suspicious looking bundle, which made him think immediately of a time-bomb. But this hypothesis proved false a few seconds later, when the bundle emitted a cry and waved a tiny hand.

Peppone moved cautiously nearer, and having lifted up a corner of the black cloth covering, discovered that the tiny hand was attached to a tiny arm and the tiny arm to a tiny baby. Never had he seen such a beautiful specimen. It couldn't have been more than three or four months old, and lacked only a pair of wings to be mistaken for an angel. On the clothes there was pinned a piece of paper with a scrawled message which read: "If yours is the poor people's party, then this is the poorest creature in the world, being possessed of absolutely nothing, not even a name. It is brought to you by an unhappy mother."

He read this incredible message several times over, remained no longer than necessary with his mouth hanging open and let forth a piercing cry. People ran out from everywhere, with sleepy eyes and nothing on but their nightclothes. And when they had read the note they were equally taken aback.

"Is it really possible that in our atomic age something of this sort can happen?" Peppone shouted. "It seems to come straight out of the Middle Ages."

"Except that in the Middle Ages, children were left on the steps of the church," put in Smilzo, who had just arrived upon the scene.

Peppone turned around and looked at him with perplexity.

"Just what do you mean by that?" he mumbled.

"I mean that times have changed," Smilzo explained unctuously. "Nowadays an unmarried mother no longer puts her baby into the hands of the priests, but . . ."

Peppone grabbed the lapels of his jacket and pulled him toward the door without waiting for the end of the sentence.

"Pick up the baby and come on in!" he ordered.

Smilzo bent over to pick up the bundle and followed him.

"Chief," he said when they had reached Peppone's private office, "why did you treat me so roughly? Have I said something wrong?"

"Smilzo," said Peppone excitedly, without stopping to answer this question, "take pencil and paper and get that idea down in writing without a single second's delay. We'll be the ones to laugh last today."

The wife of Lungo was called in to look after the baby, and

Smilzo hastened to develop his idea. He worked over it for a whole hour, and then read the result to Peppone:

"Fellow-citizens! Very early this morning, under the cover of darkness, an unknown woman abandoned her baby on the steps of the People's Palace, where Comrade Giuseppe Bottazzi found it. Pinned to its clothes was a note reading: 'If yours is the poor people's party, then this is the poorest creature in the world, being possessed of absolutely nothing, not even a name. It is brought to you by an unhappy mother.'

"Although we condemn this reckless gesture on the part of the mother, we cannot help calling attention to the social injustice by virtue of which the rich have more money than they can use and the poor have not enough to feed their helpless young.

"The mother forced to abandon her child was a commonplace of the feudal society of the Middle Ages. But today the poor no longer think in medieval terms. In those days babies were left at the church door, but now they are brought to the People's Palace. This signifies that people have lost confidence in the priests and now pin their hopes on the Communist Party, which looks upon all men as equal and entitled to an equal place in the sun.

"And so, fellow-citizens, while we take charge of the abandoned baby, we urge you to vote all together for our candidates in the coming election.

"Local Group of the Italian Communist Party."

Peppone had him read the statement again, discussed a few commas and then sent him to order Barchini, the printer, to make five hundred copies. That same afternoon the posters were ready and the paste-pot squad plastered them all over.

Almost at once there was trouble. That is, Peppone received a visit from the sergeant of the carabinieri.

"Mr. Mayor, is this Communist story true?"

"Why, Sergeant, you don't suppose I'd make it up, do you? I found the baby myself."

"And why didn't you report your discovery?"

"Well, five hundred posters are reporting it!"

"Yes, but you should have come to the police in person to make a signed statement, which we must, in turn, amplify and send on. A woman who abandons her child is guilty of

498

a crime. And how can you be sure that the baby really belongs to the woman who wrote the note? You don't even know that the writer is a woman. What if the baby was kidnapped and then disposed of in this way?"

As a result, Peppone made the required statement, the sergeant questioned other witnesses and drew up his own official account of the story.

"Where is the baby now?" he asked when this was completed.

"In his new home, the People's Palace."

"And who has charge of him?"

"The Communist Party. We've adopted him."

"But a political group can't legally adopt a baby or even hold one in temporary care. The baby has to be turned over to the proper institution. We'll get in touch with a place in the city and you can take the baby there tomorrow."

Peppone looked at the sergeant with exasperation.

"I'll not take that baby anywhere. I'm adopting him myself, personally."

The sergeant shook his head.

"Mr. Mayor, I take my hat off to your generosity. But you can't do that until we have made the necessary investigation."

"Well, while you're investigating, the baby may as well stay with my wife and myself. We're experienced parents. It isn't as if you were putting him into the hands of the first-comer. After all, I am the village's number one man."

The sergeant could find no more objections. "Let's go and take a look at the creature," he suggested.

"Don't inconvenience yourself. I'll have him brought here and you can turn him over to me officially."

Shortly after this, Lungo's wife came with the baby in her arms. And when the sergeant saw him, he exclaimed, "What do you know about that! What a handsome little fellow! I don't see how anyone could abandon him."

Peppone sighed.

"No matter how handsome a baby may be, he can't live on thin air."

The sergeant's investigations didn't have to go too far. That very evening he was called to Torricella, a couple of miles away, where a woman's dead body had been found on the railroad track. In her bag was a note saying: "Mine is just the same old story of a girl left all alone in the world and then jilted by her lover. . . ." There were also identification papers, which made it possible to write to the police of the city whence she had come for further information. A reply was soon forthcoming and brought news that this girl was, as she claimed, quite alone in the world and had registered the birth of a baby without the father's name.

"Now the way is clear," the sergeant said to Peppone. "If you want to proceed with the formalities for adoption, you can go and do so. Of course, if you've changed your mind . . ."

"Of course I haven't changed my mind," said Peppone.

The baby was a very handsome one indeed, and everyone admired him. A wealthy couple by the name of Bicci, whose only misfortune was that they had no child, took a special fancy to him and went to Don Camillo about it.

"He'd be a godsend to us," they told him. "And you're the only one that can wangle it. Peppone wouldn't listen to anyone else."

So Don Camillo went to knock at Peppone's door. Peppone gave him an unpromising welcome.

"Politics?" he asked ill-humouredly.

"No, something much more serious than that. I came to see you about the baby."

"I'd like even politics better. The baby doesn't need a thing. If you must know, he's already been baptized. His mother gave him the name of Paolo."

"I know all that. But it's not true that he doesn't need a thing. First of all, he needs a father and mother. And you don't really need another child."

"That's none of your business, Father. I'm quite capable of looking after my own family affairs. I've come to love that baby as much as if he were my own."

"I know that, too. That's why I've come. If you really love him, then you ought to give him all the advantages you can. The Biccis have neither child nor relatives. They're anxious to adopt the child and leave him everything they have."

"Is that all you came to say?" asked Peppone.

"Yes."

"Then the door's down there to the right."

But Don Camillo had a parting shot ready.

"I see. The baby is useful to you as political propaganda. You don't really care about his future."

Peppone left his anvil and came to stand squarely in front of Don Camillo.

500

"Look, I'd be justified in knocking you over the head with a hammer. But that wouldn't serve any purpose other than that of throwing me into a criminal rôle. And that's a rôle I prefer to save for you. Let's go and see the carabinieri together."

Peppone went out of the door and Don Camillo, with his curiosity aroused, followed after. They found the sergeant at his desk.

"Sergeant," said Peppone, "is it true what they said in the papers, that the poor girl left a note in her handbag?"

"Of course," said the sergeant cautiously. "It was addressed to the judicial authorities and I transmitted it to them."

"So nobody else knows what is in it, is that right?"

"Nobody."

"Well, I do."

"What's that?" exclaimed the sergeant. "Will you kindly explain?"

"Before the girl threw herself under the train she posted from Toricella a letter identical to the one found in her bag. And that letter was addressed to me."

"To you? Did you know her, then?"

"No. The letter was addressed: 'Director of the People's Palace,' and it was delivered to me in person."

The sergeant smiled incredulously. "It does seem likely enough, since that's where she left her baby, that she should have written to you about it. But how can you be sure that letter is an exact copy of the note found in her bag?"

"Because she wrote on it: 'I have sent an exact copy of this letter to the judicial authorities.' I have the original letter of hers in safekeeping. But I've brought with me a typed copy, which I shall now read to you. 'Mine is just the same old story of a girl left all alone in the world and then jilted by her lover. My betrayer is a rich but egotistical and dishonest man. Before dying I wish to leave my son in the hands of people who are against the dishonesty and egotism of the rich. I want him to be educated to combat them. My desire is not for revenge but for justice.' Now tell me, isn't that the exact text?"

"Don't ask me," said the sergeant. "I passed the note on to the proper persons, and only they can answer."

"Very well, Sergeant. Meanwhile, I have a signed letter addressed 'Director of the People's Palace.' I could have had this letter reproduced and used it for campaign purposes...."

501

Peppone turned and gave Don Camillo a withering look. "Now, do you see what material I had there for propaganda? . . . And you, Sergeant, don't you agree?"

"Mr. Mayor, that's not up my alley. I have said all I have to say."

Don Camillo and Peppone walked away in silence, until Peppone said:

"Now, wasn't I justified in wanting to knock you over the head with a hammer?"

"No, only God has a right to take away human life."

"All right. But isn't it God's duty to take away the life of the priest of this parish?"

"God has rights, not duties. Duties are what men have in relation to God."

"Perfect!" shouted Peppone. 'And before God, what is my present duty? To give the baby to the Biccis and let them bring him up to be a little egotist like themselves?"

"Or to bring him up in the school of hate to which you belong?" retorted Don Camillo.

They had reached Peppone's house and now they walked in. There was a cradle in the kitchen, and in it the baby lay sleeping. When the two men drew near he opened his eyes and smiled.

"What a beautiful child!" exclaimed Don Camillo.

Peppone wiped the perspiration off his forehead and then went to fetch a paper.

"Here's the original letter from the mother," he said. "You can see for yourself that I was telling the truth."

"Don't give it to me!" said Don Camillo, "or else I'll destroy it."

"Never mind!" Peppone answered. "Go ahead and look!"

As he handed it across the cradle, a tiny hand stretched out and grabbed it.

"Lord help us!" said Don Camillo, with his eyes wide open in astonishment.

Just then Peppone's wife came in.

"Who let the baby have that paper?" she shouted. "It was written with an indelible pencil, and if he puts it in his mouth he'll be poisoned!"

She snatched the paper away and threw it into the fire. Then she picked up the baby and raised him into the air.

Turning to Don Camillo she said, "Isn't he a handsome

fellow? I'd like to see if your De Gasperi could produce his equal!"

And she spoke as if the baby were her very own. Don Camillo did not let this remark upset him, but took his leave with a polite farewell greeting.

"Good-bye, Mr. Mayor; good-bye, Signora Bottazzi; good-bye, Baby Bottazzi!"

And Baby Bottazzi answered with a gurgle which filled Don Camillo's heart with comfort and hope.

THE ELEPHANT NEVER FORGETS

THUNDER OF course, was Don Camillo's dog. And Antenore Cabazza, known as "Thunderer," was a follower of Peppone. The dog was the brainier of the two, which fact is noted simply in order to give some picture of his two-legged namesake, with whom we are concerned in this story.

Thunderer was an enormous fellow, who, once he got into motion, proceeded with all the grace and implacability of an elephant. He was the ideal man to carry out orders but for some reason Peppone took especial care not to entrust him with their execution. And so most of Thunderer's Communist activities took place at the Molinetto tavern, where he went to play cards whenever he wasn't working. He was an enthusiastic poker player, and his phenomenal memory made him a formidable opponent. Of course memory isn't always the deciding factor in a card game, and every now and then Thunderer took a trouncing. But the experience he had one Saturday with Cino Biolchi was worse than anything that had ever happened to him before. He sat down to play with five thousand liras, and five hours later he was left without a penny. Now Thunderer couldn't stomach the idea of going home in this condition.

"Give me my revenge!" he panted, grasping the cards with shaking hands.

"I've given you I don't know how many thousand chances for a revenge game," said Cino Violchi. "But now I've had enough."

"Let's have just one game, for all or nothing," said Thunderer. "That way, if I win, I get back my five thousand liras."

"And what if you lose?" asked Cino Biolchi.

"Well, you can see I haven't got any more money," stammered Thunderer, wiping the perspiration off his forehead, "but I'll stake anything you say."

"Don't be a donkey," said Biolchi. "Go off to bed and forget about it."

"I want my revenge!" Thunderer roared. "I'll put up anything . . . anything at all. You name it!"

Biolchi was an original fellow. And now, after a moment of thought, he said:

"All right; I'm with you. Five thousand liras against your vote."

"My vote? What do you mean?"

"I mean that if you lose, you promise to vote for whatever party I say in the next election."

Gradually Thunderer was convinced that the other meant just what he was saying. And he had accepted the terms in advance. So it was that Biolchi put a five-thousand lira bill upon the table and gave Thunderer a pen and paper.

"Just write: 'The undersigned Antenore Cabazza solemnly swears to vote on June 7 for such-and-such a party. . . .' You can leave the name of the party blank, and I'll put it in when I feel like it."

Thunderer wrote it duly down and then shot Biolchi a look of resentment.

"It's strictly between ourselves," he said. "And sometime between now and election day, on June 7, you have to play off the game."

"That's a bargain," Biolchi replied.

Peppone was just leaving the People's Palace when Thunderer loomed up before him.

"Chief, I've just lost everything I have to Biolchi in a card game."

"Too bad. But that's none of my business."

"Yes, it is, too. Because I lost something else; I lost my vote."

Peppone laughed after Thunderer had told him the story.

"You don't have to worry," he said reassuringly. "After all, we have a secret ballot, and once you're in the booth you can vote for whom you please."

"No I can't," said Thunderer ruefully. "I signed a paper."

"Devil take the paper! That doesn't bind you."

"I gave my word of honour, and we shook hands on it. And I'm not the kind of a fellow that breaks his word."

Yes, Thunderer, had the character of an elephant rather than a jack-rabbit. He had a motor in place of a brain, and the motor ran with a logic of its own, which no one could stop without causing breakage. Peppone realized that the matter was more serious than he had thought, and that Thunderer was adamant on the subject of his honour.

"Keep your shirt on," he said. "We'll talk it over tomorrow."

"At what time, Chief?"

"At ten thirty-five," muttered Peppone, meaning: "Devil take you for your stupidity!"

But at exactly ten thirty-five the next morning Thunderer turned up at the workshop, saying:

"It's ten thirty-five."

It was obvious that he hadn't slept a wink, and he stood there with bewildered, drooping eyes. Peppone's first impulse was to hit him over the head with a hammer. And when you come down to it, that impulse was a healthy one. But he felt sorry for the fellow and threw his hammer down on the floor instead.

"You ass!" he shouted. "I ought to expel you from the Party. But elections are coming up and we can't let our opponents use this story. Here are five thousand liras; now go tell Biolchi to release you from your word. If he won't do it, let me know."

Thunderer pocketed the banknote and disappeared, but he came back no more than a quarter of an hour later.

"He won't do it."

Peppone put on his jacket and cap and hurriedly went out.

"Wait for me here!" he tossed over his shoulder.

Biolchi greeted him politely.

"What can I do for you, Mr. Mayor?"

"Never mind about the mayor part of it. I've come about that stupid Thunderer. He must have been drunk last night. Anyhow, take the money and release him from his word."

"He wasn't drunk at all. In fact, he was in full possession of his mental faculties. And he was the one to insist on my choice of a stake. Our agreement is crystal-clear. And I'm ready anytime between now and June 7 for the return game."

506

"Biolchi, if I were to go to the police about this, they'd lock you up. But since I don't want to make a public scandal, I'm here to tell you that unless you give me back the paper I'll flatten you out against the wall like an electoral poster!"

"And who'd go to the police, then? That would be very unwise, Peppone!"

Peppone clenched his fists, but he knew that Biolchi had him cornered.

"All right, then. But if you have any decency, you'll play the return game with me instead of with that idiot, Thunderer."

Biolchi shut the door, took a pack of cards from a drawer and sat down at the table, with Peppone across from him. It was a desperately hard-fought game, but at the end, Peppone went away minus his five thousand liras. That evening he met with his henchmen in the People's Palace and told them the story.

"That rascal doesn't belong to any particular party, but he's against us, for sure. We must settle this business quietly, or else he'll turn it into a tremendous joke. Has anybody a suggestion?"

"Well, we can't settle it at cards, that's certain," said Smilzo. "Biolchi can play all of us under the table. Let's try offering him ten thousand liras instead of five."

Although it was late at night, they went in a group to Biolchi's door. He was still up and in a restless mood, as if something out of the way had happened. In answer to Peppone's proposition, he regretfully threw out his arms.

"Too late!" I just played cards with Spiletti, and he won fifteen thousand liras off me, plus Thunderer's paper."

"Shame on you!" said Peppone. "It was agreed that the matter was strictly between you."

"Quite right," said Biolchi. "But Thunderer was the first to spill the beans, when he went to you about it. This simply makes us even. Anyhow, I got Spiletti to promise that he wouldn't tell the story and that before June 7, he'd give Thunderer a chance for revenge."

A pretty kettle of fish! The paper was in the hands of the head of the clerical party and there was no telling what use he would make of it. Peppone and his gang went back to headquarters, where Thunderer was anxiously waiting.

"This is no time for talking," said Peppone. "We've got to

507

act, and act fast. Tomorrow morning we'll post news of Thunderer's expulsion from the Party."

"What's that?" said Thunderer, pitiably.

"I said that the Party is purging you for undignified behaviour. And I'll date the expulsion three months back."

Peppone braced himself for an explosion of anger. But there was nothing of the sort.

"You're quite right, Chief," said Thunderer in a voice that was anything but thunderous. "I deserve to be kicked out like a dog." And he laid his Party membership card meekly on the table.

"We're not kicking you out like a dog!" exclaimed Peppone. "The expulsion is just a pretence, to stave off an attack from the opposition. After the elections, you can make your little act of confession and we'll take you back into the fold."

"I can confess right now," Thunderer said mournfully. "I'm a donkey, and after the elections I'll still be a donkey. There's no use hoping I can change."

Thunderer went dejectedly away, and the spectacle was such that for several minutes Peppone and his henchmen could not settle down to business.

"We'll prepare the announcement," said Smilzo, "but don't let's post it tomorrow. Perhaps Spiletti will keep his word."

"You can't know him very well!" said Peppone. "But just as you say."

For the next two days nothing unusual happened, and it seemed as if the silence would remain, for a while at least, unbroken. But toward evening Thunderer's wife came in a state of agitation to the People's Palace.

"He's stark mad!" she burst out. "For forty-eight hours he hasn't eaten. He lies flat on the bed and won't look at a soul."

Peppone went to survey the situation, and sure enough he found Thunderer in bed immobile. He shook the fellow and even insulted him, but could not get him to say a single word or to abandon for even a second his pose of absolute indifference to the world around him. After a while Peppone lost patience.

"If you're really mad, I'll call the asylum, and they'll take care of you, all right."

With his right arm Thunderer deliberately fished for an

508

object between the bed and the wall. And his eyes seemed to be saying: "If they come from the asylum, I'll give them a proper welcome."

Inasmuch as the object in his right hand was an axe, there was no need for words. Finally Peppone sent everyone else out of the room and said sternly:

"Surely you can tell me confidentially what's got into you to make you behave this way."

Thunderer shook his head, but he put down the axe, opened a drawer of the bedside-table and took out a pad on which he wrote with considerable effort: "I've made a vow to the Madonna not to speak, eat, move or get up for any purpose whatever until I recover that paper, Signed: Antenore Cabazza."

Peppone put this note in his pocket and went to call Thunderer's wife and daughters.

"Don't let anyone into the room unless he calls. Leave him strictly alone. It's nothing serious, just an attack of simple psychosis, a sort of spiritual influenza, which requires rest and a severe diet."

But he came back the next evening to inquire after the patient.

"Exactly the same," said his wife.

"Good," said Peppone. "That's the normal course of the affliction."

Things were still stationary on the fourth day, and so Peppone went from Thunderer's bedside to the rectory. Don Camillo sat at his desk, reading a typewritten paper.

"Look," said Peppone, "do you know the story of this fellow who lost his vote over a game of cards and . . ."

"Yes, I happen to be reading it this minute," answered Don Camillo. "Someone wants to make it into a poster."

"Oh, it's that rascal Spiletti, is it? He gave his word of honour that he'd make no use of it before election day, and that he'd give the loser a revenge game."

"I don't know anything about that. All I know is that we have here an interesting document signed by the loser's own hand."

Peppone took out the sheet of paper he had torn off Thunderer's pad.

"Then read this authentic document as well. That will give you the whole story, and it may be even more interesting if the signer starves himself to death, as seems quite likely."

And he went away, leaving the paper in Don Camillo's hands.

Spiletti came to the rectory a quarter of an hour later.

"Father, was there anything you didn't like in my draft?"

"No, but the trouble is that Thunderer came around here to demand his return game."

"His return game? Nonsense; I'm giving him nothing of the sort. This document is entirely too precious, and I have no intention of relinquishing it."

"What about your promise?"

"Why should we have to keep a promise made to one of that mob which deals exclusively in lies?"

"I see your point. But Thunderer is quite a menace when he's well, and now he's half crazy. If you deprive him of his revenge, he's capable of bumping you off like a fly. And although propaganda is important, it's more important for you to stay alive."

"Let's play the game, then. But what if I lose?"

"You mustn't lose, Spiletti. If you beat Cino Biolchi, then you ought to make mincemeat out of Thunderer."

"The truth is that I didn't beat Cino Biolchi, Father. I didn't win the paper away from him; he gave it to me so as to get rid of Peppone. . . . Look here, Father, why don't you play in my place? I'll say that now the document is yours, and I doubt if Thunderer will come anywhere near you."

Don Camillo was a shark at cards, and so he said laughing:

"If he plays with me, I'll demolish him! And he won't dare say a word. Never fear, Spiletti, we shall win!"

The next day Don Camillo went to see Peppone.

"The document is now in my hands. If your fasting friend wants it back, then I'm his opponent. If he refuses, then it will go on public display."

"What?" said Peppone indignantly. "How can a poor wretch who's had nothing to eat for almost a week stand up to you at a game of cards?"

"You're just as much of a wretch as he is, although you eat a large meal every day. If you like, I'll play with you."

"Good enough!"

"Then it's five thousand liras against the famous paper."

Peppone put a banknote on the table and Don Camillo covered it with the incriminating document. It was an exceedingly fierce game, and Peppone lost it. Don Camillo put the money into his pocket.

"Are you satisfied?" he asked. "Or do you want a return game?"

Peppone put up another five-thousand lira bill. He fought hard but played a miserable game. However, Don Camillo's game was even more miserable, and Peppone won.

"Here's Thunderer's paper, Comrade," said Don Camillo. "I'm satisfied with the money."

Peppone had been present for a whole hour at Thunderer's "Liberation dinner," when Don Camillo appeared upon the scene.

"Thunderer," said the priest, "you lost five thousand liras to Biolchi, didn't you?"

"Yes," the elephant stammered.

"Well, thanks to Divine Providence, here they are. Remember that when the elections come around, and don't vote for God's enemies."

"Yes, of course, that was understood in my vow," sighed the unhappy Thunderer.

Peppone waited for Don Camillo outside the door.

"You're a snake in the grass! You build up the reputation of Divine Providence with my money!"

"Comrade, infinite are the ways of Divine Providence!" sighed Don Camillo, raising his eyes to heaven.

THE BEST MEDICINE

PEOPLE COULDN'T get over the fact that Don Camillo was in such a state over Thunder.

"After all," they said, "a dog's only a dog."

But it's the last straw that breaks the camel's back. And at this time, that was Don Camillo's situation.

The day before the official opening of the shooting season, Thunder went out of the house around noon and failed to return in the evening. He didn't turn up the next day, either, and Don Camillo searched wildly for him until night. When he came home empty-handed he was too miserable to eat supper. "Somebody's stolen him," he thought to himself, "and by this time he's probably in Piedmont or Tuscany." Then all of a sudden he heard the door creak, and there was Thunder. It was obvious from his humble look that he was aware of having done something very bad. He didn't have the nerve to come all the way in, but stood half outside, with only his nose sticking around beyond the door.

"Come in!" shouted Don Camillo, but the dog did not budge. "Thunder, come here!" the priest shouted again.

The order was so definite that Thunder obeyed, coming forward very slowly, with his head hanging low. When he reached Don Camillo's feet, he stopped and waited. This was the last straw. For it was then that Don Camillo discovered that someone had painted Thunder's hindquarters bright red.

Love me, love my dog; if you insult my dog, I am insulted. This is especially true of a sportsman. And in this case, nothing could have been more cowardly. Don Camillo felt a grinding pain deep down inside and had to go and take a breath of fresh air at the open window. There his anger passed away, giving place to melancholy. He leaned over to touch the dog's back and found the paint already dry. Evidently it had been applied the day before and Thunder had been afraid to come home.

"Poor fellow," said Don Camillo. "You were caught just like an innocent puppy."

Then he stopped to think that Thunder wasn't the kind of dog to let strangers get too near him or to fall for the offer of a chunk of meat. Thunder was a thoroughbred, and didn't take to all-comers. He trusted only two people, and one of these was Don Camillo.

This shed more light on the situation, and Don Camillo impulsively decided to clear it up completely. He went out, calling Thunder, and Thunder followed somewhat shamefully after. Peppone was still in his workshop when Don Camillo appeared, like a ghost, before him. He went right on hammering, while Don Camillo went to stand on the far side of the anvil to ask him a question.

"Peppone, have you any idea how Thunder got into this condition?"

Peppone looked over at the dog and shrugged his shoulders.

"How should I know?" he said. "Perhaps he sat down on some bench that was freshly painted."

"That could be," said Don Camillo calmly. "But I have a notion you're mixed up in it, somehow. That's why I came straight here."

Peppone grinned at him.

"I'm a blacksmith and mechanic," he said. "The dry cleaner is on the other side of the square."

"But the fellow who asked me to lend him my dog to go hunting and then painted the dog red because I refused him is right here before me!"

Peppone dropped his hammer and stood up to Don Camillo with his hands on his hips, defiantly:

"Now, exactly what do you mean?"

"That your revenge was abject and unworthy!"

Don Camillo was panting with indignation. He heard Peppone shout something at him but could not catch the words. His head was whirling strangely and he groped for the anvil in order to keep his balance. Peppone eyed him coldly.

"If you've been drinking, you'd better go and sleep it off in the rectory, where it's cooler."

Don Camillo managed to grasp this last sentence and started reeling home, where he arrived without knowing how he had done so. Half an hour later Thunder's incessant barking drew the attention of the sacristan. He noticed that the rectory door was open and an electric light burning inside. And a moment later he cried out in astonishment. Don Camillo lay stretched out on the floor and Thunder was howling beside him. The priest was bundled into an ambulance and taken to a hospital in the city. And the villagers did not go to bed before the ambulance came back and they had some news.

"Nobody knows what's wrong," said the driver. "It seems as if his heart and liver and nervous system were all involved. Then he must have given his head a nasty crack when he fell. All the way to the city he was delirious, raving about how someone had painted his dog red."

"Poor Don Camillo!" the villagers murmured as they went to bed. The next day they found out that the dog really had been touched up and that Don Camillo's raving was by no means as delirious as it had seemed. And although they were still just as sorry that he had been stricken, they found his concern over Thunder exaggerated. "A dog's only a dog," they were saying.

This was because they didn't realize that the last straw can break the camel's back.

Every evening someone brought back the latest news from the city. "He's not at all well. They won't allow anyone to see him." And early every morning Thunder came to Peppone's workshop, lay down in the doorway and fixed his melancholy eyes upon Peppone. He stayed there until eight o'clock, when the square began to fill up with people going about their daily occupations. Peppone paid him very little attention. but after this performance had been repeated for twenty-five days in succession, he lost patience and shouted:

"Can't you let me alone? Your master's ill, that's all. If you want to know more than that, you'll have to go and see him."

The dog did not budge an inch and Peppone still felt

514

those melancholy eyes upon him. At seven o'clock he could not stand it any longer. He washed, put on his best suit, got on his motorcycle and rode away. After he had gone a mile he stopped to see how he was off for petrol. He found the tank full, and proceeded to check the oil and the pressure of the tyres. After this, he scribbled something in a notebook. A few second later Thunder caught up with him, his tongue hanging out with exhaustion, and jumped into the sidecar.

"Devil take you and your master!" grumbled Peppone as he started the engine.

At eight o'clock he arrived in front of the hospital and left Thunder to watch over the machine. But at the door they told him that it was entirely too early for a visit. And when they heard which patient he wanted to see, they told him it was no use waiting. Don Camillo's case was so serious that no visitor could be admitted to his room. Peppone did not insist. He remounted his motorcycle and rode off to the Bishop's Palace. Here, too, he was refused admittance, but finally his persistence and his big hands caused the secretary to relent.

The Bishop, older and tinier and whiter-haired than ever, was walking about his garden, admiring the bright hues of the flowers.

"There's some sort of ruffian outside who says he's Your Grace's personal friend," the secretary explained breathlessly. "Shall I call the police?"

"What's that?" said the Bishop. "Do you hold your Bishop in such low esteem as to think that his personal friends are wanted by the police? Let the fellow in."

A few seconds later, Peppone torpedoed his way into the garden, and from behind a rose bush the old man held him off with the end of his cane.

"Forgive me, Your Grace," stammered Peppone, "but it's a serious matter."

"Speak up, Mr. Mayor. What's wrong?"

"Nothing's wrong with me, Your Grace. It's Don Camillo. For over three weeks . . ."

"I know all about it," the bishop interrupted. "I've been to see him already. Poor Don Camillo!" He sighed.

Peppone twisted his hat between his hands.

"Something's got to be done, Your Grace."

"Only God Almighty can do it," said the Bishop, throwing out his arms in resignation.

But Peppone had an idea of his own.

"There's something you can do, Your Grace. You can say a Mass for his recovery, for instance."

The Bishop looked at Peppone incredulously.

"Your Grace, please try to understand. I'm the one that painted his dog red."

The Bishop did not answer, but walked down the garden path. Just then his secretary came to tell him that lunch was ready.

"No," said the Bishop. "Not just yet. Leave us here alone."

At the far end of the path was the Bishop's private chapel.

"Go down there and ask them for an altar boy," said the Bishop.

Peppone shrugged his shoulders.

"I can serve at the altar. I did it often enough as a boy...."

"A very special Mass, with a very special altar boy," said the Bishop. "Go on in and lock the door behind us. This is something that must remain strictly between ourselves. Or rather, between ourselves and God."

When Peppone left the Bishop's Palace, he found Thunder on guard in the sidecar. He jumped on to the saddle and rode back to the hospital. Again they were unwilling to let him in, but Peppone bullied his way through.

"We can't be responsible for what happens,' the nurses told him. "If he takes a turn for the worse, then you're to blame."

They led him to the second floor of one of the pavilions and left him in front of a closed door.

"Remember, as far as our records are concerned, you made your way in by sheer force."

The room was flooded with light, and as he opened the door, Peppone drew back in alarm at the sight of Don Camillo. Never had he imagined that twenty-five days of illness could lay a man so low. He tiptoed over to the bed. Don Camillo's eyes were closed, and he seemed to be dead, but when he opened them he was very much alive.

"Have you come to claim an inheritance?" he said in a thin voice. "I have nothing to leave you but Thunder.... Every time you see that red behind of his, you can think of me...."

"The red's almost all gone now," said Peppone, in a low voice with his head hanging. "I've scrubbed him with turpentine every day."

516

"Well, then, you see I was right to bring him to you rather than to the dry cleaner," said Don Camillo with a wan smile.

"Forget about that. . . . Thunder's downstairs. He wanted to come and see you, but they won't let him in. . . ."

"Funny people they are," sighed Don Camillo. "They let you in, and you're much more of a dog than he."

Peppone nodded assent.

"Sounds to me as if you were getting better. You're in high spirits, that much is certain."

"Soon they'll be so high that they'll carry me up into the blue beyond. I'm done for; my strength is all gone. I'm not even strong enough to be angry at you."

Just then a nurse came in with a cup of tea.

"Thank you," said Don Camillo, "but I'm not hungry."

"This is something to drink."

"I'm not thirsty, either."

"You really must make an effort to get something down."

Don Camillo sipped at the cup of tea. Once the nurse was out of the room he made a face.

"Soups and slops, for twenty-five days, without interruption. I'm begining to feel as if I were a bird. . . ." And he looked down at his gaunt, white hands. "It's no use offering to match fists with you now."

"Don't let yourself worry," said Peppone, lowering his head.

Don Camillo slowly closed his eyes and seemed to fall asleep. Peppone waited for a few seconds and then started to go away, but Don Camillo reached out a hand to touch his arm.

"Peppone," he whispered, "are you a dastardly coward or an honest man?"

"I'm an honest man," Peppone replied.

Don Camillo motioned to him to lower his head and whispered something into his ear. He must have said something very terrible, because Peppone drew himself up abruptly, exclaiming:

"Father! That would be a crime!"

Don Camillo looked into his eyes.

"Are you going to let me down?" he panted.

"I'm not letting anybody down," said Peppone. "Is it a request or an order?"

"An order!" murmured Don Camillo.

"Let your will be done!" Peppone whispered as he left the room.

The maximum speed of Peppone's motorcycle was fifty-five miles an hour, but on this occasion it made seventy. And on the way back it didn't roll over the ground, it positively flew. At three o'clock in the afternoon, Peppone was back at the hospital. Smilzo was with him, and the attendants made an attempt to block the two of them at the door.

"It's a serious matter," explained Peppone. "It's concerned with an inheritance. That's why I brought a notary along."

When they came to Don Camillo's door, Peppone said, "You stay out here and don't let anyone in. You can say that he's making his confession."

Don Camillo seemed to be asleep but he was only dozing and quickly opened his eyes.

"Well then?" he asked anxiously.

"Everything's just as you wanted it," answered Peppone, "but I still say it's a crime."

"Are you afraid?"

"No."

Peppone proceeded to take a parcel out from under his jacket and unwrap it. He put the contents on the bedside table and then pulled Don Camillo into a sitting position, with the pillows at his back. He spread a napkin over the priest's lap and moved the contents of the parcel on to it: a loaf of fresh bread and a plate of sliced salame. Then he uncorked the bottle of red Lambrusco wine. The sick man ate and drank deliberately, not in order to prolong any gluttonous enjoyment but simply to get the full savour of his native earth. For you must realize that Lambrusco is no ordinary wine but something unique and particular to that section of the river valley. Every mouthful made him homesick for the river and the misty sky above it, the mooing of the cattle in their stalls, the distant thumping of tractors and the wail of threshing machines in the poplar-bordered fields. All these seemed now to belong to another world, from which he had been taken away by a succession of malevolent medicines and insipid soups. When he had finished his meal he said to Peppone:

"Half a cigar!"

Peppone looked fearfully at Don Camillo, as if he might stiffen and die before him.

"No, not a cigar!"

Eventually he had to give in, but after a few puffs Don Camillo let the cigar drop to the floor and fell into a deep sleep.

Three days later Don Camillo left the hospital, but he did not return to the village for three months, because he wanted to be in perfect health for his arrival.

Thunder gave him a wildly enthusiastic welcome, turning around in circles and chasing his tail in order that Don Camillo might see that his hindquarters were in perfect condition. Peppone, who happened to be passing in front of the rectory, was attracted by Thunder's barking and asked Don Camillo to note that there was not a trace of red left upon him.

"Quite so," said Don Camillo. "He's all right. Now to get the red off the rest of you dogs."

"You're yourself again, all right," mumbled Peppone. "Almost too much so, in my opinion."

ONE MEETING AFTER ANOTHER

"Lord," Don Camillo said to the Christ over the altar, "this is our great day!"

Christ was obviously surprised.

"What do you mean, Don Camillo?"

"Lord, it's written in letters three inches high on posters plastered all over the countryside. The Honourable Betio is making a speech in the village square this afternoon."

"And who might the Honourable Betio be?"

"Lord, he's one of the big shots of our party."

Christ seemed even more surprised than before. "Are we enrolled in a party? Since when, may I ask?"

Don Camillo smiled and shook his head.

"Lord, I didn't express myself clearly. By 'our party,' I meant the party which supports us."

Christ sighed.

"It's all very sad, Don Camillo. To think that we have a party to help us keep the universe in order, and we didn't even know it! We're not as omniscient as we used to be. God Almighty is slipping. . . ."

Don Camillo lowered his head in humiliation.

"Lord, I failed utterly to put across what was in my mind. When I said 'our party' I meant the party of all those good Christians that rally around the Church and seek to defend it against the forces of the anti-Christ. Of course, these good Christians aren't so presumptuous as to claim that they help God run the universe."

Christ smiled.

"Don't worry, Don Camillo. I can read your heart like an open book, and I shan't judge you merely by what you say. Just tell Me this: is this party of good Christians a large one? How many people belong?"

Don Camillo replied that the party was quite strong and gave the approximate number of its members.

"Ah!" Christ sighed. "Unfortunately there aren't nearly as many good Christians as there are bad ones!"

Don Camillo told Him that beside the enrolled party members there were a lot of sympathizers. He mentioned more figures.

"But there aren't so many of them, either," Christ exclaimed. "Good, honest people are a minority compared to the number of bad, dishonest people that belong to other parties or sympathize with them. Don Camillo, you've given Me very sad news! I thought there were a great many more good people than that. But let's make the best of it. The idea of gathering all good people into one group makes our job a comparatively simple one. Those who are actually enrolled in the good party will go straight to Heaven, the sympathizers to Purgatory and all the rest can be bundled off to Hell. Please oblige Me with the exact figures."

Don Camillo threw out his arms helplessly.

"Lord, punish me! I've said too many stupid things."

"No," Christ answered. "I'm concerned not with your words but with your intentions. Your heart's in the right place, even if your tongue does trick you. Watch that tongue of yours, Don Camillo; it has a way of getting you into trouble."

Don Camillo thanked Christ for his indulgence, and feeling somewhat reassured he went out into the village. Everything was going the way it should. Busloads of people were arriving to hear the speech and their numbers were rapidly filling the square.

"Efficiency, that's what did it," someone said behind Don Camillo.

Don Camillo turned around and found just the person he was expecting, that is, Peppone, flanked by Smilzo, Brusco and three or four other members of his general staff.

"Were you speaking to me, Mr. Mayor?" asked Don Camillo.

"No sir," Peppone said with a smile. "I was speaking to Smilzo. I was saying that the success of the meeting is due to the efficiency of the postal system. If it weren't for that the pink notification cards wouldn't produce such a remarkable result."

Don Camillo took the cigar butt out of his mouth and flicked the ashes away with his little finger.

"Take it from me, Mr. Mayor," he said heartily, "an efficient postal service isn't the whole story. Sometimes an organization can send out thousands of cards and yet get no more than two hundred and twenty-seven people together."

Peppone gritted his teeth. The last meeting he had summoned, the "Peace Assembly," had been a complete flop, with no more than two hundred and twenty-seven people present.

"I don't agree with you," he retorted, "on the matter of the relationship between the number of notices sent out and the number of people actually in attendance. You can count those that turn up for the meeting, but how can you know how many notices were distributed?"

"That's easy," said Don Camillo, pulling a notebook out of his cassock: "two thousand nine hundred and fifty-seven!"

Peppone turned indignantly to his henchmen.

"There you are!" he shouted. "See what's become of the privacy of the mails!"

"Thanks for bearing out the exactness of my calculations!" said Don Camillo slyly.

"Exactness, my eye!" shouted Peppone. "We sent out exactly two hundred and thirty!"

Don Camillo put the notebook back in his cassock.

"Good! That shows the privacy of the mails is inviolate and the anonymous information given me was all wrong. As far as we're concerned, there's nothing to hide. We sent out two thousand four hundred and seven postcards, exactly."

"Six thousand nine hundred and forty-three!" shouted Peppone.

Don Camillo looked at him with a preoccupied air.

"I can draw only one of two conclusions: either the privacy of the mails has been violated or else you're telling a lie."

Peppone paled. He had fallen into the trap like a perfect simpleton.

"I heard mention of some such figure," he muttered. "I'm only telling you what people say."

"Just as I thought," said Don Camillo triumphantly. "The number of notices sent out is two thousand four hundred and seven, as I was saying a short time ago. I'm very happy to see that about three times as many people have chosen to come. And they're not all here yet."

Peppone turned around to go away, but Don Camillo called him back to look at a mimeographed sheet.

"Here's something that just happened to fall into my hands," he explained. "This is a copy of the notice of today's meeting. Since your notice wasn't very effective, I'll let you copy this one. I have an idea that the secret of success is in the letterhead. If you put 'Christian Democrat' in the place of 'Communist Party,' you might have better luck."

Peppone let Don Camillo speak without opening his mouth to reply, but his general staff had to lay hold of him and drag him away.

The square was crowded to capacity, and when the Honourable Betio appeared in the grandstand, he was greeted by a thunderous ovation. He began by speaking of the general political situation and the platforms of the various parties. When it came to the royalists, he pulled out all the stops:

"Speaking of the royalists, who want to overturn our democratic republic and restore a monarchy which in its time betrayed us, let them take note that the sovereign people . . ."

But here he was interrupted by the loud notes of the "Royal March." He tried to protest against this seditious act, but the music rang out from somewhere overhead, all the louder. Meanwhile the vastly annoyed public was aroused to commotion. Some people started to sing the republican song, "Brothers of Italy," while others embarked upon the Christian Democrat party anthem. The resulting confusion made it difficult to identify the place from which the disturbance had come. Actually it came from the fourth-storey window of the very house against which the grandstand was erected, and therefore was a real stab in the back of the republic. At least, so the Honourable Betio defined it.

Once the window was identified, a carabinieri sergeant ran up to locate the door of the apartment to which it belonged. He found it easily enough, but it was so strong and securely locked that he could not smoke out the offender and decided to call upon the blacksmith to help him. He turned around and found the blacksmith at his elbow. Peppone had availed himself of his office of mayor to come through the barrier which the sergeant had hastily thrown up at the downstairs door in order to prevent mob justice from taking over a governmental function. Now he stood on the landing, with Smilzo at his side.

"For heaven's sake, open that door!" the sergeant exclaimed excitedly.

"In my capacity as mayor or in my capacity as blacksmith?" asked Peppone.

"As blacksmith," the sergeant answered promptly.

While the criminal behind the armoured door went merrily on playing a record of the "Royal March," Smilzo dashed off to fetch the proper tools from Peppone's workshop. Because of the crowd in the square, it took him some time to get there, but he finally made it. When he came back, Peppone peeled off his jacket and hesitantly fingered the tools.

"Why don't you get to work?" the sergeant asked him.

"The blacksmith in me is arguing a point with the mayor," said Peppone, "and they can't seem to reach an agreement."

"Mr. Mayor," the sergeant muttered, "tell the blacksmith that if he doesn't hurry he'll find himself in trouble with the police."

Peppone set to work at taking the door off its hinges, while the record went right on playing the provocative tune. At last, when the door was unhinged, the sergeant made his way in. But in the presence of the disturber his anger faded to irritation. For Colonel Mavelli, an eighty-year-old retired army officer, had nothing of a dangerous rebel about him.

"Stop that gramophone, and come along with me," the sergeant ordered.

The old man obeyed, but when he had removed the record he broke it over one knee, as if it were a sword, and consigned it to his captor.

"Sergeant," he said, in a voice that seemed to come straight from the front lines, "do your duty!"

Before this unexpected demonstration of nineteenth-century heroics, the sergeant was so embarrassed that he thought it was his duty to draw himself to attention. And he was not altogether mistaken. Finally, however, he remembered the circumstances and recovered his aplomb sufficiently to tell the colonel to hold himself at the disposal of the law. And Peppone, before going downstairs, managed to whisper into the rebel's ear:

"As mayor, I told the blacksmith he'd better open your

door if he didn't want to get in trouble with the police. Now, as an ordinary citizen, I shall request the mayor to order the blacksmith to repair it."

Don Camillo was thoroughly indignant.

"Lord," he said to the Christ over the altar, "that old fool of a Monarchist ruined a magnificent meeting. I can't see where he got the idea of debating a point by means of a gramophone record."

"I'm sure I don't know," Christ answered. "Unless he got it from someone I know who once rang the church bells when the Red commissar was speaking and thereby wrecked the rally."

Don Camillo bowed his head and walked back through the sacristy.

"For they have sown the wind, and they shall reap the whirlwind," Christ called after him.

Naturally enough, Peppone wanted his revenge, and he tried to work it out so as to kill two birds with one stone. He organized a mammoth meeting, to be addressed by an important speaker who had previously come to celebrate the Red victory in the last local election. It was upon this occasion that Don Camillo had interrupted the speech by ringing the church bells.

"I want the meeting to be of historical proportions," Peppone told his henchmen. "I want to crush the enemy to a pulp."

He worked over it for a month, until finally the great day came. The speech was scheduled for four o'clock in the afternoon, but the square was teeming by three. At half-past three Don Camillo was striding nervously up and down the empty church. Finally he stopped and looked up at the altar.

"Lord," he said, "don't You think I might go and look out of the window?"

"Of course," Christ answered, "but as far as I know, the rose window above the main door of the church is the only one with a view over the square."

"There is one other," said Don Camillo, "but it's up in the bell tower."

"I wouldn't go up there," said Christ. "For one thing, it's very draughty."

"Oh, I've plenty of warm clothes on," said Don Camillo reassuringly.

"I appreciate the fact, Don Camillo, but I'd be sorry to see you repeat what you did last time and ring the bells in the middle of the speech."

Don Camillo spread out his arms in rueful assent.

"*Errare humanum est, diabolicum perseverare,*" he admitted.

"Let's hope you don't forget that on your way up the stairs."

"My memory's good enough," said Don Camillo.

He was panting when he arrived at the top of the tower and it was only natural that he should fan himself with his big white handkerchief. And it was equally natural that when Peppone saw the handkerchief from the grandstand below he should be stricken with apprehension.

"He's up there again, just as he was the time before," the speaker from the city whispered into his ear. "I trust you've taken measures to prevent a repetition of the bell-ringing."

"Don't worry, Comrade," said Peppone. "Two husky boys are hiding on the next-to-last landing, just below the bells. If he tries to start anything, I don't think he'll get very far."

Everyone in the square was aware of Don Camillo's presence, and nervousness spread through the crowd. When it was time to begin, Peppone made a welcoming speech, but the proximity of Don Camillo caused him to stutter, and when he passed the microphone to his guest, he was swimming in perspiration.

"Comrades!" said the speaker. "This is the second time I have addressed you here, and once more I see the black buzzards of Reaction perched in their nests, ready to swoop down and cloud the blue sky, with the beating of their lugubrious wings."

Peppone looked upward, but the black buzzard was perfectly quiet, and only his huge white handkerchief was stirring.

"Comrades!" went on the speaker, emboldened by the calm of his adversary, "to-day skies everywhere are darkened by black buzzards, and the dove of peace has a hard time surviving . . ."

The crowd looked upward, too, but neither buzzards nor doves were to be seen. Instead, an aeroplane flew over the scene, spiralling lower and lower and releasing tiny parachutes, which fluttered down among the crowd. The crowd became restless, because everyone wanted to grab one of them. And the restlessness grew when it was discovered that attached to every parachute were smoked sausages, tins of fruit and meat, cigarettes and chocolate bars. Except for the sausage and cigarettes, these things were all from America. The speaker proceeded at once to decry such provocatory and offensive propaganda, but he was interrupted by another visit from the aeroplane, whose second batch of parachutes met with even more acclaim than the first. A moment later the aeroplane came back a third time, but failed to calculate distances correctly, with the result that three-quarters of the parachutes fell on to the street leading from the square into the country. People started to rush down this street, and on the fourth and fifth round (it turned out that two planes were involved), the parachutes were dropped even farther from the centre of the village. Now it was plain that the purpose of the whole manoeuvre was to draw the crowd away from the meeting. And the manoeuvre was eminently successful, for at a certain point no one remained in the square except Peppone and the visiting speaker. The surrounding houses, too, were left empty, while their occupants joined the wild chase into the surrounding fields. Peppone was foaming at the mouth with rage; he shook his fist and when he was able to speak he shouted through the microphone at the placid Don Camillo:

"This is political banditry! Come on down, if you dare, you big black buzzard!"

Don Camillo came as fast as if he had flown rather than walked down the stairs and stood defiantly in front of the grandstand.

"Come down, yourself!" he shouted to Peppone.

But the visiting speaker tugged at Peppone's shoulder.

"Don't do it, Comrade. He's only trying to make trouble. I order you not to go down."

Peppone gritted his teeth.

"Come up here, if you're so brave!" he shouted, while the Party satrap tried to shut his mouth.

Don Camillo rolled up his sleeves and mounted the grandstand. By now, both men were beside themselves, and they leaped at one another, in spite of the efforts of the visitor, who was caught between them. Peppone got in the first blow, which landed on the left side of the speaker's head. And Don Camillo countered with a swat which hit it on the right. The poor man collapsed like a rag doll on the grandstand floor. Peppone and Don Camillo stared at one another. Then Don Camillo threw out his arms and said:

"There you are! Every time this fellow comes out here from the city, he seems to suffer a ringing defeat!"

He walked slowly back to his base of operations and then tried to slip noiselessly by the main altar. But Christ called him back.

"Where are you going, Don Camillo?"

"Lord," Don Camillo replied. "I didn't have any lunch, and now I'm going to bed without any supper. That way, I shan't be able to sleep a wink, and I'll have plenty of time to think over my mistakes!"

HAMMERING IT IN

AFTER THE incident on the grandstand, the atmosphere grew increasingly heated. The political truce was over and the Reds were on the warpath again. But Don Camillo seemed serene.

Only when he read in the bulletin nailed to the wall of the People's Palace Peppone's comment on the Pope's last speech did he lose patience and set forth in plain terms from the pulpit exactly what he thought of Peppone and his irresponsible band.

He must have thought and said plenty, because as soon as Peppone was told of the contents of the sermon he marched upon the rectory with the avowed intent of "bumping off that cursed priest," so as to settle once and for all the question between them.

But he found no priest to be "bumped off" in the rectory, for the simple reason that Don Camillo was in the church, in fact standing in the pulpit from whence he had thundered at Peppone a short time before. He was equipped with a hammer and chisel and intent on boring a hole in the stone column which supported the pulpit. In the course of his vehement sermon he had heard the old wood of the pulpit creak ominously, and now he was making place for a solid iron rod which was to run from the supporting column to the upper edge of the pulpit and eliminate any chance of a collapse.

Peppone, having received no answer to his knock at the rectory door, was just about to return to his home base, when the sound of hammering from inside the church caused him to change his mind. The main door of the church was closed and so was the smaller one leading through the tower, but the window of the Chapel of Saint Anthony was open. Peppone made a small pile of bricks and stones below it and stood on top of this to look through. The pulpit was directly across the nave from where he was standing and at once he recognized the nocturnal worker. His anger redoubled in intensity.

"Father, are you pulling the church down?"

Don Camillo looked up with a start and in the light of the candle burning before the statue of Saint Anthony he saw the face of Peppone.

"Not I," he answered. "Other people make that their business, as well you know. But it's no use. The foundation is solid."

"I wouldn't be so sure of that," said Peppone. "Solid as it may be, it isn't strong enough to protect the deceivers who hide behind it in order to insult honest men."

"Quite right," Don Camillo replied. "There's no salvation for the deceivers who insult honest men. Only here there's no such deceiver."

"You're here, aren't you?" Peppone shouted. "And you're a hundred deceivers rolled into one."

Don Camillo clenched his teeth and kept his self-control. But once Peppone had started, there was no limit to what he would say.

"You're a coward and a liar!" he shouted.

Don Camillo could contain himself no longer, and hurled the hammer at the chapel window. His aim was terrifyingly exact, but God willed that a gust of wind should cause a hanging lamp to swing in such a way as to deflect the hammer from its course and send it into the wall, a foot from its destination. Peppone disappeared, leaving Don Camillo in the pulpit, with his nerves strained to the breaking-point. Finally he shook himself and went to confide in the crucified Christ over the main altar.

"Lord," he said breathlessly, "did You see that? He provoked and insulted me. It wasn't my fault."

Christ made no answer.

"Lord," Don Camillo continued. "He insulted me right here in the church."

Still Christ was silent.

Don Camillo got up and paced anxiously to and fro. Every

now and then he turned around in discomfort, because he felt two eyes staring at him. He went to make sure that both doors to the church were locked fast; then he looked among the pillars and in the confessionals. No one was to be found, and yet Don Camillo felt sure that someone in the church was watching. He wiped the perspiration off his cheeks.

"Lord, help me," he murmured. "Someone's staring at me. I can't see him, but someone's here; I can feel his eyes. . . ."

He wheeled around, because he thought he could feel the stranger breathing down his neck. There was nothing but empty semi-darkness around him, but he did not feel the least bit reassured. He opened the gate of the chancel and went beyond the rail to the steps of the altar.

"Lord!" he cried out. "I am afraid. Protect me!"

Then, turning his back on the altar, he looked slowly around. All at once he jumped.

"The eyes!"

The stranger's eyes lurked in the Chapel of Saint Anthony Abbot. It was from there that they were staring at him. Never in his life had he seen two eyes like these. The blood froze in his veins and then rushed hot and tumultuous through them again as he clenched his fists and swept forward. When he came to the chapel, his fists were thrust out ready to grab the intruder. He went one, two, three steps farther, and when he thought the stranger must be within his grasp he rushed at him. But his nails only scratched the walls, and the eyes were still staring.

Don Camillo took the lighted candle from the altar and held it near to the staring eyes. Really, there was nothing so mysterious about it. The hammer which Divine Providence had mercifully deflected against the wall had knocked down a big piece of plaster. And underneath this there was a fresco, which some priest of times gone by had covered over when he decided to pierce a window.

Don Camillo proceeded to scrape off more pieces of plaster and thus to enlarge his vision of the past. Finally he uncovered the brown face and mocking smile of a devil. Was it an ingenuous figure from Hell or a symbol of temptation? This was no time for research; Don Camillo was interested above all in the staring eyes. His foot brushed against an object on the floor, and stooping down he found at the devil's feet the ill-starred hammer. Just then the clock in the tower struck ten.

"It's late," Don Camillo reflected. And he added: "But it's never too soon for an act of humility."

He walked rapidly through the darkness. Most of the village houses had gone to sleep but there was still a light in the workshop of Peppone. Don Camillo groped for the catch of the iron grille. The shutters were open and he could hear Peppone breathe heavily as he hammered out a red-hot iron bar.

"I'm sorry," said Don Camillo.

Peppone stared, but quickly took hold of himself and continued to hammer without lifting his head.

"You took me by surprise," Don Camillo went on. "I was nervous. . . . When I realized what I had done, the hammer was already out of my hands."

"You must be slow-witted, Father, if you don't wake up to your misdeeds until after you've committed them."

"There's some merit in admitting a mistake," said Don Camillo cautiously. "That's the sign of an honest man. When a man won't admit that he was wrong, then he's dishonest."

Peppone was still angry and went on pounding the iron, which had by now lost its red glow.

"Are we going to begin all over?" he roared.

"No," said Don Camillo. "I came to put an end to it. That's why I began by asking you to excuse the unforgivable gesture I made against you."

"You're still a coward and a liar. And I'll put all those hypocritical excuses of yours right here!" And Peppone slapped the base of his spine.

"Quite right!" said Don Camillo. "That's where stupid fellows like you keep everything sacred."

Peppone couldn't stomach it, and the hammer flew out of his hand. It was aimed with diabolical accuracy at Don Camillo's head, but God willed that it strike one of the narrow bars of the grille. The bar was bent, and the hammer fell on to the workshop floor. Don Camillo stared in amazement at the bent bar and as soon as he could move, he set off at full speed for home and arrived, all choked up, at the foot of the altar.

"Lord," he said, kneeling before the crucified Christ, "now we're even; a hammer for a hammer."

"One stupidity plus another stupidity makes two stupidities," Christ answered.

But this simple addition was too much for Don Camillo, who by now had a raging fever.

"Lord," he stammered, "I'm just a poor, lone priest, and I can't take it!"

After this, Don Camillo spent one of the worst nights of his life, pursued by a nightmare of hammers whistling out of his hand and then whistling back at him. The devil with the fearful eyes had emerged from the chapel wall, with a whole crowd of other devils in his train, and one of these rode astride the handle of every ricocheting hammer. He dodged them as well as he could, until weariness overcame him and they pounded his head with a monotonous "bang . . . bang . . . bang . . ." that finally sent him off to sleep.

Only at six o'clock in the morning did the banging cease, simply because at that hour Don Camillo woke up. His head was still so fuzzy that he hardly knew what he was doing and did not recover his self-possession until he stood saying Mass at the altar. The celebration of this Mass required truly epical courage, and God seemed to appreciate his effort, for he rewarded him by giving him the strength to stand on his two feet. When he had taken off his vestments, after Mass, Don Camillo went to look at the Chapel of Saint Anthony. The maleficent eyes were still there and the cursed hammer lay in a pile of plaster on the floor below.

"Aha!" said a voice behind him. "The criminal is drawn back to the scene of his crime!"

Don Camillo wheeled around and of course found himself looking into the eyes of Peppone.

"Are we beginning again?" asked the priest wearily.

Peppone shook his head and slumped on to a bench. His eyes were bleary and his hair glued to his forehead, and he was breathing heavily.

"I can't stand it any longer," he said. "Fix things whatever way you like."

Don Camillo suddenly realized that Peppone was laboriously handing him something wrapped up in a newspaper. When he took the object into his hands, it seemed to weigh a ton. He unwrapped it and discovered an elaborate wrought-iron frame which enclosed, instead of a commonplace picture, a copper sheet, and attached to it with brass wire an ordinary hammer. On the copper sheet were engraved the words:

To Saint Anthony for making me miss

533

"Lord," Don Camillo said the next day, when he was feeling stronger and more hopeful. "Thank You for Your Help."

"Thank Saint Anthony," Christ answered; "he's the protector of dumb animals."

Don Camillo looked up anxiously.

"Is that how you judge me, Lord, at this moment?" he asked.

"At this moment, no. But it was the unreasonable animal in you that threw the hammer. And Saint Anthony protected that animal."

Don Camillo bowed his head.

"But I wasn't the only one, Lord," he stammered. "Peppone . . ."

"That doesn't matter, Don Camillo. One horse plus one horse makes two horses."

Don Camillo checked the count with his fingers.

"Lord, that's not correct, because I'm a jackass."

And he said it so very earnestly that the Lord was moved to forgive him.

DON CAMILLO RETURNS

In spite of help from Saint Anthony, Don Camillo found himself increasingly provoked by the Reds as the pre-election campaigns got under way. Peppone managed to create a number of incidents in the centre of which a certain party found himself with fists flying. These incidents were deemed "unfortunate" by the bishop who sent Don Camillo (and it was not the first time) for a period to an isolated village in the mountains. There the air was cooler. Don Camillo's days were so monotonous that it was hardly worth while tearing the leaves off the calendar, for they were perfect blanks, bare of any event worth recording.

"Lord," Don Camillo complained to the Crucified Christ from the altar, "this will drive me mad! Nothing ever happens!"

"I don't understand you, Don Camillo," Christ answered. "Every day the sun rises and sets, every night you see billions of stars wheeling their way overhead, and all the while grass grows and one season succeeds another. Aren't these the most important of all happenings?"

"Forgive my stupidity, Lord," said Don Camillo, hanging his head, "I'm only a poor priest from the plains."

But the next day he repeated the same complaint. There was an ache deep down inside him, which grew every day, and was indeed the only thing to impinge upon his attention. Meanwhile, down in the little world of the river valley, nothing very remarkable happened either. Except for a multitude of petty things, which would have distressed Don Camillo had he known anything about them.

The young priest sent to hold the fort during Don Camillo's political convalescence was a splendid fellow. In spite of his theoretical outlook and his polished big-city vocabulary, he did wonders in adapting himself to circumstances and made a mighty effort not to rub the villagers the wrong way. People of every political colour responded to his courtesy and goodwill and flocked to church in large numbers, but with this gesture they drew the line. No one, for instance, went to confession. "Don't worry, Father," they explained. "It's just that we're so used to Don Camillo. We'll catch up when he returns." And weddings were put off in the same way. It seemed as if even birth and death were engaged in a conspiracy, for since Don Camillo's departure no one had either come into the little world or gone out of it. Things went on like this for months, until finally a woman came to the rectory one day to say that old man Tirelli was dying. The young priest mounted his bicycle and hastened to the bedside.

Old Tirelli had lived so many years that even a bank teller would have tired of counting them and he himself had lost track of them long ago. He had always been hale and hearty, that is until the atomic blast upset climatic conditions and a mammoth attack of pneumonia laid him low. Before entering his bedroom, the young priest questioned the doctor, who was just coming away.

"Is it serious?" he asked.

"Technically speaking he should be dead. It's an affront to medical science that he should still be breathing."

The priest went in, sat down by the bed and began to pray. Just then the old man opened his eyes and gave him a long stare.

"Thanks," he sighed, "but I'll wait."

The priest felt perspiration break out on his forehead.

"While God gives you time, you'd better put your conscience in order," he advised.

"I know," said the old man, "but I'll wait for his return."

The priest couldn't bear to argue with a dying man, so he went to talk to the members of his family, in the next room. They knew the seriousness of his condition and how miraculous it was that he should still be alive. It was up to them to persuade him to make his confession. They went to the bedside and informed the old man of the doctor's verdict, but although he respected the doctor and was in full possession of his usual common sense, he only answered:

"Yes, I know it's a serious matter. There's not a moment to be lost. Go and call Don Camillo, because I want to leave this world with my conscience clear."

They told him that, first of all, Don Camillo could not abandon his new parish in order to give one sick man his blessing, and second, it would be a matter of hours to fetch him from so far away. And this was a question of minutes. The old man saw the point of these objections.

"Quite right," he said: "we must cut down the time. Put me in a car and take me to him."

"Look here, Tirelli," said the doctor, who had overheard the parley from the next room, "if you hold my opinion in any esteem, listen to me. This is utter madness. You wouldn't last more than a mile. And surely you don't want to die like a dog, on the road. Stay in your bed and take advantage of this borrowed time to set your conscience at rest. God is the same down here in the plains as up there in the mountains and this young man is just as much of a priest as Don Camillo."

"I know," murmured Tirelli, "but I can't be unfair to Don Camillo. Surely the young priest understands. Let him come along, and if I give way during the trip, I'll make my confession to him. Let's hurry."

The old man was still alive and hence in his own house he was the master. They called an ambulance and loaded him into it, with the priest at his side. His son and the youngest of his grandchildren followed after on a motorcycle. The ambulance went as speedily as the power of its four cylinders would allow, and every now and then the old man exclaimed:

"Faster! Faster! I'm racing against time."

When the car reached the mule track leading up to Monterana, the old man was still alive. His son and grandson pulled out the stretcher and proceeded to carry it up the mountain. The old man was only a sack of bones, some nerve and an inordinate amount of obstinacy, and so the weight was not too much for their shoulders. The priest followed after, and in this way they walked for two hours, until the village and its church were no more than two hundred yards away. The old man's eyes were shut, but he saw them just the same.

"Thank you, Father," he whispered to his escort. "You'll receive some compensation for all the trouble I've caused you."

The young priest blushed, and leaped like a goat back down the mountain.

Don Camillo sat smoking his usual cigar butt in front of the hut which bore the name of rectory. At the sight of the stretcher borne on the two Tirellis' shoulders, his mouth dropped open.

"He insisted that we bring him here," explained the son, "in order that you might hear his confession."

Don Camillo lifted up the old man and all his covers, carried him into the house and laid him gently on the bed.

"What shall we do?" asked the old man's son, peering through the window. Don Camillo motioned to him to go away and then sat down beside his father. The old man seemed to be in a stupor, but he was aroused by Don Camillo's prayers.

"I couldn't be unfair to you," he murmured.

"Now you're being unfair to God," Don Camillo protested. "Priests are ministers of God, not shopkeepers. The confession is what matters, not the confessor; that's why the priest stays behind a grating which serves to hide his face. When you make your confession you don't tell your life-story to one priest or another; you speak to God. . . . What if you had died on the way?"

"I had your substitute along with me," murmured old Tirelli, "and I shouldn't really have minded unburdening my conscience to him. When a man's spent his life at hard labour, he hasn't much time left for sin. . . . The fact is that I wanted to say good-bye and ask you to accompany my body to the grave, wherever you may be. When you have a send-off from Don Camillo, you're sure of a safe arrival."

After this, he confessed his sins, and as might have been expected they were so trivial that he received an immediate absolution and blessing.

"Don Camillo," the old man said at the end, "do you mind if I don't die right away?" And he was quite serious about it.

"Suit yourself," said Don Camillo, "if you live two thousand years longer, you won't disturb me."

"Thank you," the old man sighed.

It was a fine day, with a warm sun and a blue, blue sky.

Don Camillo threw open the window and went out, leaving the old man asleep with a smile on his face.

"Lord," Don Camillo said to Christ, "something happened today that I can't understand."

"Don't torment yourself about it," Christ answered. "There are things which don't require understanding. And don't go forgetting that old man. He may need you."

"He needs You rather than me!" exclaimed Don Camillo.

"Aren't you content with the fact that he came so far in safety?"

"I'm always content with what God gives me. If He holds out His finger, I don't grab His hand. . . . And yet often I wish I could."

Don Camillo remembered that the old man's son and grandson were waiting outside and went to speak to them.

"He's made his peace with God and is sleeping," he explained. "Do whatever you think best."

"The miracle's done now," said the grandson; "there's no use expecting another. I'll go down the mountain and tell the ambulance to wait. We'll carry him back and bury him at home." Before Don Camillo could say that the old man had expressed a wish to be buried in this his new parish, the boy's father put in:

"Go down, if you like, but tell the ambulance to go away. I'll come after you and we'll go home together."

The grandson ran off, and the son turned to Don Camillo:

"We'll leave everything up to you," he said.

Don Camillo spent the night near old Tirelli. When he had to go and say Mass the next morning he called the old woman that took care of the house to replace him. After Mass he rested for a while and then, having assured himself that the old man was still alive, he went to a house near the public fountain, where he had to take something to a boy that had broken his leg. On the way back he heard someone calling him from a second-storey window. Looking up he saw a face which he was so unwilling to see that at first he actually didn't recognize it. But finally he called up to its smiling owner:

"What on earth are you doing here?"

Beside the girl's face popped up that of a sullen youth.

"We're here for a holiday," he said. "Must we have your permission?"

"Watch your tongue, young man," said Don Camillo. "If

539

you've come here to spread propaganda, I'm warning you that the place isn't healthy."

The young man cursed and withdrew his head, but the girl went on smiling.

"We'll be coming to see you," she said.

"All right, but don't come without an invitation," said Don Camillo as he went on. And he added, under his breath: "What can those two savages be up to? Who knows what trouble they're in now?"

The trouble was a sizable one, and the direct consequence of an episode in which this same pair—Mariolino della Bruciata and Gina Filotti—had already involved Don Camillo. Their courtship had been a stormy one, their families disagreed violently on political matters and it had taken all Don Camillo's persuasiveness to get them to agree to the wedding. After some months of marriage it was Gina and Mariolino who disagreed violently.

"In my opinion it's going to be a boy, and I'm glad of it, because I know you want a girl," said Gina.

"I'm positive it will be a girl, in spite of the fact that you and that family of yours all want a boy," he retorted.

"Of course. Girls take after their fathers and boys after their mothers," she exclaimed, "and I'd hate to see a girl with a character like that of the men of your family. You Bolshevik criminal! I'm going home to my mother!"

"Then good-bye for good; I'm going back to my father. Living with a reactionary's daughter is too much for me."

The logical corollary to these violent propositions was that in the absence of both of them, their baby would be left quite alone. And they made up over this discovery.

A few weeks later they were faced by another grave problem.

"We've got to think of a name," Gina declared. "Boy or girl, we must have a name ready."

The names suggested by Mariolino were all tendentious because they started with Lenina and ended with La Pasionaria. While Gina's choice ranged from Pius to Alcide. Finally they came together on Alberto and Albertina.

"And how's it to be baptized?" groaned Gina.

"It's not to be baptized at all," answered Mariolino. "But if it is, the way to do it is to take it to church and get it over with."

"To church? But Don Camillo's not there any longer!"

"That's like saying you'd rather be eaten by a lion called Leo than a lion called Cleo," Mariolino said sarcastically. "One priest's as bad as another!"

Gina started to take up the cudgels on behalf of the clergy, but all of a sudden she grew pale and sank into a chair.

"Take it easy, Gina," said her husband gently. "You keep calm and so will I."

"When I think that I married a godless individual like yourself, it's almost more than I can bear. Poor little baby boy, I'll defend you from your father's intemperance!"

"Poor baby girl," sighed Mariolino. "If I weren't here to save you from your mother's clutches ..."

They went on this way until late that night, when Gina interposed:

"After all that Don Camillo's done for us, we can't let anyone else baptize our baby. But babies have to be baptized immediately after they're born. We can't wait six or seven months for Don Camillo's return."

"That's easy enough to solve," said Mariolino. "We'll register the baby's birth at the Town Hall, because, after all, Peppone did just as much for us as Don Camillo, and then we'll take it up in the mountains to that one and only priest!"

"Impossible," said Gina. "Babies have to be baptized in the parish where they're born. And the time's getting short. I'm going to pack a suitcase tomorrow."

Six days went by without anything happening. Old Tirelli hung between life and death and Don Camillo stayed home partly in order to look after him and partly because the girl he hadn't wanted to recognize had called out: "We'll be coming to see you." Early in the afternoon of the seventh day, his housekeeper came excitedly into the room:

"Come quickly, Father. There's something very unusual downstairs."

Don Camillo hurried down and saw an extraordinary sight: Mariolino and Gina, with the village midwife between them, bearing a beribboned baby in her arms.

"Well, what's this?" asked Don Camillo.

"The lady came here for a holiday, and proceeded to bear this very fine baby," the midwife announced.

Don Camillo wrinkled up his nose.

"Did you come all this way for that reason?" he asked the young couple.

"I'd never have come," said Mariolino, "but she insisted that you baptize the baby. As if all priests didn't come out of the same pudding. . . . Well, if you don't want to baptize him, so much the better."

Don Camillo pondered the complications of the matter and made an indistinct noise. He went into the church, but the young couple did not immediately follow. Apparently, they were waiting for something. And indeed, while Don Camillo was preparing the baptismal font two groups of strangers invaded the village. One came from the mule track and was composed of members of the land-owning Filotti family; the other came up a parallel path and was, naturally enough, the Red band of della Bruciata. From opposite sides of the square they converged upon the church door, and the young parents led them in.

"Who is the godfather?" asked Don Camillo.

Old Filotti and old della Bruciata both stepped forward, gritting their teeth and reaching out for the lacy robe of their reactionary-revolutionary descendant.

"Hands off!" said Don Camillo threateningly. And he signalled to a newcomer at the church door.

"Step forward, godfather!" he commanded.

And Peppone—for it was he—obeyed, although it was plain that the honour had been forced upon him. When the ceremony was over Don Camillo was called away by his housekeeper.

"The old man is asking for you," she panted.

Don Camillo burst impetuously into the dying man's room.

"No, Tirelli," he said, most uncharitably; "you simply can't throw cold water over the celebration by choosing this moment to die!"

"Father, I called you to say that I've decided to go on living. This mountain air has healed me. Send word to my daughter to come and move me into other quarters."

Don Camillo was breathless over the succession of events. When he went downstairs he found waiting for him the young substitute priest and Peppone.

"I'm here merely as the driver of a public conveyance," Peppone told him. "The priest asked me to bring him here, and after I'd left the car at the bottom of the mule track I came to see how things were going along. Unfortunately I find you bursting with good health!"

The priest, in his turn, gave Don Camillo an envelope.

"It's a letter from the Bishop," he explained. "I've come to announce a change of the guard. You can go back in Peppone's car."

"I contracted only for a one-way trip," Peppone objected. "I have no wish to take certain people back with me."

"I'll pay extra," said Don Camillo.

"It's a question of principle, not of money," Peppone replied. "The later you come back the better. Don't get big ideas from the visit of a soft-headed old man and two young rascals. We're getting on famously without you."

"All the more reason for me to hurry back!" said Don Camillo.

Two hours later, Don Camillo emerged from the church with the crucifix over his shoulder.

"Driver, take my suitcase!" he called out to Peppone.

He proceeded down the mule track, and this time the cross was as light as a feather. At the end of the trail stood the jeep which Peppone called a taxi. Don Camillo climbed in, holding the crucifix before him like a banner.

The della Bruciata band had come in a lorry, and now they started off after Peppone. Nearby stood the two big, shiny cars of the Filotti family, and in the first of these sat Gina with the baby in her arms and Mariolino at the wheel. Mariolino skilfully steered his car in between the jeep and the lorry, while the second one, with his father-in-law driving, brought up the rear.

At this point Smilzo rode up like a demon on his motorcycle, having been worried over his chief's delay. When he saw the little procession, he turned around and rode ahead of it, in order to clear the way. When they were within two miles of their destination he responded to a nod from Peppone by stepping on the gas and leaving the others behind him.

So it was that at the entrance to the village Don Camillo found the local band ready to greet him. And the Crucified Christ came home to the strains of the "International."

"Under the rope and to victory!" rejoiced Peppone, bringing the jeep to an abrupt stop in front of the church door.

*Made and printed in Great Britain
for The Companion Book Club (Odhams Press Ltd.)
by Odhams (Watford) Limited
Watford, Herts
S.1255.ZT*